PRAISE FOR MAYA KAATHRYN BOHNHOFF

"*A Sea of Stars and Trouble* is a colorful and swashbuckling space adventure with clear, fast-paced writing and a rogues' gallery of interesting characters."

—Kevin J. Anderson, New York Times bestselling co-author of *Dune: House Atreides*

"In *A Sea of Stars and Trouble*, Maya Kaathryn Bohnhoff takes us on a grand space opera ride, with a shanghaied hero who might or might not be a hero, who doesn't know, himself—really doesn't know himself—until he's put to the test. Who is he? What's he capable of? Can he be trusted? It's a smashing good ride, with an irrepressible spirit and enough twists and surprises to carry you straight through to the end."

— Jeffrey A. Carver, author of *The Chaos Chronicles*

"… the magic of Bohnhoff's writing grabbed me (as well as her rich tapestry of story and theme), and wouldn't let me go. This woman can write."

— Linc Irvine, reviewer/author

I0587623

A SEA OF STARS AND TROUBLE

THE ANTIQUITIES HUNTER

(A Gina Miyoko Mystery)

Gina Miyoko Stories

"Tinkerbell On Walkabout"

a Book View Café novelette

"Tinkerbell and the Storybook Murder"

a Book View Café novelette

A SEA OF STARS AND TROUBLE

MAYA KAATHRYN BOHNHOFF

BVC

A SEA OF STARS AND TROUBLE

Maya Kaathryn Bohnhoff

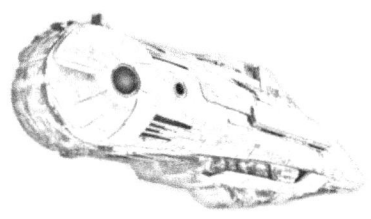

Copyright © 2025 Maya Kaathryn Bohnhoff

ISBN: 978-1-63632-334-3

Production Team:

Project Coördinator: Maya Kaathryn Bohnhoff

Cover Design: Maya Kaathryn Bohnhoff, art elements by Freepik and Vecteezy

Beta reader: Steven Popkes

Proofreader & copyeditor: Phyllis Irene Radford

Formatter: Jennifer Stevenson, Maya Kaathryn Bohnhoff

Book View Café
304 S. Jones Blvd.
Suite #2906
Las Vegas NV 89107

BOOK VIEW CAFE

www.bookviewcafe.com

DEDICATION

*For Michael Reaves, best Jedi Master a padawan could ask for, and for
Marc Scott Zicree, who introduced me to Michael at a writer's
roundtable and who always believed in me.*

*Both of these mentors enabled me to write books I would never have the
opportunity to write without their inspiring presence.*

PART 1
THE RUNNING MAN

1 / BIRTHDAY

HE WAS BORN AS HE WALKED THE ROAD INTO PORPHYRY.

At least, that's where he was when he remembered that his name was Ridley. Three steps later, he remembered that Ridley was his first name and that Matthews was the surname that went with it. Other than that, he knew of his newborn self only that he was wearing a once-blue shirt, gray breeks, and tall boots covered by a disreputable knee-length coat of indeterminate color that was vented at the sides and back.

He patted the vents over his thighs and had the vague sense that something was missing. A money pouch? A holster? A scabbard for a laz-blade? He glanced down at his hands. No rings. No tattoos. Nothing but a faint scar that ran along the inside of one wrist. He couldn't remember how he'd gotten it.

The air roared with the distant lift-off of a starship. He stopped and watched it soar toward the clouds—through them —its keel gleaming blue. The port was straight ahead, behind the walls of a city that sat on and among a range of low, rolling hills. He estimated the distance to the wall at about 400 meters and change.

Ridley knew something else about himself then—he wanted to get to the spaceport and off this world.

Which was ... what?

He did a 360 on the shoulder of the unnaturally smooth road. It had no potholes, cracks or blemishes and somehow he knew the surface was smooth to the millimeter, though he had no idea how he knew it. Beyond the road lay chaos; brackish fields and wetlands stretched out behind him; a forest of towering, crooked trees lay on one side of the road; a fen with waving reeds twice his height spread out on the other. Ahead of him, the dingy gray walls of the huge citadel rose in front of him and disappeared into the equally gray distance in both directions.

Ah. There was a sign over the gate this roadway led to: *Welcome to Porphyry.*

Right.

Porphyry. A port town on ... he racked his brain.

Nothing.

His lack of coherent memory didn't bother him too much. It would come to him eventually, he figured. He faced the city gate and began walking again, assiduously trying not to be mowed down by a variety of vehicles that were scurrying out of the twilight into the safety of the city.

He glanced back over his shoulder at the tall, waving grasses of the fen. Why was everybody in such a hurry? Did the gates—

He heard a siren go off ahead. Yellow lights flashed along the top of the gate that bracketed the roadway.

—close at dusk?

He ran, the tails of his coat flapping in the dank air. As he slipped through the pedestrian gate, barely saving the tails of his coat, he remembered something else about himself—he was running from something. Not whatever lived in the marshes beyond the city, but something else. Suddenly, his lack of coherent memory bothered him a great deal. He stepped into the shadow of the wall and searched his pockets. He found nothing. Not a credit tab, no ID, no weaponry.

The gate he'd entered through had been roughly three meters wide and constructed of aging stone with a newer metal insert. Clearly not a main access to the city. The section of Porphyry within it was a maze. This might be good, given his impression that he was on the run from ... something. The streets were narrow, the buildings old, huddled together, and decrepit. Their layout was jumbled and confusing—like a random scatter of toy blocks.

He knew about toy blocks, he realized. Knew small children played with them. Knew the sound of a child's laughter. He scrambled after the happy/sad thought then let it go in favor of dealing with his immediate situation. He seemed to recall that he trusted his sense of direction, but as darkness fell, he found he'd gone around in a convoluted circle without having realized it. It was like being lost in another dimension where the normal rules of geography did not apply. Or maybe the problem was in his addled brain.

He had apparently wandered into a dead zone. There was a distinct lack of lighting. Only the full moon, hanging huge and bloated in the sky overhead, cast its pale green light here. It was enough light to inform him that there was no one around to ask for the quickest route to the spaceport. There was no traffic. The shops were shuttered. The streets were deserted, as if the denizens of Porphyry had as much to fear within its walls as beyond them. Yet, in the distance he could hear the hum of a main thoroughfare, far-off sirens, the thunder of starship launch engines.

He looked up, scanning the facades of the buildings nearest him. Standing on a balcony some yards down the street was a cluster of robed figures, several of whom were looking right at him. Well, at least their hooded heads were turned in his direction. He couldn't see their faces. Unsettling. The ones that weren't looking at him were speaking into communicators of some sort.

P-comms, said his piecemeal memory. Short for ... something that started with a P.

The hair on the back of Ridley's neck rose, tingling, and he knew with sudden certainty that someone was behind him. He turned just in time to catch the merest glance of a gray-robed figure gripping a static-spitting staff before a jolt of freezing energy took him down. He hit the roadway like a rock and curled into a ball, bracing himself against the chill, tingling shock. Oddly, after a moment, the shock morphed into something eerily pleasant. In fact, he felt better than he had in a long time ... or at least for the past hour or so.

He'd had some expectation of the effects of the weapon based, he assumed, on prior experience—but the charge from this staff was causing his brain to explode, not with pain, but with a sense of contentment and well-being. He was suffused with a bliss so potent it was terrifying—or would have been if it didn't feel so damn good. Even the fact that he was probably about to die failed to penetrate the (insane) conviction that Ridley Matthews was profoundly right with the Universe and was fulfilling a purpose that surely had been preordained since the beginning of his existence—perhaps even the beginning of time. Everything he had ever done or experienced, whether or not he could remember it, had led inexorably to this moment, had put him just where he belonged.

He no longer felt any need to escape.

Like hell I don't, snarled a dissenting inner voice.

He ignored it. The thought of his imminent death cheered him; he wouldn't have to run anymore. He simply had to *be,* to allow events to unfold as God or the Universe had planned. So what if he didn't know who the hell he was? He was complete on every conceivable plane of existence.

Bull shit. Bull Shit. BULL. SHIT.

He *wasn't* complete. He was in a dangerous position for anyone to be in, even if they weren't a complete blank. His anger was as unexpected as the false joy, but at least it was an honest emotion, not forced on him by a neural weapon.

He was surrounded by robed figures now, all carrying similar meter-long staffs. They were swaying from side to side and chanting: "Burn, burn, burn away. Confusion, sorrow, doubt and pain. Burn away. Burn away."

Ridley gasped. Suppressing the alien bliss with a will, he stood, shaking hair out of his eyes. "Who are you? What did you do to me?"

The tallest of the monkish men—the one who'd zapped him —stopped chanting and stepped forward, seemingly surprised that their victim was speaking to them. His robe was decorated with symbols: crosses, pentagrams, cups, swords, several different kinds of stars and moons—a mishmash of religious icons from a dozen worlds and ages. Ridley could see the glitter of the man's eyes within the hood.

Good. He had a face … which Ridley was much inclined to punch.

"We are the Druud," the monk told him gravely. "The Brothers of the Rapture. We have shared the Rapture with you. You are blessed."

His companions—there were five, all dressed in similar attire —repeated the words, "Rapture. Blessed."

"Feel the burn, brother," the Druud told him. "Feel the layers of your soul sear away until your true self is revealed."

His true self. Did he want to know who or what that was? Something told him he'd been running for a while now, and until he knew what he was running *from* he'd just as soon leave his true self out of it.

"Why?" he gasped, feeling the burn. "Why attack me?"

The monk made a gesture with his staff. "We do not attack. We mean only to help you, brother." He sounded sincere.

Ridley understood. They just wanted him to join them—to be part of their cult. To belong. To them, this wasn't an assault, it was a conversion, not by faith, but by technology. Belonging wasn't bad. Belonging was good. It was necessary. He had belonged … somewhere. Hadn't he?

Ridley locked his eyes on the glowing tip of the Druud's staff.

Carrot and stick—both at once. Had they all been converted this way?

He had to wonder what made the conversions "stick"—frequent and repeated applications to weaken the mind and make it susceptible to the irresistible lure of inclusion? Was it a manipulation of the obvious loner's supposedly deep-seated desire to belong? Or was it addiction they were counting on—the mad urge to feel this overwhelming sense of wellbeing again and again?

Ridley eyed the staff, afraid the monk would use it on him—equally afraid he wouldn't. "Your rapture is false," he said through gritted teeth. He took a step, meaning to slip between two of the back-up monks, but the tall Druud cut him off, raising his staff menacingly.

"You must obey the law! Neither heathen nor holy may walk these streets at night without dispensation."

"What dispensation? I don't even live here, and I'm on my way off-world. For the love of God, just let me go!"

The tall monk looked him in the eye and lowered his staff slightly.

"I am not a cruel man. The Brothers of the Rapture is not a cruel order. We strive for justice and mercy—for harmony. Our streets are not to be walked by outsiders after the sun has set. This is the holy time, and our spiritual discipline is not to be disrupted by the presence of those who do not believe. This is the law. Therefore, you must believe."

Ah, the logic of insanity. Still, Ridley was cheered by the fact that Rapture Monk had not ended the sentence with "you must die". That was something.

"Let me see if I've got this right. You're zapping me into a religious experience because of a *zoning* ordinance?"

"Zoning ordinance? No," said the Druud. "These are the Proprieties of Herron's Hope. Here, in this sector of Porphyry, they are law."

Herron's Hope. *That* was the name of the planet. Right. He'd known that, hadn't he?

The Druud lifted his staff again and thrust it toward his would-be convert. This time Ridley grabbed it right behind the muzzle. Lightning crackled the length of his arm. He set his teeth against the overwhelming joy that came with it, wrenched the staff from the monk's grasp, and aimed a roundhouse kick at his head. Ridley's booted foot connected with a solid thud and the big man went down hard. A second monk leapt to his brother's defense, but Ridley completed his spinning move with a fist to the defender's face. He barely felt the blow on his knuckles.

When he finally stopped moving, he was outside the circle of monks, who stood and gaped as if they'd never seen anyone fight happiness with such determination. The man he had punched was warily pulling himself to his feet.

Ridley twirled the purloined staff as if it were a baton. "Go away," he said quietly, his voice a low rumble in his throat. He waited a beat, then added, "Please."

They went, scattering across the empty street, into the alleys and around the corners, three of them dragging their groaning leader to safety. The men on the balcony, who had been watching these events, withdrew to the shadowy recesses of the building.

Ridley didn't stick around to see if they were rounding up reinforcements. He started walking swiftly in the direction he surmised the spaceport lay, following the roar of engines. He'd gone several yards when the staff in his hand tugged at his thoughts. He glanced down at it. The deep feeling of contentment kickstarted by the staff remained, controlled only by the sheer force of his will. The desire to activate it again and siphon its primal energy coiled in his breast. His mind stood aloof, but emotionally he hungered to return to the pinnacle of faith and ecstasy he had attained in the moments after the monk had zapped him. Only innate stubbornness saved him from succumbing to the sudden addiction ... and perhaps the knowledge that this faith, no matter how intense, was artificial.

Leery of its insidious charms, he considered tossing the staff away into the darkness. Yet, he suspected that if he did, he'd regret it. This posed a quandary. He had no idea what he would have done under normal circumstances, but he was inclined to trust his instincts. Right now, they told him that his mind was in an altered state—the wrong state in which to make important decisions. He'd wait until his neural synapses had cleared of the staff's effects, however long it took, then he'd decide what to do with it.

As he strode briskly through the deserted streets, he analyzed his escape from the Druud. That told him something more about himself; he was a man with quick reflexes, not a little strength, and some knowledge of martial arts. What had he done back there, some sort of *kung fu*?

He flexed his hands, realizing that the one he'd used to punch the Rapture Monger didn't hurt at all. He was about to attribute that to the effects of the staff when he glanced down at his knuckles and realized they weren't swollen or abraded, as he'd expected. And the scar he'd noticed on that wrist earlier was nearly gone.

He looked at the staff with respect. Wow. That was something. It made you feel good and healed whatever ailed you. Powerful stuff. He glanced back over his shoulder, wondering if the staff's owners would be putting in an appearance soon to reclaim it, or if their beliefs would keep them from leaving their sector.

It was with a sense of relief that Ridley approached a district of bright, beckoning holosigns, crowded and noisy streets, and music pulsing from small cramped buildings. He felt oddly comfortable in the midst of all these strangers. Indeed, he felt almost as if he belonged among them … until he became aware that they were staring at him, occasionally whispering to each other as he passed them. More than a few gave him a wide berth. At first, he thought they were looking at the staff, but they weren't; they were glancing up at his face. He made a point of nodding and smiling. While being sociable seemed to come naturally (how could he know?) he suspected his internal struggle was doing something funny to his face; his smiles seemed to spook the passers-by rather than reassure them.

He slowed to peer at himself in the dark front window of a closed-up shop and smiled into the reflective surface. The man who leered back at him was disheveled, dirtied, and torn. His hair—too long, too thick and wild—framed an angular face in which pale, almost silver eyes gleamed like tiny moons and on which the twisted smile looked downright sinister. Given that he was over two meters tall, he looked like a threat going some-where to happen. But what bothered him most about this face was that it seemed only *almost* familiar.

He put a hand to his chin, seeking proof that this really was his face. It was smooth, even after however long he'd been wandering the byways of Herron's Hope before he regained a sense of self-awareness. In any event, it indicated bio-enhance-ments, or at least depilatory treatments.

How do I know that? How do I know that I know that?

He tried the smile again, tilting his head up, trying to exile the crazy from his eyes, and smiling broadly. His teeth were even and white. Eh, better, but still...

Something tugged at his consciousness. Something similar to the sensation he'd felt when the Rapture Bros were casing him. He peered into the window, no longer looking at himself, but at the people passing behind him on the walkway. His eyes darted from face to face, but he saw no one overtly watching him.

What he did see was a drunken man, with a wild thicket of white hair and a matching gold-trimmed one piece suit of some silky-looking material, walk straight into a lamppost. The drunk, who was holding a credit tab in one hand and a drink in the other, gaped at the lamppost as if it had jumped out in front of him. Then he leaned against it and tried three or four times to slip the credit tab into his breast pocket before finally succeeding. He looked this way and that, then lurched forward, taking a couple of steps before promptly bumping into a pedestrian.

Ridley swung around, his senses suddenly and tightly focused on the interaction. He was certain the pedestrian had intentionally angled into the collision. (Why did he think that? Was he, himself, a common thief? Or a policeman?) He was equally certain the pedestrian had stolen that credit tab. He hadn't seen the actual pilfering of it, and of course the drunken mark suspected nothing as he tottered off into a nearby tavern called the *Nebula.*

Ridley kept his heightened attention on the pickpocket. He was easy enough to track—he was bald, with decorative patterns tattooed on his scalp in gleaming ink. He wore a dark gray long-coat, fitted breeches, and the high boots of a spacer. Ridley followed him up the street at a discreet distance, wondering if his peculiar interest in the theft was instinctual or an effect of the Druud rapture staff. By now he had found the buttons that controlled its power charge, but he still didn't know the sequence that set off the endorphin flood. It looked like he would have to do things the old-fashioned way. When the pickpocket turned right, into an alley, Ridley stepped in after him. In two strides he'd come up behind the other man and given him a short, sharp jolt to the kidney with the butt end of the staff. The pickpocket stumbled forward, fetching up against a stone wall. He hesitated, then held up his hands as if he thought this was going to be a simple robbery.

Ridley drew up close behind him and prodded him with the staff. "You've taken something that doesn't belong to you," he observed.

"Oh, you mean this?" said the pickpocket with a nervous laugh, holding up the tab. "You misunderstand, my friend. That fellow's a friend, and this is a bad neighborhood to be drunk in. I took his tab for safekeeping until he has a chance to sober up."

"Your altruism is commendable," said Ridley. He snatched the tab, then knocked the pickpocket unconscious with one deft chop to the back of his neck. Handy skill, that. He wondered, again, where he'd learned it.

He felt that "watched" tingle again and pivoted toward the street, catching the swift movement of withdrawal—a blur of black, gray, and white. Shaking off spookiness, he returned to the *Nebula*'s entrance, where a big, burly gentleman with bio-engineered tusks and knife-sharp teeth kept a watchful eye on the patrons coming and going. Judging by the wary way he eyed Ridley, he was more bouncer than doorman.

"A street hood," Tusks said, "wearing a swell's breeches and carrying a Druud staff—not something you see every day, and not someone I think will enhance the dignity of our establishment."

Someone pushed between Ridley and the bouncer—an aging spacer dressed in an old-school dress uniform in shades of black and gray. He was short, not much more than a meter and a half in height, and his skin had the slightly waxen pallor of someone who'd rarely been out in daylight. His hair was gray with streaks of white, receding in front, but flowing down to his shoulders in the back. Ridley was struck by the absurd conviction that this was the person who'd been watching him rough up the pickpocket.

"Excuse me," the spacer mumbled.

Tusks nodded. "Yeah, sure, Cap'n."

Ridley leaned on the staff. "Why does he get in without the inspection?"

"He's a regular. You're not."

"Y'know, from what I've seen of this town so far, if you banned everyone irregular from your classy drinking establishment, it'd be empty all the time. Besides, I have business with someone inside. He lost this." Ridley guilelessly held up the credit tab.

The bouncer reached for it. "Give it to me. I'll see that the proper gentleman gets it."

"Off-worlders are wrong about the people of Porphyry," Ridley replied. "It seems they really do have a sense of humor."

Damn, but I'm a glib sonofabitch.

The bouncer eyed him, then laughed and jerked his thumb toward the interior, signaling to Ridley to go in. He did, experiencing a disquieting sense of camaraderie that was offset by suspicion and an instinctive heightening of his senses.

The place was crowded, dimly lit, and noisy. People were talking, laughing, arguing. They were also eating, drinking, and smoking a wide range of substances, most of which at least marginally bad for one's health. Or so his vague memory informed him. He'd rather have more useful information at the moment, like who he was, beyond a name, and why he was here, and how he had gotten here.

The majority of the men in the room, and some of the women, were dressed in casual attire; some displayed logograms, badges, roundels and other insignia, indicating allegiance to various factions or … no, alliances. Alliances and Guilds. Ridley noticed sigils for a handful he realized he recognized: Consonance, the Filial Pact, the Heartworlds Alliance, the Freeman's Guild, others.

Those who weren't obviously spacers tended to dress in a manner that showed off various physical assets. There were, inevitably, prostitutes of all types, some so alien in appearance, it was difficult to think of them as human. Yet they were human. In all of mankind's spacefaring history, no sentient alien species had yet been found—which could be seen as either a blessing or a curse. These were bio-engineered humans, modified to possess any number of inhuman qualities. But they *looked* alien, and that was enough to excite their adventure-seeking clients.

Their presence reminded Ridley to consider his own possible modifications—eyes that seemed to take in every movement, even in the dimmest corners of the room, ears caught and sorted through the babble of voices, extracting intelligible dialogues, skin that prickled with awareness of movement and attention. A trio of hookers had turned to watch him as he moved deeper into the room, their heads swiveling.

One of them—a woman with black hair and eyes so large and dark they seemed like rounds of polished jet—detached herself from the group and moved as if stalking him. Under the smoky light of the bar, her skin glowed golden—a counterpoint to the pale, body-hugging tunic she wore. Likely she'd seen the interaction with Tusks over the credit tab. Possibly she wanted to relieve him of it. She smiled, teeth flashing white in the golden face.

Hope springs eternal... He'd heard that somewhere.

The smell of food assaulted him then, and he forgot about the black-eyed hooker. He was suddenly ravenous. He had no idea how long it had been since his last meal. He would have to do something about that soon, but his errand came first. He scanned the tavern, finally spotting a familiar shock of white hair on a gentleman standing at the bar. The man was gesturing wildly, and Ridley had the distinct feeling he had ordered something and only now discovered he had no means of paying for it.

Ridley smiled and pushed his way to the bar, where he tapped the white-haired man on the shoulder. The old guy whirled as if someone had set him on fire, then his eyes widened as he saw the credit tab Ridley held in front of his face.

"Lose something?"

"By the Maw of Hell! You found it!" White Hair exclaimed. He presented it to the bartender as if it were a trophy. "See? I told you I'd lost it. Now I can pay for that drink!" He turned to Ridley. "And you! I definitely owe you a drink! Or three! And can I buy you something to eat?"

Ridley hesitated. This was literally *terra incognita*, but he was so damned hungry. Besides, he had performed a service; this was merely a grace.

"Come to think of it, the dishes do smell pretty decent," he said.

"That they do! What would you like? Biftek? Some fried eggs?"

Ridley shrugged. "How can I refuse?"

A few minutes later they were sitting at a table waiting for their food. The Druud staff leaned against Ridley's chair. Two beers—reportedly the best local brew—sat on the table. Ridley's new "friend" picked up his beer and gestured for him to do the same. He had just lifted his glass when someone jostled him, knocking the Druud staff to the floor. He reflexively reached down to retrieve it, glancing up briefly as he did.

The old spacer, again.

"Excuse me," the old guy mumbled, barely meeting Ridley's eyes. "It's a bit crowded in here, isn't it?"

Ridley felt the urge to explain to the fellow that he didn't rough up complete strangers without good reason. Instead, he just smiled and said: "Hope that means the food is good."

The duffer bobbed his head and shuffled off into the crowd.

"A toast!" White Hair said, words slurring.

"A toast." Ridley repeated. They clicked glasses.

"Life is good," said White Hair.

Much to his astonishment, Ridley Matthews found himself agreeing with the sentiment. He was on the run, with no memory of who or what he was, and it felt as if all was right with the universe. How wrong was that?

He felt anger trying to crawl up from his stomach. Would the effects of that damned staff never fade?

"Life is good," he agreed. He took a big swallow of beer. It was excellent.

"What may I call you, my new friend?" White Hair asked.

"Name's Ridley." He hesitated as another memory emerged. "But I go by 'Trouble.'"

"Trouble," repeated the old guy. "Now that is a most portentous sobriquet."

"I hope so," Trouble Matthews said, and was surprised to

realize he knew what a portentous sobriquet was. His meal came then, and he tucked in with a vengeance.

2 / DREAMED

Trouble Matthews dreamed. His dreams were unusually lucid, engaging all of his senses. He could not manipulate these dreams, which surprised and disturbed him; they unfolded chaotically, denying him any control. He tried to force himself awake several times. Each time he failed. There was nothing to do but ride it out.

At first, he was merely awash in a stream of images and sounds: a large, lovely room with dark gleaming floors and a glass outer wall that overlooked forested slopes. On the polished tile, a laughing child played with a doll, making it skate on the mirror-like surface while a woman sang a tune he almost knew. Then the gleaming floor became a lake with an imposing building reflected in its still waters, every door and window ablaze with light.

He beheld a council held in a room flung with the banners of all the known worlds and filled with the babble of a thousand voices. Men in uniform were stationed along its perimeter, watchful. He was puzzled by his point-of-view—not in the position of command in the circle of planetary leaders, but very near it. He was struck with the sudden certainty that something bad was about to happen.

He struggled to awaken, but he couldn't. The council

chamber was suddenly empty except for a man sitting alone in the chair at the head of the room. There was something wrong with this image. What was it? He was supposed to do something. Do what?

Before Trouble could fathom what it was, steel walls rose up around him to hem him in. He was caught in an avalanche of sensory input—the metallic stink of fear and futility, the heat of rage, the claustrophobic press of steel walls. After a single, brief, screaming moment in which he felt the walls collapse on him, he was back in the council chamber again. Again, it was empty but for the man in the chair.

It was as if his dreaming mind was trying to get him to remember, to recognize the man, to make some sort of connection. Trouble knew the face, though he couldn't put a name to it. He was arrested by its puzzled expression, the look of stunned recognition in the eyes. He was struck again by the sense of "wrongness."

Who are you? he wanted to shout. *Why are you the only clear memory I have?*

Finally, as he was trying to solve the mystery of why this man would not leave his thoughts, Trouble awoke—a process hastened by the sudden and liberal application of a bucketful of frigid water.

He gasped for breath. He was naked save for his breeches, and lying on the freezing floor of a small cell. He felt the thrum of machinery through his bones, felt the tingle of electromagnetic energy on his exposed skin. He was aboard a ship.

His feelings of goodwill and connection to both the highest and lowest elements of the universe had totally dissipated and he was kicked, head first, into fight or flight mode. Flight was impossible at the moment, so that left fight. He summoned fight to give him the will to lift himself to his hands and knees, raise his head and assess his surroundings.

Four people stood outside the cell, between him and a half-open hatch through which he could see a dimly lit corridor. He recognized only one of these people—the stumpy codger who'd bumped into him at the *Nebula*. Right now, he was looking at Trouble thoughtfully, a combination of pity and pride in his eyes, and a slight smile on his lips. He appeared pleased with himself, and he exuded an aura of authority.

Trouble had encountered people with similar auras, he realized. Male and female, generals, business magnates, politicians, leaders of government ... prison wardens—despots, all. He couldn't remember a single individual among them, but he knew the look of the dark, beaten spirit: This was a man who enjoyed squeezing the autonomy out of others because he had none of his own.

Two of the others, both in one-piece uniforms, stood diffidently near the portal. Both had been bio-engineered. One—a female—looked as if she'd been modified to work in extreme weather conditions; her skin appeared as tough as chitin. The other's skin was iridescent and a bit scaly, and when he turned, gill flaps were clearly visible just below his jawline.

Trouble immediately focused on the fourth individual—the one with the empty bucket in his hand. He was large and muscular, and his smile exposed a row of gleaming gold front teeth. From his belt hung a tubular instrument about a half-meter long, with transparent coils and two prongs at one end.

Jerkstick.

The word snuck back into Trouble's vocabulary on an ooze of anger. Technologically primitive, but damned effective for keeping recalcitrant prisoners in line. This must be the ship's enforcer. He would be, naturally, a man who not only employed violence, but enjoyed it.

Trouble turned his attention to the cell. It was simply a rounded depression in the wall, about two meters across and equally deep. The light was ambient, and not uncomfortably bright. Within the rounded back wall, a shallower cavity formed a sleeping slot. There were no bars—nothing visible to keep him in the cell.

Force field? He reached out a hand experimentally, expecting to feel a static "buzz". Maybe it was off?

He flexed his body, surprised to find that any scrapes and bruises he'd acquired had apparently been treated while he was unconscious. That made sense; if they were going to shanghai someone, they'd want to make sure he was in good condition so it would take longer to work him to death.

He shook himself to full consciousness, got to his feet, and uncoiled to his full height. Then he stepped toward the open area. The world came to a stop. It was as if he had stepped into a wall of water. Really thick, dense water. The harder Trouble tried to push forward, the more the air seemed to solidify around him, hardening like amber around an insect. He strained to the point of nearly passing out. It was impossible to breathe.

"We've recruited a moron," said Gold Teeth. "Stupid enough to fight a pressor field."

Trouble quit struggling forward, and let the pressor field push him back.

Gold Teeth grinned and the old Gray Hair said, "You see, Enoch? He's educable after all."

Trouble tapped his head with an index finger, and smiled— not caring if it was a maniacal leer. He paced, then, walking the meager circumference of his cage, assessing his situation, which was … what? He needed to get a grasp on that.

"How'd you slip me the mickey? Was old White Hair in on it?"

"I, em, added something to your beer while you were busy picking up your staff. White Hair, as you call him, had nothing to do with it. But I saw what you did on his behalf. Very noble. Though I admit, I was less impressed by your altruism than I was with the way you handled the thief."

I was impressed myself, Trouble thought. Didn't know I had it in me.

"I guess I should thank you, then," he said aloud.

The captain raised an eyebrow. "And what action of mine has earned your gratitude?"

"I was looking for a way to get off Herron's Hope. Looks like I got my wish without spending any creds."

"Be careful what you wish for," Gold Teeth muttered, just loud enough to be heard.

Trouble gave no sign that he'd heard him. "Who are you?" he asked the old man.

"My name is Erasmus Shade. I am your new employer. Your captain, in point of fact. This vessel, upon which you have so intelligently elected to serve, is the Freeman's Guild ship *Moonraker*. We are merchants."

"You're smugglers," Trouble translated.

"An honorable profession," said Shade. "One in which you are honored to take part."

"An illegal profession, in which I'd really rather not participate."

"That would be unfortunate, since you already are participating." Shade gestured at Gold Teeth. "This gentleman is my first mate and your immediate superior. His name is Rusk. You shall answer to him in all matters, mainly because, should there arise a matter in which you have to answer to me, your punishment is likely to be dire."

"Where are my things?" Trouble asked.

Captain Shade barked out a one-syllable laugh. "You mean your weapon? Your clothing was hardly worth preserving."

"It's not a weapon. And it's mine."

"It's mine now," said the captain. "I've heard all sorts of fanciful rumors about Druud staffs. I may try it on the crew to see if it assists in any disciplinary problem where the traditional methods are ineffective."

Trouble snorted. "Well, you'll have the happiest crew in the smugglers' fleet, that's for sure."

The Captain laughed again and the two bio-engineered crewmen echoed it wanly, their eyes on their commander.

"These are two of your new crewmates," said Shade, gesturing at them. "They are..." he frowned, then gave up. "Who are you?"

"Kai Jiang, sir," said the hardskin.

"Jay Blackwood, sir," said the amphibian.

"Jiang and Blackwood. I've asked them their names before, haven't I, Enoch?"

"Yes, sir, you have," said Rusk.

Captain Shade pinched the skin at the bridge of his nose, lowered his head and closed his eyes. His body language was clear: The burdens of command weighed heavily. He couldn't be expected to remember something as relatively trivial as a pair of crew member's names.

Shade raised his head with a sigh and held up a small device. "Would one of you be so kind," he said to the two mods, "as to release this gentleman and show him around?"

"Yes, sir," said Jiang.

She took the control from her captain and pointed it in Trouble's direction. It made a soft *ping*! as she used it, and Trouble felt the difference in air pressure as the pressor field shut down. He noticed Rusk had unhooked his jerkstick and held it ready for use. He'd also taken a step to his left and was blocking the half open hatch.

Shade had backed away, giving Rusk direct access to Trouble should it be necessary.

Trouble was suddenly determined that it be necessary. He leapt from the cell, pushed Jiang aside, and went straight for the hatch—and Rusk. The first mate had an almost comical look of astonishment on his face. He hadn't been expecting a direct attack—not with a jerkstick in his hand. His surprised gasp ended in a grunt of pain as Trouble drove a shoulder into his solar plexus.

The mate was only just able to activate his weapon and ram it against his attacker's torso. A wave of white hot agony lit up every nerve in Trouble's body. He'd expected the charge to leave him in a fetal curl on the floor, shrieking in pain, but it didn't. He grabbed the jerkstick and wrenched it from the first mate's hand.

Before he could turn the weapon or its master, a paralyzing shock hit his spine. He couldn't breathe, couldn't move, couldn't think. Then the wave passed, and, even as he processed that he'd been shot from behind by some sort of energy weapon, he hit the floor.

He stared at Rusk's feet; the black boots were scuffed, the heels, worn. You'd think being first mate aboard a smuggler would pay better.

Chuckling, Rusk reached down and pulled the jerkstick from Trouble's nerveless grasp. Trouble responded by aiming a vicious punch at Rusk's left kneecap. The first mate went down, roaring in pain, but not before he managed to give Trouble another jolt with the jerkstick. Whoever had wielded the weapon from behind him used it again at the same moment. Trouble's nervous system gave up on him. He blacked out.

When he came to, the pain had faded, and Jiang and Black-wood had withdrawn to the bulkhead near the hatch, as if they could hardly wait to escape the brig. Both faces were impassive masks, but with haunted eyes. Rusk sat in a foam-chair while a medi-bot administered an infuser of some medication to his damaged knee.

Trouble rolled over and looked up at Captain Shade.

Shade said, "It's impressive, the amount of punishment you can take, son. But we can keep it up as long as you maintain this rather intractable stubbornness. So, don't you think it might be in your enlightened self-interest to cooperate? There's no escape now. We're in space."

He was right, of course, and Trouble couldn't have told anyone—including himself—why he'd put up the fight he had. Or why, after all that, he was still alive. Why was he still alive? Surely any normal human being would have died. Maybe he *was* a mod. If so, until his memory fully returned, he would have to experiment—quietly, and carefully, of course—to see what his particular enhancements were.

"You win," Trouble said. "For now."

"Now is all we've ever got, son." Shade turned away, then looked back and added, "Try that sort of civil disobedience again and Rusk will make sure you rue the day you were born."

Trouble actually laughed. "Too late for that. Hell, Cap'n, I don't even *remember* what day I was born."

Without warning, Rusk grabbed the jerkstick and delivered a measured jolt to the base of Trouble's spine. Trouble, gritted his teeth so hard, his jaw ached, but he did not pass out.

"That was for talking back to the captain," the first mate said.

"Play fair, Enoch," Shade admonished mildly. Then, to Trouble: "What's your name, son?"

Trouble's teeth were chattering; Rusk's last strike had sent uncontrollable spasms ricocheting through his muscles. "R-ridley M-matthews. People ... call me T-trouble ... I think."

"Trouble. How appropriate. Welcome aboard *Moonraker*, Mr. Trouble," the captain said. "I trust your voyage will be an interesting one."

3 / RUSK

First Mate Enoch Rusk of the *Moonraker* didn't think of himself as cruel, or detached, or indifferent to the hardships of others. He was just someone who had a job to do, and that job entailed making sure others did their jobs, by any means necessary.

The duties of *Moonraker*'s crew were long, hard, and tedious. No denying that. There was a phrase that he'd heard applied at one time or another to just about any line of work one could think of, but one which he felt described space travel with extreme accuracy: weeks of boredom broken occasionally by moments of stark terror. Nine-tenths of the work involved in flying a starship between systems was vigilance, and nothing was as boring as keeping a constant lookout for something that rarely happened. That was why almost every member of the crew was trained in every essential duty, regardless of their specialty, and rotated through shifts on those various duties. The theory—which belonged to Captain Shade, not to Rusk—was that this would keep them relatively fresh and gave them redundancy at key positions.

There were, to be sure, areas in which this was more important than others. When it came to monitoring the ship's engines, for example, a moment of boredom could result in disaster. The crew assigned to Engineering had to know the Keplinger drive like it was an old, eccentric relative. They had to be on hand in case something went wrong. And if something did, they damned well better act quickly. Space was a cold-hearted bitch; she had no patience for the indecisive or the ignorant.

For this reason, when Erasmus Shade requested that the new guy be trained up on engineering and cargo duty as his first rotation, Rusk was skeptical. No, he was more than skeptical; he was outraged, but he did his best not to show it. Standing in the Captain's ready room, which was adjacent to the bridge and just forward of the Master's quarters, Rusk gritted his teeth and glowered at the clear portal that afforded the captain a view forward over the bow.

"Are you sure that's for the best, sir?" he asked. He'd almost asked if Shade thought it was *wise,* and was profoundly glad he hadn't. He respected Shade, even as he coveted his position as ship's master, but he respected his family ties more. Clan Shade was the powerhouse of the Freeman's Guild and if Erasmus was not the most powerful of the house, he was yet part of it.

Rusk heard the older man shift in his chair and set his teacup and saucer down on the little wooden tray-table he affected in his attempt to make his ready room resemble the captain's quarters of an ancient, wooden sailing vessel. Shade insisted on calling it his Map Room. You could hear the capital letters when the old man said the words. There was a squat, cylindrical teakwood-clad navigational station in the center of the chamber. It housed a relatively modern tactical display that could either call up star charts on a faux three-dimensional screen or—when it could be persuaded—display a real three-dimensional model in a spherical display above the station.

"What is your objection, Mr. Rusk? Mr. Matthews is clearly intelligent, quick, and able-bodied. I should hate to waste him in the galley. I would like him trained up to his more important duties while we are sailing in relatively calm waters. In any event, I should like to have him learn those duties sooner rather than later. Our crew is too small to allow anyone much time for stargazing."

Rusk pulled his own gaze reluctantly from the view the portal afforded. One half of the sky was filled with the brilliant froth of stars and nebulae that comprised the Milky Way. In the other half, save for the lonesome glow of a few isolated stellar wanderers, the pitch blackness of the Rift stretched outwards—over a thousand light-years from this point—toward the blue-white shoals of the Orion Arm.

No one on this crew had time for stargazing. Certainly not Rusk. Indeed, there had been precious little time in his entire life for anything save locating and securing his next meal—at least until he'd fallen in with Erasmus Shade. Before that, he'd been a weapons runner for the Black Heart League—a nasty cadre of smuggler-pirates that worked at the fringes of the Heartworlds.

Smuggling, even smuggling unusual contraband like their current cargo, was a Goldilocks orbit compared to that. The position of first mate, even on a bucket like this one, was an enviable one. That was the real reason Rusk did not want to show Matthews anything of significance. He distrusted the man's easy, watchful manner; it spoke of a natural confidence that could be dangerous if the new guy decided he wanted to rise quickly through the ranks. Rusk's future plans did not include "accidentally" stepping out an airlock or any one of a hundred other unimaginative ways in which his position might suddenly become vacant.

Rusk turned to look at his captain. "I'm not sure we can trust Matthews, is all, sir. We don't know squiddle about him."

"Nonsense. I know he is capable of honest and altruistic behavior. I know he can intimidate even someone who is, themselves, intimidating. I know he can handle himself in a fight. I also know that he is capable of controlling his temper. A sterling quality when it comes to life aboard a freighter."

Shade picked up his tea and took another sip. "On the surface, Mr. Matthews is no more or less obstinate than many shanghaied crewmen you've supervised over the years. Most of them have adjusted to the rigors of space flight, and accepted the necessity of working cooperatively with the rest of the crew. Some have actually embraced their role aboard *Moonraker*. I think they learn to appreciate the rewards that can come at the end of a long voyage." Shade set his cup and saucer down with a click. "Or he might turn out to be a reactionary, ungovernable pain in the ass. I trust you will keep me informed as to which he is."

"Yes, sir," Rusk said. "I'll see to it, then, sir. As soon as he's fit for duty, I'll assign him to the roster."

What he didn't say was that Trouble Matthews was different. Not different in the way the weird net-head helmsman, Cyber, was different. Not different in the way the biologically altered Jiang and Blackwood were different, though clearly he'd been modified in some manner. Trouble Matthews was different from the inside out. Rusk was determined to find out how different.

The last thing Shade told him was, "Make sure he gets a meal and a night's sleep first. I don't want him to make mistakes because he's hung over from the recruitment process."

As Rusk left the captain's quarters, he knew Matthews was already being escorted to the Retreat, a relatively spacious recreational area on Epsilon Deck. There the crew enjoyed their few precious hours of R&R. They exercised, played games, watched trivee, and jacked into VR scenarios. The Retreat also boasted a few private cubicles to which crew members could retire with little fear of being interrupted or even noticed, except when they were entering or leaving. If there was a place where unrest was going to start, it was the Retreat. The crew expected it, and the officers bore with it. All of which meant that the Retreat was the de facto place the crew sized up new recruits. Rusk had seen a number of such initiations in his day, and of course he had been the object of one, many years ago.

He'd once thought his own initiation had gone well. He'd stood up to the hazing; it was not in his nature to suffer such nonsense silently. He had established a zone of respect and limited the amount of humiliation he'd had to endure. All it had taken was rearranging the facial structure of some of the more hostile hazers. Even so, the path to his current position on *Moonraker* had not been as smooth as he'd planned, forcing him to commit a few surreptitious murders. He'd likely have been drummed off the *Raker* if Shade got wind of it. The Guilds did not function like the rogue operations Rusk had grown up in. Here, his position obligated him to publicly frown on unsanctioned violence among the members of the crew, and to mete out justice as he saw fit—at least until the captain told him he was going too far. Old habits, Rusk found, were hard to break.

If this Matthews bloke was going to be a problem, the best indications would come during his initiation into ship's society. Naturally, Rusk wanted nothing more than for Matthews to do something so stupid that even Erasmus Shade would consider it punishable. But Rusk knew well that if he instigated the stupid something, there'd be hell to pay.

Fine then, Rusk thought. No point in Heisenberging things up by being present in the flesh. He'd watch remotely so that he could neither start something nor finish it. He took the lift down to Epsilon and went forward past the Retreat and all the way to the heart of *Moonraker's* operational network—the Core.

On his way, he passed a few members of the crew who saluted or otherwise acknowledged him. The *Raker* wasn't a military vessel; there was no formal protocol for greeting the mate, but he noted who acknowledged him and who did not. He knew them all on sight—the *Raker's* crew was only twenty-five strong at present—and he was fully aware of their strengths and weaknesses. He liked none of them and trusted none, least of all those who might have their eyes on his position. Rusk was not worried about this; he was first mate because that was his proper station in the moment, but he intended to be captain of his own ship some day.

Captain Shade knew this—he was no fool—but Rusk would

not challenge him openly. The old man was strong and crafty; even if he seemed occasionally whimsical to the point of daftness, the crew respected and even admired him. They'd be unlikely to vote anyone else into the Captain's chair without a seriously dire reason.

More to the point, Erasmus Shade's family held a controlling interest in the Guild.

The Core was a darkened, low-ceilinged hive of computers, cameras, and sensor devices. It was good-sized—about twenty meters square—and the temperature was always cool, to keep the outmoded and overworked electronics from malfunctioning. It was also the home of four stasis pods equipped with neural nets.

On a fully crewed ship, at least two would be occupied by techs at any given time, one conscious and piloting the ship, the other asleep, but a mere failsafe's signal away from being awakened if a situation needed to be manually monitored. Theoretically, the electromagnetic wards of the ship's Castellan shields would protect her from space debris and warn of the approach of other vessels. In practice, those aging shields needed human backup.

Because the *Raker* was running light on crew, only one of the workstations was occupied at the moment,. It was manned by a shanghaied crewman who called himself Cyber. His real name was Trevor something. Rusk only knew that because he thought Trevor was a wimp name that he converted to Tremor in his mind. He approached Cyber from behind, loomed over the back of the station chair and reached over to jiggle the tiny antenna jutting from the skull plate behind the tech's right ear.

Before his fingers could come within five centimeters of it, Cyber said calmly, "No touchie, Ruskie, or the biofeedback shock'll knock you on your ass."

Rusk straightened, disappointed. "How did you know it was me?"

"I'm a net-head jacked into a sensor network. I don't really have to explain that, do I?"

Rusk regarded Cyber with something akin to respect. The net-head was spare and wiry. He had the almost luminescent skin of someone who'd spent a lifetime in space. Even in the subdued lighting of the Core, Rusk could see the network of blue capillaries beneath his bald scalp; he could also see the more delicate skein of glowing, silvery circuitry overlaid and intermingled with it—a literal net.

Cyber had come aboard a little less than a year ago. Like the new guy, he'd been scooped up on Herron's Hope. Initially, Rusk had taken him for a mere "wire-flyer," a stim addict he'd doubted would last more than a week. But Tremor had surprised them all by not only getting his addiction under control and spending the majority of his time in the real world, he'd also whipped his body—wasted and frail from years of jacking in for days on end and pushing IVs for nourishment—into shape. Cyber now used his abilities primarily to pilot and protect *Moonraker*. While it could truthfully be said that Rusk liked and admired no one, he came damned close to admiring Cyber.

"Need you to show me the Retreat," he said. "New fish, name of Trouble. Big, shaggy-haired, moves like a damned ninja. Seems a little ... wrong, somehow."

Cyber didn't reply, didn't even blink, but several monitor screens abruptly changed from views of various cargo holds, corridors, rooms, service tunnels and the like to different angles of the crew's recreation area—including the private cubicles.

It took hard work and strong structural materials to create the tiny bubble that is a starship, and keep it stable against a hungry vacuum; these things always translated into money. Consequently, space of any kind was at a premium, which was why only the captain, the mate, and a few other officers had the luxury of sleeping in private compartments; the rest of the crew lived in open quarters—or cryo-pods. Therefore, the retreat cubicles—and the seclusion that supposedly came with them—were extremely popular. Only Cyber and Rusk knew that the seclusion was a lie; the place was liberally salted with closed-circuit cam bots Rusk had had the tech deploy for his private amusement.

Cyber now used them for his own entertainment as well. In fact, he was still chuckling over his latest "peep show"—an amorous encounter he'd recorded the previous evening between Jiang, the hardskin, and Blackwood, the amphibian. The tryst had just been wrapping up on one of the monitors, when Rusk entered he Core.

Rusk raised his eyebrows and emitted a low whistle. "I had no idea their physical differences were so—uh—pronounced."

"Yeah," said Cyber as he switched to a live feed and mentally positioned surveillance cams to watch the main room. "What they lack in eroticism they more than make up for in comic relief. ... Huh. Speak of the devils ..."

The couple in question were just entering the main room of the Retreat in the company of the new man. The latter was obviously still groggy from his encounter with Shade's drugs and Rusk's discipline, but a close-up of his face left no doubt that this fish knew he would be making one of the most important first impressions of his life, and was determined to enter the Retreat walking without assistance.

Rusk frowned; he hadn't expected Trouble to recover that much of his self-awareness so soon.

The crew members present had been involved in a variety of activities—eating, arguing, playing games—but upon Matthews's entrance, all ceased whatever they were doing and looked at him as if linked by a hive mind.

The first to approach him was Hackett, a brawny mesomorph who had been raised third generation on some world out in the Pleiades Cluster, with a gravity field heavier than standard. The man looked like a collection of rocks with skin stretched tightly over them.

"Here we go," Rusk murmured. "Let the games begin."

Cyber snorted. "You don't have to sound so gleeful. Were you like this at my initiation?"

"I was in the room, if you'll recall."

"Oh, yeah. I *do* recall, now that you mention it."

Some things about human nature were eternal, Rusk mused. No matter if the ship in question was seafaring or starfaring, no matter if the crew was composed of different nationalities or altered genomes, there would always be a rite of passage.

"Someone's always got to be the low man on the totem pole," he said. He smiled and settled back in a station chair to watch the show.

Cyber cleared his throat. "Uh, about totem poles..."

"Shut up, Tremor."

"Shutting up, sir."

4 / DESPAIR

TROUBLE STIFLED A SIGH AT THE LOOK IN THE EYES OF THE BIG MAN approaching him—a look reflected in the eyes of everyone around them, a feral anticipation of blood and pain. It was familiar in a way that brought him up short. He had a strong mental image of a dark warren full of the stench of human fear, hatred, longing, and despair.

The despair was the worst.

How did he know that? How did he know that place? What the hell *was* that place?

The word sprang to his lips before he could stop it, so that when he faced the big guy—who was chewing a food bar, it almost seemed some sort of eccentric greeting.

"Slam."

The big guy stopped. Although he was Caucasian, he was wearing an exercise loincloth of an ancient Asian style. His thin, brown hair was bound up in a topknot. Given visual clues like these, it wasn't hard to guess what style of fighting he favored. Trouble stepped carefully around him.

Topknot regarded him with a sneer. "That your name, newbie, or an invitation?"

"Just an expression. I meant to say, 'damn, but I'm hungry'."

"Yeah? Want something to eat?" Topknot threw the food bar at Trouble's chest. It bounced off and hit the floor.

Trouble knew better than to let his eyes follow the movement. Such a distraction would open him to attack. He simply stood there, head cocked slightly, watching his adversary.

"No, thanks," he said, smiling, amiable.

Topknot grinned. "Afraid of my germs? Worried about your health, huh?"

"No," said Trouble, softly, reading the immediate future in the other's eyes. "Worried about yours."

It took Topknot as long as Trouble anticipated to decide he'd been challenged, and when the last circuit fired in the rock man's brain, he reacted as expected. He came at Trouble with a speed that was surprising in a man of that size.

Trouble wasn't surprised; he was easily able to sidestep Topknot's charge, taking advantage of the ship's slightly lighter gravity. Topknot was operating in the same field, but had considerably more momentum to deal with. As a result, he blundered a good meter and a half past Trouble before wheeling and turning to attack again.

Someone laughed. The rest of the audience remained silent, but the high-pitched adolescent chuckle obviously annoyed Topknot.

"Shut up, Lucas!" he snarled, glaring at a dark-haired teenager who looked about sixteen or seventeen, Standard. "Or we'll find out if you can laugh without a voice box."

The boy paled, cleared his throat, and cowered between two older crewmen.

It was then that Trouble decided he actively disliked Topknot. Adults who bullied kids were in a special class of vermin. He wondered if that was a memory or a simple reaction to the present situation. Didn't matter, really. His dislike was active but agnostic.

Topknot turned his attention to his prey. "Now I'm going to swab the decks with your brains."

"Colorful imagery," Trouble said.

Before Topknot could attack again, a female voice snapped: "Back off, Hackett!"

A woman stepped between the combatants. She was ginger-blonde, muscular, and obviously afraid of neither of them. It was this last fact that intrigued Trouble. He regarded her as one might a strange new life form.

"And you are—?" he asked.

"Name's Morgan."

"Morgan. Is that a first name or a last name?"

"It's all the name you need."

Trouble nodded, shifting his eyes to the hulk glowering at him over her shoulder. "I think someone wants to talk to you."

Morgan turned and looked up at Hackett. She was a tall woman, but she still barely came up to the big man's chin.

"Get out of the way, Morg," he growled.

But Morgan refused to move, much to Trouble's growing amusement. Something in him responded warmly to the moment, though he half suspected the woman would end up as a grease spot on the big guy's boot.

"Leave him be, Hackett," Morgan repeated. "He's one of us, now."

"That's open to debate," Trouble said, before Hackett could reply.

Surprised, Morgan looked over her shoulder at him. "Shut up," she said, "or Hackett'll spread you over this deck like paint."

"Actually, I think the plan was to swab the deck with my brains."

"Oh, *well*, then."

"But that's not likely to happen either."

Morgan looked closely at Trouble. He smiled and met her eyes. They were green.

"Give me a hint about the subtext here," she said. "You're asking me to butt out?"

"I'm just saying, I can take care of myself. I'd rather not shed blood, but if I have to…" He gave her a shrug with the smile; she stepped aside.

Hackett came forward. "Okay, pile rat, why don't you show me—"

Trouble didn't wait to hear what Hackett wished to be shown; he took a quick step in and popped him in the solar plexus. Five times. Very fast. Short, strong blows, driven by Trouble's powerful shoulders and arms, but calculated not to break anything. He did those calculations unconsciously, aware only of amazement that he did them at all.

Hackett's face took on the shade and waxy gloss of a pale cheese. His breathing sounded like … like air whistling through a micrometeorite breach. He slowly sagged to one knee.

Trouble glanced at Morgan. "I'm new here," he reminded her. "Little help on protocol?"

"He's down, but not all the way. As long as he's still partly upright, he ranks you."

Trouble nodded. He turned back to the big man, put his foot against his shoulder, and gave him a gentle shove. Hackett toppled and hit the deck with a crash that probably registered on the outer hull sensors. The audience was silent.

Trouble glanced over at Morgan. "We done here?"

She nodded, her eyes amused. "Oh, yeah."

"Good." Trouble started toward the hatch.

"I thought you were hungry," Morgan called after him.

"Lost my appetite."

"Want me to show you around?" she asked next.

"Maybe later," said Trouble, and left the Retreat.

Slam, he thought as he headed down the corridor toward the quarterdeck. Where had that come from? He knew without knowing how he knew that he had been in a place like that, had *survived* a place like that. He looked at his hands, surprised/not-surprised to see that his knuckles were unscathed by the number of punches he'd thrown. He noticed something else: His skin was not as pale as most of his new crewmates which suggested that he wasn't a spacer himself and that if he'd been in the slam, he hadn't been there too long.

Question was, what had he done to put himself there in the first place?

Just now Trouble Matthews had no answers to that, but his fighting skill put uncomfortable ideas into his head.

Rusk watched Trouble walk out of the room, leaving one of the best fighters aboard the *Raker* unconscious behind him. And he'd done it in two moves. *Two moves!*

Rusk realized he was gripping the arms of his chair so hard that his fingers were cramping. He looked over at Cyber.

The net-head looked back, brows raised. "Little-known fact about totem poles," he said. "In most First Nations lore, the lowest position was usually occupied by the figure with the most power." He blinked, and the monitor winked out. "Just thought you'd like to know."

Rusk growled, stood up, and stalked out.

5 / FLIES

Lucas Shade had never seen anything like it. Mouth agape, he watched the new man saunter out of the Retreat as casually as if he had just brushed away a fly, and not decked one of the most brutal members of the *Raker*'s crew.

This was especially fulfilling to Lucas because Hackett often took pleasure in tormenting him. Nothing really serious, of course. After all, Lucas was the captain's nephew. And even though Erasmus Shade had made it quite clear that Lucas was to be accorded no special treatment, the relationship kept the boy safe from Hackett's bursts of temper. There was some irony in that; it also made him the target of Hackett's resentment.

As Lucas watched, he saw Hackett stir. The big man would regain consciousness in a few moments, and Lucas decided it would be prudent to be somewhere else when this happened. His duty rotation was coming up, anyway. He might as well get a move on.

He left the Retreat quickly, heading aft toward Hydroponics. He liked the botanical section of the cargo holds—plants were quiet, restful to be around, and mostly not dangerous.

All things considered, life as a smuggler wasn't bad, even with assholes like Hackett to contend with. Lucas had spent most of his life learning to deal with his father, whose swift but icy temper made Hackett look as if he had the patience of a saint. When he'd finally had enough of his father's emotional abuse and petitioned his uncle for a berth on the *Raker*, he'd had no real idea what it would be like. He'd only been sure of one thing—it couldn't be any worse than the life he'd left.

Most people would scoff at that. The only son of a wealthy and influential man lived a life of moneyed privilege. An outsider would call him a fool to give all that up to become a glorified cabin boy on a piecemeal freighter running contraband. Let 'em call him whatever they wanted. It was better than the alternative—his mother disappeared, his father a cold uncommunicative bastard he could never impress or even please. Hell, he'd realized finally that he didn't *want* to please him. Along toward the end, he'd gone out of his way to *displease*. And, in the end, his father had been only too happy to let him go to his uncle's ship with some clichéd speech about the experience making him into a man Julian Shade could respect.

He wasn't sure he ever wanted to be that.

Hydroponics was far astern; in fact, you couldn't get much farther aft without running out of ship entirely. Made sense. Using an aft cargo space for the various botanicals allowed them to be kept in whatever climate required for their transport. In this case, Captain Shade had put their Lerandia "grove" as far away from the bridge as possible because of the smell. The stuff that nourished the valuable growth stank like the lair of an incontinent carnivore. Lucas, Morgan, and the other tenders wore air filters made from Delus sea sponges. Even with those, the stench was irksome.

Other than that major cavil, it wasn't a bad job; Lucas at least knew where he could go when he wanted to get away from his uncle. Better still, the potential profits would be high. Many members of the Guild smuggled illicit botanicals, often in the form of seeds because it was easier to slip smaller items through customs undetected, but the profit was way higher for the sporules from a mature plant. Even if you had to bribe a few officials not to notice them.

Smuggling was not considered a particularly unethical profession, but it was still risky. The penalties for being caught carrying some items were extreme, depending on local law, but this peril was rendered acceptable by the payoff. Captain Shade had assured them that Lerandia produce would pay very well, indeed. He had not divulged anything about the state of its legality.

That was a little worrisome, and neither Lucas nor any other member of the general crew knew why that was or what properties the plant possessed that made it worth the risk of smuggling it. Certainly, the ship's botanist knew, and Lucas had asked him, but he'd just smiled and said, "Sorry kid. That's on a need-to-know basis, and you don't need to know."

It was ironic, really—at home on Caledonia, his father told him too much too often. He went on and on and on about what he expected, what he wanted, what he deserved from his young son. Nor would he shut up about all the ways in which Lucas failed to meet those expectations, desires, or just desserts. The communication was mostly verbal—Julian Shade had a tongue that his son believed wasn't human flesh, but carved from an iceberg's lethal underbelly. But occasionally his father went beyond the verbal and sent Lucas into a realm of dark unknowns and terrifying suspicions about what had happened to a cherished book, a beloved pet, a friend ... a mother.

Lucas always shied away from those memories, and he did so now, putting himself firmly back aboard his uncle's aging vessel. No doubt about it—stench, risk, mystery, and the occasional painful attentions of thugs like Hackett aside, Lucas was happier by far on the *Moonraker* than he had ever been back on his homeworld under the coldly critical eye of his father.

He reached the Hydroponics hatch and went through the lab into the tiny break room where he logged himself in for duty. Then he went to the lockers and slipped into a thin protein sheath uni-suit—designed to be worn for one rotation before dissolving—pulled a botanics kit out of the equipment locker, and stepped through into the long forward bay where the crew's food staples were grown.

The air was cool, moist, and smelled fresh and green. He'd love to linger here, but he had to tend to the money cargo. Still, he moved as slowly as he dared to the aft hatch. He took a deep, longing breath, then activated the hatch and slipped into the aft bay's thick, humid jungle air.

Lerandia plants—trees really, their botanist had informed him—required room to grow and fructify. A typical plant must have at least seven or eight meters of stalk to put out seed-bearing fruit, which was why their bay rose vertically from Zeta deck to Epsilon. They also seemed to require a certain congestion of growth to generate fruit; the thick boles were barely far enough apart to allow someone to squeeze between them. They were grown in square plots circumscribed by a network of catwalks and ramps that ran from its lowest point on Zeta to nearly the ceiling of Epsilon.

Oddly enough, it wasn't the fruit that made Lerandia so valuable, but the leaves. Lucas wasn't quite sure what benefit was derived from them, but, given their black market value, it was obviously significant.

The leaves were broad, flat, and vaguely heart shaped. Each mature specimen was roughly 20 centimeters in diameter. They were crimson instead of green; Lucas knew this was because they metabolized light through an iron-based molecular structure, instead of chlorophyll, but that was as far as his knowledge went. One didn't have to be an exo-botanist to do the scut-work required to keep the plants healthy.

The Lerandia root system sent a series of nodes and fibrous tendrils through the nutrient. Without soil to impede growth, the interweaving mass had to be lasered back regularly. The nodes were also prey to a leprous blight that turned their glossy black surfaces a sickly mottled gray, and which had to be painstakingly scraped away with a cryoplane, which froze the softer, water-heavy blight, leaving the dense fiber of the roots intact.

This was how Lucas spent much of each day—crouched in the vile nutrient muck, fishing out nodes and carefully freezing, then scraping away the blight-ridden bits. He wore gloves for this particular task, after once nearly losing a fingertip to frostbite. Now he pushed and clambered through, under, over, and around the dense, twining mass, until he reached the pulse-marker that told him where he'd left off yesterday.

He opened the botanics kit, fished out long synthetic gloves, pulled them on, and hitched them up above his elbows. Then he took the crescent-shaped cryoplane in hand and flicked it on. It hummed, and a blue-white light arced from one tip of the crescent to the other. Lucas could feel the supercooled backwash glide over his gloved hand and ride up his arm to kiss his cheek. It was pleasant, really, and effectively banished the feeling of being in a swamp.

Now came the unpleasant part. With a grimace of distaste he groped around in the slimy feed liquid until he found a node, and pulled it into view. Each node was basically egg-shaped and about a foot long, with a thick root stalk connected to either end and, depending on its size, had anywhere from six to twenty tendrils erupting from it—each a potential Lerandia plant.

Lucas hummed while he worked, scraping a few spots of blight off the bole before letting it slide back into the "juice" and selecting another. He'd lost track of how many he'd done when he pulled up one that was different. Radically different. First off, it wasn't oval, but more of a flattened sphere, as if someone had partly deflated a ball. Second, although it had stalks attached to it on both ends, it had no tendrils growing from it. Third, it was gray instead of black; but not the gray of the blight. This had a metallic sheen. And it was heavier than a normal node.

Lucas tapped the cryoplane's handle against it, and swallowed in surprise. It wasn't just a metallic color; part of it *was* metal. What he held in his hands was not a natural growth, or even an unnatural one. It was a device that had been attached to the root stock—a device that had certainly not been on the Lerandia when it was brought aboard. Lucas's mind scrambled to make sense of it. The bay was monitored constantly. Only someone whose presence here would arouse no suspicion could have done this. Which begged the question: *Why* would they do it?

"Whoa, shit," he said softly, lowering the thing back into the murky fluid. He rose and backed away from it.

I should've known, he thought as he splashed and floundered toward the lowermost catwalk that led to the compartment's hatch. Things had been just too freakin' easy lately. Everything going the way it should. That was *never* a good sign. He had to tell someone.

He scrambled up onto the catwalk, hurried to the hatch and slapped the lock cycle control. His first impulse was to go to his uncle, but Erasmus Shade was a stickler for protocol. He'd insisted on treating his nephew like any other member of the crew.

Which means I'd have to go through Rusk. He snorted. Yeah, right. The bastard's probably in on it.

He'd tell the botanist, Sanchez, he decided. The plants were his special charge, after all. Lucas felt comfortable with this decision. If he was circumspect, Rusk wouldn't even have to know about it until after the whole thing had been—

The light went green. The hatch opened. Hackett stood framed in the opening, looking at Lucas, jerkstick in hand.

"In a hurry, are we?"

6 / ADJUSTMENTS

THE INVITATION FROM THE WOMAN NAMED MORGAN FOR A TOUR had its appeal, but Trouble had been smothered in people since first coming to on Erasmus Shade's old freighter, and he was determined to take the grand tour on his own. His sudden memories of the narrow, humanity-clogged confines of what was most certainly a prison (or perhaps a prison ship) made being alone suddenly preferable.

He wondered what he had done that would have landed him in a slam. He wondered how he had gotten out and how he had lost all memory of either fact. He wondered who the child in his dream had been, and who the woman who sang and laughed in the background. He wondered about the man sitting alone in the council chamber. He wondered those things, but refused to pursue them. At this point in time, pursuit made no sense and offered only frustration.

He glanced up at what was undoubtedly a cam bot in the corner above the doorway of a forward lift on Epsilon Deck. It was no bigger than his pinkie nail, but he could see it clearly—a pimple in the otherwise smooth surface of the wall where it met the ceiling. He smiled at it and sketched a salute.

He'd start at the topmost deck, he decided, and work his way down until he had either traveled the ship's corridors from stem to stern or had been summarily called to duty. He didn't expect to finish the tour.

In the lift, riding up to Alpha Deck, he pondered what his response to that call would be. He could be stubborn and fight, he supposed, with predictable results. Or he could acquiesce. The first option didn't seem to lead much of anywhere—after all, he couldn't take on the entire crew. The second option was just plain distasteful. This seemed a further confirmation that he despised bullies, even if they out-ranked him. Was that why he'd been in the slam?

The lift doors opened, letting him out onto the forward observation deck. The light was muted here, so that visitors could see the stars through an arching vault of transparent flexiglass. Trouble was certain that even if the lights were turned up to full throttle, someone half-blind would still be able to see the Milky Way trailing its blaze of glory across the void.

He raked hair back from his eyes and turned to look across the curving chamber, past the lift core to the blackness of the Rift. It was as if someone had sliced the universe in two, swept all the stars and planets to one side, and left the other side empty except for a few random motes missed by the cosmic janitor's broom.

Feast or famine. All or nothing. His life was like that, he realized, crowded as that swath of star stuff one moment; the next moment as empty as the road to Porphyry, or as empty as this observation deck. He found that curious. Did spacers become so blasé that even the stars lost their wonder? Did that idea—that one could always find wonder in the stars mean he hadn't been a spacer before?

Before what? He contemplated that, then realized that he felt natural here—whatever that meant. He felt comfortable on the ship. He knew the parts of the ship more intimately than someone who merely took passage.

Okay, so he'd been in space before. Good to know.

Trouble moved across the deck to the Rift side, gazing up at the paltry spatter of pinprick lights. He walked up to the transparent, curving wall—close enough that another long stride would carry him into space, were that possible. He could see his reflection in it, shortened, dwarfish, then looked past it to a star that distinguished itself both by its brightness and by its sheer solitude.

A rhyming verse emerged from memory. "Starlight, star bright," he murmured at the radiant bead of light. "First star I see tonight. I wish I may, I wish I might, have the dream I dream tonight."

Where the hell had that unmitigated whimsy come from? And even if he could order up a dream, what would it be? A habitable world on which he could lose himself? There must be such worlds. Worlds on which one could become permanently and irretrievably lost.

Why do I need to be lost?

Trouble chuckled inwardly. Hell, it didn't matter what questions he asked. He didn't know the answers and probably shouldn't want to.

Behind him, the lift doors hissed softly. A mirror image of the rectangle of light opened in the polished surface of Trouble's window on the universe. Someone stepped out onto the deck, backlit by the wash of light from the lift, then turned and moved toward him.

It was the hardskin, Jiang.

"You okay?" she asked.

"What do you think?"

"Okay, then ... you lost?"

"In a way, yeah."

"I can show you to the crews' quarters—"

"Not that kind of lost."

"I don't—"

Trouble turned to look at her. "You came up here looking for me? Why?"

"Rusk's going to be looking for you any time now and ...

well, I just wanted to give you a heads-up. If you're thinking of hiding from him, you can't."

"Hey, I'm just taking the whirlwind tour. Getting a sense of the ship. I don't generally hide from men like Rusk."

Oooh. Tough talk. He almost laughed at himself.

"Yeah. I kind of got that feeling about you. Something about the way you kept running into Rusk's jerkstick down in the brig."

Trouble took a couple of steps toward the woman, noticing the way her eyes widened and she lifted her head, warily. Was he really that scary?

"Why the solicitude—Jiang, is it?"

"Yeah. Jiang. Kai Jiang. Not all of us are as callused as Hackett and that bunch. I didn't particularly like watching what they did you to when they brought you in. I signed onto *Moonraker* willingly. So did Jay. So did most of the others. I kind of figure that's the way it ought to be. Ripping people off the streets when you don't know what—or who—you're taking them away from..." She shook her head, starlight rippling across her short dark hair. "That's not right."

"Softer on the inside than you are on the outside, huh?"

"Look, Trouble, the way you got here was bad enough. I just wanted to make sure you don't do stuff that's gonna make things even harder for you. So, take my advice: Do what you're told and don't be a smart ass. You should be okay if you can do that."

"Yeah, well, thanks. But I'm beginning to think I'm a natural smart ass."

She shrugged. "You want me to show you the rest of the ship?"

"Thanks, but I prefer to explore on my own. Don't worry," he added as she hesitated. "I'm not stupid. I get Rusk. I've met men like him before."

"Didn't think you were. Stupid, I mean." She smiled (an act

that did not crack the dark, shiny skin of her cheeks) and turned away.

"So who else came aboard like I did?"

She looked back over one shoulder. "Why do you care?"

Trouble shrugged. "I figure if they're still alive, there's a chance for me to survive, too. Might want to talk to them."

"There's Cyber for one—you haven't met him yet. He's our navigator—a net-head. And Sal Sanchez—he's the resident expert on our cargo. Captain Shade acquired him and the cargo as a sort of package deal. And Rainor Glass, I think, although I'm not real sure about him. Those are the ones I know of. I suppose there might be others."

"How'd they take being shanghaied?"

"About the way you'd expect. But they adjusted."

"What happens to the ones who don't adjust?"

She turned away from him and started toward the lift. "I'll bet you can guess."

"Hey, Jiang … Kai."

She stopped as the lift doors opened and looked back at him again.

"Thanks for the heads-up."

"Sure." She disappeared behind the lift doors.

Madelen Morgan was doing biceps curls in the exercise area of the Retreat. She'd already jogged around the perimeter several times and had worked up a good sweat but she wasn't done yet. During the downtime shift, she'd dreamed she was a little old lady who depended upon the kindness of strangers. All right, it was a freaking nightmare, and since then she'd imagined feeling her muscles atrophy with accelerated decrepitude.

The underpinnings of the nightmare were, unfortunately, well grounded in scientific fact and personal experience. She feared becoming weak. Too many years spent in the confines of artificial gravity inhibited production of certain amino acids necessary for building protein, as well as slowing the pituitary's production of Human Growth Hormone. In short, past a certain point, muscles atrophied regardless of how much exercise one did, or how many vitamin and supplement patches one wore.

While some of her crewmates used electrostim devices to maintain muscled tone. Morgan was a purist; she preferred the stress and burn of lifting real weight. It was more protracted and painful, but she'd never let pain stop her. It was a reminder that she was alive.

Morgan didn't think of her life as having been arduous, degrading, or even dangerous, though at times it had been all those things … often all at once. She had come a long way since her days as a street urchin on Rogue's World, when she'd had to do things to survive that she didn't think about now, things that surfaced only occasionally in nightmares she'd trained herself to forget upon awakening. At nineteen, she'd stolen away on a smuggler's ship to get away from her fagin, who had become more deranged and cruel than even she'd been used to, pimping her out to a radiation-damaged spacer who couldn't even get it up in Z-Grav, and who took out his frustration on her. The ship hadn't been out for three hours before she'd been discovered.

Interstellar protocol permitted punishments of varying degrees of severity, everything from forced labor to ejection from an airlock without a spacesuit. Usually the crew dictated a stowaway's punishment, subject to a vote supervised by the captain or first mate. Morgan had been lucky. Not only was she attractive, but the crew was undermanned, and in dire need of novices to do such dirty, dangerous, yet necessary work as replacing drive rods, patching the hull, and checking the quantum drive for radiation leakage.

During her "hearing", Morgan let it be known, through a combination of defiance and flirtation, that she was willing to perform all those tasks … and more. A few crew members took an immediate liking to her. Morgan had no problem letting their imaginations run wild, at least until the outcome of the vote. Then she let it be known in no uncertain terms that she would entertain only the best offers. By the time she'd been voted to a full-fledged membership on the crew she was, for the first time in her life, in control of her destiny.

So long as she remained in space, that is. Spacer prospects weren't so good on land, be it planet, satellite, or wheelworld, unless one had a stake, and wanted to settle down with a partner and work a mundane job for a living. Being crew on the *Moonraker* could be monotonous, but you could never say it was dull. Especially when there was ever the possibility of someone new and interesting showing up.

Morgan found Trouble Matthews especially interesting. That he had a questionable past went without saying. He had the watchful, wary aura of someone who had been in the slam and he was clearly dangerous—more so because of that deceptively easy-going attitude. Still, Morgan had worked side-by-side with all sorts of low-lifes; Trouble Matthews definitely did not fit the profile of a hardened criminal. He was a bizarre combination of confidence and acquiescence, toughness and amiability, and though he wasn't sly or ambiguous, she couldn't quite figure him out.

He seemed to use the minimum amount of violence necessary to get his point across. Few of the men she had met had that kind of restraint. He hadn't—so far, at least—lost control, whereas a lesser man in the same circumstances might have done just that out of fear. She wondered if he had blood on his hands. If he did, she wagered he hadn't had a choice about shedding it. Trouble was unquestionably an outlaw, but she didn't believe he was a criminal.

And he was undeniably attractive.

"Working something out of your system, Morgan?"

Morgan set the weights down and turned to face the man who'd just stepped into the gym. "What do you want, Cyb?"

"Nothing," said the net-head with a shrug. "Just happened to catch you working out and thought you might have something on your mind. You looked ... pensive."

"Pensive. And what might I be pensive about, Cyb?"

"I wouldn't know. I was just hoping that you might confide in me."

Morgan wiped off her face, then her bare underarms with a towel. She knew what this was about. Cyber got a bump in his pants every time he got within ten meters of her. It was almost Pavlovian, and he didn't seem to care that he would never be rewarded for his response. Nor did it stop him from finding every excuse he could to leave his dark cubicle and attempt a human interface with her.

Morgan supposed she should be flattered. After all, Cyber could immerse himself in a virtual encounter with any woman he could imagine yet, he lost no opportunity to pursue Morgan. She often wondered why. She was taller and harder than those cyber-women, and her body bore the scars of countless little accidents and fights and sexual encounters gone awry. She supposed that, by landfall standards, she was attractive. She was also fairly certain she would never know, because being that kind of woman didn't interest her. She'd had more than enough of male fantasies.

Morgan had nothing against Cyber. In fact, she'd grown to like him. He was wicked smart, funny and perceptive in ways that surprised her. But his veiled desperation reminded her too strongly of other men. He didn't leer—that wasn't his personality, and she appreciated it—but he watched her too closely with eyes that were too omniscient, and too needy. Most of the time, she wished he would just leave her alone.

She turned and began performing her *tai chi* routine. She closed her eyes and imagined Cyber was not there. The ship was not there. The universe consisted solely of her body and her mind, working in tandem. There was no time. No past, no future. There was only the moment…

"What do you think of Trouble?" Cyber asked, utterly destroying her concentration.

"What?"

"You do have some thoughts about Trouble. I saw you step between him and Hackett in the Retreat today."

"Yeah, and then I stepped back out again. The guy can take care of himself, that's what I think."

Cyber grinned. "Is that admiration I hear? C'mon, admit it: You like him. I think you liked him the first moment you saw him."

She turned and faced him. "And if I did?"

He hesitated, then: "Nothing."

Morgan scowled at the navigator. She wondered just how much he knew about her and her ambitions. Even in her worst moments, she had nurtured them, and been sustained by the belief that she not only deserved better in life, but was capable of making better happen. Her life aboard the *Raker* had been characterized by a slow but steady progression up the crew hierarchy, until she was a trusted, respected, experienced hand who lacked only one thing: rank, and the extra percentage of the profits that came with it. The latter was a secondary concern, but significant nonetheless, because for her a greater share of the profits would be an indicator of greater respect.

Moonraker was an excellent ship for her age, but Morgan had been stuck at the same level for too long, with Rusk standing squarely in her way. He was cruel, and mistook his cruelty for strength and control. She wanted his job, knew she could do it better. She feared Cyber was beginning to comprehend what she hungered for. She'd been thinking about making her move, and a man like Trouble Matthews would make an excellent partner. Despite the fact that she theoretically had more important matters on her mind, Morgan found herself wondering what he looked like naked. That conjured a smile.

Cyber was watching her, watching the thoughts tumble

through her head, making her feel transparent. A grin hovered on his lips.

"So, how is your love life, Morgan?"

She glared at him. "None of your damn business, that's how," she said.

He took a step back. "Understood. No problem."

Morgan started to turn away from him, then paused. "By the way, Cyber…"

"Yes?"

"Those remote cams in the Retreat cubicles?"

His eyes darted nervously from side to side, though they were the only two in the immediate area. His thoughts might as well have been floating in a big, fluffy thought balloon over his head: *How the hell does she know*?

"Get rid of them."

7 / WALKABOUT

TROUBLE COVERED MORE TERRITORY ON HIS GRAND TOUR THAN HE expected to. Although he did encounter various crew members, no one stopped him, tried to talk to him, or even looked at him sideways. As a result, he went from the Observation Deck to the Retreat on Epsilon without interacting with any of the *Raker*'s crew. It was almost like being alone, and it gave him ample opportunity to take the measure of the ship.

She was clearly not a new vessel. He figured she was at least thirty years old. There were discolorations in the bulkheads, the decks were worn shiny in places with the passage of many feet, there were consoles and lighting panels held together with gaftape. There were also newer accoutrements, to be sure; some of the hatches were of a dilating design that was a decade old at most, most of the maintenance consoles he'd seen were fairly new, and the surveillance system seemed to be state-of-the-art. Trouble gave one of the cams an amiable glance. Paranoid bunch, these smugglers, but then what they did probably warranted an obsession with security.

He started to walk past the Retreat, then changed his mind and stepped through the doorway. The room was empty except for one crewman who sat at a table, torturing a long, thin piece of mylar. Trouble turned, surveying the room. A quick glance showed that the commons was flanked with cubicles of some sort. Trouble had no curiosity about what they were or what their uses might be, though he did note that red lights on several doors seemed to indicate some were occupied. Through the open hatch at the far end of the room, he could see part of an exercise area.

"You Ridley Matthews?" asked a soft voice from behind him.

He swung back to fix the crewman with a neutral gaze. The man looked Hispanic, maybe with a little Asian thrown in. Age uncertain—he could have been thirty or fifty. He wore his curly, black hair long enough that it almost fell across one dark eye. Probably wreaked havoc with ladies and gents alike, as likely did the smooth walnut brown skin and guileless expression.

"That's me."

"I hear they call you Trouble—and that you apparently deserve the nick."

Trouble brought up an easy smile. "Guess my fame precedes me."

The other man laughed and did something to the strip of mylar that made it look suddenly like a double-helix strand of DNA.

"I'm Salazar Sanchez. Ship's botanist."

"Botanist? Jiang mentioned you. Said you were the cargo expert. I take it that means the cargo is botanical?"

"Indeed." Sanchez's smile was rueful. "Pardon me for being tight-lipped, but if Rusk hasn't mentioned our cargo, I don't think I should."

"Jiang said you were shanghaied. Like me. Must've been a while back."

Sanchez looked down at his handiwork, twisting it in his long fingers. "A while."

"And you're still here?"

"I have little choice, Mr. Matthews."

"Just Trouble. I think a man always has choices." *Well, that was philosophical of me.*

Sanchez shrugged, still examining his mylar sculpture. His eyes flicked briefly to a corner of the ceiling, then he said: "I have a place to sleep, plants to care for, something to do with my hands." He held up the double-helix and smiled again, showing even, white teeth. "What else could a man require?"

Trouble shrugged. "Freedom?"

"A much-touted, over-valued philosophical construct, my friend. 'Freedom consists not in refusing to recognize anything above us, but in respecting something which is above us.' Goethe said that. I respect what is above me, *Mister* Matthews."

He laid subtle stress upon the 'mister,' which Trouble did not miss or misinterpret. "'The man who trades freedom for security does not deserve or receive either.' Benjamin Franklin said that— or something like it."

Sanchez sat back in his chair, and fixed Trouble with a bemused look. "Follow that aphorism, Mr. Matthews, and believe me, your life aboard *Moonraker* will be brief and unpleasant."

"It is what it is," Trouble said, and left the botanist to his art project.

Cyber jacked in. The initial rush never failed to take him by surprise—suddenly he had a thousand eyes, a thousand ears. His senses were augmented beyond comprehension. He was everywhere.

He loved this; the rush, the crystalline avalanche of multiple camera points-of-view, cacophonies of conversations, music, the animal grunts and sighs of sex ... if it was happening anywhere aboard *Moonraker*, he knew about it. He was the ultimate voyeur. Then there was the data stream from the ship's systems. That provided a whole different smorgasbord of information.

At first, he could do little more than just surf the sensory waves and let the data wash through him. It was always like that when the time between cyber-journeys was too long. He wasn't addicted to the experience—not in his opinion, anyway—but he much preferred having it to not having it.

He jumped from monitor to monitor, from sensor to sensor, feeling, as he often did, that if his mind could somehow grow large enough, it would encompass the entirety of the ship all at once. He could have as much control over the mechanics of the *Raker* as those of a religious persuasion believed the Grand Designer had over the mechanics of the universe. In fact, he sometimes thought his experience in the net was evidence for the existence of such a Designer. One point of view or infinite points of view—perhaps that was the difference between being human and being God.

Jacked into the net, Trevor Marsden aspired to be a real ghost in the machine. But it wasn't within his grasp right now, and he wasn't sure if it ever would be. He wasn't sure if he wanted it to be; he'd heard of wire-fliers who'd gotten in too deep and couldn't find their way back from virtuality to reality. Sometimes the idea frightened him. Sometimes it held a strange appeal.

For now, anyway, he was satisfied with knowing things piecemeal. It was one of the few ties to humanity he had left when he was jacked in, harnessed to the body-fitting, reclining couch-cum-stasis pod in his cubicle while his mind ranged the electronic highways and byways of the ship. He was mostly self-aware during the times he was uplinked to the ship's systems. Although the enhancements he'd had made to his neural net—enhancements he suspected had gotten him shanghaied onto the *Raker*—had somewhat altered his sense of self.

The mods were experimental and potentially unhealthy, but he'd had himself retrofitted anyway when the opportunity had presented itself, about a year ago. Less than a week later, he'd gone to sleep in his six by ten room on a ring station orbiting Herron's Hope, dreaming of the lucrative contracts he'd be able to land with his souped-up bionics. He'd awakened in *Moon-raker's* brig.

It was one of those good news/bad news scenarios: he was an unwilling recruit, but so far, the pay and the duty had been pretty good. His enhancements had made him far more skilled at riding the virtual stream than any of the other techs then aboard. Erasmus Shade had rewarded him well enough that he didn't regret the improvements to his system. He might be facing mindmelt in another ten years or so, but for now he liked having that edge.

He also liked following Mad Morgan around the ship. In fact, he liked Morgan, period. There was a part of him that wanted to get rid of the cams in the retreat cubicles as she'd asked—but not the greatest part. If nothing else, they were justified by Erasmus Shade's need to know if any of his crew might be plotting something against him from the privacy of the Retreat, or simply doing something that could provide fodder for future extortion. For now, he simply moved the cams, hoping that Morgan wouldn't notice they were still there. Mounted in miniature bots, he could order them to new locations in the cubicles as he chose. He brought them down from the ceiling to positions on the furniture frames, on which they looked convincingly like tiny rivets. He was surprised he hadn't thought to do that before.

He blipped into the feeds cursorily. There was a couple doing the wild thing in Cubicle Three; otherwise the little rooms were untenanted. The pair—two drive techs, he didn't know their names—were too involved in their own endeavors to notice a tiny gray welt toodling down the wall. Cyber used them to adjust the focus, which set his libido tingling. It was a good thing the rest of the crew had no idea he could flit from monitor to monitor like a tinkerbell and catch an eyeful of anything he wished.

His work in the Retreat done, he moved to catch Morgan in the mister, where she would invariably go after her workout. As always, his focus wandered to the myriad scars on her body, the souvenirs of her unhappy and mysterious past. They fascinated him; they were extensions of her spirit, of her fortitude and determination. They were the physical synergist, the flaws that paradoxically enhanced his idealization of her. His desire for her ... his love for her.

He did love her. He would never admit it—least of all to her. She'd laugh at him, or worse, pity him. He didn't want her pity; he fantasized about having her respect.

Respect? Hell, where had that come from? Her desire was what he wanted, but he stood a comet's chance in a supernova of getting it. Still, Cyber believed himself blessed, for his abilities at least allowed him the privilege of this vicarious intimacy. No one else could see Morgan like this.

Morgan stepped out of the semi-opaque cabinet, skin gleaming with gel mist, and set to patting off the cleansing salve with a towel. Cyber, who almost knew what it was like to be a starship, now wished only that he knew what it was like to be a man that Madelen Morgan wanted.

Today, Morgan departed from her routine. Instead of giving her short hair fifty strokes (with an allegedly real boar's bristle brush she had bartered for in a Heartworld market), pulling on her uniform and returning to duty, she moved to the lone mirror in the mist booth and turned before it, seemingly admiring her naked body.

No, not admiring, for when she turned back into Cyber's camera eye, he noticed the slight frown between her brows, the assessing quality of her gaze. She ran her hands over the most prominent scars that decorated her ribs and abdomen, and as she did so her mouth tugged down at the corners. Cyber's imagination supplied a vivid fantasy in which he stepped, naked and real, from the tiny eye of his camera and told Morgan that she was perfect, that she had no right to look at herself with a critical eye, and that he wanted nothing more from her than to kiss every scar on her body.

With a shake of her head, Morgan pulled a pair of underwear

and a bra out of her duffle and put them on. Then she drew out a small, metal cylinder and sprayed a soft cloud of mist into her face. She stood motionless for a moment, eyes closed, then moved to inspect herself in the mirror. Her cheeks now glistened with a soft dew as if a cluster of tiny stars clung to them. Her eyelashes were tipped with jewels. Her lips looked moister and softer than they had a moment before. They looked ready for kissing, and as if that thought was also in her mind, she aimed a kiss at the mirror, then laughed and shook her head again.

"Get real, Maddie," she murmured, and pulled out her hairbrush.

Her hair got a hundred strokes today, and as he watched her finger-style it so that it curled softly over her forehead and around her ears, Cyber recognized the emotion he was experiencing—jealousy—for she was obviously doing this for *somebody*. He could not even pretend, could not even begin to hope, that this transformation had anything to with his interruption of her workout and his obvious attraction to her. To his knowledge, she had never taken a companion into a recreation cubicle. He couldn't imagine such a vivid woman suppressing or ignoring her sexual desires completely, but he assumed she satisfied it discreetly while on leave. He tried not to think about that. But he did anyway, of course, and it made him want her even more.

Now, suddenly, it appeared she intended to be noticed. And she would be; there wasn't a man aboard the vessel who wouldn't notice this sudden change in Morgan. It was not random, and the target for it could only be one person: Trouble. The new guy. The amiable tough guy, who made even Enoch Rusk uneasy.

Cyber fumed as he watched Morgan dress in a spotlessly clean uniform, which she left open at the neck. He followed her from the showers, his consciousness jumping from cam bot to cam bot, as she walked the corridors, whistling a tune he recognized—"The Green Hills of Earth"—and seemingly oblivious to the surprised stares from a crew that thought they had seen

Morgan in every mood. More than a few gave her second looks without realizing it. One crewman walked into an undilated hatch.

Cyber checked the log data. Morgan was slated for a shift in hydroponics. Her normal duty was engineering, but everyone but the captain and Cyber (being the lone navigator) worked shifts in 'ponics because the current cash cargo was there and that cargo belonged to the entire crew.

Now he was really confused. 'Ponics duty was dirty, sweaty, exhausting work. He didn't see the point of getting beautified if you knew you would be covered with soggy filth in short order. The concept of looking one's best at all times, even if it was futile, was beyond his comprehension.

Of course, maybe she just hoped someone would see her. Someone in particular. That made no sense either—she could have no idea where Trouble was.

Cyber made a quick check of the ship, beginning with Alpha Deck and moving down. Trouble was on Epsilon, strolling at a leisurely pace. He seemed merely to be checking the ship out. Walking the corridors with his eyes roving here and there as if memorizing each passage, each bulkhead, each panel. The net-head brought himself back to where he expected Morgan to be, which was on her way to her workstation. She wasn't. He found her, instead, heading for the Retreat. Where Trouble had just been. Cyber savored the irony.

Morgan reached the Retreat, poked her head in the door, and took quick inventory, failing to react to the surprise on the faces of the three crewmates she found there.

"Any of you seen the new guy?" she asked. "Rusk wants to put him to work."

A true lie. Of course, Rusk wanted to put Trouble to work, but that was hardly of interest to Morgan. Cyber felt a viscous tide of black emotion rising in his reptilian cortex.

Jiang was crossing to a table with a coffee cup in hand. She looked up and gave Morgan a long, speculative look before saying: "Last time I saw him, he was on Alpha Deck stargazing. That was a while ago, though."

"I think he's playing tourist. You just missed him," said Sanchez, not taking his eyes off the sculpture he was molding from the remains of his own cup. A strangely twisted piece of mylar computer printout sat atop the table already. He paused to admire his handiwork—in his nimble fingers the bio-foam cup had morphed into a tiny castle with a dragon peeking over the battlements.

He rose and headed for the door, stopping before Morgan to offer her a mocking bow. He handed her the castle. "Good hunting, fair lady," he said, and left.

Cyber's first impulse was to shut down and disconnect. He didn't want to see Morgan hunting Trouble, or snaring him, or, least of all, indulging in the spoils of victory. Still, he found himself following her from the Retreat, and was surprised when she continued on down to Hydroponics. Perhaps she thought that Trouble's journeys would inevitably take him there, and when they did, she would—what? Pounce on him, drag him into one of the bays, and devour him amongst the plantlife?

Cyber cursed himself for an over-imaginative fool and jumped ahead of Morgan into a 'ponics cam. The place seemed unusually quiet. Beneath the gurgling of the water filters and the steady whisper of the circulating air, there was silence. That wasn't right. There should be crewmen on duty here, complaining about the stench and the muck, breathing loudly through their filters, tramping about on the metal walkways.

A quick jump and a check outside the chamber: Morgan was still approaching, taking her time, still humming to herself. The poor woman couldn't carry a tune in a magnetic bottle; Cyber found that endearing.

He ran the 'ponics duty roster. Redfield and Duff were supposed to be on duty this shift, but they hadn't reported in yet. The last check-in had been Lucas, and that was hours ago.

His shift overlapped with Redfield and Duff's, but he was nowhere in sight.

Cyber ran through the ship-wide monitors next, looking for the missing crewmen, knowing they were not above bending protocol if offered the appropriate inducements. He'd bribed them himself on occasion for small shit. He found Duff asleep in a cubicle in the Retreat ... alone. Redfield was in the Ship's Mess on Gamma Deck, playing Sabot, apparently with real credit chips.

This boded ill.

The hydroponics farm was large, a hundred yards square. The scarlet Lerandia leaves were wide, and grew thick on the branches. There were a lot of places where his tiny, robotic snoops could not see. Cyber figured maybe twenty percent of the area was hidden from his view.

Hidden.

He had the uncomfortable feeling that the word was appropriate. He began systematically filtering all the ambient noise from the monitor's audio input. The whisper of air circulation, the soft drip of nutrients, even the almost undetectable drone of the engines themselves; he stripped them all away, one by one, until there was only one sound left.

A low frequency. It barely registered.

The sound of someone breathing.

Barely breathing.

8 / WHISTLING

THE HYDROPONICS BAY HATCH DILATED AND MORGAN WALKED IN, still whistling, still feeling pretty good. There was every chance that Trouble would happen by soon enough that she wouldn't be sweaty and stinky when he did. At least his appearance might give her a welcome break from the tedium of watching plants grow. She wasn't trained to do the root-planing or any of the other hands-on work and there were only so many times you could check the nutrient flow or gather up leaves that had fallen to the catwalks.

The chamber was silent and still. She looked around, frowning in puzzlement. "Anyone here?"

She turned to the small computer console just inside the hatch, set Sanchez's little castle on the top of the display, and punched up the duty roster. Redfield and Duff were listed for this shift. Okay, so where the hell were they? She gazed down the leaf-laden central aisle.

"Hey! You guys here?"

There was a long, unbroken silence, punctuated only slightly by a faint hiss of air from the ventilators.

"Great. Just great. Now I'm gonna have twice as much work to do because of those lazy—"

A high-pitched, metallic shriek made Morgan yip and clap

her hands over her ears. The shriek cut off with a sound like a blast weapon firing, and sparks flew from a point high up on the chamber wall about three meters from where Morgan stood. The sparks came to rest in the broad crimson leaves of the nearest Lerandia plant, and smoke curled out to waft on the canned breeze.

Uttering a stream of profanities, Morgan dashed to the nearest fire extinguisher and yanked it from the wall. She bulled her way through the stalks while trying to free the safety catch. She was rewarded for her efforts by having the entire firing mechanism break off in her hands.

"Oh, you *bastard!*" she snarled. She tried the spigot futilely, then threw the useless tank aside.

Two or three leaves of the plant nearest the little explosion were smoldering. Morgan cast a baleful glance in their direction, then turned and started for the hatch. It opened as she reached it, bringing her into forceful contact with Trouble, who thrust her away, then held her at arms' length.

Morgan blinked mentally. She couldn't have written a better entrance for him; too bad it was at the wrong moment.

"Why the hurry?" he asked. "Plants attacking?"

"The plants are *burning*," Morgan gasped.

She turned her head, drawing Trouble's eyes to where several of the great, broad leaves smoked and smoldered. As they watched, a tongue of flame flared, crawling up the branch toward the tall central trunk. It burned with a strange rainbow of colors, as if the plant were giving off some exotic gases or liquids —which, for all Morgan knew, it was.

Trouble said nothing. He released Morgan so suddenly she reeled, then leapt toward the burning plant. He put one foot on the root tank and literally vaulted up into the foliage. In an instant, he was hanging by his arms from the affected branch, while the fire scorched toward him, flaring ever higher.

With a sudden burst of energy, the flames shot out and jumped to another branch, thick with the precious leaves.

Morgan wanted to yell, to do something besides dance futilely in the aisle, but she held her tongue and caught up the fire extinguisher again, in the vain hope she might somehow coax it into working.

The vivid flames were almost licking Trouble's left arm when he wrapped his legs around the central stalk of the plant and, with a lithe convulsion of his lower body, ripped the entire burning branch away. He let it fall into the nutrient bath, where it sizzled and smoked as the fire went out. He twisted to reach the second burning branch and tore it down as well, nearly sending himself into the drink in the process.

Morgan used the defunct fire extinguisher to push the broad, smoldering leaves beneath the noisome water.

Trouble twisted his body upright and stretched up through the Lerandia foliage to pluck the still sparking camera from the wall. It followed the branches into the nutrient tank. Then he dropped back to the deck, landing neatly in front of Morgan.

"That was quick thinking," she told him. "I don't know that I—"

Trouble silenced her by clamping a hand on her shoulder and holding a finger to her lips. She caught her breath and started to protest, but he shook his head.

"Hear that?"

"Hear wh—?"

Trouble left her reeling and off balance a second time and began moving between the plants, pushing away the leaves to scan the root tanks. About halfway down the bay he stopped and knelt between two of the tanks.

"What is it?" Morgan rushed to follow, stopping behind him to peer down through the leaves into the dark slot.

Lucas lay there, wedged into a trough meant for blight scrapings. The boy was bruised and bleeding.

Morgan felt her uterus contract as her maternal instincts put in an unexpected appearance. "Oh, my God! Lucas! What happened?"

Trouble shot her a cool glance. "Someone beat the living shit out of him, is what happened."

Morgan bit down on her fury, wondering who she should aim it at. "Yeah. Let's get him into the break room, out of this stench. It's hard to breathe in here."

They got Lucas to his feet, then helped him out of the Lerandia grove into the little ante room. The poor kid was a mess: two black eyes, a swollen lip, a bloody face. And Morgan was sure he had bruises hidden under his shirt. She wasn't going to ask to see; at least spare the boy that much embarrassment.

"Who did this to you?" she asked.

Lucas shook his head. "Doesn't matter," he mumbled through swollen lips.

"Of course it matters! Your uncle is going to want to know who did this so he can bust his ass. And I'd kind of like to see it busted myself."

Lucas met Morgan's eyes. She could see the stubborn light in them and knew it was futile to prod him. Short of murder, you didn't squeal to the captain about anything and get someone in trouble, no matter how much they deserved it. Even though the conspicuously absent Redfield and Duff very likely knew who did this, there was little chance they'd talk, beyond giving some lame alibi. Lucas was the only witness to his own abuse, and he was the new kid on the block—only Trouble was newer. Whoever had done this had seniority and possibly more of Erasmus Shade's trust than his own nephew. If the accusation did not end in the perpetrator's banishment or incarceration, Lucas's life aboard the *Raker* could easily become a living hell.

Then again, perhaps it was already.

"Lucas, c'mon. There's nothing to be gained by silence. Tell us who—"

"I'm not saying who," Lucas told her. "You wouldn't either if it was you."

"The hell I wouldn't," Morgan protested.

The kid spat out a splatter of blood. "No, you'd probably kill the son of a bitch."

"It was a man, then."

"Whole gang of men, actually," Lucas mumbled. "Don't know how many. I gave 'em what-for. Had 'em on the run until they resorted to violence."

"You dickhead," she said, with a fondness for the young and weak that she suspected was hardwired into the human female's psyche. "C'mon, Trouble, let's get him to the infirmary."

"Just a minute." Trouble, still on his haunches in front of Lucas's chair, hadn't taken his eyes off the boy's face for a moment. "Why?" he asked the kid, making a zipping gesture across his own mouth.

"I just—I don't want to make any enemies."

"It's pretty obvious that you've already made at least one, kid. If you won't tell us who, tell us why. Why'd somebody do this to you?"

Lucas's gaze moved to Morgan's face and back to Trouble's again. "I—I laughed at him, and he—" His mouth closed so fast, Morgan could almost hear the snap of his jaws.

She said, in a voice filled with disgust, "Hackett."

"Okay," Trouble said. "So now we got the who. What about the why?"

Lucas winced. "I laughed at him because of what you did to him."

Trouble nodded dispassionately, then directed his next words to Morgan, though he didn't look at her. "You know, maybe he's right—maybe the reason he got his ass kicked isn't any of our business. Maybe it's not important to any one but Lucas—I get your name right, kid?"

The boy nodded and fell silent.

The kid's expression was eloquent. This was no petty revenge ass-kicking, but something else entirely. Cyber used the cam to move in on Lucas's face, then watched Trouble and Morgan take him to the infirmary.

Cyber's disembodied mind dithered. What was Hackett's real reason for thrashing Lucas Shade? There might be a monitor log somewhere that would provide a clue. It was worth investigating. Cyber checked the last two days' cam records for Lucas's comings and goings, but found nothing that would have threatened the loutish Hackett.

He went back to the 'ponics duty log and there he discovered something interesting: not only was the vid of the shift Redfield and Duff had missed erased, but so was a significant portion of Lucas's shift. The part still in existence showed nothing much. Lucas had entered the bay, signed in, then pulled out a botanical maintenance kit. He'd started in to work, quickly disappearing from the cameras' view behind a screen of foliage approximately ten meters from where he'd ended up, and on the opposite side of the central transverse aisle. He'd been de-blighting the nodes, Cyber surmised, and had been at it for only a few minutes when the record suddenly ended.

It was disturbing. All of it. The beating, Lucas's reluctance to speak, although this was clearly about more than Hackett's wounded pride, and—worst of all—the idea that someone had managed to enter Cyber's domain without his knowledge or permission to manipulate information for which he was responsible.

He wasn't thrilled about the loss of the cam bot he'd had to fry in order to draw Morgan's attention to Lucas, either. He'd replace it immediately, of course. Maybe even add to the collection of 'ponics snoops. Clearly this area of the ship bore more watching.

Cyber returned to his body with more haste and less reluctance than he'd ever known. He had to know what was going on and, odd as it seemed, his lanky, clumsy body was the best vehicle for his next task.

9 / CARGO

WITH THE SHADE KID SAFELY IN THE HANDS OF THE SHIP'S DOCTOR —a cadaverous undertaker of a man named Pike—Trouble cleaned up, then accompanied Morgan forward to the ship's mess. He was hungry for both food and information; she was talkative from the adrenaline flush of their brush with disaster ... and, perhaps, something beyond that. He hadn't missed the speculative looks she'd aimed at him on the journey from the infirmary.

He let her rattle on for a bit about the weird love-hate relationship between Erasmus Shade and his nephew and the dynamics between Rusk and the rest of the crew, filing it all away for future use. Then, as they sat down at a table, each carrying plates filled with steaming green blobs of something he suspected would kill a wild hellion boar, Trouble asked, "So, what are they?"

Morgan glanced down at her plate. "Boiled t'whill, I think."

"I meant the plants down in Hydroponics. Never seen them before." *And wouldn't remember them if I had, most likely.*

She did a quick check around to make sure no one was within earshot. The place was empty but for them and a lone crewman at a table across the room. "Ever heard of Lerandia?"

"That a planet or a person?"

"Neither. It's our cargo. Lerandia plants … trees … whatever. I'm not surprised you haven't heard of them—they're apparently a well-kept secret."

Trouble didn't look up from his chow as he shoveled it in. It tasted even worse than it smelled, if that was possible, but who knew when he'd get another chance at a meal?

"Whose well-kept secret?"

"Well, Captain Shade's for one. I'd never heard of Lerandia plants until these came aboard."

"Are you telling me you don't know what they're for?"

"Not precisely. The leaves have some sort of medicinal value. That's what we've been told. Beyond that…" She shrugged. "I'm sure Shade knows, and Sanchez. Rumors are rampant, though. Blackwood thinks they give people psychic powers."

Psychic powers. Trouble shook his head. "We talking about levitating things, making things disappear, deadly eye-beams—what?"

"Who knows? Like I said—rumors. Duff thinks it's a hallucinogen. He'd probably smoke the stuff if he thought he could get away with it, Chen says it's an aphrodisiac." She smiled at him. "She would."

He smiled back. "So, doesn't that make you a little nervous—not knowing squat about your cargo?"

She shrugged. "Why should it? Captain Shade's never screwed us over. If he pays up at the end of the trip, that's all I really care about. I don't think he'd ever take on anything really dangerous. I think he just wants to make a killing. He's got a hot new product he wants to spring on the market before someone else beats him to it, that's all."

Trouble nodded, sipping his coffee. It wasn't bad. Tasted real. He wondered if they grew that in their hydroponics bays, along with the Lerandia.

Morgan's eyes targeted a spot over his right shoulder, her face, which had been animated, went deadpan. "Speaking of dangerous…" she murmured.

Trouble sensed Rusk's presence before the first mate loomed behind him. It surprised him—not that he'd known someone was there, but that he'd known, without any doubt, that it was Rusk.

Trouble shrugged. "Nah. He's mostly harmless."

Surprisingly, Rusk ignored him. "Morgan, what the hell are you doing in here having a tea party with this scum? You're supposed to be on duty in Hydroponics "

"I *was* on duty in Hydroponics ... sir. Oddly, the overlap shift wasn't. Lucas was there, though—barely in once piece, but there."

Rusk shoved past Trouble's chair, deliberately striking it with one hip. He stood where he could look from one of them to the other and did so for a full five seconds before saying, "What're you talking about? Lucas would have been off-shift hours before you went in. Redfield and—"

"Duff—yeah, I know. But they weren't there, and in their absence someone beat the crap out of Lucas. Trouble found him and helped me get him to Pike. After all the excitement, we were just a little hungry."

"And just what was this scum doing there?"

"Why don't you ask the scum?" Trouble asked mildly.

Rusk glared at him. "Well?"

Trouble kept his attention on his food. "Just taking the ship's tour. Thought I'd drop by and see if what we're carrying was worth me being shanghai—ah, recruited. Sir."

Rusk laid his jerkstick almost gently across Trouble's shoulders. "Look at me."

"I'd rather not. This stuff's hard enough to keep down as it is." Trouble cringed. He was already regretting this rediscovered facet of his personality—he really was a wise-ass.

Rusk slapped the plate, sending the remnants of Trouble's meal flying across the table and onto the floor. No big loss, really; he'd had about all he could take of it. He noticed that a trio of crewmen had entered the room and were now were watching the confrontation.

Rusk saw them too, and stiffened. "Don't mouth off to me, asshole," he growled.

"Or?"

"Or what?"

Trouble gently put down his spoon and folded his hands atop the table. "That's what I'm asking: or what? Planning to zap me again? You already tried that."

Rusk put his face down on a level with Trouble's. "You think you're so damn tough. I'm going to take great pleasure in showing you how wrong you are, when this run is over."

Trouble could smell the other man's sweat, his anger, and his fear. Authority only worked if everybody recognized it. Trouble didn't—and Rusk knew it. Worse, he knew the crew knew it.

"Why wait?" Trouble asked mildly. He slowly stood up, unfolding his body until he was eye to eye with the other.

The mate straightened, backing away from the moment. "You were recruited for a purpose, Matthews. We need all hands aboard this vessel. When your hands are no longer needed, you'd better watch your back. Right now, the two of you are under disciplinary action. Get your butts down to Hydroponics. You're going to pull a double shift."

Trouble glanced down at Morgan, who looked back, deadpan. Neither of them moved.

"Now!" growled Rusk, and brought the jerkstick down on the center of the table, coating it with clotted gravy.

Morgan rose, a smile hovering about her lips, her eyes still on Trouble. They moved in unison toward the exit. Halfway to the hatch, she looked back over her shoulder at Rusk.

"Oh, by the way, you might want to tell Sanchez he should take a look at the plant closest to the explosion."

"What explosion?"

"Oh, didn't I mention that? Just before we found Lucas, one of the ship's monitors blew out and started a little fire."

"A little fire? You dumb bitch, there's no such thing as a little fire in the cargo hold!"

Trouble swung around to face Rusk. As he suspected, the mate was about to bust a seam. His face had gone a mottled red which made the squeezed bloodless furrows between his brows look like white war paint. Kind of comical, Trouble thought.

"Relax," he said. "I put the fire out."

Rusk's face shifted toward the purple end of the spectrum, but he seemed to be speechless; his mouth opened, his jaw worked, but no sound came out.

Trouble liked him that way. He sketched him a salute as he and Morgan resumed their trek to Hydroponics.

"So are we really going to pull a double shift?" he asked her as they exited the mess.

"Oh, yeah. I smart off to Rusk—which seems to come easier since you came aboard—but in the end, I do what I have to do to keep him from coming unglued. I'm not a masochist."

She looked up at him and grinned, and their eyes locked for a moment. He noticed, again, that hers were green ... or blue ... or maybe gray. He also noticed that her breathing was a bit faster than the pace she had set warranted.

Was that normal? To be that aware of another person's physical responses? Trouble catalogued another apparent sensory enhancement and smiled a slow, lazy smile. Morgan, to his surprise, blushed. They continued wordlessly to the cargo hold, a subtle tension arcing between them. Trouble rather enjoyed it. It called up an echo from his past—from someplace he couldn't reach. There had been a woman, but when he reached for her memory, all he found was a deep, impenetrable fog.

Cyber was at the computer station just inside the bay that held the Lerandia grove when they got there. Alone. Morgan's surprise was palpable.

"A little out of your element, aren't you, Cyb?" she asked him.

The guy was sweating, and not, Trouble could tell, because of the jungle atmosphere. He seemed nervous, his eyes shifting, his hands working, unable to hold still.

"I was checking out the damaged monitor and..." He looked from Trouble to Morgan. "Lemme show you something."

He shoved his way down the central aisle through the encroaching crimson leaves and took a left turn onto a transverse catwalk. Trouble and Morgan followed him down to a tank a little over ten meters beyond where they'd found Lucas. He herded them to a position in the center of the leafy avenue, then, turned, squatted down, and pointed up through the branches of the Lerandia plants to their left.

"There's a cam mounted up there underneath that branch with the torn leaf. See it?" He spoke in a near whisper. "Looks like a large thorn."

Trouble hunkered down behind Cyber and followed his pointing finger. Morgan did likewise, leaning into Trouble and all but breathing in his ear. There was a cam there, all right—a larger, bulkier version of the ones that dotted the *Raker*. It was approximately the same shade as the branch beneath which it hid.

"I see it," Trouble said, keeping his own voice low. "What about it? You've got those things all over the ship."

"That one's not mine."

"Then whose is it?" asked Morgan.

"I don't know. Maybe it belongs to the person who ripped Lucas up."

"What do you know about that?" Morgan's voice rose and Cyber stood up and beckoned them away from the camera.

When they'd reached the privacy of the break room, he slid into a chair, where he sat, gangly legs crossed, bouncing his foot up and down.

"I found Lucas," he told them. "I didn't see the beating, this was after the fact. I was ... doing some system checks and I heard him breathing down there between the tanks. When you came in, Morg, I blew out a cam bot close to him by reversing the feed on the microphone and blowing the diaphragm to hell. I hoped it'd help you find him."

"So what's this other camera got to do with it?" Trouble asked.

"That cam is trained on the area where Lucas was working this morning. I don't know why. I can't exactly get in there to look without being seen. But I do know that's not the only rogue cam in there. There are at least two more."

Morgan sat down in the chair across from the net-head, her hands between her knees. "So what're you saying? That Lucas saw whatever it was that cam was monitoring and that's why he was beat up?"

"Could be coincidence, I suppose."

"That'd be a pretty big coincidence," said Trouble.

Cyber sat forward in his chair. "Don't you see? This is major. You don't mash the captain's nephew on a whim. All that 'Hackett did it 'cause I laughed at him' bullshit—"

Morgan stiffened. "You heard that?"

Cyber found the table top suddenly fascinating. "Well, yeah ... I wanted to find out what happened to him. And I have to say, the kid's reaction when Trouble was asking him questions ... I don't think this is about Hackett's fragile ego."

"Then what is it about?" Trouble asked, wondering why he cared. The answer to this puzzle might be useful, he supposed ... or it might be dangerous to life and limb.

"The plants. It's about the plants, I'm pretty sure."

"Do *you* know why they're of value?" Trouble asked the net-head.

He nodded. "Yeah. The extract contains high levels of androstin."

Morgan frowned. "As in Andro*stim*? The radiation treatment?"

Cyber nodded again, light shimmering along the traceries of circuitry beneath his scalp. "Yeah. If the levels are what Sanchez says, Lerandia's pretty much off the charts when it comes to a single organic source for the drug. That's what the latest scientific literature says anyway."

"Why didn't anyone tell the rest of us about it?"

"Oh, nobody *told* me," Cyber said. "I got curious and checked it out."

Morgan's eyes narrowed. "You just said Sanchez told you about the elevated levels of androstin."

Cyber's mouth quirked up at the corners. "Yeah, well. I sort of pretended I knew about it because the captain told me."

"Maybe the other cameras are the captain's," Morgan suggested. "If these things are that valuable, maybe he's taking out a little extra insurance."

"Then," Trouble interjected, "why didn't he respond to his nephew's beating? Shade may be an eccentric old coot, but he didn't strike me as being bloodless or mean."

Cyber and Morgan both shook their heads.

"No," said Cyber. "He's not mean. If he'd seen what happened to Lucas, I think he'd be all over whoever did it."

"So what do we do?" asked Morgan. "Should we tell Shade?"

"About the beating?" asked Cyber. "I don't think so. Lucas sure didn't want him to know."

"Then we don't tell," Trouble said.

Cyber nodded. "Good call. I'm gonna go back to my little cubby and see if I can locate the controls for this upstart surveillance system. It's probably a freewire, which means it won't be linked into the ship's monitors, but it's got to be drawing power from somewhere. And if I can locate a power drain that's not accounted for by the ship's systems, that will give me the location of the control console. If it's not too much of an antique, I might be able to hack it."

He grinned suddenly, as if the idea of counter-espionage tickled his fancy. "Just call me Cyber-dick."

"Cyber-what?" asked Morgan. "Why? I mean, yeah, you're a dick, but—"

"Dick as in detective, gumshoe, private eye ... huh, that's appropriate."

"I'm glad you think this is all so amusing," muttered Morgan. "In the meantime, what the hell do we do about those rogue cams?"

"We don't do anything about them," said Trouble, drawing a nod of quick agreement from Cyber. "If we so much as breathe on them, whoever's using them will know they've been found. You want to end up like the kid?"

"Okay, so we ignore them," Morgan agreed. "For now. But at some point we've got to let the captain know what's going on under his nose."

"And what would that be, exactly?" Trouble asked. "We don't know anything. And we won't know anything until Cyber-dick here hacks into that system. Am I right?" He gave Cyber an assessing glance.

Cyber nodded, then caught the look in Trouble's eye. "Yeah, uh, I'll get on that. Right now. Right this minute." He popped out of his chair as if some unseen puppet master had jerked all his strings at once, and departed, casting one transparent glance back at Morgan.

Trouble gestured after him. "You and him got something going on?"

"Something ... ?" Morgan seemed to shake herself. "What— me and Cyber? Hell, no. What'd make you think that?"

The way he looks at you. Watches you. Which is a lot like the way *you watch me.*

She turned away from his gaze. "No. Cyber and I don't have 'something going on', though it's painfully obvious he wishes we did. He's a puppy. A big, clumsy, hyper puppy. I stick to my own species in these things." She looked up and met his eyes again. "I like *men*, Trouble."

Trouble let his mouth curl up at the corners into something that was not quite a smile. "I'll be sure to remember that. So, you wanna show me the ropes?" He nodded toward the Hydroponics bay.

Morgan grimaced. "Not especially. But we should get on it. The first thing you'll need is a filtration mask. Then, I'll show you how to check the nutrient flow."

"Yeah, it is a little pungent in there, but I've smelled worse."

She gave him a look that said she thought he was yanking her chain and led him to the equipment locker.

10 / PILGRIM'S PASSAGE

ERASMUS SHADE SAT AT HIS MAP TABLE NURSING A FIZZING MIXTURE of soda, water, rum, and mood elevators. The Druud staff he had taken from the new recruit lay across his lap. Above the table's console was a holographic star map of local space. The map showed a glittering ball of twinkling white lights and shimmering fields of muted color. The lights were stars and the fields nebulae—the birthplace of stars. The *Moonraker* was that tiny red pin prick smack in the middle. Erasmus knew this map as intimately as if it were the deck plan of the ship he had grown up on. A forest filled with alpha predators contained less peril.

For most men, this reality might cause extreme stress. An abortive attempt at taking extended shore leave some years ago had taught Erasmus Shade that he needed stress—and a ship—to survive. In the absence of either, he wilted. In the grip of stress, on the deck of a ship, he felt totally at home.

Only one factor in his professional and personal life saddled him with a form of pressure he did not weather well. The pressure that came with his brother Julian's ascent within the Freeman's Guild. In the past year, Julian had amassed unprecedented power in the Guild—systematically consolidating a control invigorated by the mysterious and catastrophic explosions aboard smuggling ships captained by two of his most inveterate rivals. No one could prove Julian had been responsible for the explosions. Certainly, there were no living witnesses willing to accuse him. Nevertheless, a clear message had been sent to every smuggler in the Freeman's Guild that they should pay their duties on time and support Julian Shade in the next election for Guild Exec.

Erasmus had withdrawn his own candidacy and supported his brother's bid. It was a way of showing loyalty that did not require him to ferry unsettling contraband hither and yon. He was not averse to smuggling items of questionable provenance, or ones he knew had been obtained under sketchy circumstances, but there was cargo for which the penalties were so severe as to condemn a captain to a life of imprisonment and a crew to exile. Since becoming Guild Master, Julian had suggested several times that the *Moonraker* take on such cargo; Erasmus saw the suggestion for what it was—a sword of Damocles that Julian could dangle above his brother's head.

The cargo *Moonraker* currently hauled was not dangerous, but its legality was in a gray area. Most freighters hauled the fruit or foliage of a botanical, or the processed product of same. In the case of Lerandia, which was a protected species on its homeworld, there were no legal ways to acquire the unprocessed leaves, and the sporules for planting were exorbitantly expensive from legal sources. It would have been punishable to have, say, removed saplings from the swamps of Pangloria and carted them into space.

Erasmus had not done that … he had simply hijacked some saplings from another smuggler who had. And he had done it in such a way that Sanchez, who'd tipped him off to the existence of the rare cargo, could swear on any holy book you put before him that he had grown this grove in *Moonraker's* belly over a period of years from sporules he assumed were legal when he acquired them. This did not mean that there would not be serious repercussions if they were caught transporting the trees. They could prove that they were nowhere near Pangloria when a small stand of saplings went missing from a larger grove in a massive swamp, but getting caught with them would still tie Erasmus Shade, his ship, and his crew in legal knots for years.

His mind wandered to the new recruit, Trouble. The man possessed a potentially dangerous asset: the charisma of the unpredictable. He had flummoxed Rusk and bested Hackett in a fight in which the odds had been well-stacked against him. Whatever his morality, he possessed many of the ingredients necessary for command. Hackett had already been taken down a peg. Shade didn't doubt that Trouble would eventually challenge Rusk as well. And as able as he thought his first mate, Captain Erasmus Shade was no fool. If Trouble stayed aboard the *Moonraker*—which, given their current itinerary, he must—Rusk stood every chance of being replaced or removed.

And then ... well, there was nowhere for Trouble to go but up.

Erasmus decided he would let the new man off the ship at the earliest opportunity. Clearly taking him had been a mistake, but there was nothing he could do about that now. What he *could* do was to pull off a coup of his own—a financial one, one that would ingratiate him with his crew and make them unlikely to elect someone else Captain in his stead or allow anyone to challenge him. The sooner he could manage this, the better.

Within the three-dimensional star map hovering in the air before him was a tiny cobalt blob which presented a possible solution to his difficulties. His original plan for getting their cargo safely to market was to avoid established space lanes—superluminal "expressways" which used the convolutions and manifolds of hyperspace to increase a ship's speed. This lessened their chances of becoming a target for piracy, but it also eliminated their chances of getting their cargo to market quickly. The *Raker's* profit margin would be higher if they arrived at their destination before other Lerandia smugglers did—if indeed there were any. They were losing precious time by not following the established routes.

But there was a way—a bold way—to make up that time, and more.

Erasmus Shade pressed his finger over the blob. It represented Einstein-Rosen Bridge L971. In layman's terms, a wormhole. An artificial wormhole. Spacers called it the Pilgrim's Passage.

No one knew who had built the Pilgrim's Passage; it was a relic of an ancient civilization—the titular Pilgrims—that had inhabited or passed through the galaxy while Earth was still prebiotic, and tideless seas had washed the surface of Mars. But the how and the why of it weren't important to Erasmus. It was a relatively stable hyperspatial shortcut, a passage that could shave more than four light months from their schedule with a subjective travel time of less than a standard week.

There was just one problem—a significant portion of the crews aboard the few ships that had braved the Passage had disappeared, or had died, or had come out the other side stark raving mad. Cryosleep was no sure refuge; the survival rate for crewmen in stasis was only fifty percent. The sane survivors, who were pitifully few, spoke of strange and impossible happenings: the dead returning to them to offer rewards or to exact retribution, bulkheads and decks becoming transparent or fluid or vaporous, air supplies becoming unbreathable for no reason, people unable to distinguish the living from the "ghosts" and blasting both indiscriminately, killing crewmates, and tearing holes in the fabric of their ships.

Shade couldn't imagine why anyone would intentionally create an interstitial passage that caused madness. He theorized that perhaps, millennia ago, the Pilgrim's Passage had been more stable, and such problems had not existed. Or perhaps the Pilgrims had simply been immune to the psychosomatic stresses that drove humans mad.

Unfortunately, one fact made that irrelevant: the crew of the *Moonraker* was human and would go quite mad, unless he found a way to prevent it. To that end he pondered the Druud staff and its effect on brain chemistry. If he could but unlock some of the mysteries of this device, or at the very least find new uses for its properties, they might protect *Moonraker's* crew in the Pilgrim's Passage. Otherwise, they would have to go the long way round, shaving off some time with a series of short jumps in less-traveled space lanes. He had tried tunneling across the hyperspace corridors once before. He would not make the same mistake twice.

"Captain?" said a soft voice, the focused sound waves making it seem that the speaker was right next to his ear. He jumped, startled, and the Druud staff tumbled to the floor.

"Damn it, Cyber! I told you I was not to be disturbed!"

"Yes, sir, I know."

Cyber was an obsequious little squirrel, in Erasmus's opinion, but he was a squirrel with myriad talents. One of these was that he saw more than he should and could usually be convinced to part with whatever information he'd gleaned.

"It's your brother, sir. On hyperwave."

Erasmus took a deep breath, let it out slowly. "All right. I'll take it. And Cyber..."

"Sir?"

"If you eavesdrop on this conversation, I'll have you dragged in the ion vapor, understood?"

"Yes, sir. Understood, sir."

"Now go away." Erasmus sat back and pretended to be comfortable as he opened communications with his brother. He was not comfortable. Not in the least.

The brothers Shade had a rivalry that went back to the childhood they'd shared aboard their father's ship—a childhood throughout which the vicious old bastard had enjoyed pitting the two boys against one another. The old man had favored him, Erasmus assumed, because he seemed the more ruthless of the two. He had thought he understood what was expected of him, and he'd pushed himself and his ships and his crews. When he'd risked all to get a cargo to market before the nearest competitor, nearly losing his ship in the process, he thought the old man would applaud him.

He'd been dead wrong.

Horace Shade had been appalled by his elder son's willingness to risk the safety of an entire crew and cargo in order to shave time off a run. What Erasmus had meant to be daring and aggressive, his father had seen as a miserable lack of judgement and a violation of Guild codes of conduct. He had sacrificed his personal ethics and his material position along with his father's approval, and Horace Shade did not allow second chances.

The brothers' relative positions were altered profoundly: Julian rode a rising star, Erasmus found himself at the helm of a sinking ship.

Once upon a time Erasmus had thought of his father's attitude as a betrayal. The old bastard had taught him greed, had schooled him in expediency, and then, when he'd performed his great feat, had all but disowned him. Now he no longer believed his own excuses. He had made those decisions on his own, and he had learned a painful lesson about interdependence and loyalty. It could not be said that Erasmus Shade was a kind man. But he tried to be fair to his crew and careful of their welfare ... within reason.

Julian seemed to have learned a different lesson altogether.

A translucent, three-dimensional image of the man's head appeared above the console to the left of Erasmus's chair. He smiled at it stiffly. "Julian. How are things?"

"Good," said Julian, his tone indicating that when he said 'good' he meant something entirely different than the dictionary definition of the word. "And you?"

"Well enough," said Erasmus, neutrally. "How's business?"

"Quite good," said Julian, just as neutrally, "though there are disturbing trends."

"Oh?"

"I have it on good authority that there is a sudden interest in your cargo among your fellows."

"My—why would anyone have any interest in a hold full of—"

"Lerandia?" Julian's smile was brittle. "Don't bother with the canned lies. I know what you're carrying and I know where you got it. I do owe you some small thanks. It seems your little—ah —encounter with that New Osiran freighter convinced the captain he needed to purchase an insurance policy from the Freeman's Guild to make sure such a thing doesn't happen again. In fact, he's considering becoming a full, paying member."

Erasmus had to admit, his younger brother had cultivated a spirit of malevolent gamesmanship that outstripped anything he could imagine doing. There never had been love lost between the two, but now, Erasmus regarded Julian with an unease that bordered on fear. Julian would not hesitate to eliminate him if he felt Erasmus threatened his position in the Guild. Which was why Erasmus had thought it a minor coup when he'd taken taken his nephew Lucas aboard *Moonraker*. It at least ensured that the boy's father would not simply destroy him on a whim. For all that Julian felt Lucas was weak and indecisive —a poor prospect for a spacer—he was the Guild Exec's only heir.

Julian was a cold, analytical bastard but, as far as Erasmus knew, prone to neither physical violence nor verbal abuse. And yet, Lucas curled in on himself and shut down whenever his father was around. Perhaps it was the mere threat of violence, so icily controlled, that terrified the boy. Or perhaps he was more his mother's son than his father's ... if he was Julian's son at all. Whatever his paternity, the boy was insurance against Julian's machinations as long as he served aboard *Moonraker*.

The challenge now was how he might keep Julian Shade from absconding with the lion's share of the prize at the end of the voyage, because this voyage—this cargo—would command a king's ransom.

"All right, so you know about the Lerandia."

"So do a few other people. I thought I should warn you.

Chances are you're being dogged. I'd advise you to jump to hyperspace at your earliest opportunity."

"We'll jump as soon as we are clear of this star system. But why merely warn me? Why not call the dogs off? As Guild Master you have that authority."

"Aye. I do have that authority. But some of our captains are fools who would raid you, then deny having done it, or who would cite the original articles of the Guild Charter, under which piracy is legal, if not ethical. If they're *not* Guild, there's literally nothing I can do. They don't have to play by our rules."

"Ah. You mean if they're Black Heart—or pretending to be. You cannot be content to allow for the possibility that your own son's life may be snuffed out."

Julian's pale eyes glittered with antipathy. "Why do you think I'm warning you? And let me make my priorities clear: If you have a choice between saving your cargo and saving my son, you will choose my son. Understood?"

Erasmus gritted his teeth to keep from saying something Julian would make him regret. "Understood. Thank you for the warning."

"Just remember that I didn't do it for you," Julian said.

"Oh, heavens, no. For Lucas."

His brother laughed aloud. "And perhaps to preserve the honor of thieves."

Erasmus couldn't contain a chuckle. "Sounds like a case of diminishing returns to me."

His brother's expression turned suddenly serious, and his eyes lost their remoteness. "Something's happening aboard your ship, Erasmus. Something you seem not to know about. Worse, it's something *I* don't know about. Find out what it is, if you want to survive. What I do know is that the captain of the freighter you pirated was not the source of the leak about your cargo. In the meantime, until you can jump, damp your fields and run silent."

"We're doing that already," Erasmus said, but he spoke to empty air. The hyperwave image was gone.

Erasmus was at sea. His brother—his detached, aloof younger brother—suddenly seemed very much attached to the outcome of this run. Why? Lucas? The honor of the Guild? A potential loss of revenue? Or deeper political reasons?

Motive didn't matter, Erasmus supposed, but the warning did. The odds had suddenly become even: They kept to a conventional road and risked piracy—or worse—or they went through the Pilgrim's Passage and risked ... everything. He glanced at the star map again, calculating how long it would be before they could jump. If they were being dogged, their pursuer would be expecting the *Raker* to make a jump to hyperspace, but they would also expect her to travel one of the commercial spaceways.

Erasmus picked up the Druud staff from the floor and stared at it pensively. If he could get his ship into the Pilgrim's Passage before any would-be pirates put in an appearance, only a fool or a madman would follow.

11 / WAKING

On the empty observation deck, Trouble felt as if he had the universe to himself. It was his. All of it. He wanted just one small piece. That one small, out-of-the-way planet on which there was no one to run from, fight, or answer to; no snarling, conniving bullies; no needy, pathetic underdogs. A place where he could lie low and try to recover his memory, his sense of Self.

Or not. It was possible he might not be able to reclaim his Self. It was possible he might have to build a new Self. It was also possible that building a new life was preferable to remembering the one that had led him here.

Perversely, Trouble found himself processing the tidbits of information he'd gleaned about himself. Heightened senses, accelerated reflexes, strength that seemed inordinate even for a man of his height and weight. Then there was his instinctive use of martial arts. The confidence that he knew how to handle himself in a fight. Clearly, he'd undergone enhancements. The question was: Why? What had he been and done before now to have needed those particular modifications? How could he find out without drawing attention from the wrong people—whoever the hell they were?

He wondered if Cyber could help him. Or *would* help him.

He was reluctant to ask for help, and not just because he wasn't sure whom he could safely trust.

Trouble's senses twitched. He spun to see a looming silhouette backlit by the light spilling through the open lift hatch. But the perspective was all wrong. The figure loomed over him—was right on top of him, without him being aware of its presence.

How was that possible?

The world tilted crazily as memory hijacked him and took him back to the slam—to waking up in a freezing sweat with cold, implacable hatred looming over him.

He came awake with a start, one hand shooting with whiplash speed toward the looming figure. His hand latched onto a broad, almost non-existent neck. He didn't complete the move and crush the man's larynx, though; he recognized him by his body odor. Rusk.

Trouble now remembered where he was: not in the slam, after all, but in a bunk on a lower deck of a ship named *Moonraker*. He'd been dreaming—if you could call his highly manipulative processing of accumulated data dreaming.

He released Rusk, who backpedaled a step or two and glowered at him. "You're in trouble, smartass."

"I was sleeping. You can't tell me my dreams are out of line."

"I went down to 'ponics. I saw how you put out the fire. You just about killed a plant doing it."

Trouble blinked up at him. "And...?"

"You know how valuable those damned leaves are?"

"It's called acceptable loss, Rusk. If I hadn't ripped those leaves off that plant you might've lost the whole crop. Those things burned like their sap was some sort of accelerant."

Rusk ignored him. "Those leaves were worth more than your miserable life, Matthews. Fortunately for you, Captain Shade is a kinder man than me. I'd like to hardwire this jerkstick to your balls, but the captain would rather I put you to work. So, you're going into the duty rotation officially, as of now."

Trouble considered telling Rusk what they both knew: that the mate was hiding behind his captain. He didn't want a confrontation with Trouble, at least not until he was ready. Trouble considered precipitating something.

No, there was no purpose to that. He shrugged off the impulse and sat up.

Rusk shifted his stance slightly and tightened his grip on the jerkstick.

Trouble swung his legs over the edge of the bunk and stood. "Aye, aye, sir. Looking forward to being a productive member of this crew, sir," he said, his tone a drawl that stopped just short of insolence.

The glower etched itself even deeper into Rusk's face. "Go to Supply and get fitted for a rad suit. The Cap wants you in Engineering today."

"Okay."

"Okay, what?"

Trouble smiled. "Okay, *sir*." He leaned hard on the last word.

Rusk's grip tightened on the weapon, turning his knuckles white, while his face went crimson. His desire to inflict blinding pain on Trouble for the loss of those few leaves was palpable and toxic. The only thing holding him back now was the fear of the unknown—the unknown being how Trouble would react. He knew that without knowing how he knew it. It was obvious that Rusk did, too, because Trouble could see—hell, he could *feel*—the effort it took for the mate to control his rage.

As they left the crews' quarters, Rusk said, "You ever rotated the rods on a Keplinger drive, or do I have to teach you?"

Trouble grasped a fleeting memory. "Yeah, I have. At least once. You don't have bots to take care of that?"

"We do have robotic backup, but the captain, you might have noticed, can be quite particular about certain things. He doesn't trust bots to do a proper rotation. He's afraid they might crack the rods. You know what happens if you crack a drive rod?"

That didn't require memory, just logic. "Yeah. The engine

destabilizes. If you're in superluminal space, you fall out. If you don't shut down the drive in time, the ship shakes itself to pieces. Not to mention the flood of radiation. Not pretty."

"Bear all that in mind and I'm sure you'll do an exceptional job."

"Thanks for your confidence," said Trouble. "Makes me feel all warm and cozy inside."

Rusk actually smiled at him. Which did not improve his face any. It also set off Trouble's internal alarms. He'd seen that look before on other faces, made equally as ugly by hatred. He wasn't sure he wanted to remember them.

"Was that a smile?" Trouble asked. "Or just gas?"

Rusk poked him almost gently with the butt of the jerkstick. "You're a funny man, Matthews."

"Ha," Trouble said. "So, did you ever find your delinquent crewmen?"

"Yeah. I found 'em."

"What was their story?"

"Duff said he was sleeping off a drunk; Redfield said he lost track of time because Duff never came to get him for duty."

"And you believe that, do you?"

Rusk scowled. "Why is that any business of yours?"

Trouble shrugged. "Might give me some insight into what sort of bald-faced lies I could get away with on this boat."

Rusk glowered. "They didn't get away with shit. They said someone suggested they skip their shift—made sure they had the creds to do it."

"They say who?"

"They said they don't know who. They *say* that the 'suggestion' they skip their shift was waiting for them when they rolled out for the day. Two neat bundles of credits wrapped in hand-scribed messages, left in their boots."

Trouble nodded. "Bribery. A time-honored tradition. So, you let them get away with it? Or is that sort of thing actually punishable here?"

The creepy smile was back. "Redfield and Duff are doing a double shift in 'housekeeping'. That give you any insight into what you can get away with on this boat?"

Trouble had already been warned that "housekeeping" was a euphemism for maintenance of the ship's waste management system and her many heads. It was, by all accounts, foul beyond description, since the *Raker*'s waste system was as old and piece-meal as the rest of the ship's systems.

"I feel positively enlightened," Trouble murmured. "Which way is Supply?"

The question gave Rusk reason to direct him with the butt of the jerkstick. "That way."

That, Trouble thought, is going to get old very fast.

There were two engine rooms on a superluminal vessel; one for the subluminal ion drive and maneuvering engines, another to house the Keplinger drive core that opened jump points and powered the ship in hyperspace. On *Moonraker*, the Keplinger sat just forward of the ion propulsion system. The long, crystalline Quadrium-D rods of the drive extended from the engine housing on Delta up to a terminus in a squat turret on the outer hull of Beta deck. There were nine of the translucent rods, each one a decimeter in diameter and ten meters in length. They formed an inverted cone with the broadest point housed in the turret.

On Gamma deck, a maintenance gallery extruded into the circular space at the center of the array of drive rods. It was here that Trouble stood, clad in a silvery, form-fitting rad suit designed to give him one-half hour of protection from the sigma radiation that pulsed from the idling Keplinger drive. Behind the suit's clear polycarb mask, his eyes adjusted easily to the soft blue-white light radiating through the rods from the drive below. The visible light was harmless, of course, and the dosimeter on his suit would warn him well in advance of a lethal dose of sigma rays. At least, that was the theory...

Normally, a rod rotation was done by three people—one working each end, and a third on the central gallery to coordinate their movements and stabilize the rod. Rusk had quite intentionally saddled Trouble with the sole responsibility for this rotation. The reason he gave was that every crewman who worked engineering must be able to perform the rotation on his or her own—just in case. Trouble suspected Rusk simply hoped he'd screw up and crack one of the rods, thereby requiring the administration of appropriate punishment. That would explain Rusk's comparatively sunny disposition this morning. A broken rod did not spell disaster for a ship, as long as there were replacement rods on board. But Quadrium-D wasn't cheap, and paying for a broken rod would take quite a big bite out of Trouble's potential share of the cargo. No doubt all this had occurred to Rusk as well.

Trouble had been given two adjustable length metal poles with padded flanges at each end. These were used to unlock the collars that held the ends of the rods in place. The poles were ancient, he quickly discovered, and very much the worse for wear. The telescoping mechanism on one was bunged up and wouldn't allow the pole to extend to its full length. The other lacked padding on its flanges and had a crimped cable in the flange control mechanism that made the mechanical fingers move awkwardly. Rotating Keplinger drive rods required delicacy. A flaky cable control was going to make delicacy difficult, if not impossible. And the shorter of the two poles was worse than useless.

"I don't suppose you've got any better poles?"

"Not for you," Rusk told him, and left the drive core, chuckling.

Trouble smiled and shook his head. Rusk had stacked the deck, that was for sure. Which was both pathetic and cowardly. He shrugged off his contempt and returned to the equipment area to see if there might be any other poles. Of course there were not. Nor were there any replacement parts that he could see. But there were a couple more rad suits and some gaffer's tape—a product Trouble suspected had been around since the Big Bang. He wouldn't be surprised to find that God—if there was indeed a God—had used gaffer's tape to hold the universe together.

Trouble snitched the gloves from one of the rad suits and used a laser tool to dissect them. Then he pulled two of the fingers over the bare metal flanges of the longest pole and secured them with the tape. The cable control was still screwed, but it would have to do.

He returned to the drive core and looked up to where the rods connected to the broad drive turret overhead.

"This is going be a considerable bitch," he told himself, and climbed up into the maintenance gallery.

He chose a rod and lowered the flanged end of his pole down to where it was coupled to the lower drive housing. It took him a good twenty seconds to get the mechanical hand firmly around the rod's protective collar, but after that, a deft twist of the pole rotated the collar open. The rod itself stayed put, held inside the collar by its own weight.

Next, he went after the rod collar in the upper housing. This was the tricky part. The rods canted out at about a seventy-five degree angle; loosen the collar without securing the rod and it could slip right out of the housing to shatter on the deck below. The way they were aligned, a falling rod could easily take out one or more of its brethren on the way down. All this would, of course, contaminate the deck with deadly radioactive fragments that someone (guess who) would be obliged to clean up.

Trouble considered his options, then glanced around for the ubiquitous cam bots. "Rusk," he said amiably, "if you're watching this, I just want you to know how much I appreciate the challenge."

He raised the flanges up to the top of the rod and worked

them into position around the collar. It took him five tries to get it right, during which time it seemed he could hear the cosmic clock ticking and feel the invisible radiation from the Keplinger beating against the rad suit with every audible pulse of its idling drive.

With the clamp finally in place, Trouble leaned out over the gallery's waist-high railing and gave the rotator pole a twist. The collar refused to budge.

"*Damn* it! What'd you do, Rusk? Glue the damn rod in there?"

He tried again. And a third time—which turned out to be no charm. On the fourth twist, the collar gave with an audible snap, and Trouble felt the weight of the rod in his hand so suddenly, it almost toppled him over the gallery rail. Smiling grimly, he propped the long pole against the railing, then used both hands to turn the drive rod one-quarter turn to the left. The action prompted the memory of an inane rhyme. "Less than a quarter or more than a quarter—that will make your drive life shorter."

Where had he heard that? He had no time to ponder it now. He hefted the pole a second time, using it to twist the collars back into place.

He checked his chronometer. Five minutes. If he took that long on every rod he'd exceed the safe limits of the rad suit by a good ten minutes. They went faster after that first one, though, and he had about six minutes left when he got to the ninth rod. He was doing the procedure almost by muscle memory now.

He went after the ninth rod with the same combination of care and expediency he had the others. He was lowering the pole when he felt the gallery rail give slightly. It wasn't much— maybe a few centimeters—but it was enough to torque the upper end of the drive rod out of its collar. The weight of the suddenly free rod pulled Trouble off balance and up against the gallery rail, which gave even further.

"Sonofabitch!"

He swung his right leg over the railing in an instinctive quest for leverage. The bottom of the rod came free then, putting its full weight into Trouble's left hand. He dropped the rotator pole to the lower deck and grasped the rod with his right hand as well. The rod swung dangerously, whispering past its next door neighbor, and nearly kissing the gallery rail.

Trouble growled aloud as the unbalanced weight of it carried him over the edge. Pitching forward, he hooked his feet through the railing's metal balusters, simultaneously swinging the rod away from an impact with the gallery. If he could just keep the ends from striking anything...

He reached the bottom of his arc; his legs, entwined with the balusters, took the combined weight of his body and the rod. His muscles held, but the damned railing shifted outward even further, metal groaning under the strain. He hung up-side down now, his entire focus on the fragile thing in his hands. It was inert; no light emitted from its glossy core, but the soft blue light from the Keplinger drive poured from the open coupling below, filling the chamber with more radiation than any rad suit aboard the *Raker* was built to take all in one shot.

Trouble's adrenaline kicked into overdrive. He scanned the room below his head for a possible out. If he could slide the rod to the floor ...

But no, he was too high up for that. He could just drop it, he supposed, which was what Rusk had likely hoped for all along. He'd survive and the rod wouldn't. Or he could just hang here until he'd soaked up enough rads to kill him, the rod would be shattered just the same and Rusk would be rid of him.

Can't have that.

He lowered the rod toward the floor below to minimize the impact and resulting glassy shrapnel.

"Trouble?" Morgan's voice came to him through the comm.

"Yeah?"

"I need to talk to you."

"I'm a bit indisposed right now. Got a loose rod and a lot of radiation washing around in here."

He saw movement out of the corner of his eye and looked aside to see Morgan peering through the flexiglass panels of the lower engine room. She took the situation in at a glance and disappeared. Moments later, the engine room hatch dilated and Morgan appeared below in a hastily donned and badly fitting rad suit.

She said nothing, quickly moving into position below him.

He lowered the rod into her hands. She had just managed to fit it back into its collar when the railing holding Trouble aloft gave by a good half-meter. He swore eloquently but managed to keep his hands on the rod, sliding down its glossy length until the railing jerked him to a stop.

He took a firmer grasp on the rod. "It's gonna give any second, Morgan. Can you get up here—?"

She was on the move before he'd finished the sentence, disappearing from his line of sight.

He counted the seconds out in the pulsing of the drive core. At least, he told himself, he was no longer dangling in a fountain of radiation.

He felt a hand on his leg.

"I'm here," Morgan said.

A second later, he felt the rod quiver in his hands as she took it. He jack-knifed his body, hurling himself up into a tight somersault that brought him back to the gallery in a landing a cat would have been proud of.

And where, he wondered, did I learn to do that?

The broken section of railing did not do the predictable thing and tear away to fall with a crash at the foot of the drive core. It merely toppled until it was hanging from the gallery by its two central balusters. Trouble could see from where he stood that the handrail along the top had been very neatly lasered almost through. Several of the balusters looked as if they had received similar attention.

He ignored the implications of that for the moment and moved to Morgan's side. While she grasped the back of his rad suit to keep him from falling, he rejoined the top of the rod with its collar.

"The pole—" he began.

Morgan placed it in his hand. "All comes with Mad Morgan's Rescue Service."

"Yeah?"

"Yeah. Wanna know what else comes with the service?"

"Ah ... maybe later," he said. "Little busy at the moment." Hell, even in that damn rad suit she was distracting. He brought his focus back to the rod, relocked the upper collar, then tossed the pole aside.

"I think I need to have a word with First Mate Rusk," he said and moved toward the exit.

Morgan trailed him. "Not just yet. You should get down to the infirmary for radiation treatment."

Outside the drive core chamber, safely shielded from further radiation, he checked his chronometer.

"No problem. I only went two minutes over."

They peeled off the rad suits and dumped them into a reclamation bin. Trouble started for the corridor. Morgan reached out and laid a hand on his arm. He was surprised at the strength in it.

"I outrank you, Trouble. I said, 'You should get down to the infirmary.' That was an order, not a suggestion. I'm taking you to Doc Pike."

He acquiesced.

Dr. Baron Pike frowned, an expression that made his long, narrow face look as if it was made of wrinkled fabric. "Are you sure you went over the rad limit?"

"Uh, yeah. Pretty sure. By at least two minutes."

"Not showing up in the scan or in your blood. Highly unusual." The doc turned an inquisitive gaze on his patient. "You have some sort of experimental mods done?"

"Not that I know of," Trouble replied in all honesty, then added, "To be completely honest, I don't remember."

The doctor looked at the blood sample he'd drawn as if it were some rare gem and set the vial carefully in a specimen rack on one end of his work counter. The counter took up the full width of the pocket lab along the Medbay's outer bulkhead. The larger portion of the almost square space contained a set of six bio-beds that were some of the most modern tech Trouble had seen on the aging vessel. The one furthest from the Medbay entrance was occupied by a sleeping Lucas Shade.

"Well, I'm going to dose you with serum anyway," Pike said. "Unless you have some objection to that."

"None, thanks." Trouble watched as Pike administered an infuser full of anti-rad serum.

"Mr. Matthews," the medic told him, "if you were a perfectly normal human being, that dose of radiation you took would have been barely survivable. Even with your … amazing constitution, I'd advise against basking in sigma radiation for extended periods of time."

"Trust me," Trouble said. "It wasn't intentional. Someone … complicated things for me. Something in the nature of an initiation prank, I suspect."

Pike grunted and seated himself at his workstation. "A prank? Sounds more like attempted murder, to me. You should watch your step, young man."

"Yeah, I'll do that."

Morgan was waiting for Trouble in the corridor when he emerged from Medbay pondering how he wanted to handle Rusk. Apparently, this showed in his face, because Morgan gave it a good read, then said, "All right, then. Go beat the crap out of Rusk. You have my blessing. But first..."

He tilted his head and gave her a look of keen interest. "First?"

She didn't go where he expected her to. "I just talked to Cyber."

"Yeah? News?"

"Quite a bit, actually. First thing is: Hackett doesn't have a console—at least not in his private quarters."

"No surprise there. Hackett isn't smart enough to think of using something like that, let alone hiding it. Someone else is running the show. What else?"

"He's located about eight of the rogue cams. He thinks that's all of them."

"How can he be sure?"

"Apparently, they put out a frequency signature. He found eight cams on that frequency. He's also sent a bunch of his own snoops to the Hydroponics bay. The Watcher is being watched."

"But no console yet, huh? I thought finding this power drain was supposed to be a piece of cake."

"Apparently, we're dealing with someone pretty clever."

"Well, that lets Hackett out."

Morgan laughed and Trouble noticed that her eyelashes were spangled with what looked like dew drops. He recognized the effect; she was wearing face spritz, which he vaguely recalled seeing on glitzy planetside billboards *(He's on his way? Use Glamor Spray!)* He thought he'd noticed it on her face yesterday in Hydroponics, too, but he'd had other things on his mind. Now, he was coming down off a super adrenaline rush, and he noticed these minute details.

The expectation of dying did that to a man.

"You polishing up your face for anyone in particular, Morgan?"

She looked him square in the eye. "A girl likes to look her best."

"Girl? I'd say you haven't been a 'girl' for a few years."

She started to protest, but he added, "And that's fine by me. I like mature women."

She smiled. It was a good smile. A beautiful smile, even.

Trouble's pulse hiked back up, but in a good way this time. He took a deep breath. "You were going to show me what all goes with Mad Morgan's Rescue Service?"

Her brows lifted. "Right here in the corridor? A little public, isn't it?"

"I'm open to suggestions." He was, he realized. And open to starting something with Mad Morgan.

She lifted an eyebrow. "I thought you were going to go bust Rusk's ass. I'd hate to come between Rusk and a good ass-busting."

"I'm not gonna waste all this adrenaline on Rusk. He can wait. Not like he's going anywhere."

Her smile deepened toward the flirtatious. The look was slightly incongruous with the short tumble of hair and the crew coveralls. But the coveralls wouldn't long be an issue, he figured. Desire uncoiled in his groin and stretched itself. He didn't know if he was ready for this, but he *wanted* to be ready for it.

They moved side-by-side to the Retreat, where they saw that there were no open cubicles. Morgan swore, practically dancing from one foot to the other.

Trouble felt the heat of her anticipation like tiny hot pin pricks down his spine ... and other places. Hell, she was putting out more radiation than the damn Keplinger drive.

"Time for Plan B," Morgan murmured in his ear. "Let's hit the showers. You'd be surprised the things you can do with that minty shower salve. Cyber's got the Retreat pretty well plastered with snoops anyway. I told him to get rid of the damn things, but Cyber's Cyber. He just moved them."

That gave Trouble a moment's pause. "You mean he'd be..."

She grinned at him. "Watching? Yeah. That's how our cyber-boy gets his thrills. Bother you, does it?"

"Now you mention it, yeah." He glanced warily at the occupied cubicles. "Kind of makes me want to take a shower."

Morgan laughed.

Cyber was not happy. Returning to his roost to find Rusk hovering over his monitors made him damn nervous and he was already damn nervous. The mate had mumbled something about keeping track of Trouble, then beat a hasty retreat. Cyber had followed his progress all the way to the mess where the big man sat down with a big-man-sized snack that consisted of a whole, real roast chicken—one of the perks of being an "officer" aboard a smuggler.

Cyber wondered about Trouble's whereabouts, himself. Morgan had taken off to give him the latest news from the "cyber-detective" unit and he'd hoped to have heard something from them by now. Cyber smiled. Espionage with a purpose was more fun than garden variety voyeurism, which was incongruous, considering that what he found out might very well affect their livelihood—or at the very least what they stood to pocket from this run.

He dived into his work, checking the program he'd set running to find and tag any unusual power usage, firing through his cams one by one. He started in 'ponics today, but things looked boringly normal there. He moved on, checking on Lucas in the infirmary—asleep—then deciding to look for Morgan. He was tripping through the cams on Epsilon Deck when he thought he saw her enter the showers.

Serendipity! He zapped his consciousness there, mentally salivating in anticipation of the usual striptease as she removed her coverall and undergarments. But today there was nothing usual about it. Trouble was with her. *Really* with her. And there was no tease to the strip whatsoever. That the coveralls remained in one piece was a credit to the manufacturer.

Cyber was stunned. Well, yes, of course he'd expected it to happen at some point. Morgan had been wearing her pheromones on her sleeve and Trouble was apparently not a man to pass up an open invitation to ... *this*. But he hadn't expected to see it, to hear it, to almost *feel* it.

He tried to imagine that was him doing those things with Morgan, but any resemblance between him and Trouble... Well, there was no resemblance. He was all gawk and gangle where Trouble was sleek and muscular. Trouble was Morgan's match—physically as well as temperamentally. He even wore old scars in many of the same places she did.

Cyber's libido vacillated between a roar and a whimper. In

the end, he shut down the cams in the shower and turned his full attention to finding an unaccounted-for power flux. He tried to tell himself he was doing the decent thing, giving them their privacy.

Keep telling yourself that, he thought. You might even believe it—someday.

13 / WEAPONS

Rusk took a deep breath as he entered the corridor leading to Captain Shade's private quarters. He was no stranger to the captain's inner sanctum; many private conversations had taken place between them there. But a summons always piqued his curiosity and his concern. When the captain wanted to talk to Rusk in his quarters, it meant he didn't want the conversation to be overheard by anyone else. The Captain's cabin and ready room were possibly the only places on the ship that Cyber did not have a presence. Not because he hadn't tried to establish one, but simply because Captain Shade employed the latest in snoop jammers.

Rusk could not help but wonder if somehow his own recent activities had come to the captain's attention. He had dispatched a repair crew to Engineering to clean up the mess Matthews had made and replace the broken section of gallery railing. That would soon be almost as good as new, and no rods had been broken after all.

On the downside, Matthews was still alive, was not suffering from radiation poisoning, and was probably pissed as hell. Any hope Rusk harbored that the younger man might not realize how he'd been set up had pretty much evaporated as he'd eavesdropped on his conversation with Morgan just outside Medbay.

Rusk puzzled over the last he'd heard of that dialogue. On the heels of Lucas's beating and the "little fire," all that stuff about rogue cams in Hydroponics made him uneasy. Cyber's return to his lair had been poorly timed.

Rusk was still juggling it all mentally when Shade answered his door comm. As the hatch dilated open, the captain said, "Enoch, we have a problem."

He was seated at his personal computer console, his back to the holopad. The Druud staff Trouble had brought aboard was lying across his knees.

"Sir?"

"It seems we may have a traitor aboard."

Rusk was completely blindsided. "A traitor, sir?"

"It's related to the cargo," said Shade, catching and holding his first mate's gaze.

Rusk had had a lot practice pretending he didn't know what his captain was talking about. At this moment, none of that practice was necessary. He legitimately did not know what Shade was talking about, except that it had nothing to do with his own perennial attempts to generate extra credits by caching his private contraband aboard the *Raker*, or his attempt to get Trouble Matthews killed, maimed, or thrown in the brig.

He cocked his head and raised an eyebrow, trying not to look relieved. "What about the cargo, sir?"

"According to my source, it's no longer a secret among our fellow smugglers."

Rusk brought himself upright. "You can't mean … did the Osiran Captain talk? That man was a quaking mass of jelly when we left his ship. There's no way—"

"No, you're quite right about that. He was terrified of us. He didn't talk." Shade stood and paced the floor of his cabin, casually twirling the Druud staff as if it were a pike. "My source says the leak came from someone aboard the *Raker*. I want you to find out who."

Rusk, opportunist to the core, jumped at the opening. "That new guy—"

"'That new guy' didn't know what we were carrying until he saw it. And then he had no idea what it was."

"Might've been an act. Maybe he allowed himself to be shanghaied because he knew and just pretended he'd never seen Lerandia before. You said yourself that he followed you into the Nebula."

"I didn't mean he *intentionally* followed me. In point of fact, he reached the door before I did, but Tusker held him up briefly. He came into the Nebula to return a stolen credit tab. For which honest act I richly rewarded him by flinging him into my brig and forcing him to sign onto this tin can. No, Rusk, think it through. In order for Trouble to have known about the Lerandia as an outsider…"

"There had to have already been a leak." Which meant there was no way to convince Shade that Matthews might be culpable. Rusk was unable to hide the disappointment in his voice.

"Precisely. No, it's another member of our loyal crew. You will determine which one."

"Right. I'll start by putting people on watch in pairs, and put everyone on notice to stay alert. And … I'll have Cyber add some cams to the Hydroponics security system. If the traitor realizes we've been tipped off, he—or she—might do something stupid."

"No. Leave the crew out of it—except for Cyber. I want you to keep this quiet. If our saboteur thinks we've been tipped off, it might also precipitate an immediate attack on the *Moonraker*. But the cams are a good idea. Also, without making a show of it, I would accelerate some of the combat and self-defense sessions. Make sure everybody's sharp. We may have some time, and then again, we may not. Lerandia may be a tempting cargo to the occasional pirate who knows its worth. And you know what occasional pirates must do to keep their records clear and their prizes to themselves."

Rusk nodded. An "occasional pirate" was a ship of the Guild

that went rogue when presented with an irresistible opportunity to liberate a good haul from another Guild member. Unfortunately, getting away with such piracy usually meant making sure that none of the crew aboard the target vessel lived to tell the tale. After all, though the spaceways were well-traveled and had been for centuries, they were still dangerous. Many a ship had disappeared on the most commonly traveled routes without leaving any more trace than vapor and a few pieces of debris so tiny they weren't worth recovering. The *Moonraker's* pilfering of the Lerandia saplings had worked only because the Osiran freighter had not been on Guild registry and therefore had no real legal recourse. The vessel's captain was hardly able to complain to authorities about the loss of a cargo that violated transportation, patent, and conservation laws.

"Don't worry, sir," said Rusk. "Our crew is tough. They can take care of themselves."

"Only a few of them have been in any battles more rigorous than a tavern brawl." Shade hesitated, then added, "Matthews can take care of himself quite well though, can't he?"

Were the old man's glances just a little too keen?

Rusk shrugged. "From what I've seen, he might be pretty effective in repelling a boarding party."

"He's fearless, from the scuttlebutt that's reached my ears." There it was again—that odd glint in the old man's eyes.

"Sir?"

"I assume you knew he put out a fire in Hydroponics yesterday."

Damn. "Yes sir. Of course, sir."

"Yet, you didn't mention it to me. I had to hear it from Cyber. That surprises me ... and concerns me."

"I didn't want you to worry, Captain. The fire was out, and I saw to it that Matthews was disciplined for having damaged the plants."

Shade stopped twirling the staff and turned to look at him. "Disciplined?"

"I gave him a double shift in 'ponics with Morgan. She was with him when he destroyed the leaves—"

"Really? I was thinking he deserved a reward."

"But he ... he destroyed several fully leafed branches. Around two dozen leaves by my count."

"He saved the cargo, Enoch." Shade shook his head and made a clucking sound with his tongue. "First Mate Rusk, your personal biases are showing. You don't like the man. He threatens your authority. You shouldn't let that blind you to his value. Or to common sense. Or to the fact that I gave you a direct order to give him a day of rest before you put him on rotation. I gave that order for the safety of the crew. A good commander treats his crew with neutrality. If you single people out for either reward or punishment based purely on personal bias, you undermine your authority. Imagine what the crew would have done to Lucas if I had treated him with favoritism. Imagine what they would have thought of me."

Shade resumed his pacing. "Don't make an enemy of Matthews. Make use of him ... and of reason, rather than force, for a change. Point out to him that if rogues seize this vessel, he'll be just as cold in the vacuum of space as the rest of us."

Rusk covered his smile by pretending to thoughtfully rub his face. If the *Raker* was boarded, if there was a fight and he could be absolutely certain the right crew was going to win, and if the opportunity presented itself, well then, Trouble Matthews just might die a hero in spite of himself.

"Anything else, sir?"

"I would think the possibility of a hijacking is plenty for one conversation, don't you?"

"Yes, sir. I suppose it is."

Rusk was relieved that this particular conversation was over. He turned to leave.

A hot jolt of energy struck him at the base of the neck. He went down like a felled tree, unable to catch his balance or prod his body to defend itself. He expected to be dead in the next moment or two. He thought he must have passed out. The next thing he knew he was looking up at Captain Shade's expressionless face.

"How do you feel, Enoch?"

How did he feel? His Captain had just attacked him while his back was turned—how was he supposed to feel? He wanted to grab the captain by the throat and crush his larynx ... didn't he? That brief impulse was swamped by sheer disgust. Such violence suddenly seemed wholly alien—repugnant, in fact. The captain was Lord of his ship; by Guild Code he had the right to punish as he saw fit any crew, at any time, for any infraction, real or imagined.

God knew Rusk had committed some very real infractions. At this moment, he regretted every single one of them. He saw now how faithless he had been—hiding private contraband, pursuing his own agenda with Trouble to the point of potentially sabotaging the vessel, and neglecting to tell Shade what had happened to his nephew.

His conscience urged him to come clean with all of it. He loved his captain, would do anything for his captain, would die for him, if necessary. He forgot the throbbing of his head; he was being swept into an ocean of pure, bright good will. Yet beneath the brightness, lingering below the warmth, was an icy black chill unlike any he'd ever known.

"The staff!" he whispered.

"Very good, Enoch," said Shade, still rotating it slowly in his hands. "Now, answer my question: How do you feel?"

"Great." Rusk rose to his elbows and scooted back a couple of inches. He wanted to put as much distance between himself and the captain as possible, and that was the best he could do. "Actually ... I feel ... complete."

"I'm sure you do," said the captain, returning to his chair and crossing his legs. He appeared very relaxed, yet his eyes were alert and steely. "I used myself as a test subject with this Druud staff last night. And do you know how I felt, Mr. Rusk?"

"About like I do," said Rusk, without thinking.

"Indeed. I felt grand. And grandiose. I was connected to the universe, and everything in the universe was connected to me. I guess you could call that a religious experience."

"I could," said Rusk, with a laugh. "Except I don't believe in religion. I mean, maybe as a way to keep order. Every society needs a way to keep order—"

"Shut up, Enoch."

Rusk shut up without a trace of resentment.

"Last night, I also felt the prickling of conscience. I felt like righting wrongs. Evening scores. Answering questions. Luckily for me, there was no one around to ask them. But I suspect that, like me, you've suddenly found yourself in a cooperative mood. Is that right, Mr. Rusk? Are you willing to answer some questions?"

"Yes, sir!" Rusk had never been so afraid in his life, but the fear was buried too deeply to be heard above a whimper.

"I'm afraid you've already been asked these. I just need to make sure you didn't accidentally give me incorrect answers. Now, tell me—what do you know about a mole among our crew?"

"Only what you've told me. I never would've thought—"

"No, of course not. What about the fire in the cargo bay yesterday: Have you told me all you know about that?"

In his head, Rusk quailed and exulted simultaneously; here was his chance for repentance. The whimpering deep inside his head grew louder. "Not ... everything."

"What have you not told me?"

"I ... I haven't put it all together yet, but Hackett is involved somehow, and crewmen Redfield and Duff. They skipped duty yesterday, which enabled someone to ... to rough up Lucas a little bit."

The old man's eyes focused on Rusk's face with an intensity that made the mate want to sink through the floor. "Roughed up Lucas? How badly?"

"Bruises, cuts, split lip, black eyes."

"And you didn't think I needed to be told? Who did this?"

"I don't know. The kid—I mean, your nephew—isn't talking. But Matthews and Morgan seem to know something. I heard them talking about Cyber sending extra cams to the 'ponics bay. Something about a rogue surveillance system down there. They were going to 'watch the Watcher', Morg said."

Shade stood, once again turning the staff in his hands. His eyes went, unfocused, to a point over Rusk's head. Rusk shivered and pressed himself against the legs of a table.

"So, someone aboard is showing an undue amount of interest in the cargo."

He took a couple of paces, then turned to face Rusk, faster than the younger man would have thought possible.

"Why was my nephew beaten, Mr. Rusk? Can you tell me that?"

"No sir. I can't, sir. Only that it's somehow connected to the fire, and maybe to the rogue surveillance cameras."

"Now you see? This is exactly what I was talking about."

Shade came to squat next to Rusk, leaning on the Druud staff, his hands wrapped about it. He rested one weathered cheek against his knuckles and gave Rusk a look of almost gentle reproach.

"If you had treated Mr. Matthews neutrally; made an ally of him instead of an enemy, you might know what it is that he and Morgan know. But as it is, they know something you don't. And as a result, I don't know it either. I'm in the dark, Enoch. I can't see what's going on under my own nose, because you can't see it. Or won't."

Rusk felt a surge of contrition that nearly brought tears to his eyes. "Oh, sir," he whispered. "I'm sorry. I don't hate Matthews. It's just that he ... he's such a smartass. He ..." *He terrifies me*, Rusk thought, but even the effect of the Druud staff couldn't make him say the words aloud. "He makes me nervous. But I'll try to be more careful with him. I'll stop sabotaging him. I'll—"

Shade shook his head. "You'll do what it is you do, Enoch. Which, unfortunately, means that as soon as the effects of this" —he waggled the staff— "have worn off, you will go back to fearing and hating Trouble Matthews to the exclusion of common sense or reason. And you will very likely go back to selectively informing me about what's going on aboard my vessel."

"No, Captain. Never that."

Shade smiled and cast the staff a wistful glance before turning his attention back to Rusk. "You said Hackett was involved in my nephew's beating. Will you ascertain the facts surrounding that please, and report them to me? If Mr. Hackett is the person who injured my nephew, he will have to be punished for it. And of course, I will want to know why. It sounds as if Trouble is your best resource in that endeavor."

Trouble, his best resource. The man he'd just tried to kill or maim. "Anything, Captain. For you—anything."

Shade sighed. He stood, held out his hand, and helped Rusk stand. "These are dangerous times, Enoch. A man must be sure of both his allies and his enemies."

"I understand," Rusk said, by which he meant he understood that if ever a man deserved not to be trusted, it was him.

He looked down at the old man from his superior height and recognized in him both nemesis and mentor. In that moment, he experienced a profound emotion that had nothing to do with the staff. An emotion dredged from the repeated boyhood experience of looking into the loving face of his habitually inebriated father.

He felt his throat constrict. "Captain..."

"Shut up and get out of here," said Shade, "or I'll strike you again with this mind-wrecker."

Rusk exited as quickly as his body would let him. His mind was already working on what he had to do. First, he had to find out for certain who had beaten Lucas and turn them over to Captain Shade. That wouldn't square him with the captain, but it would be a start. Then he must get every scrap of information he could about this situation with Lucas and the fire and the rogue surveillance system and see if it did, indeed, lead him to the mole. That meant sucking up to Trouble or Morgan or Cyber, who was also apparently involved.

Or perhaps it merely meant threatening Cyber.

Rusk's conscience bit back sharply. Allies. He needed *allies*, not enemies or even terrified toadies. If he made allies, they might help him smoke out this mole and present him to Shade on a silver platter. And he'd get back into the captain's good graces.

He sweated, suspecting that Trouble, Morgan, and Cyber were way ahead of him on this. He had to get up to speed. Somehow.

Any doubts Erasmus Shade might have had about using the Druud staff on his second-in-command vanished with the realization that he couldn't really trust the man. Worse, the first mate's hold on things was slipping. His personal dislike of Matthews was blinding him to all else. That made him a liability.

A shame. Rusk had showed promise once upon a time, but he had proven to be a man too easily controlled by his passions. That made him a danger to himself, his crew, and his captain. It also meant Shade was without a trustworthy source of intel. Which was something he could not afford.

He returned to his computer console and opened a closed communications link.

"Cyber, this is Captain Shade—are you on duty, son?"

"Well, uh, yes sir. Of course I am, sir."

"Very busy, are you?"

"Ah ... part of me's very busy. A little security project, you might say."

"Having to do with the rogue cams in Hydroponics ... and my nephew's beating?"

There was a moment of deep silence, then Cyber said. "Yes. Yes, sir. Having to do with that, sir."

"Good. I would like you to summon Matthews, Morgan, and Lucas to the Map Room immediately."

"Y-yes sir. Immediately."

"And I'd like you to join them."

"Sh-sh-ure thing, sir," Cyber said, but Shade knew he had been about to say something else.

14 / PASSION

"I've got bridge duty in ten minutes." Morgan slid into a chair at one of the Retreat tables, a cup of coffee in her hand.

She looked about ten years younger than she had half-an-hour ago, Trouble thought. Her eyes were bright, her cheeks were flushed with color, her hair had that windblown look he recalled women paid big money for in some societies. He smiled, sloshing coffee into his cup. Amazing what a little animal passion could do.

She caught the smile and returned it, leaned toward him as he sat down across from her. "I'm glad we had that little accident with the light switch. I'd have never known your eyes glow a little in the dark. Very sexy."

Trouble laughed. "Yeah, right."

"Is it a genetic thing or did you have it done?"

He read her expression and narrowly avoided choking on his coffee. "I ... uh ... I had it done," he lied glibly. "Knew it'd play well with the X chromosome crowd."

As if he'd known that his eyes did anything of the sort. When he'd looked at himself in a reflective surface last, he'd thought that slight gleam had been reflected light. Actually, it *had* been reflected light in both cases, but light his irises apparently absorbed and then released. His night vision was exceptional.

Was it a genetic anomaly? An environmental adaptation? A bad case of vanity? He didn't know, couldn't say, didn't remember, but he had to believe it went with all the other little "differences" he'd catalogued. He remembered that some lifeforms—both plants and animals—reflected absorbed light. Bioluminescence. He tried to remember if he'd ever heard of people being modded with bioluminescent eyes. Tried and failed. Maybe he could learn something from Sanchez. He put it on his list of things to do.

"Trouble?"

Speak of the devil...

Trouble and Morgan both looked up to see Sanchez standing in the hatchway. He came over to the table, looking extremely distraught. Probably not a good time for a chat about bioluminescent modifications. Trouble leaned back in his chair and put down his coffee cup. Usually when someone was sending out that much angst, they were either scared shitless or ready for a fight ... or both.

"Matthews, I understand I have you to thank for rescuing my plants yesterday."

Trouble relaxed just a bit. "Both of us, actually." He nodded at Morgan.

Sanchez pulled up a chair and sat down. "What happened?"

"Monitor shorted out," Trouble told him. "Leaves caught fire. Morgan and I put them out. Pretty simple. Are you planning to bite my head off for it?"

"What? Don't be ridiculous. I'm thanking you. You probably saved the whole crop."

"That's a refreshing change. First Mate Rusk was ready to rip me a new one for destroying a bunch of the leaves."

"Rusk is an idiot. So you dunked the leaves into the tanks. That's fine—they'll just be absorbed into the nutrient bath." He looked from Trouble to Morgan. "But that was it? The monitor shorted out? How does something like that happen?"

Morgan said, "Well, Cyber actually blew it—"

Trouble caught her with a small shake of his head.

Without missing a beat, she continued: "I don't know if Cyber would *admit* that he blew it. He got a cam too close to the misters and water got into it." She made a boom gesture with her fingers.

Nice save. Trouble was impressed.

Sanchez sat back in his chair. "Really. Is there any chance something like that could happen again?"

Trouble shook his head. "Cyber's learned his lesson. He's moving his little snoops out of harm's way."

Sanchez's brow was still furrowed. "It's just bizarre, I think, that as often as we've had live cargo in the hold, this is the first time something like that has happened. So you think he just got careless?"

Trouble shrugged. "Maybe. Or maybe the equipment's getting old."

Sanchez nodded and started to rise, then had second thoughts and lowered himself back into the chair. He folded his hands in front of him (they were empty of sculpting material, for once) and leaned in.

"I don't know how to put this, or if I should even mention it but ... some strange things have been going on in Hydroponics lately."

"Such as?"

"Well for one thing, the place has apparently been abandoned by crews at least twice that I know of, and when I've gone back over the duty logs to see who the guilty parties were, I find that Cyber can't come up with the audio-visual records from his monitors. It's like that time just— disappeared."

"Maybe the crews were abducted by aliens," Trouble said dryly. "They say that's what it means when people go missing randomly."

Morgan snorted. "Come on, Trouble, Sal is serious. Yeah, we've noticed some irregularities. When I went in yesterday,

Redfield and Duff were nowhere in sight." She glanced at Trouble then added, "They never even signed in."

Sanchez nodded. "And then one of Cyber's cams just happens to malfunction when you were all alone on the floor with a dead fire extinguisher. Quite a coincidence."

"How'd you know about the fire extinguisher?" Morgan asked.

Sanchez gave her an odd look. "I found it floating in the tank with the firing mechanism broken off—ergo, I assumed it didn't work. The absence of retardant foam was another clue. I'm going see if I can't requisition some more of those. Or maybe we can move them from somewhere else on the ship. After all, if anything happens to that cargo, we're all pretty much screwed financially. Anyway—thanks, again, you two. I'll have to make you some special trophies for going above and beyond the call." Sanchez stood and headed for the hatch.

"A moment," Trouble told Morgan, then followed Sanchez into the corridor. "Hey, Sal, got a minute?"

Sanchez turned and shrugged. "Sure. What do you need?"

My memory back would be a good start. "I just have a question about something you might know about in your line of work. Bioluminescence."

Sanchez's dark brows rose, but he nodded. "Yeah. There are a number of plants, animals, and fungal forms that absorb and reflect light. Even some that produce it chemically without an external light source."

"Produce it how?"

"Chemical compounds called luciferins. They emit light as they oxidize. Why?" He looked suddenly uneasy. "Are you about to tell me something is glowing in Hydroponics?"

"No, nothing like that. I was wondering if that sort of thing could be adapted for human use—as an eye mod, say."

Sanchez's gaze immediately locked with his. "*Your* eyes?"

"Yeah. Just noticed it. I mean, they've always been kind of a weird color, I just realized they gleam in dim light."

"Wow. Interesting. Could be a modification aimed at giving you exceptional night vision. Do you have exceptional night vision?"

Trouble vividly recalled his after-dark tour of Porphyry. And even more vividly, Mad Morgan's wet body glistening in the darkness of the shower.

"Yeah, I do."

Sanchez looked bemused. "Cyber said something about your memory being jinked. You don't remember having your eyes modded?"

Trouble shook his head. "No. But it's possible? It can be done?"

"Sure. It's done through an alteration of the pituitary gland. I could probably find some papers on it, if you—"

"No, I'll take your word for it. I just wanted to make sure it wasn't, you know, experimental or illegal or anything."

"No, neither. What were you—"

"Just curious. Thanks ... Sal." He sketched a salute and returned to the Retreat where he rejoined Morgan at the table.

She looked at him suspiciously. "Why all secret all of a sudden?"

"Nothing secret. I just wanted to ask him about this glowing thing." He gestured at his eyes.

Morgan leaned forward, lowering her voice. "You didn't tell him how we found out—"

"Didn't mention it." He grinned. "I don't think I'm a kiss and tell kind of guy."

"Speaking of telling—any reason in particular you didn't want me to tell him about Lucas or the rogue snoops?"

"I just wanted to get his take on things. Maybe he noticed something we didn't because they're his plants. Or at least he's responsible for their health. If we'd told him about Lucas, his emotional reaction might've blown anything he noticed right out of his head or at least prejudiced his observations. Besides, we don't know who put those cams there. What if Sanchez shoots his mouth off to the wrong person?"

"Right. Yeah, I should've thought of that. Seems he's suspicious of Cyber."

"And that his plants are a target."

"For sabotage? Why? Who'd sabotage that valuable a cargo?"

"Don't know. But he's worried about them. Huh. Maybe the rogue snoops are Sanchez's."

"But then why would he ask us what happened?"

Trouble's eyes were drawn to the hatch again as a long, lanky body unfolded through it. "Hey, Cyber-man, we were just talking about you."

"What? Oh, great. I'm ... I'm flattered as hell. Look, we've been summoned. To the captain's quarters—I mean the ready—I mean the Map Room."

Trouble gave the net-head a sharp look. He was paler than usual, if that were possible, and was practically bouncing out of his skin.

"You drink coffee, Cyber?"

"Uh, yeah. Why?"

"Don't."

"What do you mean we've been summoned?" Morgan asked.

"You, me, Trouble, Lucas. Captain called me and said he wants us in his ready room right now. I ... figured you guys might be down here. I already pinged Lucas and told him to meet us in the mess so we can get our stories straight."

"I'm on duty in five minutes," Morgan protested. "Bridge engineering station—not something I can just blow off."

Cyber gave her a pointed look.

"Yeah, okay, I get it. I've just never been summoned to the captain's quarters before."

Trouble did a quick check of the several other parties in the room. They seemed to be engaged in conversation, not eavesdropping—but then you never could tell. "You think this has to do with the fire?"

Cyber was bouncing again. "I don't know, but whether it does or not, I think we've got to tell him what we know."

"The way you're dancing around, I'd guess that's more than we knew this morning," Trouble said.

"Tell you on the way." Cyber turned and fidgeted his way out of the Retreat.

They headed forward, Trouble and Morgan side-by-side and Cyber in front, dancing sideways and sometimes even backwards as he filled them in.

"So, literally a second before the captain linked, I found it."

"The power drain?" asked Morgan.

"Yep. And you know where it is? It's in a little access bay practically on top of the aft sensor array. That's what made it so hard to find. It was where the power usage tends to be in flux anyway. It's the way the sensors work," he explained when Trouble raised an eyebrow at him. "They use a fairly steady rate of power most of the time. But when they ping something that requires more detailed analysis, they draw more power. Naturally, they find things that require more analysis pretty randomly, so irregular power spikes from that area are common."

"Then how'd you find it?" Morgan wanted to know.

Cyber looked so pleased with himself, Trouble almost laughed out loud.

"I was monitoring the sensor array when it blipped—it found something. I was patched in, so I thought I'd take a look at what it had found. It was another ship way out on the grid's edge, crossing our forward port quarter. I stuck with it until the sensor analysis was complete and guess what?"

"There was still extra power being drawn," Trouble guessed.

Cyber snapped his fingers and pointed at Trouble's nose. "That! Just a little ghost. But more than the array draws when it's just scanning."

"That doesn't tell us whose toy it is, though, does it?"

"It may tell us whose it *isn't*," Cyber said as they entered the lift. "Gamma Deck," he told the lift computer.

"Does it?" Trouble asked.

"Well, it's got to be someone whose longterm presence in that part of the ship wouldn't draw any attention—not even from me. That lets out most of the crew right there."

"So ... who'd be able to gain access to that part of the ship without tweaking you?"

"Well, the captain, the mate, Sanchez, Redfield, and Glass are the ones who come to mind."

"Because...?"

"The captain can go anywhere he wants, and he and Rusk both have access to the *Raker* during times when the rest of us aren't even aboard. I mean, it's entirely possible that the rogue snoops are Captain Shade's. Maybe he wanted to make sure we had an extra layer of security—"

"Captain Shade wouldn't have his own nephew beaten to a pulp," argued Morgan.

"You sure?" Trouble asked.

She gave him a wry look. "Not funny. And Sanchez sure as hell wouldn't do anything to his own plants. They're like ... babies or pets or something to him."

Trouble nodded. "Which leaves Rusk, Redfield, and this other guy."

Cyber returned the nod in double-time. "Rainor Glass. He's a Slinky."

"Yeah?" Trouble had heard of Slinkies somewhere, he realized, but he was pretty sure he had never met one. "Modded to work in zero gravity?"

Cyber nodded. "Uh, yeah. Light bones, triple joints—"

"Triple-jointed? That can't be right..."

"No, it is. Triple-jointed. He's a walking ad for DeNA-Gen— Slinkies are one of their greatest success stories. And his bones aren't just light, they're hollow."

"Then how does he get around in normal gravity? Exo-frame?"

Cyber gave him a "what planet are you from?" look and nodded again. "Yeah. He and Redfield are both sensor hardware guys. Rain specializes in the outdoors work, naturally."

"How are those mods done?"

That *look* again. "Bio-mod nanites."

The lift doors opened and they stepped out into the short corridor that linked the mess, which was forward of the lift, with the aft section of Gamma Deck containing the infirmary and ship's stores.

The small mess was pretty full of just-off-shift crewmen in some phase of chowing down. Lucas sat at a table by himself, nursing a bottle of something and looking edgy and miserable. He was clean and tidy, but still a wreck from the beating. The pinky finger on his left hand was wrapped tightly in med tape. The trio started to move across the room toward him when they were blocked by First Mate Rusk, who planted himself right in front of Trouble, hands on hips, jerkstick dangling from a strap on his right wrist.

"You know, as nice as it is to see my crew bonding, some-thing about seeing you three together sets my teeth on edge."

Morgan said, "Look Rusk, we don't really have time—"

"Crewman Morgan, you're supposed to be on the bridge. Take a wrong turn somewhere?"

Trouble stepped forward, smiling. "Down, Ruskie."

Rusk's face ran a gamut of emotions, some of which Trouble had no names for. Finally, he said, "What? What did you say?" His voice was pitched low, almost a growl. He took a step into Trouble, color rising in his neck.

Morgan stepped between the two of them. "Look, I'm seri-ous, Rusk. Captain ordered us to the Map Room. We were just coming up here to get Lucas."

Rusk's color shifted suddenly toward the ashen. He stepped back and glanced at each of them, his eyes coming to rest on

Trouble. "You're lying. Cap would have told me if he was going to call you in. In fact, he would have had me deliver the message."

Cyber cleared his throat. "Actually, he had *me* deliver the message. He really did ask to see us, sir."

"Well, you're not gonna see him unless I say you can. And I don't. Morgan, get up to the bridge for your duty. Matthews, I've got a couple of jobs for you."

"Like the last one? The one that was supposed to get me killed?"

"I'm s-so..." Rusk took another step back and shook his head.

Trouble could have sworn he saw a flash of contrition in the mate's eyes before he put his game face back on. Then the man did something that surprised the hell out of even Trouble: He laid the serious end of the jerkstick in the palm of his own left hand and fired it.

The resulting roar got the attention of everyone in the mess. The first mate doubled over, shuddering and breathing hard. When he straightened, his earlier confusion seemed to have vanished. There was no contrition in his eyes now; there was only cold, hard hatred. He raised the jerkstick again, this time targeting Trouble.

"That's more like it," said Trouble. "Now I won't feel bad about doing this."

He reached up, intercepted the jerkstick with one hand, and jabbed Rusk solidly in the gut with the other. He followed the jab with his right shoulder, bored into Rusk's mid-section and flipped the big man heels over head.

Rusk landed on his back at Morgan's feet.

Morgan found herself staring down into Rusk's beet red face, half-expecting to hear the classic cartoon sound of a tea-kettle getting ready to boil over. She scampered quickly out of the range of the jerkstick, dragging Cyber with her.

Trouble turned to face his fallen adversary and waited.

Morgan gritted her teeth. He was too casual. Too damned relaxed. Only the slight tilt of his head hinted that he was even watching Rusk's movements. And the mate's next movement was a doozy. Without seeming to have twitched a muscle in preparation, Rusk flung his legs up over his head in a backward somersault clearly intended to bring his booted feet into sharp contact with Trouble's face.

It would have been an effective move, too, except that Trouble was no longer where the mate had aimed. With a move too fast to follow, he darted aside and brought his clamped fists down in a lightning chop to the back of Rusk's now-exposed neck. The big man went down again, this time face first.

A timid cheer rippled through the mess.

Trouble stepped back, just at the edge of Rusk's reach, and began pacing around him. "Hey, Cyber," he said.

"Huh?" The net-head looked up from Rusk's prone form, blinking.

"You better hail the captain and send him our apologies. We're gonna be just a few minutes late for tea."

"Oh. Uh. Yeah." Cyber wriggled through the hemming crowd of crewmates, raising a hand to the sensor on his internal p-comm.

Rusk had not moved. Morgan could see that he was perfectly conscious; his eyes tracked Trouble's progress around him like a venom-spewing sensor array. She fought the tightness in her throat. Trouble was good. Damn good—at a number of things. But Rusk was Rusk, and he hadn't risen to first mate on his sterling character. He had earned the post, in large part, because he was a heller in a fight.

She glanced at Trouble, and saw Lucas's mottled face staring back at her from a knot of crewmen just beyond him. The boy seemed transfixed with terror, and she suspected his thoughts were similar to her own. After herself, Trouble was the closest thing to an ally Lucas had aboard the *Moonraker*. All others either ignored him or actively twitted him because of his age, temperament, and bloodlines.

"Come on, Rusk," Trouble crooned. "You've got to have more than that. You know what your problem is? You think too much. You plot and scheme against a guy instead of just having it out. You think I can't see what's going on in that big, fat head of yours right now? 'How do I trick him into coming too close? How do I get him to think I'm down for the count'?"

Trouble stopped circling and squatted about four feet from Rusk's head—out of reach of his big hands, but not out of reach of the jerkstick.

"You hate me. I get that. I think I even know why. But you've got a lily-assed way of showing it—if you don't mind my saying so. You could just get in my face and say, 'Trouble, you sonofabitch, I hate your guts, and I'm gonna kill you.' And then try to do it. That, I think I could respect. But no. Not you. Big, powerful First Mate Enoch Rusk. No, you set me up to take a long fall down the drive core, maybe flood Engineering with enough radiation to make everybody on shift glow in the dark."

He paused to shoot Morgan a cock-eyed grin. She could hear the murmurs from the crewmen at her back. She felt the sudden tension as Trouble's words hit home.

"What are you talking about, Trouble?" Jiang asked from across the circle of watchers.

"You want to tell them, Enoch?" Trouble asked mildly.

Rusk moved then, again, with a speed that caught Morgan off guard. He brought the jerkstick around and over his head in a swift arc, firing it as it came.

It should have caught Trouble in the back of the leg, but Trouble was suddenly airborne, rising more than a meter off the deck, his legs drawn up beneath him, his arms spread to either side. It was an incredibly powerful and graceful leap; the jerkstick passed well beneath him.

He touched down with his full weight on Rusk's extended forearm.

The first mate roared in pain and frustration, and tried to flip himself over. But his arm was pinned at an awkward angle. Instead, he wrenched up, pulling his arm out from under Trouble, and rose for another sweep of the jerkstick.

Trouble leapt a second time, lashed out with one foot, and caught Rusk squarely in the jaw.

The mate went down again, this time on his side. He didn't stay down long. He rolled to his feet, forcing a section of the audience to scurry backwards in an attempt to get out of his way. Enraged, he fired the jerkstick randomly, sweeping it around him and jabbing several of his fleeing crewmates with it. They shrieked and fell.

Trouble shook his head as if he were watching the tantrum of an incorrigible toddler.

Rusk was losing it, Morgan thought. Letting his anger drive him. She prayed God that would make him stupider than usual.

On his feet for the first time since the fight began, Rusk moved in on Trouble with the jerkstick at the ready.

Trouble circled just out of reach, shaking his head and chuckling. The incongruous sound sent chills down Morgan's spine, and liquid warmth through her core. The last time she'd heard that sound was under very different circumstances, in the moist dark of a shower cubicle.

"You're a piece of work, Mr. Rusk," Trouble said. "Did you just happen to find broken rod rotators for me to use, or did you screw them up just for me? Did you know that gallery rail was hacked, or did you cut it as a gesture of respect?"

The crew was murmuring again. Absorbing every word.

Finally, Rusk spoke. "Don't listen to him! He's full of it. Got delusions of grandeur. As if I'd care enough to do any of that—"

"I fixed that railing myself, Rusk," said Jiang from the sidelines. Her gleaming face allowed her little expression, but her voice was sharp with disgust. "Trouble's right, it was cut.

Almost clean through in a couple of places. And keeping those rod rotators to spec is my job. I *do* my job."

Trouble nodded, stopped moving, and gestured at Rusk to come at him. "Time, Enoch. Time to pay the piper."

Rusk came at him full-throttle with a roar of pure rage. At the last second, he feinted left and brought the jerkstick around from the right, trying to squeeze Trouble against the crowd.

Instead of retreating, Trouble stepped into his mad dash, grasped the jerkstick just behind the coils, and aimed a chop at the inside of Rusk's elbow. The elbow buckled, Trouble ducked, and the momentum of Rusk's own arm brought the coils up against the side of his head.

Trouble bobbed up again and grabbed the stick in two places: One hand held it to the side of the mate's head, while the other grappled for the trigger, covered by Rusk's fist. Rusk staggered backwards and sideways, but managed to keep his feet. He brought his massive left hand up and wrapped it around Trouble's throat.

Morgan leapt forward, intending to wade into the fight herself, but a strong hand clamped on her forearm and restrained her. She glanced aside, a curse on her lips, and found Captain Shade standing beside her.

"Patience, Mr. Morgan," he murmured. "The best man will win."

She brought her eyes back to the struggle. Trouble was on his knees before Rusk, looking like a penitent in front of an over-sized priest. Though his face was reddening, he still held the jerkstick against Rusk's neck. But she knew the strength of Rusk's hands. They were like the jaws of a predator; once they had locked onto you, they didn't let go.

Panic exploded in her. "For God's sake, Trouble!"

As if at her cue, Trouble launched himself forward and up, driving his head into Rusk's mid-section. The mate let out a woof of surprise and pain, and the jerkstick fired, sending its full load into his unprotected temple. He didn't even cry out. He simply went rigid, then limp, all fight extinguished by the neural overload. He hit the floor in a crumpled heap.

There was total silence in the mess as Trouble pulled himself to his feet, rubbing his throat. He stood, weaving only a little, and gazed down at his adversary. "That's gotta hurt," he said. The words were almost a croak, but they were enough to send the crew into fits of laughter and cheering.

Morgan looked at Erasmus Shade. He seemed older suddenly, the lines on his face folding in on themselves. Then the moment passed. Shade took a deep breath, let go of Morgan's arm, and went to stand over his fallen first mate, facing Trouble.

"Congratulations," he said.

Trouble inclined his head.

Shade bent and, with difficulty, pulled the jerkstick from Rusk's slack hand to hold it aloft. Turning in a full circle, he addressed the crew, asking, "What say you?"

"Trouble!" shouted Jiang, thrusting her fist into the air.

Everyone in the mess joined in, shouting: "Trouble! Trouble! Trouble!" in rhythmic unison.

Facing the bemused victor, Captain Shade held the jerkstick out to him on open palms. "It's unanimous and official, young man. You are *Moonraker*'s new first mate."

15 / BECOMING

"And if I don't want it?" Trouble's eyes were on the jerkstick in Erasmus Shade's gnarled hands.

"Don't want it?" repeated Shade. "Does it mean nothing to you that you've gone from recruit to first mate elect in two short days?"

"Actually, they've been pretty damn long days, and yes, it means nothing to me. No wait, I take that back. It means I won't have to put up with *him* anymore." He pointed at the recumbent Rusk. "It doesn't mean I want to *become* him."

Shade merely nodded, as if this turn of events was unsurprising. "You're sure? Yes, of course, you are. I suppose you always are. In that case, it falls to you to nominate someone else from among your able crewmates." He offered the jerkstick again, gesturing at it with his head. "The choice is yours."

Trouble took the stick and walked the circle of crewmen, looking into the faces of each man and woman there. In the end, he came back to where Morgan, Cyber, and Lucas stood flanking their Captain.

He smiled. "Yeah. That's it. Hey, Cyber-man! Catch!" He tossed the jerkstick at Cyber, who caught it, juggled it, and finally held it before him as if it were a frozen snake in danger of instantaneous thawing.

A few of the crew laughed. Others broke into applause.

"What say you?" asked Erasmus Shade.

"Yeah," said Jiang, turning to look at the crewmen nearest her. "Yeah!"

They all applauded then, with varying degrees of enthusiasm, while Cyber continued to stand and stare at the weapon as if he had never seen it before in his life.

Trouble chuckled and leaned into Morgan. "He'll never use it," he said. "Probably pull the power pack out and put it into a sex toy."

Morgan let out a crack of laughter that, at last, drew Cyber's attention from his new acquisition. He smiled uncertainly as various crewmates patted him on the back and offered congratulations and sarcastic bits of advice.

Erasmus Shade brought the party to a close. "Smithson, Blackwood, take Mr. Rusk down to the brig. Then clean out his quarters and remove his personal gear to the barracks. Matthews, Morgan, and Lucas, if you don't mind I still need to speak to you privately. Would you be so kind as to join me and my new first mate in the Map Room?"

Shade couldn't seem to take his eyes from Lucas's mangled face—something Lucas was obviously uncomfortably aware of. When finally the captain spoke, it was to ask: "How did this happen?"

Trouble looked at Lucas. So did everyone else. The boy fidgeted, unable to meet their eyes. "I nuked someone off."

"Hackett?" asked Shade.

Lucas stared at him. "How...?"

"Mr. Rusk overheard a conversation between Morgan and Trouble. About the fire and a rogue surveillance system. Mr. Hackett's name came up. Did Hackett do this to you?"

Lucas stared at the floor.

"Lucas..." There was a growl of warning in Morgan's voice. "Do you want *us* to tell him?"

"Okay. Yeah. It was Hackett. He was nuked because I—"

"Lucas," said Cyber. "There's a rogue snoop aimed right at the spot you were working that day. I know where the control console is now, so there's probably a record in it of what happened to you, but it would save us some time if you just told us."

The boy looked at each of them in turn, lastly turning to his uncle. "I found something. In the Lerandia grove."

Shade stiffened. "What?"

"I don't know what it is. I don't even know how to describe it."

"Try."

"There's something ... attached to the root nodes. I don't know what it is, exactly, but it doesn't look natural. Hell, it *isn't* natural. It's some sort of ... device. I couldn't even guess at what it's for. I just know it doesn't belong there. I think maybe I got beat up because I saw it."

"Makes sense," said Cyber. "You stumble across this what-ever-it-is, it turns out the whatever-it-is is being monitored, next thing you know Hackett shows up and beats you senseless. I think that's a little too much to chalk up to coincidence."

"I agree," said Shade. "First Mate Cyber, as your first official duty, I would like you to see to it that Mr. Hackett is remanded to the brig. Tell him I'll be down soon to have a talk with him. I'd also like you to assign a guard detail to the Hydroponics bay."

"Yes sir." Cyber headed for the hatch.

Trouble noticed that he'd left the jerkstick lying on the captain's nav console. He picked it up and balanced it in his hands. Had to admit it did look pretty out-of-place in Cyber's.

"Hey, Lord Cyber."

Cyber turned back at the hatch.

"You forgot your scepter." He tossed the stick.

Cyber caught it at the last minute, giving it a look of pure loathing.

Trouble grinned. "You don't have to use it. Just act like you might."

"Yeah. Right. Thanks."

When Cyber had gone, the captain turned to Trouble and Morgan. "While he's doing that, I want you to tell me everything you know about this situation. Everything."

Cyber caught up with Hackett during his duty shift in Hydroponics. He was dreading this with every fiber of his being, but it couldn't be helped. He'd recruited a couple of the usual security detail to go along as enforcers, choosing two crewmen who'd been in the mess when Trouble had taken Rusk down and passed the "scepter" to Cyber.

Hackett refused to believe, at first, that Rusk was no longer mate and that Cyber was. He laughed out loud at the idea that Cyber meant to haul him to the brig for Lucas's beating. Cyber noted that he didn't deny having administered it.

Even after both security guys corroborated Cyber's story, Hackett still resisted arrest. Cyber threatened the jerkstick; Hackett laughed in his face; the guards jumped him; he put up a fight.

After dithering for a moment and enduring a couple of eloquent glares from his security detail, Cyber sighed, said: "I'm really sorry about this," and let Hackett have it with the jerkstick.

It took them about three minutes to get him down the lift to the brig, where they delivered him, snarling and snapping, into a pressor cell. There, his eyes still watering from the pain, Hackett turned to snarl obscenities at his captors. His voice cut out on him in mid-oath as he caught sight of Rusk lying on a cot in another cell.

He brought his eyes back to Cyber, who was standing uneasily in the center of the room, the jerkstick clipped to his belt.

"You ... you weren't kidding."

"I wasn't kidding."

"Matthews did that?"

"Uh-huh."

"Then why isn't *he* first mate?"

Cyber shrugged. "Didn't want it. So, he passed the baton to me." He waggled the jerkstick.

Hackett goggled at him in disbelief.

"Yeah, me too. I don't think I could've imagined this in a billion years. Look, Captain Shade is going to come down in a while to talk to you about what happened with Lucas. We know this wasn't just a personal vendetta. We know it had something to do with those ... devices attached to the Lerandia. I think it would really be in your best interests to come clean."

Hackett did not have a poker face. Every emotion he felt as Cyber spoke played out on his stubby features: alarm, anger, despair, sly calculation, panic.

"I'm serious, Hackett. We pretty much know that someone put you up to beating Lucas—that it was your job to make sure he didn't tell anybody about the devices. Shade is going to want to know who your boss is."

Hackett's eyes darted about as if in fear that that person was going to appear out of the brig bulkheads.

"He can't get to you in here. I've got guards posted with instructions that only Captain Shade, Trouble, or Morgan are allowed to see you."

Hackett relaxed and sat down on his cot.

"Vengeful guy, your boss?" Cyber asked.

"Go screw yourself."

Cyber took a step toward the cell and was surprised when

Hackett actually sat up straighter and eyed him warily. He'd never had anyone look at him that way before—with fear.

He didn't like it. That was good. He hoped he would never come to like it. *Anyway, it's not me he fears,* he told himself. *It's the stick.* He laid his hand on it, saw Hackett's eyes follow the gesture.

"If you're afraid of your boss, Hackett, let me assure you that Captain Shade will be far worse. I wouldn't disappoint him if I were you."

"I ain't afraid of anybody," Hackett lied.

"Right." Cyber rubbed his hand along the barrel of the jerkstick and saw Hackett wince. "What are they?"

"What are what?"

"The things on the Lerandia roots. What are they supposed to do?"

"I don't know. And that's the truth. I was just supposed to discourage anybody who might find them from talking about them."

"For who?"

"The Pilgrims," said Hackett, grinning.

Cyber thought about using the jerkstick on him again—for an entire point two seconds. Then he glanced over at Rusk, still lying inert in his corner. What was it Trouble had said? *I don't want to become him.*

Cyber let go of the jerkstick and turned to go.

"Hey, can I get a drink in here or you gonna let me die of thirst? I was doin' hard labor when your goons grabbed me."

"Yeah, okay. I'll have something sent down. If you're lucky it'll get here before the captain does. He probably wouldn't let you have it."

"Yeah, you've got a soft, squishy center."

"That's 'you've got a soft, squishy center, *sir,*'" Cyber reminded him, and slipped out through the hatch.

Trouble didn't miss the malevolent look in Hackett's eyes when he stepped into the brig. Glancing aside, he saw that Rusk was conscious and sitting up on the edge of his cot with his head in his hands. The ex-first mate cast Trouble a look of pure hatred from red-rimmed eyes.

Trouble smiled. Loathing in stereo.

Beside him, Erasmus Shade caught his eye and echoed the smile with some irony. The captain stepped farther into the room, flanked by Cyber and Trouble. Morgan hovered behind them near the hatch, the Druud staff in hand.

"Mr. Hackett," said Shade, "I understand you had a disagreement with my nephew yesterday. Is this true?"

Hackett pondered his answer with apparent care, his eyes on the captain's face. Trouble could almost hear the squeaky little gears turning in his head.

"Well, Mr. Hackett? Did you thrash Lucas Shade?"

Hackett paled a bit at the captain's pointed use of the surname. With phony ease, he took a final slug of his drink and put the cup down beside his cot. Then, he stood, stretched and said, "Well, maybe I did, and maybe I didn't."

Shade grimaced. "Oh, please, Hackett. Don't be an ass. He's accused you. I believe him. If for no other reason than the bruises and lacerations on your knuckles."

"On-the-job accident," said Hackett.

"Come on, Hackett," said Cyber. "You admitted it to me. You said you were supposed to discourage people from talking about anything going on with the Lerandia."

"Maybe I was just yanking your chain."

"And maybe you're just afraid to admit the same thing to me," Shade guessed. "After all, I could have you tossed out an airlock for beating up my nephew. Heaven knows, if his father were to find out, your fate would be many times worse."

A shadow of doubt flickered across Hackett's face. "His father is ..."

"Our Guild Master. And you are right in supposing that even were you to extract yourself from this brig, you would not be safe aboard this or any other Guild vessel."

"So if I admit smacking the boy around, you won't tell his pop, is that what you're saying? Fine. I smacked the boy around."

"Why?"

"He nuked me off."

Trouble took a languid step toward the cell. Hackett eyed him warily.

"Yes," said Shade, "I certainly could have Mr. Cyber shut down the pressor field and let Mr. Matthews have at you. Are you sure you'd prefer that to being thrown out an airlock?"

Trouble looked into Hackett's beady, near-set eyes and shook his head. "I believe your logic is falling on deaf ears, Captain. May I suggest you cut to the chase?"

"Very well. Cyber, please drop the pressor field."

The field shut down and Shade held out his hand to Morgan, who stepped forward and placed the Druud staff in it.

"Do you know what this is, Mr. Hackett? This is a Druud staff. Mr. Rusk will vouch for the fact that it has a peculiar effect on its victims. A liberating effect, you might say. It makes a man want to clear the slate, make a clean breast of things, utter sterling and often startling truths. ...Am I making my point, Mr. Hackett?"

Apparently he was, for Hackett's eyes widened to their maximum, and he stood and held up his hands.

Time for the unexpected, Trouble thought.

He plucked the staff from Shade's hands and took the last step into Hackett's cell, bringing the staff around, intending to discharge it against Hackett's chest.

The other man took a step back, went rigid, and fell to the

floor as if he'd been pole-axed. Trouble stood over him, surprised to the soles of his boots. He shot a look back over his shoulder at Shade.

"I didn't touch him," he said.

16 / DEVICES

"DEAD. STROKE, APPARENTLY."

That had been Dr. Pike's laconic assessment of Hackett's demise. It was too convenient, under the circumstances, to strike anyone as being coincidental. Shade had been immediately suspicious of the cider Hackett had been drinking and had turned the cup over to Pike for analysis.

Now they stood in Hydroponics, sweating next to a nutrient tank—the nutrient tank at which Lucas had been working when he'd found whatever it was he'd found. Cyber had climbed into the sensor array access and shut down the rogue surveillance system manually. With any luck, it would take the saboteur some time to realize he'd been off-lined intentionally. Without that luck, he'd tumble to the fact that he'd been made the moment his cams went down, and would take counter measures.

Trouble expected the latter; in his recent experience luck was the most fickle force in the universe.

Lucas donned long protective gloves and began feeling about in the fetid water. After a couple of false tries, he came up with the ersatz node. As he had said, it was clearly a device. A device that to all appearances was feeding a toxic-looking orange liquid into the Lerandia root system. After further search, they came up with a total of eight of the devices, each under the careful watch of a rogue snoop. With great care, Morgan and Lucas detached one of them and brought it out of the tank.

Under the canned lighting of the Hydroponics lab, they examined the thing with exaggerated care. It had an intake system that apparently sucked in water from the nutrient tank, processed and supplemented it, and fed it out again into the root system where it was passed from plant to plant.

"Definitely sabotage," said Morgan, frowning over the device's configuration.

"But to what purpose?" asked Captain Shade. His face was ashen. "The plants look healthy. What do these devices do?"

"I don't know," Trouble said, "but I bet Sanchez does."

"Of course," Morgan nodded. "After all, he's the botanist."

Trouble chuckled. "After all, he's probably the saboteur. Or he knows who is." He glanced around at the others. "Is this a surprise to you? You think someone could do this to Sal's plants without him knowing about it?"

Morgan raised her eyes to Trouble's face. "Shit."

Cyber mumbled: "I tried to hail him. While you were poking at our little thingy there. No response."

Shade exhaled sharply. "First Mate Cyber—"

"Say no more, sir. I'm on it."

Cyber left the room at a dead run, no doubt to return to his cubicle, from which he stood a better chance of finding Sanchez than he did roaming the passages of the freighter or ordering a crew detail to do it.

The Captain immediately opened a ship-wide comm link and broadcast to the rest of his crew that if they saw Salvador Sanchez, they were to restrain him for questioning with regard to the sabotage of their cargo.

"That ought to put a significant charge into them," Shade said grimly. "These plants are as much their fortune as they are mine."

"Now what?" Morgan asked. "If this cargo has been screwed up in some way ..."

"Mr. Sanchez might be the only person who can tell us that with any certainty," said Shade. "But I want to take this thing, a leaf, and a piece of the root system to Dr. Pike. He might at least be able to render some sort of preliminary analysis."

"Wouldn't the quickest way to tell what these things were doing be to brew some Lerandia tea?" asked Trouble.

Shade raised snowy eyebrows at him. "And are you volunteering to test the brew, Mr. Matthews?"

"Me? No, thanks. But Rusk might volunteer. If it got him out of the brig and back on the crew. Of course, since we don't know how that orange goo alters the androstin..."

Shade glanced from Trouble to Morgan to his nephew. "You know, then."

"Cyber figured it out," said Morgan.

"I see. Then you may know that Lerandia's prodigious production of androstin is a fairly recent discovery, and the plants are not widely grown. I had hoped to get these plants to market before this becomes common knowledge and they pop up in every environment capable of sustaining them. Now, I think it's past time I contribute something else to this discussion. I received some information last night that makes me think it extremely likely that this ship will be the target of piracy. Someone here has let it be known what the *Moonraker* is carrying."

"You think the two things are connected?" asked Trouble. "Your mole and this sabotage? I don't get it. If this guy wants to turn the whole cargo over to someone else, why would he screw with the plants?"

"A very good question, Mr. Matthews. One to which I have no answer at this moment. Perhaps, when we find Mr. Sanchez—"

He was not to finish the thought. The comm link sprang to blaring and urgent life.

"Captain Shade," said Cyber's voice, "we've had an unauthorized shuttle launch. It's Sanchez, damn it, and he's gotten clean away. He overrode the shuttle bay sensors so no one would pick up the launch. The bridge crew thought it was a system glitch and rebooted the sensors in that section. He's been gone at least ten minutes."

"How far can he go in ten minutes in a shuttle?" Morgan asked.

"Far enough for his buddies to pick him up," said Trouble. "You do remember how Cyber found the rogue surveillance console?"

Morgan paled. "A ship. He said there was a ship off our port quarter."

"I have been an idiot." Captain Shade thumbed the comm link on. "Cyber, track the shuttle. That will at least tell us what direction to expect an attack to come from. Morgan, Matthews, you're in Engineering. Get the K-drive ready to go on line if it becomes necessary."

"Captain," said Morgan tightly, "we won't be in optimal jump position for—"

"We may not have the option of waiting for optimal jump position." He paused to give them a look that made Trouble's skin crawl. "If we find ourselves under attack, I may be forced to take extreme measures to save this vessel. If we are boarded by a pirate crew, our chances of survival are nil. I want you to know that going in, so you'll understand that my plan may be our only chance of survival."

"I just realized how much I hate mysteries," said Trouble. "What the hell are you talking about?"

Shade shook his head, already moving toward the hatch. "No time."

"What about me?" asked Lucas quietly.

His uncle turned to look at him, clearly at a loss to know what to do with the boy.

"Since he's got one good hand, we could use him in Engineering," said Morgan, for which Lucas shot her a look of pure gratitude.

Great, Trouble thought, as they scrambled to their station. *We just bought ourselves a puppy.*

Glass and Jiang were on duty in Engineering when Morgan and Trouble arrived. The two were full of questions about the ship-wide broadcast commanding Sanchez's capture and suitably stunned when Morgan explained the situation to them.

"Captain wants the Keplinger ready to go online at a moment's notice," she told them. "So let's get cracking. Jiang, you ride the power couplings, start bringing them online now. Rain, since your exo is rad shielded, take a position in the core gallery—just in case. Lucas, you know how to read engine flux?"

The kid nodded. "Sure, Morg."

"Do it. Keep your eye on the negative field profile. You see anything out of line in those readings, shout out, okay?"

She turned to Trouble. "I figured you and I should suit up, too—just in case. You know the jump sequence for a rig like this?"

He searched his memory. Tech stuff like this seemed to come with relative ease. Body memory, or whatever they called it.

"I've been on one or two jumps. The jump controls seem familiar. I can handle them." *I think,* he did not say aloud. He moved to pull a rad suit out of the equipment locker. "You got a clue what the old guy's plan is?"

Morgan looked grimmer than Trouble had ever seen her. "Half a clue. You heard of the Pilgrim's Passage?"

Trouble frowned. He *had* heard of it. What had he heard of it? "It's a wormhole, right?"

"An artificial, alien wormhole," Morgan clarified. "And if half of what I've heard about it is true, we could all be brain dead before we come out the other side. *If* we come out the other side."

"You think that's the captain's plan—diving into an ancient alien wormhole?"

Morgan shrugged. "Well, judging from our present location, he might be thinking about taking the plunge. We'll know when he lays in the course for the jump."

"Holy Hell," Trouble muttered.

"Yeah, but which would you prefer—a fifty-fifty chance of being brain dead, or a hundred percent chance of being completely dead?"

"Let me think on it." Trouble snapped his mask into place and slipped into the engine room.

Morgan followed after donning a suit of her own.

From his vantage point at the drive controls, Trouble could see the Slinky, Rainor Glass, high above him on the gallery. He was admiring the graceful movement of the man's spidery limbs when the ship suddenly rocked—hard enough to throw him sideways against the drive console. A thunderous rumble, conducted by the hull, enveloped them for several seconds. Klaxons keened and a voice began a repetitive litany: "Emergency alert! Emergency alert!"

They were under attack.

"Stations!" yelled Morgan. There was fear in her eyes, but she kept it there and did not let it spill over into her voice. She turned to give Trouble a grim smile.

"Here we go."

17 / PURSUIT

THERE WERE FEW THINGS MORE FRUSTRATING, IN TROUBLE'S opinion, than being stuck in the bowels of a ship during a running battle. You were blind, cut off from the action, unable to do to anything but wait for it to be over—one way or another. And you were deaf, too, or at least deafened, by the klaxons and by the sound of the ship recoiling from each blast.

As soon as he had the thought, he wondered how the hell he even had an opinion about being in a space battle. He grunted as a memory sliced through his mind, fleeting and sharp.

Darkness riven by slashes of boiling light. Searing heat. The shriek of rent metal and torn human beings.

He shook himself. Where had that come from? If it was a memory and not a nightmare, how had he even survived it?

The klaxons, mercifully, shut off. Trouble shook his head as if that might makes his ears stop ringing.

"He won't destroy her," Morgan said into the relative silence. "Whoever he is, he wants the cargo. He just wants to force us to roll over."

Trouble opened his mouth to say he didn't need the reassurances, then realized she wasn't talking to him. Lucas, hovering over the engine status display, looked as if all the blood had drained out of him. The boy swallowed, taking as tight a grasp on the console's hand-holds as his injured hand would allow.

"Captain won't roll over," he said, and Trouble could hear the pride mixed with his fear.

Morgan grinned at him. "Damn right."

"Engineering. Prepare for jump to superluminal." Cyber's voice was so present, Morgan jumped, then glanced sheepishly at Trouble.

From her station at the base of the drive core, Jiang brought the last power coupling fully online, then nodded back over her shoulder at the group near the controls. "Ready."

"We're just going to buy some time," Cyber told them. "Dazzle 'em with our footwork and get ourselves out of the way long enough for the captain to plot a new course. So be ready to shut down again on my mark."

Trouble wedged his right foot further under a deck ring and put both hands on the jump controls.

"Cyber, do you recognize the ship?" Morgan asked.

"It's the *Agni Devi*."

"Damn," Morgan growled.

"That mean something?" asked Trouble.

"Vishnu Chowdury's ship. He's a mean sonovabitch. Makes Rusk look like a cuddly toy. He's gone rogue before. Keeps that scow of his armed to the teeth. We've got some firepower, but nothing like what the *Devi* packs. We're talking plasma cannons, neutral-particle beams, tritium torpedoes—"

The *Raker* swung suddenly down and to starboard. There was no way to tell this except by the instrument readings and a slight vibration, of course, as the ship's inertial dampers compensated for such movement.

Cyber's voice came sharply through the comm link: "Jump!"

Trouble locked the hyperdrive controls on, feeding the power build-up from the Keplinger engine up through the drive rods. The subluminal engines shut down, while in the drive core, blue-white brilliance shot up through the rods to the field generator's broad turret.

The ship seemed to hold its breath for a moment, hanging on the threshold of hyperspace; then she dove in. At least that's what it felt like to Trouble; a heartbeat of vertigo, followed by an incredible head rush. It was a familiar feeling, he realized. Then came what veteran spacers called 'The Hush.' The Keplinger purred when idling; at full power it was virtually silent.

"Engines look good," murmured Lucas.

Trouble shook his head. People always seemed to whisper in hyperspace. He felt the tug of curiosity about how he knew that.

"On my mark," said Cyber. "Three ... two ... one ..."

Trouble tightened his hands on the drive controls.

"Mark!"

Trouble shut the Keplinger down. It wasn't like braking as such, more as if the wind had gone from a full gale to a dead calm. The sub-light engines kicked back in and filled Engineering with their tuneless humming.

"Okay," said Trouble. "Now what?"

"I don't know how much time we have," said Cyber. "No way to tell. Theoretically, Chowdury can't track us in hyperspace, but thanks to Sanchez, he probably knows our general heading and where we planned to make port. Obviously, that's gonna have to change. Anyway, if there's one chance in fifty we're going to end up in the Pilgrim's Passage, I can't pilot this thing manually."

Cyber sat on the edge of the 'couch' at his station in the computer core, still connected by fiber-optic filaments to the external sensors, but offline from the navigational controls, which were now literally in the hands of the bridge pilot. He looked a bit sick, Erasmus Shade thought. The words "Pilgrim's Passage" had that effect on most spacers. And with good reason.

"What do you recommend we do?" Shade asked.

"Okay, I'm about to suggest something that is theoretically possible, but pretty radical."

"Theoretically possible?"

Cyber ran a shaking hand over his bald pate. "It's been done, experimentally. I've read all the literature, absorbed the data—"

"I'm sure at this juncture our friend Mr. Trouble would say: 'Can you cut to the chase?'"

Cyber smiled. "Well, it's like this. We put my 'couch' in stasis and hardwire me to the ship's systems. Without the distraction of my autonomic reflexes and other external factors, my mind is free to pilot the ship—to *be* the ship."

"This is possible?"

"Oh, yeah. I mean this is a cryo-chamber, after all." He patted the headrest of the "couch," which had more in common with an escape pod than a piece of furniture. "The difference is, I'll be completely jacked in and my mind will be fully awake. And there'll be no lag time at all between me and the navigational controls."

Shade grimaced. "I should hope so. What do we need—"

The lift doors slid open to disgorge Dr. Pike. He stopped just inside the chamber and blinked at the other two men with almost reptilian calm.

"We need a trained medic," said Cyber. "Which is why I invited the Doc. What d'you say, Captain—do we do it?"

"Have we a choice?"

"Not if we end up in the Pilgrim's Passage." Cyber hesitated, swallowed noisily. "Do you think we might?"

Shade looked directly into the net-head's eyes. "I cannot rule out the possibility, but it's not a decision I will make lightly. What's the danger to you?"

Cyber laughed nervously. "None of the test pilots died."

"Yet the procedure is still experimental ..."

"Because it causes mental changes they don't understand yet. Apparently, the test subjects ... look at the world differently afterward."

Pike spoke. "I've read the literature, too. The pilot and ship merge, Captain. She'll become an extension of Cyber's mind. The air exchangers are his lungs, the sensors his eyes and ears ... it changes the body image. It's hard for someone to go back to being ... small ... after something like that."

Cyber looked uncomfortable. "It's okay. I'm not much of a party animal anyway. I think it's necessary to do this. Quickly."

Shade nodded. "Will we be able to communicate?"

"I can manipulate the comms audio output directly. A voice is just sound waves." He shrugged.

Shade took a deep breath. "Do it," he ordered. "Do you need anything else?"

"Nope. Just Doc Pike."

"How long will it take?" Shade glanced at Pike.

Pike said, "Five minutes for the uplink, another ten for stasis to be established."

"Fifteen minutes?" Erasmus shook his head. "An eternity. Vishnu could locate us at any moment. Can you control engineering functions from here?"

"No more than I could before. The *Raker*'s systems are too piecemeal for that. I'll be able to navigate and throttle what power I'm given, but I can't handle the interface between the two drives because there isn't one. I'll still need warm bodies in Engineering to do that."

As he spoke, Cyber was already sliding into his station, jacking more fibrous connections into the plate behind his right ear.

Pike moved to assist, readying the cubicle's life support systems. "By the way," the doctor said, "my autopsy indicates that Hackett died of an overdose of Lerandia serum. A massive overdose. Induced a stroke."

Shade stopped on the verge of stepping into the lift.

"Lerandia serum? But how … the sabotage? Have the plants been poisoned?"

"I've seen no evidence of it. Seems to have been a simple overdose. Lerandia affects the blood cells. Hackett's thrombocytes literally exploded. Anaphylactic shock, followed by stroke. Probably introduced through ingestion. He had cider. Odd though. I wouldn't have thought you could get enough of a dose into a cup of cider to kill someone."

Captain Shade entered the lift and returned to the bridge considering the irony of Hackett's death. Sanchez was a man of science with the soul of an artist, Matthews a complete mystery even to himself, but who seemed capable of extreme and almost casual violence. Yet if someone had stood them side-by-side and asked him to predict which one would murder a crew mate in cold blood, he would have been dead wrong.

He grimaced at the unfortunate phrase. Trust. If it were a black market commodity and not a philosophical chimera, it would be worth more booty than even Julian Shade could earn in a lifetime.

18 / CYBER

"Trouble? Morgan? Hear me?" It was Cyber's voice, but somehow not Cyber's voice.

"Yeah," said Morgan. She was manning a display terminal that Shade had patched into the bridge systems to give them an external view off the bow of the ship. "You sound ... weird."

Trouble, who hadn't moved from the engine controls since their brief dive through hyperspace, glanced over at her. He could just see the screen over her shoulder. It was filled with anonymous, unmoving points of light—the star field.

"I'm using a voice synthesizer," Cyber said. "I'm going into stasis, Mad. Doc's putting me under right now." His voice was beginning to slur. "Feel ... fuzzy. Need to make sure I can talk to you guys before ... I'm fully committed."

There was a funny scraping sound that Trouble thought might be laughter. "I ought to be committed ... for doing this ..."

"Doing what?" Morgan's concern was evident. "Cyber?"

"Oh, wow. This is different. Didn't think ... it would be ... somehow. Okay. Okay. Captain? Am I coming through to the bridge?"

"Yes, Cyber. I can hear you." Captain Shade's voice came through the comm link, sounding normal.

"Okay, good," said Cyber, sounding a little drunk. "I'm

gonna leave the channels ... 'tween bridge'n Engineering open ... so everybody can hear everybody ... and you'll all hear me ... alla time."

Trouble traded glances with Morgan, then Morgan said, "Cyber, what have you done?"

There was a moment's pause—then the disembodied voice, now sounding crisp and more artificial than ever, came on again. "Who's Cyber? Just call me *Moonraker*."

"Oh, shit," murmured Morgan.

"Just kidding," said Cyber.

The change in his voice was subtle, but definite. Although it still came from the speaker, it also seemed to be emanating somehow from all around them—the decks, the bulkheads, the air itself.

"Captain? We have company. Do you see her?"

"I see her," said Shade's voice, tersely. "Aft guns, Cyber. Target their forward weapons array."

Trouble's eyes jerked to the external monitor. The star field swung drunkenly, and then he was staring the length of the *Raker* at a sleek ship bearing down on them. Before he could do more than draw a breath, its guns fired silently, blazing a trail of golden light from the bows of the *Devi* to the *Raker*'s stern.

The hit sounded like a squadron of drummers. *Raker* shuddered.

Trouble felt another slap of sudden recall—hearing a voice shouting orders in a similarly dire situation. Crewmen scrambled to obey ... no, not crewmen. Soldiers or some sort of armed operatives.

"They're not going to go for blood," said Morgan quietly. "They can't if they want to get this cargo off in one piece."

"I hope," Trouble said, "we won't be so polite."

Their gazes were fixed to the external monitor, watching the *Agni Devi* gain on them. She was a bigger ship than the *Raker*—sleeker, newer, and painted in shades of red and gold. Her forward guns blazed again, and *Raker* released an answering volley. The two streams of energy met just meters off *Raker*'s stern devouring each other in a spectacular spherical aurora.

The ship shuddered again.

Trouble watched the star field on the monitor cant momentarily. The internal gravity told him they hadn't moved, but obviously they had; that last blast had packed a heavy punch.

Lucas doubled over his console, gripping the handholds so tightly his knuckles were white.

"Sit down, Lucas!" Morgan told him. "Strap in."

He shook his head. "You guys aren't strapped in. If the footholds are enough for you—"

"Do it, kid," said Trouble. "She ranks you."

Lucas shot him a desperate and furious look. "I'm not a kid. I'm a smuggler. Same as you. I'll strap in when you do."

Had to admire that, Trouble supposed. Probably get the kid killed, but he'd die proud.

Moonraker was running, her thrusters firing to catapult her forward, but she was no match for the *Agni Devi*. The larger vessel seemed to leap at them, her ion guns firing again and again as she gained, intent on drawing parallel. *Moonraker* shuddered and shook, and the sharp percussion of an explosion sounded through the comms. Someone on the bridge screamed.

Shade's voice overrode the scream. "Cyber! If he levels a broadside, we're through."

"Keep firing!" said Cyber. "Keep—"

He cut off as a bright barrage from the pirate drilled into *Raker*'s aft section. The ship bucked, then swung hard to port, slewing around in a pendulum arc until she faced the *Devi* dead on. Her forward batteries fired. Once. Twice. First port guns, then starboard. Then she dove straight at the *Devi*.

"What the hell's he doing?" cried Morgan.

Trouble laughed. "Playing chicken. See who blinks first."

They were accelerating toward the other ship, holding dead steady. She grew in their monitor, swelling. She'd soon take up the whole screen.

"Trouble ..." Cyber's voice sounded in the room, coming from every comm link at once. "Superluminal. On my mark."

"Got it."

"Ready ... and ..."

The *Devi* was so close Trouble could read the letter designations on her forward cargo bay doors, see that there was a stylized golden tree painted on her port bow.

Then *Moonraker* broke sharply upward and Cyber yelled, "Mark!" so loud the word seemed to bounce off the walls.

Trouble fired the idling drive and the ship popped into hyperspace like a stopper shot from a bottle. The *Devi* disappeared from the view screen. Starlight blue-shifted, flared—and vanished. From her station near the drive core, Jiang made a strangled mewing sound. It seemed abnormally loud in the strange silence.

Moments ticked by.

"Status, Lucas," Morgan murmured.

"Uh ... engines are okay. Normal. Almost."

"'Almost'? Are they normal or aren't they?" Trouble asked sharply.

"Well, there's a funny flutter at the beginning of each pulse."

Trouble left his station and moved across the chamber to Lucas's side. "Yeah, I see it. Harmonics are a little out of phase."

Morgan said, "Probably the way we've been abusing the drive. I don't think it was made for these short bursts."

"Will it be a problem?" asked the captain's voice.

Morgan hesitated, then said, "Don't know, sir. Doesn't seem to be destabilizing the envelope. Still ..."

"Cyber," Shade said, "I think it's about time."

"Yes sir. Uh, Trouble ..."

"Offline the Keplinger on your mark. I'm ready."

He was, too. Damned ready. He'd come to the decision that he didn't like being in Engineering during a superluminal jump. The silence was eerie. Unnatural. He could hear everyone in the room breathing. He could hear his own blood

pulsing through his veins and imagined that it had synchronized with the pulsing of sigma radiation up the long drive
rods.

"Mark," said Cyber.

Trouble responded, and the ship slipped back into normal
space. The view screen showed stars again—and something else.

Morgan gasped.

Dominating the lower half of the view screen was something
vast and beautiful: a huge cube, over a kilometer on a side,
according to the readouts, and constructed of exotic matter. It
gleamed an intense, cobalt blue that hurt the eyes and teased the
brain, as if it wasn't completely a part of the visible spectrum.
Likewise, the cube didn't seem to exist entirely in three dimensions; some trick of perspective kept the eyes from grasping its
entirety.

"Oh," said Lucas, in a voice tinged with awe. "Is that ...?"

"Yeah," Morgan said.

It was beautiful ... and dreadful—a stabilized "tunnel"
through the higher dimensions, a cosmic short-cut that could
shave parsecs from their route.

And sanity from their minds ...

"Hey, Cyber," said Trouble. "You watching our drift?"

"Very carefully," said Cyber, sounding oddly subdued. "I ...
we've taken some major damage. I'm hoping we'll have time to
repair some of it before we have to do anything else. Rain, I need
you to suit up and do a little EVA. I think they blew away one of
our aft thrusters on that last pass."

"I'm on it," the Slinky said, and disappeared from the gallery.

"Cyb, will Chowdury be able to find us again?" Morgan
asked.

"Hell, I don't know. I'm not sure how he managed to find us
the first time."

"A beacon," said Trouble. "If I were setting a ship up for
piracy, I'd set a beacon on her somewhere."

"Yeah," said Cyber quietly. "That makes sense. If I had time,

I'd track it down. But I don't, so I'm gonna hope he got caught in our jump wake."

"Which would do what?"

"I'm not sure. I don't think anyone's ever tried it before. Could be pretty nasty." The nervous scratching sound filled the engine room as Cyber laughed.

"Don't be enjoying this too much, Cyb," Trouble told him. "How bad's the damage?"

"Apart from the thruster, we took a hit to one of the dry-cargo bays; it's decompressed, but the emergency bulkheads are holding. The bridge took some damage; we lost one of our subluminal navigation panels and we had to send Tully to the infirmary with second degree burns. The aft sensor array isn't responding. And if they attack our port side, I don't have any way of targeting them."

Trouble grinned humorlessly. "That all? I thought you said it was major. What now? What's the first thing we have to do?"

"We repair that thruster, 'cause if I fire thrusters right now, we'll go in a circle, and if I don't fire them we'll have all the acceleration of a slug."

"You sure the Slinky can do this gig solo?"

The Slinky in question stepped out onto the lower Engineering level into the middle of the conversation, his thin face tense.

"Some reason you suppose I can't?"

Trouble shrugged. "External engine repair's gotta be a big job. Two can do the work faster than one."

"Are you volunteering, Mr. Matthews?" asked Shade from the bridge.

Yeah, he supposed he was. Where did he get these suicidal urges? "Hey, I just asked a question."

"Can you work in a weightless environment?" Shade asked.

Oh, hurrah. Another newly remembered talent. "Like I was born there."

19 / E.V.A.

STANDING MAGNETICALLY ANCHORED ON THE HULL OF A STARSHIP was an experience that filled a great many men with quaking dread. Trouble was apparently not one of them. He'd meant it when he'd said he was comfortable with EVA. That, too, was apparently part of his life experience—the part that had been stripped from his memory ... or that he had jettisoned.

Scary thought.

He was aware that he'd volunteered for this duty as much to get out of the tin can atmosphere of Engineering as to help get the *Raker* back in service. Maybe more so. The EVA suit was a pain; it wasn't exactly state-of-the-art, unless the art in question was ancient.

Trouble's was a hardsuit, picked up cheaply as surplus, Glass had told him. Its multi-layered, carbon-fiber weave and thermo-mechanical circuitry added bulk, making movement awkward despite the pressurized joints. If all that wasn't bad enough, the heads-up display inside the helmet had developed a flicker that gave him a walloping headache within minutes of putting it on.

He shifted so he could look toward the bow. Beyond the ship, the gleaming cube that formed the entrance to the Pilgrim's Passage rippled like an angelic halo around the mouth of Hell. He'd donned goggles for the EVA, and he could tell his enhanced eyeballs were compensating, as well, but still the light of the aurora was so vibrant a blue that it made him want to pinch his eyes shut.

Still, the light was was hypnotic, alluring. Pain and promise. The cycle of addiction. With a measure of relief that he didn't have any personal recollection of that, he pulled his attention forcibly back to the job at hand. Their best chance of preempting the captain's wild idea of diving into madness was to get the *Raker* back in running condition ... and then fly like hell. He was damn glad the rest of the crew had no idea what their captain was contemplating or Shade would probably have a mutiny on his hands along with his other problems.

Trouble looked over at Rainor Glass, who had already advanced aft toward the thruster tube. Without his exo-skeleton and wearing a specially designed vacsuit, the Slinky moved through the weightless environment like an exotic sea creature— a starfish with only four limbs. Trouble watched him glide over a blackened area of the hull just below the fantail, then stop to inspect the damage.

His voice crackled over the comm. "Shit!"

Trouble moved after him. They both had laser cutters tethered to their suits—devices shaped like spear guns, and capable of producing a beam that could easily shear away any damaged plates or other debris. From the sound of Glass's explosive expletive, it appeared he'd found whatever was blocking the thruster.

Trouble settled behind the Slinky, his boots lightly touching down on the hull plating.

"Bad?"

Glass moved to one side and made a graceful gesture at the hull. "Look."

It was worse than bad. The thruster assembly was shot. The tube was crushed, the hull around it buckled. Through a rent in the hull, Trouble could see that the internal gimbals were fused.

"Good thing the fail-safes worked and shut the sucker

down," said Glass. "Otherwise the explosion could have ripped the whole stern apart."

"Cheerful thought. Got any more good news?"

The Slinky gave him a look, his elongated features seeming alien through the faceplate. "Let's just get it done."

Trouble unfastened his laser cutter from his belt.

Glass already had his in hand. "If we work on opposite sides, we'll finish faster. Try not to slice your suit."

"Thanks. I'll do that."

The Slinky didn't respond; he merely took his cutter and settled in on the port side of the thruster assembly. Trouble took the starboard side.

The thruster tube was over six feet in diameter where it exited the hull; Trouble could have easily stood up in it before it collapsed. Now it looked like a slag-filled abscess. There was no telling how far into the hull the damage went.

He fired up his cutter and started in to work, taking a quick peek out into space beyond the ship's stern. No sign of the *Devi*. Good.

"So what kind of name is Glass?" he asked, once his laser blade had begun to make some progress on the ruined assembly.

"Dutch. Why?"

"It's one of those names that suits—you know? Like a policeman named Courage, or a teacher named Lerner."

"Yeah? And how does it suit?"

"You look kind of like a brittle star. Glass is brittle ..."

Glass glanced up at him momentarily. "That's lame, Matthews. Really lame."

"Just trying to make conversation."

"Yeah, I get it. Keep the jitters down. Fine. What kind of name is Trouble?"

"An acquired one, I think. I'm pretty sure it's not a compliment."

"I find you a bit annoying, myself, if that's any consolation."

"You were shanghaied, too, weren't you? Can't imagine you were any more thrilled about that than I was."

"Yeah, well, you adjust."

"How about Sanchez? Did he 'adjust'?"

The laser sliced through a lump of fused metal that broke free and started to float away. Trouble glanced out past the fantail again. Still nothing.

"Apparently not."

"Did you have any idea what he was planning?"

Glass stopped cutting. "Why the hell would I?"

"Thought maybe he'd confide in another conscript."

"Well, he didn't. And I don't like what you're hinting at, Matthews. Sanchez was a loner. Kept to himself. Spent his free time on those weird little art projects of his. Thought he was better than anybody else because he was a real scientist, and the rest of us ..." He trailed off, shook his head.

"The rest of you?"

Glass was glaring at him through his faceplate. "Were just grunts and sideshow geeks ... in his exalted opinion. Look, are you getting anywhere over there?"

Trouble shifted his position toward the overhang of the ship's stern. "Yeah. Slowly. How about you?"

"I might, if you'd shut up."

Trouble shrugged and bent back to his work. After a few minutes of industrial strength laser surgery, another piece of the crumpled hull broke free and floated away. He'd barely made a dent in the main blockage, however.

He looked back out into space again. One of the stars had grown a bit brighter since the last time he'd glanced in that direction.

"How much longer, Glass?"

"If you're as far along as I am, another five or ten minutes."

"We don't have that much time."

The Slinky didn't ask what he meant, but lifted his helmeted head to look aft. "Damn."

"Trouble?" Cyber's voice sounded inside his helm. "We've got company."

"Saw it. What's his ETA?"

"He'll be in firing range in seven minutes. Are you done?"

"Not even close."

"Then you'd better get back in here. Now. We're going to need every bit of time we can steal to get this crate moving."

"Moving where?" But he already had a pretty good idea.

"Get inside," Cyber's eerie voice replied. "Now."

"If we can just cut through a bit more over here," said Glass, "we might be able to blow the blockage out when we fire the thrusters."

"Can you guarantee that?" Cyber asked.

"No, but—"

"Then get inside. Now."

Glass ignored him and kept cutting.

"You planning on staying out here so the *Devi* can use you for target practice?" Trouble asked him.

"Keep cutting!" There was panic in the reedy voice. So much for the calming strategy.

The laser's blue-white brilliance cast Glass's face in a nightmarish glow. The utter silence, save for the voices and the crackling carrier wave over the comm, added to the surreal atmosphere.

"Trouble, Rain. This is your first mate speaking. This is a direct order: Get the hell off the hull! We need to move *now*!"

The next voice they heard was Captain Shade's. "Gentlemen, if you don't re-enter the ship in one minute, we will be forced to engage sublight drive with you still out there. Am I clear?"

"Damn clear," Trouble said.

He turned off and stowed his cutter. He had no intention of being on the hull when the *Raker* started her engines. While it was true that there was no slipstream in the vacuum to tear him off his perch, the stream of charged particles from the working ion thrusters would be anything but healthy. He knew he could take some radiation above and beyond the norm for a human being, but he had no idea how much, or if the mod was specific to a particular type of radiation.

On the opposite side of the thruster tube, Glass kept working.

Trouble started toward him around the blasted perimeter of the tube. "We're done, Glass. Let's go."

The Slinky merely growled something Trouble couldn't make out and kept at it. A moment later a man-sized chunk of tortured tube debris parted company with the hull and floated free. Glass moved sinuously to avoid it, arching backward and stretching his elongated frame.

Trouble used the opportunity to wrap a muscular arm around his slender torso.

"What the hell are you doing?" Glass snarled.

"Don't worry, I'm not being romantic, just saving your narrow ass. You can thank me later."

Trouble turned in the direction of the cargo bay airlock. He started to move, but Glass's struggles brought him to a stop.

"Don't you get it?" Glass twisted in Trouble's hold until their face plates were mere centimeters apart. His pale eyes were wide and wild, and sweat stood out on his thin face. "Don't you know why he's brought us here? What he's planning to do? He's going to take us down the Pilgrim's Passage. Without thrusters, there's no other way to lose Chowdury. We either finish this job, or *we're* finished. I'd rather die clean than—" He cut off, panting, his gaze going down the length of the *Raker*'s hull to the wormhole's terminus.

He had a point; maybe it was better to die quickly in a blaze of laser and plasma fire. Trouble almost let him go. He looked from Glass to the approaching pirate vessel and back.

Nope.

Trouble tightened his arm again, and dragged the Slinky forward toward the airlock. Even a million-to-one chance was a chance. And who could say? Maybe there was such a thing as dying happy. He only knew—and knew it with every fiber of his body and soul—that he could not let Rainor Glass commit suicide when there was a chance they could all survive.

They'd gone half the distance, with Glass struggling against Trouble and making incoherent noises, when the Slinky suddenly twisted his long body in a quick jackknife. Trouble all but lost his hold. He turned, tried to renew his grip on the other man, felt something tap his faceplate, and found himself looking into the sharp gleam of a laser cutter.

Momentarily blinded, he let go, narrowing his eyes against the brilliant light, pulling back before the tool could be angled to cut into his faceplate. Glass, having cut his boots' grip on the hull, pushed away and soared upward, but Trouble's reaction was too quick. His right hand shot out and clamped on one fragile ankle. Glass cried out in pain.

Glass swung the cutter downward, aiming for Trouble's head, but Trouble blocked, grabbed the slender barrel, and yanked the tool from the Slinky's grasp. He jerked him back down until they were face to face again.

"You're in such a hurry to die, Glass, I can expedite the process for you." His voice was soft with menace.

Glass panted. "What d'you mean?"

Trouble lifted the Slinky clear of the deck, hoisting him easily over his head. He aimed him at the starless void of the Rift.

Glass let out a high, thready wail. Trouble smiled grimly—suddenly, his EVA buddy seemed not to find the prospect of death quite so appealing.

Cyber's voice crackled over comms. "Trouble! Don't do it!"

"What, after he tried to ghost me?"

"We need him!"

"Yeah? Why's that?"

"If things go wrong in the Pilgrim's Passage ... there are places on this ship only a Slinky can reach—junction boxes and control nodes, shunts, routers ..."

Trouble sighed melodramatically. "You hear that bullshit, Mr. Starfish? Our crucial backup systems are inaccessible to everyone but you. Apparently, you are essential personnel and I am not allowed to dispose of you."

"Trouble," Cyber said, "this isn't funny."

Trouble was still holding the hapless Slinky over his head. "Cyber," he said, in an amiable tone, "this fully-poseable idiot just tried to slice my face off with a laser cutter. Can you explain to me why I should care that he doesn't float away with the other debris?"

Cyber's voice, still tinged with that strange non-human brittleness, said, "Because without him, our chances of surviving the Pilgrim's Passage drop significantly. And because if you let him go, it's murder, and I'll see that you join him. Every lock and hatch on this ship is under my control now. Ghost the Slinky and you'll never get back inside."

Trouble turned Glass so that he could see up through his face mask. "Hear that? We need you, Glass. The ship and the crew need you. Apparently, I also need you if I want to get back inside. I guess I can't kill you today, after all."

He grinned and started for the nearest hatch, towing Glass behind him like a sentient balloon.

Cyber spoke again, sounding relieved this time. "Thanks, Trouble. Hurry, because—"

"I know."

They were three meters from the hatch; he glanced back over his shoulder. The *Devi* was the size of a tiny, squashed moon.

"Fifty-five seconds until the *Devi* is in firing range," said Cyber. "The captain's trying to negotiate with Chowdury, but—"

"We're there." Trouble hit the airlock cycle with his boot, counted to three as the hatch slid back into the hull. He leaned in, pushing the Slinky before him. Glass stumbled as he entered the artificial gravity field. Trouble stepped in, cycled the lock ... and felt the hull shift beneath his feet as the subluminal drive kicked in.

The hatch slid shut and the chamber compressed. As gravity stabilized, the Slinky rose from the floor, leaning against the bulkhead for support. Trouble watched him carefully. When a man took it into his head to die, it was sometimes difficult to talk him out of it. Glass's repenting of his death wish had seemed sincere, but you never could tell.

The inner hatch dilated, revealing the tall, spare silhouette of Dr. Pike.

"Good day, gentlemen," he said. "I've been asked to ascertain if either of you are injured, and if you're able to stand, to bring you to the bridge immediately."

"Another crisis?" Trouble asked. "Or more of the same?"

"Depends on your definition," Pike replied dryly. "But, given as our choices seem to be capitulating to Vishnu Chowdury or letting the Pilgrim's Passage swallow us, I'd say this qualifies as a crisis." He glanced at Trouble, a frown rippling his brow. "Looks like we'll have to retire that helmet, Mr. Matthews. It's unsafe."

Trouble popped the pressure clamps and pulled the thing off his head to look at it. Unsafe was an understatement. Glass's cutter had caught the faceplate where it joined with the helm and sliced through the grommet. Trouble realized that Glass was staring at it right along with him.

The Slinky raised his pale eyes to Trouble's face. "Why aren't you dead?"

20 / RUNNING

"We are out of options." Captain Erasmus Shade spoke to the three crewmen gathered in his ready room and to a fourth, present via the monitor system. "My 'negotiations' with Chowdury consisted of him demanding our unconditional surrender and expressing an unwillingness to discuss the disposition of my crew. Which is understandable, given the situation. He's attacking another Guild member. We can't be allowed to survive regardless of any promises he might make. If our ion thrusters had not been damaged, we could have outrun the *Devi*. But as it is, he's sure to overtake us before we reach jump velocity—unless we go into the Passage."

The words hung in the air for a few moments. No one seemed inclined to address them, but Trouble could feel the sudden surge of fear in the room. Hell, he could *smell* it.

"Maybe we could change course at the last minute," suggested Morgan. "Leap in another direction. Put Vishnu off the trail."

"Thought of that," Cyber said, seemingly from the four walls. "Did the math. By the time we got to the right velocity, the radial tension and tangential pressure factors of jumping this close to a negative mass structure the size of the Pilgrim's Passage would rip the *Raker* to atoms."

"Got it," said Morgan. "Not pretty."

Trouble turned to Shade. "You've been thinking about this for a while, Captain, so I imagine you've got at least half a plan. What is it?"

In answer, Shade lifted the Druud staff from where it leaned against his map table. "It would seem that the worst of the wormhole's effects are psychological. If we can adjust the psychology of the crew, it might—indeed it *should*—ameliorate those effects."

Trouble could only stare at the old man. "That's your plan? Shoot everybody up with the happy stick? What are you going to do, Cap—run around the ship zapping people one at a time, or did you want us all to stand in line?"

Shade's face went red with sudden rage. "Mr. Matthews, sarcasm is not helpful in this situation. I could have you thrown out an airlock—"

"But you won't, because you need able-bodied crewmen who won't be paralyzed at the thought of where you're planning on taking them. So, let's say your crazy idea works. Let's say we're all blissing on joy jolts, and nothing that happens raises anyone's pulse. What's next?"

"When we reach jump velocity, we engage the Keplinger drive to throw us farther into the Passage—out of Vishnu's reach. Then we shut down the field and run sublight, of course."

Trouble frowned, considering that. "Why? Why not stay superluminal? That'd get us farther away."

Cyber answered. "Because you don't ride a hyperspace field into a hyperspatial fold. No one knows what that would do. It might produce resonating quantum fluctuations that could conceivably collapse the wormhole while we're in it. Or, the negative energy string scaffolding might convert the ship and everything on it to a negative mass state. Unless ..." His voice trailed off.

"Can't hear you thinking, Cyber," Trouble said.

"On the other hand, that might just work. For one thing, it

might shield us from the worst effects of the wormhole. I mean, think of it—a negative field envelope inside another envelope. It could serve as a buffer zone. The downside is, we'd have to stay superluminal until we exit Pilgrim's Passage—if we drop down below the light barrier while we're still in it, well ... it could be bad."

"Define bad," said Trouble.

"That rending, tearing thing I was talking about. Plus the effects of the ... whatever it is the Passage does."

Shade glanced thoughtfully at Trouble. "Cyber, where's the *Devi*?"

Cyber brought the monitor in the Map Room online, showing the view aft. Above and behind them, Vishnu Chowdury's ship was in pursuit, and seemed to be gaining, but not as swiftly as Trouble had expected.

He could make out details now. The vessel's colorful, rakish prow was misshapen, crumpled. Apparently, Cyber's hopes had been met and the *Agni Devi* been damaged as a result of *Raker*'s last jump. No way to tell how badly. The rest of the vessel, from bow planes to fantail looked untouched and, as duly noted, she bristled with weaponry. Even from this distance, he could see the laser cannon slung under the curving, flared keel.

Shade was nodding. "Yes. Yes, we'll try it. We can at least use the staff on ourselves, the bridge crew, and other essential personnel. Then I may ask people to stand in line. Mr. Cyber, what's our time to jump velocity?"

"Fifteen minutes, thirty seconds. I recommend we man stations and ... what the hell is that?"

The monitor shifted suddenly to an interior view of a corridor and a face, blurred because it was so close to the lens of Cyber's cam. It moved away, resolving into Salvador Sanchez's face. His dark eyes peered at them intently. Trouble saw fear in them.

As they watched, Sanchez held all ten fingers before the cam, then two. Then he made a gesture over his shoulder and pulled out of view, revealing the back of a soldier armed with a rifle Trouble recognized as a scatter gun—a weapon that fired a spread of energy pellets, making it useful for riot control. You could spray minor damage across a small group of people— without doing any serious damage to, say, a starship's bulkheads or hull.

The soldier glanced back at Sanchez. "Sanchez, you comin'?"

"Yeah. I was just making sure this thing was dead." His hand came toward the cam and the monitor went black.

Cyber made a completely inhuman sound that just about took out Trouble's eardrums. Morgan flinched and Lucas turned three shades whiter than he'd been.

"Talk to me, Mr. Cyber!" Shade cried, clutching the staff. "What's happening?"

"We've been boarded. Shit! She deked us—the *Devi* deked us! They came in above, played wounded quail, drew my attention. Then, while the aft sensors were down, they sent a boarding party back in our own damned shuttle. Had to have been, to engage the shuttle bay doors with no alarms."

"Did you make their location?" asked Shade.

"Yeah. Just outside shuttle bay, heading for Epsilon."

"Get a security team on it," ordered Shade. "As many as you can scramble. Tell every one else to stay where they are and lock down. But quietly and subtly. We don't want to tip the pirates off." He hesitated a moment, then added, "Let Rusk out of the brig. We'll need him."

"Aye, sir."

"What the hell was Sanchez doing with them?" asked Morgan. "Why would he come back?"

"Looked like he was ratting them out," Trouble said. "Making sure we saw them."

"But why?" asked Lucas. The quiver in his voice betrayed his fear, but his face was composed.

"Why don't I just wander down there and find out?" Trouble proposed.

Shade managed a grimace that Trouble took as a smile. "Permission to kick butt granted, Mr. Trouble. Morgan, report to Engineering. Lucas—"

The boy drew himself upright. "I want to go with Trouble, sir. After the pirates." He was pale, but determined.

"Crewman Shade ..." the captain started, but stopped when Trouble gave him a pointed glance and swung toward the hatch.

"If you're coming, Lucas, get a move on," he tossed back over his shoulder.

"Lucas, it seems you're with Mr. Matthews," said Shade.

"Sir!" said Lucas, and scrambled after Trouble.

Trouble had stopped at the hatch and let the boy go through ahead of him.

"Mr. Matthews," said Shade quietly.

Half-in, half-out of the hatch, Trouble turned back.

"Please ... my nephew ..."

Trouble nodded. "Understood, sir." He followed Lucas onto the bridge.

21 / BOARDED

"THEY'LL HAVE SCATTER GUNS OR SLAP GUNS, I FIGURE. ONLY A complete idiot would fire a laser pistol inside a starship. And hotrods or jerksticks—they might have those, too. Probably shivs for hand-to-hand—"

"Lucas, does your mouth ever run down?" Trouble inquired.

The boy dropped his gaze. "Sorry."

Trouble pulled a pair of slap guns out of the weapons locker and handed them to Lucas. They were sonic weapons and far from deadly at distances over three meters, but up close and aimed at the head or internal organs, they could cause severe head trauma or impair the heart or lungs long enough to kill.

"One in hand, one in your belt. This is for the other hand." He held out a hotrod about the length of the boy's forearm.

Lucas took it uncertainly.

"Like this." Trouble slipped the strap of the rod over Lucas's left hand and pulled it up to his elbow, then laid the barrel of the weapon down the inside of his arm, wrapping his fingers around it just above where the prongs protruded. "Keeps your enemy from seeing it, and you can use it one-handed. Just bend your elbow to fire."

Lucas did and was rewarded when the prongs lit up. He grinned. "Slick. Where'd you learn this stuff? You military?"

"I don't know where I learned it. And yeah, it is slick. But don't get cocky. Weapons are only as good as the man holding them."

Trouble was vaguely aware of having given that little speech before. The impression that he had commanded armed troops was strong. Maybe he *had* been military. He armed himself with a scatter gun, a slap gun, a hotrod, and a shiv, which he tucked into the top of one of his boots.

"Where's our posse, Cyber?" he asked as he and Lucas emerged into the corridor.

"Gamma Deck, approaching the forward lift tube."

"How many?"

"Uh, seven. Rusk's with them. ...Just thought you might want to know."

"No skin off my behind. Where are our guests?"

"Still on Epsilon."

Trouble frowned. "Haven't gone far, have they?"

"Hard to get around a ship when the lifts are out." Cyber's synthesized voice conveyed a certain smugness. "They're trapped on Epsilon until I decide to send the lift down for them."

"Correction," said Trouble. "They're stuck on Epsilon until *I* decide to send the lift down for them."

Salvador Sanchez was sweating bullets. He stood in the rear-guard of the *Agni Devi's* boarding party, watching as the tech they'd brought along worked on the disabled lift. He was hoping that the non-functioning lift was part of a plan on Shade's part, and not just a result of the damage Captain Chowdury had inflicted on the *Raker*. If it were part of a plan, there was an armed security team on the way and this nightmare would soon be over. He might even live through it.

He patted at the padded pouches in the flak jacket he wore

beneath his coverall. Two contained serum he'd brewed from his augmented Lerandia plants, and two more contained packets of enhanced sporules. Both of these items would be worth a king's ransom ... if he could get them to market.

There was a sudden buzz of activity around the lift door. The tech was giving a thumbs up. They could hear the quiet whir of the mag-lev generators as the platform lowered toward Epsilon Deck. Sanchez held his breath and started to fade back down the corridor toward the shuttle bay.

"Shit. Shit. Shit!" The mission leader exploded as the lift stalled again. He kicked the doors.

Sanchez shook his head. Neanderthals. He was surrounded by Neanderthals.

He glanced back over his shoulder and contemplated making his way aft to the Hydroponics bay. It was tempting to go there and hide among his plants. But he couldn't do that. Not yet. He had to make sure things turned out as he needed them to.

There was renewed activity around the lift door. This time the tech really seemed to have done it. The lift was descending once again. Sanchez took a deep breath and weighed his options. He still had not decided what to do when the lift doors slid back to reveal an empty, darkened car.

The mission leader stepped into the lift, signaling his men to follow. He was in the act of turning when something—no, *someone*—dropped on him from the ceiling of the car.

Sanchez gaped. Trouble. Bloody Trouble!

In one deft move, Trouble had stripped the pirate of his weapon, whirled him around in a neck lock, and used him as a shield while he fired a series of blasts from the slap gun he'd shoved between the man's arm and rib cage.

He took down the tech and three other men before anyone got a shot off at him. When they did, the barrage of sonic energy from the slap hit his human shield in the upper body, crumpling the man like a wad of waste paper.

Hardly knowing what he was doing, Sanchez drew his own weapon.

The pirate was suddenly dead weight. Trouble let him fall and tumbled with him. He got off one more blast with the slap gun, which took out another pirate—though probably not permanently. Trouble had mixed feelings about that.

Still, it was six down, six to go.

Halfway to the decking, Trouble rolled aside, against the wall, coming up with the gun ready. Two of the pirates were headed for the bend in the corridor, where they could fire from cover. In seconds, they'd be out of range of serious damage from the sonic weapon.

Trouble holstered the slap gun and pulled the scatter pistol from his belt. He fired one shot from the energy pellet gun just as the pirate closest to him swung about and fired. They both missed badly, and it wasn't until the pirate flung himself against the wall and took aim again, that Trouble realized he wasn't the target.

There was a high-pitched yip from the general direction of the lift that could only have come from Lucas.

Damn it. Why do kids never stay where you put them?

Roaring, Trouble charged forward, right at the enemy, that being the most unexpected move he could make. As he'd hoped, the pirate was taken by surprise; before the man could retarget, Trouble was on top of him. He brought his left arm around, hotrod extended, and connected with the guy's ribs. The hotrod fired; the pirate stiffened.

Trouble knew what he was feeling. His rib cage was on fire; his diaphragm was spasming; he couldn't breathe. The pirate surprised him, though; he managed to stay conscious long enough to twist Trouble's arm and shove the still-sparking end of the hotrod back against his belly. Trouble grunted as explosive pain lanced through him. The pirate slumped against him, pinning his gun hand; the hotrod clattered to the deck.

Now two more of the pirates appeared around the corner, snarls on their lips and kill-gleam in their eyes. Trouble pulled his right hand free of the dead weight to take aim, but one of them kicked the gun out of his grasp while the other drew down on him.

Trouble rolled backward, pulling the unconscious pirate with him. He was surprised as hell when the man's comrade fired the slap gun. The body absorbed the shock, but the other pirate was on top of them, literally, his foot pinning Trouble's right hand to the floor. Trouble's left hand was still encumbered by the other man's weight—probably dead weight, now, depending on where the shot had been focused.

The pirate above him—a bald guy with a face like a rock—smiled and aimed the slap gun at his head. That was a death sentence. Trouble coiled like a spring, whipping his legs free. But before they could connect with the pirate, the man toppled forward, landing full-length atop his dead crewmate. There was a second percussive blast followed by the sound of a body falling farther down the corridor.

Then, silence.

Into which Lucas Shade whispered, "Holy shit."

Trouble heard his soft footfalls, then: "I'm sorry, Trouble. I didn't mean for him to fall on you like that—"

"Down!" Trouble snarled. "Three more around the corner."

Lucas hunkered behind the pile of bodies. "Only two. You got one on the run."

"Cover the corner."

"What? Oh ... oh, yeah." Lucas pressed himself up against the starboard bulkhead, then rose slowly, his weapon raised.

Trouble rolled the pirates from his body. He lost the hotrod in the process, but he didn't figure he'd need it again. He still had both guns—and the shiv, which he trusted more. He slipped to the wall in front of Lucas, gun up and ready, and began a slow advance on the corner.

"Hey, Sal!" he called. "That you down there?"

There was a whispered conversation, then Sanchez said, "Yes, Trouble. I'm here."

Trouble heard the raw terror in the botanists's voice, smelled its bitter tang, even over the stench of death that pervaded the corridor. "They're all dead and dying, Sal. Every last one. Why don't you two just come on out? Or would you rather be sent back to Chowdury posthumously?"

Again, the whispered conference, and then the last pirate swung around the corner, his gun drawn.

Trouble tensed to fire, but the man was already falling, nailed by a blast from behind. He collapsed into the intersection.

"Whoa," Lucas breathed.

Trouble took three long, quick strides to the corner and stopped, gun ready. "Come on out, Sanchez."

There was no answer. Trouble dropped and rolled into the cross corridor. The adjoining hallway was empty.

"Where's this go?" Trouble asked Lucas.

"Shuttle bay."

Trouble nodded. "Cyber, we have a runner."

"On it." Cyber's voice fell into the corridor from unseen speakers. "He's not going anywhere by shuttle."

Trouble looked up at the sound of footsteps in the hallway beyond. A moment later *Raker*'s security party came into view, with Blackwood leading. They came up short, staring across the intersection at the scattered bodies of the dead and wounded pirates.

"We ... we got here as fast as we could," stammered Blackwood. "I expected you'd wait for us to get into position."

Trouble shrugged, slipping his weapon back into his belt. "Apparently, I like to do the unexpected." He glanced into the stunned faces of the security team. "You lose somebody, Blackwood?"

"Huh?" The amphibian turned to glance back over his shoulder. "Hey, Rusk's gone. Wonder where?"

"Wonder why," countered Trouble. "Sanchez is gone too. Neither of those things makes me feel particularly cheerful."

Blackwood turned back to him, his expression darkening, his webbed hands tightening on his weapon. "Sanchez? Sanchez was with these guys?"

"Yeah, but don't punch holes in him if you see him. He shot that guy before he could shoot us." He nodded down at the corpse at his feet. "We might want to ask him why."

Blackwood nodded, then turned to his team. "Let's clean this up. Shove the dead ones out an airlock. Maybe Vishnu will get the message."

Trouble became aware that Lucas was staring at him. The kid's awestruck look made him flush ... and wish he still had that hotrod.

"What?"

"You didn't mention the real reason we want to find Sanchez," Lucas observed.

"You think it's a good idea to tell four armed smugglers someone's been dicking with their cargo?"

"Um. Probably not. What're you gonna do next?"

"Find Sanchez before he gets wherever he's going or he does whatever he came here to do."

Lucas swallowed. "Great. I'll—"

"Report back to your captain."

"But—" Lucas looked up into Trouble's face and the argument died on his lips. He holstered his weapons and headed for the lift.

Trouble headed in the opposite direction, shaking his head.

Apparently, I am a very scary man.

Lucas and Blackwood reported to the bridge together, Blackwood still shaking his head over Trouble's performance in the corridor, Lucas still smarting slightly for having been remanded to the bridge. Each had his thoughts blown completely out of his head by the view from the holo-screen.

The *Raker* was heading right for the center of that great, shimmering cube.

Blackwood stopped so suddenly, Lucas ran into him.

"Oh-my-God," Blackwood whispered. "You're going to do it. You're really going to do it."

Sitting in the command chair with the Druud staff across his knees, Erasmus Shade appeared to have aged decades since Lucas had seen him last. Then, diving into the Pilgrim's Passage had been a possibility; now it was inevitable.

Morgan stood beside the captain, disheveled and weary; Jiang sat at the bridge Engineering station, her glossy face expressionless.

"We have no choice," Shade said. "So, I've ordered all but on-duty personnel to quarters. I've told them it's because we may be boarded again. But we've taken countermeasures that we're hoping will shield us from the worst effects. And we have this." He held up the staff. "Those of you who have been called here, will be 'treated' with the Druud staff, which will alter your brain chemistry sufficiently, I hope, to offer more shielding from the wormhole ... mirages."

"Hope?" repeated Blackwood. "Exactly how much hope are we talking about? A ghost of a prayer? A dead lock? What?"

"Jay," Jiang shook her head, her eyes warning ... pleading.

"Captain's right," said Morgan. "We don't have a choice. With our port thruster gone, we've got one chance of making it." She nodded toward the wrap-around holo-screen/window with its paralyzing view of the Pilgrim's Passage.

Blackwood swallowed, hard. "There's got to be another way, sir. Find it, for God's sake." He took a step toward the captain's chair, perhaps to plead, perhaps to attack.

In answer, Shade swung the Druud staff about and tagged Blackwood on the shoulder with it. There was a zap of energy, and the crewman staggered to his knees.

Jiang rushed to his side, helping him to stand. "Jay?"

The amphibian looked from her to Shade, fear and anger washing away in a flood of endorphins. Lucas could see it moving across his face and behind his eyes like the radiant tide of a sunrise.

Blackwood smiled. "I ... I understand, Captain. Sorry. I don't know what I was thinking."

Jiang looked up at her commanding officer. "Sir?"

He let her have it next. Then Morgan. When all three were smiling and using the word 'glorious' to describe the terrifying sight at their bow, and 'adventure' for what was going to happen to them in there, Lucas figured the prudent thing to do was to present himself before his uncle to be zapped.

It wasn't anything like he'd expected. He'd feared it, oddly enough, and afterwards felt stupid for having done so. He was flushed with possibilities. The Pilgrim's Passage *was* glorious, and beautiful, and awe-inspiring. He'd never thought much about it before, but now he was certain there was a God. The sight of this creation made him want to cry "Author! Author!" What an adventure to sail there!

He smiled at his uncle, who held out the staff to him and said, "My turn. Will you do the honors, son?"

Lucas felt as if he'd been knighted. This is what Galahad or Lancelot or one of those other mythic figures must have felt like when receiving their commission from their king. And he had called Lucas "son". Even his own father had never called him that with any affection.

He lifted the staff, but hesitated at the sudden look of dismay on his uncle's face. He started to turn to see what the captain was looking at, but the staff was ripped from his grasp. A second later, he was flung violently aside to collide with one of the duty station chairs. He tumbled over it onto the deck, rolling beneath a console.

"What are you doing?" asked Morgan's voice from behind him. "You shouldn't—" Her words ended in a ringing slap.

Lucas struggled to sit. Morgan lay crumpled by the command chair while Rusk, staff in hand, towered over his uncle. Before the captain could object, Rusk lifted Erasmus Shade from the chair and flung him against a bank of system monitors. The old man's head hit the metal surface with a resounding crack, and he slid limply to the floor.

Then Rusk was gone, and the staff with him.

Lucas scrambled to his feet and staggered to where his uncle lay. Shade was bleeding from the back of his head and from his mouth. Lucas felt his heart melt with compassion and concern.

Cyber would know what to do. Lucas looked up into one of the bridge cams. "Cyber! We need Doc Pike on the bridge! Rusk's got—!"

"I know. I saw it, Lucas. Don't worry. He won't get far."

Trouble had searched the shuttles and shuttle bay, prowled the connecting corridors, checked all the storage areas and access crawl-ways. He had found nothing and no one. Now he stood in a darkened corner of the shuttle bay, listening, scenting, observing. His senses took in the whole chamber, huge though it was, like a surveillance net. He smelled machinery, heard the soft breathings of the ship's life support systems, saw ... nothing.

"Hey, Cyber," he murmured, "Where's Sal gotten to?"

There was no response. Odd. He slid further into the shadows. "Cyber? You takin' a nap?"

Cyber's voice came back suddenly, loudly, echoing through the bay. "Forget about Sanchez, Trouble. We've got bigger problems. Rusk just attacked Shade and took the Druud staff. He's headed aft, but he knows this ship well enough to know where I don't have permanent cams."

"The captain okay?"

"No. Rusk knocked him senseless. I sent Doc up to him, but Doc says he's not looking good. He's unconscious. Head trauma."

Trouble was already moving toward the hatch that separated the shuttle bay from the rest of the ship. "Headed aft ... that the best you can do?"

"Engineering, possibly. Maybe he wants to shut down my engines so we can't jump into the wormhole."

"Would you like to give me a good reason to stop him? I'm not that keen on diving into the Pilgrim's Passage, to tell you the truth."

"C'mon, Trouble. You're not stupid. You know what Chowdury will do to the *Raker's* crew if he takes her."

"Maybe we should take our chances with Chowdury. I can fight men. I can't fight wormholes. Eventually he'll run out of boarding parties and—"

"All he has to do is blow the forward section of the ship apart and send a team in EVA suits over to get the booty. They don't even need the trees. The sporules will be enough." There was a metallic hiss that Trouble took as a sigh of exasperation. "Look, Trouble, you know all this. There's no other way. And this is me talking, not Shade. Shade's in bad shape, which means I'm in command of the ship. They're going to bring the captain down to the computer core and get him into cryo. Doc says that's his only chance of survival. Lucas and Doc and Morgan have started down with him already. I've sent Jiang to Engineering; we're about thirty seconds from jump velocity. She'll be firing the Keplinger in thirty-five. Blackwood's on the bridge keeping an eye on the instruments. Oh, and I think Chowdury's seen the bodies. He's gaining on us."

Trouble had reached a cross-corridor. He turned aft, sprinting, his footfalls soft and certain on the decking.

"Where are you going?"

"Engineering, you said."

"Yeah, but I'm not sure. It occurs to me he might also be trying to reach the Lerandia. Maybe he figures to grab some booty and cut his own deal with Chowdury."

"Only if he gets off the ship, which he can't if you depressurize the shuttle bay."

"Right. I'm on it." Cyber hesitated, then added, "What if Sanchez is still in there?"

"He dies."

The words came so easily to Trouble's lips, he wondered once again what sort of man he was.

Shade looked so frail lying there in the cryo pod. Just a fragile old man who was powerless without the people around him. People who would die if this didn't work.

Morgan watched Doc Pike's long fingers tethering Shade to his lifeline, placing an oxygen mask, slipping the neural sensor helm over his head. The Brain Pattern Monitor came up, displaying the captain's vitals on the screen at the foot of the pod's couch. It didn't look good—ragged, weak.

She glanced aside at Lucas, wondering what he was feeling. He was little more than a boy, really. A boy about to lose the only man in his family who'd ever taken any sort of interest in him. She slipped sideways and put her arm around his shoulders. He looked up at her and smiled, gratitude in his eyes.

"He'll be okay," she said. "This is going to work."

Even as she spoke, Pike turned the old man's autonomic functions over to the ship. The BPM stabilized. Shade's chest rose and fell regularly, a quiet beeping echoed the rhythm of his heart.

"There, see? The ship will take care of him now. Cyber will take care of him." She glanced at the net-head, lying next to Shade in his own pod. He seemed almost as young as Lucas in cryo sleep, kind of sweet and vulnerable.

A chill ran down Morgan's spine.

Vulnerable ...

"Five seconds to hyperspace jump," said Cyber's voice.

23 / HUSH

AT THE TRANSVERSE BULKHEAD THAT DIVIDED THE CREW FACILITIES from Engineering, Trouble had turned left, bypassing the aft lift core. He never even considered the emergency ladders. Both offered too easy access to the aft sections of the ship, and therefore were good places to set up traps. Instead, he had chosen an access tube with foot and handholds set into the curving walls.

He was on the main Engineering deck, just below the lip of the access tube, when the ship's superluminal engines came online. He felt the moment of vertigo, sensed the Hush through the interior plating. The thrum of the ion drive stopped, turning the *Raker* into a faster-than-light glider.

Cyber's voice came to him hushed, as well, as if his lips were against Trouble's ear. "ETA in two minutes, thirty seconds. I hope your plan works."

"Seen Rusk?" Trouble murmured.

"Not a twitch. But then I can't see you right now either. I did see you go past the lift. Figured you'd take the hard way up."

Trouble listened to the corridor before he lifted himself over the lip of the access. The corridor was empty. He looked left toward the starboard emergency stairs, then right toward the lift and, just beyond it, the entrance to Engineering. He slipped out onto the deck, moving toward the Engineering hatch. He'd gone maybe two yards when he noticed that an instrument panel almost directly across from the lift door had been left open.

Trouble's senses went on high alert. He pressed himself to the bulkhead opposite the lift core, drew his slap gun, and slid silently to the open panel. Just short of it, he paused to listen.

Nothing.

His eyes caught a faint trail of ruddy light that spanned the corridor from the panel to the lift door. On the door itself, at dead center, a tiny bead of brilliance—a laser targeting beam.

He lowered himself to the floor and rolled beneath the beam, peering up into the open panel as he did. A laser cutter sat atop the instrumentation, tethered there by a network of fiber-optic filaments. That was one serious trap.

Trouble came smoothly to his feet beyond the targeting beam and crossed to the wall next to the lift. He couldn't risk raising Cyber, so he waved his hand in front of the lift's sensor. In mere seconds, the lift came down from the upper levels of the ship and the doors slid open. Its target lost, the laser fired with a high-pitched whine, burning a hole in the back of the lift car; the doors slid shut; the laser fired a second time, this time boring into the door.

Trouble hit the deck and rolled to the opposite side of the corridor, just in case Rusk showed up to check on his work. He didn't. Trouble moved on to the Engineering hatch then, pressing himself to the wall before activating the door mechanism. The hatch didn't open. He tried again. More nothing.

"Okay, Cyb, we've got a problem. If Jiang's in there, she's locked down the hatch."

A second later the comms panel by the door went live and Cyber said, "I can't raise her."

Trouble stepped back from the hatch and blasted the controls with his slap gun, denting the panel and exposing the fiber optics. He reached into the cavity and ripped out a handful of control filaments. The hatch irised half open, then stopped.

It was enough. Trouble dove through the aperture, rolling to a stop beneath a duty station. The hatch that led to the drive core was just sliding shut. Jiang lay next to it, unconscious or dead. He couldn't tell which.

He took out that hatch mechanism too, then fired a blast into the inner chamber before diving through, coming to a crouch and firing again. Rusk was halfway across the chamber headed for the drive controls; Trouble's shot blasted the chair at the drive console into twisted wreckage, stopping the big man in his tracks.

"Entering the Pilgrim's Passage," said Cyber's oddly dispassionate voice.

Rusk snarled and launched himself at the drive console. Trouble anticipated it and lunged to meet him in mid-air. To Trouble it seemed they were caught in a suddenly thickened atmosphere, their bodies pouring from one point to another like half-warmed molasses, stretching, distorting, then hanging motionless in time and space. Time, too, distorted—dilating, oozing almost to a stop before snapping back into its normal shape. But snap it did. Trouble hit Rusk mid-torso, ramming him into the bulkhead next to the drive core's monitor station.

Trouble regained his feet and his balance in a nimble flip, bringing the slap gun to bear on the other man's head ... which he could see through. Rusk glared up at him, one eye dead centered over a blinking red light from the monitor panel. He took advantage of Trouble's instant of bemused hesitation, lashing out with a foot. The slap gun flew between a pair of drive rods, to land in the hub where the rods met.

Trouble made a lightning fast grab for Rusk's foot, grasping it with both hands and flipping him over. The big man hit the deck with an almost gentle bounce, as if the metal beneath their feet had morphed into something infinitely softer and springier—or as if they'd lost gravity.

The effect didn't last. When Trouble dragged Rusk to his feet, the guy seemed to weigh a ton.

"Hey, Trouble," said Cyber, conversationally. "Seems you

were right about the envelope in an envelope deal. It's like I'm wearing a giant EVA suit."

"A little busy right now," grunted Trouble, knocking Rusk's hand away before it could fasten around his throat.

"Yeah, I see. You need some help?"

"Sure. What have you got?" Trouble punctuated the last word with a head butt. It felt as if he'd only face-palmed vigorously.

Rusk snarled, then recoiled as a miniature lightning bolt leapt from the power monitor panel to his backside.

"That," Cyber announced.

Trouble let out a crack of laughter, which was cut off when Rusk's fist connected with his head.

"Sonofabitch! Zap him again!" Trouble snapped, and Cyber obligingly sent another arc of energy through the panel into Rusk's body.

A neat trick, Trouble thought, as Rusk spasmed. Trouble rolled him to the floor and landed atop him with a knee on each of his biceps. "Okay, Rusk, where's the staff?"

"Where you won't find it," Rusk sneered, but his eyes had twitched infinitesimally toward the drive gallery.

Trouble bounced Rusk's head off the deck plating. "What's the plan? You going over to Chowdury?"

"Survival. That's the plan. If you were half as smart as you think you are, you'd help me shut that drive down."

"Too late, Rusk. We're in the Passage."

"No. Not too late."

"Too late," Trouble repeated and aimed a blow at Rusk's head.

Time hiccuped again, slowing his punch; Rusk bucked, dislodging one arm enough to wrench away from it. Trouble grasped his coveralls and rolled with him, coming into painful contact with the footholds in front of the power monitor panel. Rusk used every muscle in his massive arms to break Trouble's grip on his uniform, and with a speed and agility belied by his bulk, he scrambled to the drive controls.

Trouble came up in a crouch and leapt after him, grabbing the ex-first mate's uniform in both hands and dragging him back. But Rusk had a bulldog's grip cn the drive controls. He moved, but they moved with him.

The Keplinger drive dropped offline.

The encapsulated world of the *Moonraker* became an infinitely weirder place than it had been the moment before. Suddenly Trouble could see through everything—every panel, every monitor screen, every duty station chair, as if the ship were made of smoky glass. Stranger still, he could see through Rusk—layers of skin, the tightly-woven blood vessels beneath, viscera pulsing in the basket of his transparent ribcage ...

Rusk roared with laughter, shrugged off Trouble's loosened grasp, and ran. After the first few steps his feet left the deck, and it seemed to Trouble's beleaguered senses that Rusk either swam or flew toward the hatch.

"Trouble! The Keplinger's offline! Navigation's responding erratically—if we hit the tunnel wall the stress will—"

Trouble let Rusk go. He spun back to the drive controls, reaching for them, seeing his arms and hands moving in a series of strobing, overlapping images as he shoved the sliders up in a desperate bid to reactivate the drive.

Nothing happened. No green lights answered Trouble's attempt to re-engage the Keplinger. No power pulsed up through the rods. No Hush pervaded the chamber.

He pulled the sliders back, zeroed the ignition sequence and tried again. He could see the red handles of the sliders through his hands. Hell, he could see his bones through his flesh.

He rejected what his eyes told him. It was a lie. He was solid. He closed his eyes, shook his head.

I'm solid. The ship is solid.

He opened his eyes and was relieved to see that the room, its accoutrements, and his body were now comfortingly opaque.

"Cyb, I can't bring the drive back up," he said. "Ignition sequence won't fire."

"It's okay—for now. I've stabilized our course." Cyber's voice seemed slightly relieved.

Trouble let out a gust of air, took his hands from the controls, and turned to go after Rusk.

A woman stood between him and the hatch, beautiful and familiar. And alive. This he knew, with a sudden return of recall, was a lie. She smiled at him, her eyes full of warmth and love.

Janina. Her name was Janina. Jani.

"You're dead. They killed you." Memory stabbed through him. "God ... they *killed* you."

The smile left her face—was replaced by stark fear. (Lying on the gleaming floor of their home, she had looked as if she was merely sleeping.) A man stepped from behind her, as if he had materialized at that exact moment. He had cold eyes, a mouth that was little more than a slash. He was dressed entirely in black from his thigh-length cutaway coat to his breeks and boots.

"Fool," he called Trouble. "You could have had everything a man could imagine wanting. Wealth, adventure, a life. But you don't have much imagination, do you? You have duty. You have scruples. How comforting is that on a lonely night with her gone, knowing you got her killed?"

Light flashed from a medallion pinned to the man's coat. No, not a medallion—an antique timepiece. A pocket watch. He held a beam weapon in one hand. Trouble forced himself to believe it was not real. He started walking again. He would walk through both of them.

"We warned you about what would happen if you screwed up, Matthews. If you didn't do your part. There's still time—"

"Don't," the woman said, her voice desperate. "Ridley, for God's sake, you can't do this. It will destroy you. It will destroy our family."

Trouble kept coming.

Janina stepped into his path. He paused, wary, and she put

her arms around his neck. They felt warm, and solid, and familiar. She kissed him, and that too felt solid and familiar. He felt her breath on his cheek, her tongue against his, smelled her perfume, something spicy—sandalwood and nutmeg. He had loved her scent. He had loved her.

Had, had, had.

Jani Matthews was in the past tense—gone, dead, though he had no memory of how she had died.

He pushed her to arms' length. "You're not real," he told her.

She reached up and caressed his face, her gaze holding his. He felt the touch, saw the love in her eyes.

"Ridley ..." she murmured, then she stiffened, eyes wide, as a tiny, neatly cauterized hole appeared in the middle of her forehead. He watched the life drain out of her eyes. Then she was gone like the popping of a bubble, leaving empty air in her wake.

Trouble stood, shaking, gutted.

No time for this. No. Time.

He shook off the lingering feel of her touch, shoved the sudden, eviscerating grief aside, and made his feet carry him into the outer corridor.

"How're we doing, Cyber?" he asked, and was relieved that his voice neither cracked nor trembled.

"Still holding, so far."

In the corridor, Trouble turned right and stopped. Rusk lay in a disjointed heap in the center of the hallway, a faint scent of burnt flesh wafting up from his body. Above him, the laser beam kept silent guard on the lift. Now that was a booby trap.

"Trouble?"

Trouble spun back toward Engineering, his shiv already drawn.

Salvador Sanchez stood just outside the hatch, the Druud staff in his hands.

"Were you looking for this?"

24 / SHADE

ERASMUS SHADE WAS A SECOND-RATE SMUGGLER, NEITHER enterprising enough to be successful in his own right, nor smart enough to use his family affiliations to their best advantage. At least, that had been Captain Vishnu Chowdury's opinion of him since his brother Julian's seemingly meteoric rise to power in the Guild.

Erasmus had had some backbone before that—had been willing to take risks, play large. Since then, however, he had grown so timid he had become all but invisible, losing everything he had won until he was left with one aging starship, patched together with kitchen-sink technologies and a ragged-ass crew, which Shade had resorted to chicanery and outright kidnapping to piece together. This was something Chowdury considered foolhardy and dangerous, since impressed hands were not likely to be loyal hands.

Captain Shade's vessel was the laughingstock of the Guild, which was why Chowdury had been stunned to learn that Shade had hijacked a cargo of Lerandia from a non-Guild free trader. If he had heard this bit of news about any other Guild smuggler, he might have simply stood aside and applauded. But because it was Erasmus Shade, Chowdury saw an opportunity to strike an easy target. His confidence had only increased at the ease with which one of *Moonraker*'s shanghaied crew had been turned.

He mused now on how radically perceptions could change. Since Chowdury had embarked on this act of piracy, Erasmus Shade had surprised him several times. None of those surprises had been pleasant. Shade had eluded him rather cleverly during his first attempt to take the ship, damaging the *Agni Devi*—not critically, but significantly. Then *Moonraker*'s crew had repelled his boarding party. Worse, he had lost eleven good men, and most likely his mole, Sanchez, as well. They had counted only eleven bodies. He assumed that Sanchez had been held for special treatment.

Now Shade was threatening to leap into the Pilgrim's Passage.

"About thirty seconds before we'll be in range to do some serious damage, Captain." The helmsman's eyes were locked on his tactical display. "He's heading straight for the Passage. Can he be that stupid?"

"Yes. Which is why when I promise to spare his crew, he'll believe me and capitulate. He's not going to leap—"

"Captain! *Raker*'s gone superluminal!"

Disbelieving, Chowdury drew himself upright in his command chair. "Course!" he demanded.

The helmsman shook his head. "Still heading straight into the wormhole."

Chowdury ground his teeth. "Jump."

"Captain?" The man turned in his chair to stare at him.

"I said jump! Go to translight speed, Mr. Conally."

Conally swallowed. "Aye, sir."

The helmsman activated the *Devi's* Keplinger drive; they jumped. Judging by the Sigma signature trace the *Raker* left behind, their aging drive was as substandard as anything else aboard that vessel. Chowdury was gratified to see that their belated jump actually closed the gap between the two ships.

"Course, Mr. Conally?"

"She's still headed for the Pilgrim's Passage."

"She'll veer off."

"Begging your pardon, sir, but she's running out of time to veer off."

"How long until she's past the point of no return?"

The helmsman checked his tactica display. "About fifteen seconds, sir. But we'll still be able to pull out of it for another ... twenty seconds or so. Our drive has a lot more punch than his."

"Damned idiot. He had to choose this moment to grow a spine? Give me a mark when he's fully engaged."

Vishnu Chowdury expected to never hear that mark; expected to hear instead that Shade had veered off or dropped out of hyperspace at the last possible moment, in another attempt to deke his pursuer. He was therefore completely stunned to hear his helmsman shout, "Mark!" loudly enough to startle him.

In a disbelieving voice, Conally added, "She's committed, Captain. She's going in."

Vishnu nodded, chewing his lip. "Be ready to pull out on my mark. Make your heading toward the Euphrates system."

Conally looked so relieved, Chowdury wanted to snarl at him. He'd gone to too damn much trouble to have it end with the *Moonraker* getting away. Even if they were able to do an end-around the wormhole to its other mouth, they'd arrive as much as a week later, and in that time the *Raker* would be in port, or salvage, or destroyed. He had lost eleven crewmen; he stood to lose that very valuable cargo ... and the respect of his crew. And he had spent significant funds to buy Sanchez's complicity.

"Ten seconds. Captain?" Conally's voice had a peculiar edge to it. "Shade hasn't dropped to sublight speed."

Chowdury rose from his command chair to hover at his helmsman's shoulder. The tactical display showed the *Raker* riding toward the wormhole, still wrapped within her superluminal cocoon. He opened his mouth to give the command to veer off, then stopped as the meaning of what he was seeing sunk in.

"*He bhagavaan,*" he murmured. "My God."

"Sir?"

Conally's eyes met his, lapping over with fear.

"He's more clever than I thought," Chowdury said. "Hold your course, Mr. Conally. We're going in."

Trouble had never heard of an apparition being capable of picking up a real three-dimensional object. But then, neither had he heard that you could feel an apparition's embrace, or their breath on your skin, or the caress of their lips. Allowing the possibility that the Druud staff in Sanchez's hands was a mirage, Trouble approached the botanist warily, his hand outstretched.

"Will you give it to me? And I mean that in a straightforward, non-violent way."

In answer, Sanchez merely smiled and laid the staff in Trouble's hand. It certainly felt real enough.

Sanchez nodded toward Rusk. "I saw where he hid it. Can I ask what makes it so valuable?"

Trouble ignored him and slipped back into the engineering chamber to retrieve his slap gun. He checked on Jiang while he was at it. She was unconscious, but seemed to be breathing regularly. There was a lump the size of a plum at her temple. She was probably better off than the conscious members of the crew. He chose to ignore the rippling of what were supposed to be solid titanium bulkheads and the will-o-the-wisp transparency of the control panels.

Trouble returned to the corridor and realized he was surprised to see that Sanchez (or his doppelgänger) was still there, poking around the booby trap. He turned as Trouble approached.

"Pretty clever. Did you do this?"

Trouble moved to the open panel and disengaged the laser cutter, removing it from the makeshift brace Rusk had set up, and clipping it to his belt. He glanced over at the ex-Mate's corpse.

"Nope. This was *his* bright idea."

Sanchez followed his gaze. "Huh. Never knew he had it in him. Too bad for Rusk his memory wasn't as good as his capacity for sabotage."

"Speaking of sabotage, I don't suppose you feel like telling me what you did to the cargo."

"Nothing devastating, I assure you."

"You'll excuse me for not having a lot of faith in your assurances."

Trouble turned and headed down the transverse hallway away from Engineering, making his way to the longitudinal corridor that would take him toward the bow. It seemed to have acquired kinks and bends it hadn't had before. He strode off down it, regardless.

Sanchez trailed after.

"You're a strange one, Mr. Matthews. I'd at least expect that you'd want to know why I came back. Hell, I expected you'd probably knock me up against a wall the moment you saw me. That's why I appropriated the staff—as sort of a peace offering ..."

Trouble turned, caught the man (or mirage) by his uniform, lifted him half off his feet and pinned him to the bulkhead, surprised at how solid he felt. "I don't remember you being this gabby when you were alive," he said. "Why don't you just disappear like the other ones?"

Sanchez's dark eyes widened with alarm, and his voice came out in a frightened rasp. "The other ones what? Oh ... oh, you think I'm a psyquam? I'm not. I'm me. Salvador Sanchez, in the flesh. Ouch. Very tender flesh. Would you let me down, Mr. Matthews? Please?"

Trouble released him, stepping back warily. "A what?"

Sanchez winced and massaged his throat. "Psyquam. Silly neologism, short for psycho-quantum manifestation. Time gets kinda wonky in places like these. Effects precede causes, life and death are—"

The deck beneath them suddenly heaved and rolled like an ocean wave, throwing Trouble and Sanchez toward the junction with the longitudinal corridor.

Sanchez picked himself up, wiping blood from his lip. "I guess we're really in it, now, aren't we?"

He gestured down the corridor ahead where the decking suddenly looked as if it were boiling. Large bubbles rose and grew and then flattened out again as if the air had gone out of them.

Trouble watched the blood trickle from the other man's cut lip. It looked real enough.

"You're really Sanchez?"

When the botanist nodded, he moved on him with lightning speed, pinning him to the wall again. "You're right—I probably should kill you. But I'd really like to know what you did to the plants. This whole crew's got a pay day riding on them, after all. And, well, I discover I'm a very curious sort of person."

Sanchez licked his lips. "So, it's true—that you've got no memory."

Trouble thought fleetingly of his encounter with the Janina psyquam in Engineering. He grimaced. "I have just enough to make me wish I didn't. But that's enough about me. What did you do to the Lerandia?"

"Take me to Captain Shade. I'll tell him."

"Captain Shade is injured. Severely. He may not even make it through this alive. I'm thinking you'd better tell *me*."

Sanchez thought about it for a moment too long. Trouble shook him hard enough to rattle his teeth. "You'll have to speak up, Sal."

"I modified them!"

"Modified?"

"Improved. Vastly."

Trouble loosened his grip.

Sanchez coughed, then spoke in a strangled whisper. "The genetic mutations I induced should triple the value of those plants. Triple, Matthews. If it's administered in time, serum from a normal Lerandia plant will cure the symptoms of sigma radiation sickness by means of an interaction with the damaged blood cells. The plants I modified prevent the radiation from affecting those blood cells in the first place. It's a radiation shield."

"And you came back—why? Because you had to leave your mutant spores behind?"

"I came back," said Sanchez, "because I realized—belatedly, I admit—what Chowdury meant to do with you people."

"You're kidding me."

Sanchez's eyes darkened in fury. "I'm a botanist, damn it, not a smuggler or a pirate. And I'm sure as hell not a murderer. I don't know the rules of the game or the-the protocols of the damned Guild. I only knew I wanted off this ship. And I wanted to be able to make enough money from this cargo to get me as far away from port towns as possible. And yes, I wanted some revenge on Shade for pulling me out of my life and dumping me on this wreck. I had a research post at a prestigious university. I had a *life*—" He shook his head. "Why am I telling you this? You don't give a shit. And—hell—we'll be lucky if this bucket holds together long enough to get us through the Passage at all."

A life. Trouble had apparently had one of those, too, before ...

Before what? What had that psyquam scene been a re-enactment of? He remembered the moments; he remembered the emotions; he just couldn't remember the context or *why* any of it had happened.

What had the mirage man said? *You didn't do your part.*

He only realized he'd said the words aloud when Sanchez said, "I know, damn it! I've explained why. I'm sorry, all right? If you want to kill me, do it. But just remember, I'm the man who discovered how to mutate Lerandia. That means I'm worth something. And I'm the only one who knows how to distill this new serum."

Trouble shrugged and let Sanchez down, then turned to face the central fore-and-aft corridor that ran down the ship's axis. It still resembled the innards of a gigantic worm; appropriate, given the anomaly they were traveling through. It twisted and turned, wriggled up and down or right and left; sometimes it seemed to extrude through the ship's external plating. Trouble ignored the gyrations of the corridor and moved doggedly forward, his eyes on the deck just ahead of him. Sanchez tagged along in his wake.

They were approximately amidships when every light in the corridor went out and the ship's gravity failed. Trouble found himself floating toward the overhead. He adjusted quickly, thanking his extraordinary night vision that he could see the handholds set into the bulkheads. The handholds—built into every starship in the event of just such a situation—were evenly spaced throughout the vessel. He latched onto a grip with his free hand and used it to propel himself forward.

Sanchez followed, swearing non-stop.

They'd gone maybe three or four yards when the gravity engaged again. Trouble managed to keep his grip on a handhold and let himself carefully back to the deck. Sanchez landed behind him with a resounding thump. His swearing accelerated —vivid, juicy spacer's oaths that caused even Trouble to raise an eyebrow. He glanced aft. It was almost totally dark, but he could see the botanist kneeling in the center of the corridor, frantically patting at his coveralls. He unzipped them and reached in to poke at something in an inner pocket.

"Damn it," he muttered. "Damn it, damn it!"

Trouble moved several steps toward him. "What is it?"

Sanchez withdrew his hand and rubbed his fingers together. Trouble could see a dark, viscous, green liquid on them. Definitely not blood ... unless the Passage was colorizing it.

"Nothing ... It just—just startled me."

"What's that on your hands?"

Sanchez hesitated, clearly reluctant to admit anything. Finally he said, "The top came off one of the phials when I fell. Thank God it was only one. These are worth more than—"

"More than the lives of the people on this ship?"

Sanchez struggled to his feet. "I told you. I didn't know what Chowdury was planning for the *Raker's* crew. When I found out, I volunteered to come back with his boarding party. A show of good faith. I was supposed to help them take over. Notice that I didn't do that. Notice that I helped you, instead."

"Get up and walk," Trouble said.

"How? I can't see a damn thing... How can you—oh," he murmured as Trouble swung back to face him. "Your night vision ... I forgot—you're a mod."

"Yeah, or maybe my mom was a cat."

"Either way, you'll forgive me if being alone in the dark with you doesn't inspire confidence."

"Just follow the sound of my voice," Trouble said, turning his attention to the corridor ahead.

"That's not going to work unless you keep talking and you're not exactly loquacious."

"I'll hum. Work for you?"

The melody came spontaneously to mind. He knew it, but not what it was. It reminded him of ... a doll. A child's toy. Why? He found the possible answers terrifying.

They managed to go another couple of meters toward the bow, when Sanchez said, "Hey, the walls are starting to glow. It's like ..." He paused for a couple of paces, then gibbered, "Oh, my God, I know what those are! I saw them on Ceti Alpha Seventeen. Those are flesh-eating rangeomorphs. I saw what they left of the settlers. Trouble, we can't go this way!"

Trouble didn't answer. He didn't see any glowing walls or rangeomorphs (whatever the hell those were), but he had just noticed someone moving toward them in the darkness of the corridor. Someone he couldn't put a name to, but who was familiar to him, nonetheless. It was a man, wearing a long, formal fly-away dress coat and a black shirt, instead of crew's coveralls. He had dark hair with silver at the temples and he moved toward Trouble and Sanchez as if he had seen them despite the stygian dark.

Trouble realized, with a peculiar jolt, that he knew the man well. He'd been hired to kill him.

25 / MIRAGE

KAI JIANG HADN'T ALWAYS BEEN A HARDSKIN. SHE'D BEEN BORN A "soft"—a normal human—on Pele. Like so many others of that world, she'd been a victim of the heavy mutation rate caused by periodic solar storms on the system's hot white star. Her skeleton had been warped and twisted until it would no longer support her. So she had opted for bio-reconstruction. Picotech "factories" established in her bone marrow had secreted a metal alloy to strengthen her bones, while other nanites had coaxed her into growing a thin, chitinous layer of skin to protect her from further radiation damage.

She'd always wanted to be a soft—ever since she'd found a holo-image of her grandmother in her mother's private diary. She'd imagined herself looking just like her grandmother: beautiful, with a full, curvaceous figure instead of the small, wiry frame she had grown up with. What might it have been like not have to settle for men so hard-up they didn't care about either the personal or physical qualities of the females they hooked up with? Might she have been rich, or famous, or elegant? Or all of the above? Might she have belonged somewhere—had a family?

She could not conceive of an alternate reality where beauty could be as much a curse as an asset. Yet, in this curious dream she was having, those were exactly her circumstances. In a few seconds of dreamtime, she amassed a lifetime of being watched by countless eyes. Eyes that desired, envied, even hated her. Eyes that watched her every move—in private, in public, at work and at play.

She was pursued by men and other women. Most of the men wanted her; most of the women who didn't also want her wanted to know how she came to be wanted. There were reporters and pictographers, as well, who wanted to know everything. Her beauty secrets, her diet, her reading list, her passions, her phobias. Her opinions. And if her opinion on a given subject was not especially interesting (after all, she hadn't dreamed of being an intellectual), no one seemed to care. They were content merely to look at her and hear the sound of her voice, and she was, at least at first, content to let them look and listen.

The eyes were everywhere. They followed her as she went about her day-to-day business which, oddly enough, was still aboard *Moonraker*. They followed her into Engineering, where she still contrived to look beautiful as she showed the media how she rotated the drive rods. They followed her into the head, into the Retreat, into the shower. They watched her eat, sleep, and have sex—which, oddly, always seemed to be with Blackwood, the gill-neck.

She couldn't hide from them. She couldn't escape them. Everywhere she looked, everywhere she was—so were the eyes. They wouldn't leave her alone. They wanted something from her, those eyes. They wanted a relationship with her. No, they believed they already *had* a relationship with her, whether or not it was true. And because of the eyes, she could have a real relationship with no one. In her dream, she was as lonely as if she had been orphaned on a barren asteroid.

Between one heartbeat and the next, she found herself alone on a precipice that overlooked the boiling waters of a volcanic lake on Pele. She recognized the place. She had been here once, before she'd shipped out on the *Raker*, before she had met Jay

Blackwood. She had been desperately alone then, and had thought of diving into that hot, vent-fed lake in the hope that she might drown, for it certainly would not harm her rock-hard carapace. Now she thought of diving again, but this time for reasons so opposite, they were truly alien.

She let herself pitch forward over the precipice, and felt the eyes follow her down. They followed her into the water. They watched coldly, dispassionately, as the hot springs scorched her beautiful skin and made it peel away in bloody patches. She was melting, like the witch in that old tri-vee her mother had loved so much.

Melting ...

Jiang awoke to find herself lying on the deck in Engineering, her chitinous skin cracked and smoldering. The hair that grew through the shell over her skull was wet, dripping warm water onto her neck. Her head throbbed like a sonofabitch. She put a hand to her temple and winced as her fingers found the knot there.

Fighting dizziness, she pulled herself upright and listened. The hum of the ion drive gave her the bad news: The Keplinger was offline. She culled through her memories to see if she knew why.

Rusk. Rusk had come into Engineering, had headed for the drive controls. She had moved to intercept him. That was the last thing she remembered.

Jiang hauled herself to her feet and shuffled to the drive console. The controls looked ... wrong. Warped. More than warped, they looked ... alive. The drive levers wove and curled like the strange sea creatures Blackwood had shown her on his home world when they'd made port there last year. The mixture filters looked like the bio-luminous jelly-birds of her own world. She reached for the levers, but couldn't get her hands on them; they simply bobbed out of the way.

Her eyes blurred, her head swam. She was probably

concussed, which meant she had to get to the infirmary. She left Engineering and hauled herself forward.

"Trouble?" There was real panic in Sanchez's voice. "Trouble, the walls—!"

"Not real. It's a mirage."

"No, it—"

"Sal! I don't see it. Get that? This is your own personal hallucination."

"Not real ..." Sanchez said. He repeated it like a mantra. "Not real ... not real ..."

Trouble heard him begin to move again, now about a meter behind.

The man he'd been ordered to assassinate (by whom?) was about two meters in front of them. The man opened his mouth and said, "You stood them up."

Blood ran from his mouth, down his chin, in rivulets. There was a hole in his chest the size of Trouble's fist.

"You backed out on them. And I'm still dead."

"That's not my fault," Trouble said, though he was far from certain of that. "I didn't kill you."

"You should have told me. If you'd told me, *she'd* still be alive and you wouldn't be here."

"Shit," Trouble said and swung the Druud staff at the Dead Man.

The psyquam stopped to watch it pass through his torso. He said, "You didn't kill me, but maybe you should have." Then he exploded in a burst of white light.

"Who the hell were you talking to?" panted Sanchez, hurrying to catch up. "A psyquam? I didn't even see anything. What'd you mean, 'I didn't kill you'? Who didn't you kill?"

"I don't remember. Now shut up and move." Trouble pressed

on, seriously considering using the Druud staff on himself, but knowing he couldn't trust Sanchez not to take advantage of any temporary lapse of reason on his part. He supposed he could use it on Sanchez first—make him cooperative—and then use it on himself.

No. He hated being out of control. *Hated* it. Besides it was discharging with every use, and he had no idea if they could recharge it. So, he kept on, wondering if the effects of the staff would keep him from seeing any more specters from his mostly forgotten past.

I was ordered to kill someone? Me? Is that what I am—an assassin?

They hadn't gone more than another three meters when Trouble heard a horrific scream ahead of them. He kept moving, not missing a step. It was a man's voice, and in a few more steps they rounded a corner and Trouble could see the source of it; a crewman had literally fallen through the deck, which must have been not quite solid when he'd stepped on it. It was solid now, and he was stuck in it up to his armpits. He was, not surprisingly, dead.

Trouble moved to step around him, turning back to guide Sanchez. At this point the lights in the corridor flickered and came on with just enough power to illuminate the hallway dimly. Trouble blinked once—his eyes adjusting immediately to the dim light—and kept walking, mulling over the list of mods he suspected he'd had. Superior night vision—yeah, that'd be useful in an assassin. Had he been modified for that purpose? He already knew he had heightened senses, abnormally quick reflexes, and more strength than he could account for by any normal means. And combat training. *Serious* combat training. Plus, an apparent resistance to the effects of radiation.

That one bothered him and caused him to recall Doc Pike's question about "experimental" modifications—a question he hadn't been able to answer.

Behind him, Sanchez gasped, "Oh, my God." Then: "No, no. Not real, you said. None of this is real."

"That one is."

"Oh ... oh, God ..."

Behind him, Trouble heard the sound of Sanchez retching and figured this might be a good time to inquire about another facet of the botanist's treachery.

"So, where'd you put the telltale, Sal?"

"The what?" Sanchez gagged again.

"The beacon that Chowdury's been using to track us."

Sanchez waited a hair too long to reply and Trouble rounded on him. "Where is it?" he asked, his voice soft with menace.

"It's in my office. Off the 'ponics bay. In the console. Looks like a data chip."

"Thanks. Hey, Cyber. Talk to me. I've got some intel for you."

There was no answer.

"Cyb? What's the situation up there?"

The response was as disorienting as it was unexpected: the gravity dropped off to about fifty percent of normal and they were plunged back into darkness.

Trouble grabbed a handhold and swore. "Damn it, Cyber, what the hell's going on?"

There was a strange bleat from the comm links up and down the corridor, and then a new voice came through every one of them.

"Cyber can't hear you right now. He's 'offline', I suppose you would say, and I think he must remain in that state."

Trouble noted the change in vocabulary and cadence. He knew both better than he really cared to.

"Captain Shade, where's Cyber?"

"He's incapacitated at the moment. He was standing between me and something I wanted."

"Which was?"

"Revenge, Mr. Trouble. Against the man who has loomed over me like a thunder cloud since time immemorial. The man who has harried and harassed and belittled me and who now seeks to take from me my best chance at fortune."

"Captain Chowdury?"

"Your thinking is too small, Mr. Trouble. Vishnu Chowdury is merely a pirate. I refer to Julian Shade, my brother. The architect of my humiliation."

Trouble kept moving, thinking. They'd taken Shade to the computer core, Cyber said. They'd have to plug him into a cryo pod—into a brain monitor. And that, in turn, would plug into the ship's systems. The same systems Cyber was interconnected with.

"Captain," Trouble said quietly, reasonably, "can I talk to Cyber?"

"I told you. Cyber is unable to respond right now. I suppose you could say he's in the brig, metaphorically speaking. He refused to help me get to Julian."

"Captain, in case you hadn't noticed, we're in the middle of a wormhole, coming apart at the seams. Your brother—"

"Is pursuing me, Mr. Trouble. Always pursuing me. I can feel him out there—ahead of us now, since we went subluminal. But he'll realize that he's overshot us and he'll lie in wait. But I know he's there, and I'll be ready."

Sanchez broke in now, confused, scared. "What's going on, Matthews? What's he babbling about? Does he really think that's his brother out there?"

There was the metallic scraping sound Trouble had come to associate with laughter. Then Shade said, "Vishnu is only a proxy... Why, it's Mr. Sanchez, isn't it? I can see you now. You're a traitor, sir. I'm disappointed in you. And I will deal with you later. Right now, I need all my faculties to deal with *him*."

Sanchez sidled up to Trouble and murmured, "He's crazy. What are you going to do? We've got to regain control of the ship."

"I heard that," said Shade. "You'd be amazed at what I can hear. I'm amazed at what I can hear ... and see." His voice dropped, took on an introspective tone. "For the first time, I am truly master of this ship. I *am* this ship. Vishnu, the puny Preserver, inspires no fear in me; I am become Shiva, shatterer of worlds! My senses are expanded, multiplied ... a thousand eyes, a million ears ... Oh, yes—I hear you and Trouble down there plotting against me. I see Morgan and Lucas in the infirmary, plotting with the doctor. And others in pockets all over the ship, terrified of this new paradigm, wondering what's happening and how they can fix it. But I'm not something that can be fixed."

A muted alarm sounded, two urgent notes, rising and falling. Trouble doubled his pace, dragging Sanchez in his wake. Captain Shade spoke again, an unmistakable note of triumph in his electronic voice.

"There. Fix *that*, if you can."

"Fix what?" Sanchez asked, panic making his voice sharp and thin.

"I just flooded the engineering section and the lift tubes with sigma radiation from the drive core. This ship is mine—and no one is taking it from me."

Trouble had meant to ask how the Pilgrim's Passage affected people in cryo-sleep. Now, he had some idea.

26 / GLASS

Rainor Glass walked without the aid of his exoframe. He walked on solid earth beneath a clear blue sky, in normal earth gravity. His step was light and easy, his joints bent in only two directions. This was familiar, as if he had been doing it all his life.

He had no idea of the how or when or why of it, just that it was so, and had always been so. And this was odd, because the movement of these leg muscles, this jaunty footstep, this easy, regular breathing ... they were like a drug to him, new and intoxicating. When he was thirsty, he was able to take the water bottle and bring it to his mouth with the ease of thought. This was at once mundane and breathtaking.

He took a moment to notice his surroundings. It seemed a rather small planet, perhaps even an asteroid. The horizon's curvature was noticeable. And it was barren beyond the emptiness of any desert on any world he'd ever seen. It reminded him of images he'd seen of the sun-blasted surface of Hel. Yet here the climate was temperate, the air rich and breathable. Despite the mild weather, there was scarcely any vegetation, and no signs of animal life or civilization.

He came to a stop, looked about. Where was he going on a world where there was obviously no place to go?

It occurred to him that he was dreaming. He determined to wait the dream out to see where it would take him. He was in no hurry. He'd dreamed of walking before, but never this vividly.

Something struck the earth between his feet, sending up a tiny puff of dirt. He paused, thinking someone had thrown a pebble at him, but there was no one to be seen and nowhere for them to hide. In a matter of moments, several more tiny explosions dotted the dust about him. Rain, he thought, savoring the sound of it hitting the dust, and anticipating the sweet smell of wet earth he knew must follow.

But it did not follow.

Puzzled, he looked up at the sky, which was now a velvety shade of purple. A moment ago the sun had been shining, but now it was night. Bright streaks of light etched paths between the stars, flared to brilliance in the atmosphere of his tiny world, then went dark. The rain-like patter continued, accelerated. Not a gentle rain—not rain at all—a micro-meteor shower.

Something struck him a glancing blow just above his right knee. It sent an explosion of pain up and down his leg.

He set himself in motion again and had taken several limping steps when a knuckle-sized micro-meteorite landed on the ground not twenty feet away, setting off a blast of dust and debris and leaving a small crater. Rainor, rocked by the concussion, stumbled and nearly fell. He staggered upright and picked up his pace. It was only a matter of time before something that size struck him directly—perhaps crippling him. The thought was horrifying. He didn't want to lose his newfound ability to walk unaided so soon.

In the sky, the streaks of light showed no sign of stopping. They seemed to be in infinite supply. He had to keep moving. Ignoring the pain in his leg, he began to jog, then to run. Still the meteorites fell, blowing dust and rock into the desert air. He saw a small hill topped with a clutter of large boulders. He made for it, thinking it might offer some shelter, feeling—even through the fear of injury—the thrill of having muscles that supported his weight, that worked without artifice.

He reached the bottom of the hill, breathing hard. Sweat trickled into his eyes. He blinked in astonishment ... and found himself back at his point of origin—the flat, dry, featureless plain on which he'd entered this dream.

He stared about frantically, looking for cover. The smallest meteorites now were the size of his fist. They pummeled craters as big as flitters all around. The scream of their descent, the thunder of their impact, were overwhelming. Rainor was amazed he hadn't been hit already.

He tried to remember which way he'd run, and started out again. Again, he found the hill and again he made it to its base, only to be blinded again by sweat and dust; only to realize he'd returned again somehow to square one; only to have to start running again, certain that at any moment a falling star would find him and destroy the strong bones, the resilient muscles, the strong, flexible spine he had inexplicably acquired.

The Slinky looked up into the beautiful violet sky and saw a ball of light streaking right for him. There was no time, no way to dodge. It grew, filling the sky, blinding him—

Rainor awoke with a gasp, his breathing labored and his legs in cramped agony, as if he'd been over-exerting himself. He gritted his teeth and waited for the analgesic drip in his exo-suit to kick in, then realized he wasn't in his exo. He was lying on a bio-bed in the infirmary, which was bathed in the amber glow of emergency lighting.

He managed to lift his head, to look down at himself—and saw, to his shock, that he was covered with bruises and lacerations—exactly as if he'd been subjected to the shrapnel of the meteor bombardment.

Out of the corner of his eye, he could see three blurred forms huddled around a computer console. He blinked, and they resolved into Mad Morgan, Doc Pike, and Lucas Shade. He opened his mouth to call out to Pike, to beg for something to knock down the pain of his injuries, when the infirmary hatch opened and Trouble Matthews stepped through the iris, seemingly in slow motion. Sal Sanchez was right behind him.

"You son of a bitch," Rainor growled. "You stupid, greedy, sell-out son of a bitch!"

Trouble glanced over at him, eyebrows raised, then looked back at Sanchez. "I don't think he likes you, Sal."

Pike glanced at Rainor. "Ah, you're awake. You'd probably like some morphatrine." He began filling an infuser with the painkiller.

Rainor wished with all his soul that he still had the lithe, strong muscles of his—dream? Hallucination? Out-of-body experience? Whatever it had been, he was once again a prisoner of gravity and genetics.

"The lifts are out," Morgan said. "The bridge is cut off from the rest of the ship, system for system. I don't know if Blackwood's still alive. I don't even know if there's life-support up there. We've managed to disable all the snoops in here and in the corridor as far back as the emergency stores. I figured if we needed to get anything out of the emergency supplies, we didn't want him to see us. We also rewired the comms so we can hear him, but he can't hear us unless we manually restore contact."

When Morgan finished her report, Lucas added, "We can put it right again, of course. I mean, we'll need to have comms working once we've taken the ship back." His gaze swung to Trouble. "Right?"

"Right," Trouble said. "You got some plans for this mutiny?"

Lucas winced at the word. "No. But I'm sure we'll think of something."

Morgan said, "The only way to get to the computer core from here is to go down the forward lift shaft. The car is stranded up on the Observation Deck." She smiled at him. "I'm glad you're still alive, by the way."

Trouble returned the smile, if grimly. He could see how hard she was having to concentrate on the problem at hand. He remembered what that was like—fighting the effects of the staff. It was a good thing that she was still under the influence. He'd checked the charge on the thing and realized that it didn't have much power left. There were no weapons chargers in the infirmary nor in their meager emergency stores, and no guarantee they'd work on this thing anyway. He figured it had two, maybe three shots left. That would have to be enough.

He looked over to where Doc Pike was working on the Slinky, who'd come out of his altered-space dream with some very peculiar side effects, which included, according to Pike, slightly increased muscle mass and stiffer joints. Not to mention looking like he'd been through a war. At fifty percent gravity he wouldn't need his exo-suit, and if they had to go down the lift shaft, he'd still be an asset.

Trouble turned his attention back to Morgan and noticed that her eyes had changed color. They'd been hazel. Now they were brown, like—

He blinked and she became fully Janina. The urge to go to her, to hold her ...

"What?" Morgan said, apparently seeing the change of expression on his face.

He blinked again. Schooled his face. Shook his head.

Focus. "Shade flooded the lifts with sigma radiation."

Morgan's face (and it *was* Morgan's face) lost most of its color. "So if we save the ship, we die anyway, is that what you're telling me?"

"Yeah, we'll probably die, but not from radiation." Trouble moved to stand in front of Sanchez, who sat sulking in a makeshift holding cell between two bio-beds. He held out his hand, palm up. "Give it over ... please."

"What?" Sanchez withdrew even further into his corner, his

eyes measuring the chances he might get past Trouble to the hatch.

"The Lerandia serum. We're going to have to dose up before we go save the universe."

Sanchez crossed his arms across his chest, as if to shield his stash of drugs. "I don't think so."

Morgan shook her head impatiently. "Trouble, Lerandia serum only works after the fact."

"Ordinarily, yes. But this is new improved stuff your botanist friend's got in his pocket."

Lucas stared at Sanchez. "*That's* what he did to the plants? That's the mutation? He created a vaccine?"

Sanchez met Trouble's eyes defiantly, then rose from the chair he'd been sitting on. "If I give the serum to you, I'll come out of this with nothing. I'll have to start all over."

"You don't give it to me, you won't come out of this, period. None of us will. You're a smart man, Sal. You know I'm right. We're going to have to go down that shaft." He hesitated, then added. "It's your choice as to whether we have to step over your corpse on our way."

Sanchez glanced toward the hatch, then sidled a couple of steps toward it.

"I don't think you want to do that, Sal," Trouble told him.

Sanchez hesitated, then dove beneath the bio-bed. He had probably intended to hit the deck and roll to the hatch, but the weakened gravity turned his somersault into a chaotic tumble. He pitched up against a diagnostic station with enough force to knock himself senseless.

Trouble moved to squat by the unconscious botanist. "Well, I *thought* you were a smart man. Shows you what I know."

He unzipped Sanchez's coverall and relieved him of the packets of serum and sporules. He gave the sporules to Lucas for safe-keeping. The serum he handed to Pike.

"There enough of this here for three of us?"

Pike opened one of the phials and used a pipette to collect a drop of the serum. He inserted the pipette into one of the contraptions on his workstation and tapped a sequence into a keypad on its small console. His eyebrows rose.

"There's enough of this for three hundred of you. This is pure distillate. I'll have to dilute it."

"Which three?" asked Lucas.

Trouble just looked at him.

"You, me, and Morgan, right?"

"Wrong. Me, Morgan, and Glass."

Lucas's face darkened with sudden anger. "Why? Why *not* me? Why can't I go with you? Because you think I'm just a kid? Didn't I help you out with the pirates?"

"Lucas ..." Morgan put a hand on the kid's shoulder. He shoved it off.

"Trouble, I saved your ass!"

He tried to draw himself up to his full height, but only succeeded in overbalancing in the decreased gravity. He sat down on the deck, bouncing slightly.

Janina was suddenly standing behind him, looking at Trouble. "Don't do it, Ridley. Don't give in to them."

What did she mean? The memory eluded him and he had no time to pursue it. He kept a stone face. "Look, we don't have time for this. Lucas, if you want to be treated like a man, act like one. We'll have to slide down the shaft on ropes. Somebody's got to make sure we don't slide all the way to the bottom."

"Can't Doc do that?"

"Yeah, he could. But then who'd keep an eye on our old buddy Sal? Or d'you trust him suddenly?"

Lucas glanced at the unconscious botanist. "We could strap him to a bed."

"He's got a point," Morgan said. "And we could probably use Lucas's help. But Lucas, that's your uncle down there. I don't know what we'll have to do to take the *Raker* back."

"Do what you need to do," said Janina, clutching the front of Trouble's coverall. "But don't give in to them."

The man with the pocket watch was suddenly standing at her shoulder, the shiny carapace of the antiquated timepiece visible through her body. "Your wife has a death wish, Captain Matthews. A sad commentary on the sort of man you are."

Captain Matthews?

"My first duty is to the ship and my crewmates," Lucas said. "Besides, he wouldn't be doing this if he was sane."

"Duty," repeated Trouble. He closed his eyes to Janina and her murderer and focused on Lucas. "Okay. Morgan, we need something long enough to get us down that shaft."

She nodded, already moving toward the hatch. "Emergency webbing. It's in the EMG stores."

Trouble turned his attention to Pike. "Doc, how long on the serum?"

"Give me ten minutes."

"What about the Slinky? Is he in any condition to go?"

"The 'Slinky' is fine." Glass slipped gracefully from the diagnostic table. "In fifty percent gravity, I'm going to be more of an asset in that lift shaft than you are, Matthews. I won't even need the webbing."

"Now you've gone and hurt my feelings. I thought we were destined to be fast friends. Lucas, help me with Mr. Deadweight here."

"No follow-through," said Pocket Watch. "Any way you cut it, you're a traitor." He morphed into the Dead Man, who added, "Why were you silent, Captain?"

Trouble shook his head as if that might clear it. Later, he would deal with these ghosts, maybe understand why they were haunting him. Maybe remember all of it.

Then again, maybe he'd be dead ... which might be a mercy.

They were in the process of anchoring lengths of webbing around a bio-bed pedestal when the comms crackled to life and spoke to them in Shade-Cyber's voice.

"Trouble? Are you there? I've been looking for you all over the ship. The only place I can't seem to see is the infirmary. I assume that if you're still alive you must be there. Answer me, please."

Trouble traded glances with Morgan, but ignored the summons. "How's it coming, Doc?"

"Working on the last dose. Eight in all."

"Eight?" asked Morgan.

"Five of us—and Sanchez, Cyber and the captain. You unseal those doors, you defeat the wards; any connected compartments are going to be flooded."

"Trouble?" Shade's voice filled the room. "I don't believe for a moment that you're dead. You're with those traitors in Medbay. I'd advise you not to plot against me. I have no desire to harm any of you, but I will if it becomes necessary."

"Let's go," Trouble said. "Dose us up."

Doc Pike administered the Lerandia serum to everyone in the infirmary, then handed Trouble two full infusers—one each for Cyber and Shade. Trouble tucked them into the top left pocket of his uniform and sealed the velcro.

Pike returned to his workstation. "I'll have doses for the rest of the crew in half an hour ... if we last that long."

Under other circumstances Trouble might have been amused by the fact that, even under the thrall of the Druud staff, Pike was as much a pessimist as ever.

"Count on it," Trouble said. He picked up the staff and stepped from Medbay into the corridor. The others followed, including Jani, Pocket Watch, and the Dead Man.

27 / TRAPS

THE AMBER EMERGENCY LIGHT FOLLOWED THEM FROM MEDBAY INTO the corridor, but it was weak and threw strange shadows. Morgan turned on a hand light, which she fastened at her belt.

"What are you going to do with that?" Morgan asked Trouble, nodding at the staff.

In return, Trouble asked, "You hear that?"

She paused and listened, brow furrowing. "What? I don't hear anything."

Trouble could hear it plainly enough: the wails and screams and desperate profanity of the crew trapped somewhere astern. Trapped by the unimaginable, the possibly unreal, the potentially deadly. Was it his natural or mod-heightened senses or the twists of wormhole space that allowed him to hear these things? Or was he hallucinating?

It didn't matter.

"There are dozens of people trapped somewhere on the ship, each in his or her private hell. If we're going to have a functional crew when and if we pull out of Pilgrim's Passage, hell has to be overthrown, and this"—Trouble lifted the staff—"is the best—no, the *only*—chance of that happening."

Morgan was peering at him strangely. "What—you're a believer now?"

"After Shade blasted you with the staff, how'd you feel?"

"Great. I still feel ... better than I ought to." She grinned. "I'm ready to save the universe."

"You seen any psyquams?" Trouble looked over Morgan's head at the Dead Man, who now hovered there like a well-dressed but bloody ghost.

I should know who he is.

"I don't think so." She glanced at Lucas, who shook his head.

"Me neither," the boy said. "But like you told the captain, you can't go around the ship zapping people."

"I know," Trouble said. "But Cyber gave me an idea awhile back. Maybe it'll work; maybe not. Worth a try, I figure. Ready with the webbing?"

"Ready." Lucas handed the rolled-up end of the heavy duty webbing to Trouble.

Trouble pried open the lift doors.

The sigma radiation was invisible, odorless, and soundless, of course. There was no physical sign of its outrush into the corridor, but it seemed to Trouble that he could feel it anyway, assaulting his body, making his flesh creep, being repelled (he hoped) by the Lerandia serum. He dropped the roll of webbing down the shaft.

It did not get far. Gravity shut down suddenly and completely, and the webbing simply remained rolled-up on itself, hovering uselessly in the shaft. Trouble, Morgan, and Lucas were in free fall, trying desperately to find handholds, their lamps spraying the dark corridor with erratic flashes of light.

Rainor Glass, engineered for just such an environment, adjusted swiftly, his elongated, strangely jointed limbs steadying him against the bulkheads and ceiling.

He moved to each of the others in turn, guiding them to handholds in the corridor. He went to Trouble last of all, holding his long, delicate fingers out for the webbing.

"I'll take it down. In zero-gee I can do it faster than any of you. I'll anchor it below the door on Zeta Deck."

Trouble relinquished the webbing into the Slinky's hands, then peered over the lip of the shaft. Glass slipped past him and down into the abyss, pulling himself swiftly via the handholds. The blue-white beam of his lamp—clipped now to the shoulder of his coverall—sliced through the gloom, bright enough to make Trouble wince. He concentrated away from it, on the point far below where the doors of the lift opened directly onto the computer core on Epsilon. The walls of the shaft seemed to breathe, pressing in and out. Trouble ignored them.

There would be no snoops in the lift shaft, but the mutineers would be targets as soon as they opened those doors. And in opening them, they might just give Shade all the advance notice he needed that his sanctuary was being invaded. Trouble hefted the Druud staff. He might only get one chance to change Shade's mind.

"Trouble." The captain's voice was smug. "I don't know what you're doing, but I suspect you're still trying to take the ship back. You'll fail, of course. To paraphrase Louis the Fourteenth: *Le bateau c'est moi.* I am the ship, and I'm learning to use all of her systems."

Trouble glanced down the shaft. Glass was already several meters below him, almost to Gamma Deck. If Shade was learning the ship's systems, it would be only a matter of time before he turned them against those he considered enemies.

Lucas had pulled himself to the hand hold next to Trouble's. "Trouble, there's something wrong."

"Really? I hadn't noticed."

"No, I mean back there on Beta Deck. There are little lights everywhere."

"It's the effects of wormhole space," said Morgan, still clinging to a handhold across the hall. "You're seeing stars through the hull."

"No, that's not it. Look!" He tugged at Trouble's coverall.

Trouble turned to look back down the corridor behind them. To his light-sensitive eyes, it appeared that the ceiling several meters astern was populated by a froth of tiny, opaque bubbles, each carrying its own fleck of light. There was a small constellation of them—minuscule, colorful—and moving closer.

"Shit!" Trouble swore. He pulled the slap gun from its belt clip, aimed, and fired. He blew away about half of them and left a depression in the overhead. It took a second shot to get them all.

"Trouble?" Glass's voice came to him up the shaft, fear in it.

He looked down. The Slinky had stopped about halfway to his goal and was peering back up toward Beta Deck. His lamp, directed upward.

Trouble blinked. "Keep going!"

Glass hesitated, then turned his attention and his light back toward Zeta Deck.

"What was it?" Lucas asked.

"Shade was moving snoops."

"Then he knows what we're doing," said Morgan.

"Maybe not. But he sure as hell knows where we are—or thinks he does. Lucas, why don't you go have a talk with your uncle?"

"About what?"

"The price of goose eggs on Euphrates. I don't give a rat's ass what, just talk to him."

Lucas's eyes showed sudden comprehension. "Yeah. Sure." He by-passed the comms panel by the lift, floated himself carefully to the one just inside Medbay, and thumbed it on. The boy wasn't stupid—he'd immediately recognized that using the comms panel by the lift would alert Shade to their attack from above.

"Uncle Erasmus? It's me, Lucas. How ... how're you feeling?"

"I'll tell you how I feel, boy. I feel powerful. Capable of surviving this wormhole. Capable of surviving anything. Anything your father can throw at me."

Trouble went back to monitoring Glass's progress, half-listening to Lucas attempting to distract his uncle.

"My father?" the boy asked.

"Surely you realize that's who's out there in that other ship. Controlling Vishnu like a puppet master. Controlling everything from his seat of power."

"I ... I don't like my father very much," Lucas said. "Maybe that's why—because he always has to control everything. I was glad when he sent me to serve aboard the *Raker*. I'd rather be here with you than with him."

"You're a good boy, Lucas. Much more intelligent and capable than your father gave you credit for. You understand why I have to do what I have to do."

Lucas glanced down the hall at Trouble, who made a 'keep rolling' gesture at him. The Slinky had reached Zeta Deck and was making the webbing fast to a magnetic cleat below the doors.

"Uh ... what exactly do you have to do, Uncle Erasmus?"

"I have to kill your father, boy. You understand that, don't you?"

"Yes. Yes, sir. I do understand. He ... he stole your life. Just like he stole mine."

"A thief. Yes. Julian Shade is the quintessential thief. The ultimate pirate. A pillager of lives."

"You have to do what you have to do," Lucas repeated, watching Trouble.

"You won't try to stop me?"

"No, sir. I won't try to stop you."

"You won't let Trouble try to stop me?"

"Trouble doesn't want to stop you. None of us do."

"Then why did you destroy the cam bots I sent down to see what you were doing? If you're not trying to stop me, why don't you let me see where you are and what you're doing?"

"I'm in Medbay," Lucas said. "And I don't want to stop you from killing my father. I don't care what you do to him. Neither does Trouble. He fired on the cam bots because he thought they were more wormhole ghosts. He just wants to get out of Pilgrim's Passage. We all do."

"Oh, but *I* don't, Lucas. I like it here. I'm powerful here. Once I've eliminated Julian, I may stay."

Trouble signaled Morgan into the shaft, then turned on his hand lamp and flashed it in Lucas's direction. The boy shook his head and pointed at the comms panel. Trouble drew one finger across his throat in a "cut" sign and waved the light toward the shaft. Lucas ignored him, seemingly entranced by his uncle's monologue.

"Imagine it, boy," Shade was saying. "I could lie in wait here, like a great mechanical spider in its web of exotic matter, salvaging the cargo of any ship foolish enough or desperate enough to fall into the Pilgrim's Passage. None could resist me."

"But, what would you do with the cargo? I mean, if you never leave Pilgrim's Passage, if you're a ship—not a person— what good would it do you to have any of it? And what about the crew? You'd need a crew to salvage cargo, wouldn't you? But if you stay here, won't we all die?"

There was a sudden, heavy silence, during which Trouble swore under his breath and pulled himself back to the infirmary. Lucas had just backed Shade up against a wall of logic, and who knew how the desperate, delusional old man would react to being cornered?

Trouble made the infirmary entrance and reached through to grab Lucas's shoulder. When the boy turned to look at him, Trouble scowled and shook his head.

Shade came back on comms. "You're trying to confuse me. You don't want to stay here—you said so yourself. You destroyed my cam bots. You're plotting against me. You and your friends down there in Medbay. I'm very sorry, Lucas. I have become quite fond of you."

Trouble wrenched Lucas through the hatch and shoved him out into the corridor, where he bounced off the wall and half spun around before gaining purchase on a hand hold. Trouble turned back into Medbay.

"Pike! Get out of there! Now!"

The medic, his feet tucked into foot holds below his workstation, was in the process of packing a med kit with infusers and phials of dilute Lerandia serum. He hesitated only an instant before redoubling his efforts. He was reaching for the tray of raw serum phials when the data panel of the bio-bed closest to him blew out in a blinding shower of sparks.

Pike twisted and tried to duck out of the way, but only succeeded in pulling his feet out of the foot holds. He flipped backwards, heels over head, toward the hatch. Another diagnostic panel blew and Trouble dove—not away from the explosions but into the midst of them, toward the workstation where the precious med kit still sat open. He snagged the back of the workstation chair with one hand and used the other to slow his spin. Still clinging to the chair, he shoved the last phials of pure serum into the kit, closed the lid, and slipped his arm through the strap, orienting himself toward the open iris of the hatch in the same smooth movement.

He'd no more than gotten his head pointed in the right direction when the workstation itself blew. He found himself soaring toward the hatch at a dizzying speed. Every data panel in the room seemed to explode at once. The sparks seared his eyes and stung his exposed skin. He felt a sharp stab of pain in his right side, but balled himself up in spite of it, tumbling in mid-air.

Trouble shot through the iris and collided feet first with the opposite wall, letting his lower body take the impact. His ribs screamed in pain, but he cradled the med kit, protecting it. The reactive force of his impact had sent him sailing off again, but then a pair of arms grappled him and stopped his mad flight.

It was Doc Pike. His hair was slightly singed, his uniform likewise, but he seemed otherwise intact.

Trouble steadied himself against the bulkhead and thrust the med kit into the doctor's hands. "Take care of this. We're gonna need it."

"Optimist." The medic dropped his gaze to Trouble's midsection, illuminated in the fitful light from the Medbay, where the fire suppression systems had at last engaged. "You're bleeding."

Trouble followed his gaze to where a thin shard of metal about the size of a knife blade protruded from between two ribs. "Yeah, I guess so."

"Let me—"

"No time." Trouble pulled the sleeve of his coverall down over his right hand, grasped the shrapnel and gave it vicious yank, gritting his teeth against the renewed agony. He left the bloodied spike to float aimlessly. Pike had pulled an orthobond patch from the med-kit, enlarged the tear in Trouble's coverall, and slapped the patch against the wound. Trouble grunted in thanks, then turned and pulled himself to the lift shaft.

Looking down into it, he saw Morgan and Lucas staring back up at him, white-faced.

"What happened?" Morgan asked as Trouble pulled himself down to meet them.

"Shade blew up the infirmary."

"Doc?"

"He got out okay. With the serum. Not sure about Sanchez."

"No big loss," said Morgan. She angled her light around so that it picked up a pattern of gleaming ruby droplets hovering between them. "That's blood."

"Mine. I'm okay. Here, take this." He handed Morgan the Druud staff. "Use it on me if I start acting too weird."

"How am I supposed to tell?"

"Didn't know this thing made people think they were comedians." He nodded down toward Zeta deck. "Where's Shade's cryo pod in the room?"

Lucas answered him. "Um… There are four stasis pods

directly across the room from the lift. The ones in use will be lit. Cyber's on the left, so the captain's on the right."

"Got it. Let's move before he figures out we're still alive."

Trouble hauled himself down to Epsilon hand-over-hand, concentrating on the feel of the flat synthetic mesh under his fingers, the ripple of his shoulder muscles moving him smoothly down into the heart of the ship. The fire in his side diminished as the patch did its work, seeping painkillers and tailored amino acids that would more quickly heal the wound.

Trouble descended the shaft swiftly, leaving Morgan and Lucas to fumble along in his wake. Below him, Rainor Glass looked like a spider lounging at the end of a strand of web. The beam of his hand light was trained on the lift doors.

He looked up as Trouble lowered himself to a point just above the entrance to the computer core. He pantomimed prying open the doors.

Trouble shook his head and loosed the laser cutter from his belt. Glass's eyes were huge as he flattened himself against the wall opposite the doors and snuffed his hand light. Trouble adjusted the laser beam to a narrow setting, then flicked it at the control panel contacts arranged in neat rows to the left of the portal. The thin, red beam lanced out, cutting through the back of the panel, melting the contacts and severing the fiber optic traces beneath.

The doors slid back silently upon darkness broken only by the blinking of a handful of pinprick lights from the instrument panels in the chamber. Glass reached across the shaft to anchor himself to the door frame, then pulled himself gracefully to the threshold.

The door sill erupted with a sudden storm of electricity. Twisted fingers of vivid, violet-white lightning reached out to the Slinky, caressing his body, stabbing at him. His limbs whipped as if caught in a high wind, and he let out a keening wail of agony. Then there was a final, blinding flash, and Glass pitched backwards into the shaft just as gravity cut back in with full force.

CHAOS.

Dark, screaming, clawing chaos. Gravity was a ravening beast, grasping at Trouble, dragging him down into the black well of the shaft. It broke his grasp on the webbing, ripped his hands free and flipped him upside down. His entangled legs kept him from tumbling down the shaft, but he was jerked downward, head first, catching the webbing with hands and feet just as he would have slipped free. He felt a trickle of warm blood begin to spread across his chest as the med-patch loosened.

A hand light tumbled past. A second later, someone collided with him from above, nearly tearing him free. Instinct kicked in, and his arms shot out to wrap around Morgan's torso, taking her weight in addition to his own. His torn side screamed, but the webbing and its anchor, far above in the damaged infirmary, held. Morgan let out a trembling sigh.

She had fallen feet first; Trouble's face was buried in the front of her coverall. He turned his head and looked down toward her feet, hearing her heart hammering in her breast. The Druud staff still dangled from her belt. He grasped her more tightly with his left arm while he reached his right over to relieve her of the staff, which he clipped to his own belt.

She tensed as Trouble lowered her toward the gaping computer core doors. But she made no sound that might give them away. When they were eye-to-eye, he began to swing the webbing back and forth, perpendicular to the door sill.

He put his lips to her ear. "Roll for cover," he murmured, then gave one last swing and flung her through the doors.

She disappeared the moment she crossed the threshold; he heard her touch down. The door sill lit with sudden lightning, but there was no one there to absorb it.

Trouble hauled himself more or less upright and found himself staring into Lucas's terrified eyes. "You're next," he mouthed silently, and shut off the kid's hand light.

He tossed Lucas across the sill, inciting yet another fireworks display, then lowered himself until he was opposite the doors. Looking across the shaft, the room seemed cavernous. He could see Morgan and Lucas peering at him from behind a workstation near the doors. He unholstered the slap gun from his belt. Then he carefully disentangled his legs from the webbing, taking his weight on one arm. He began swinging.

When he'd gathered enough momentum, he let go of the webbing and shot through the doorway, pulling his knees tight to his chest and spinning through the darkness into Shade's domain. He hit the deck, absorbing the shock with his legs, rolled to the center of the room, and up onto his haunches, the gun ready to fire.

He located Shade's cryo pod. A sudden streamer of electricity arced across the room, scorching the deck less than a foot from where he knelt. He ducked and rolled, again coming up with the gun ready—an effort as useless as it was instinctive. His reflexes were preternaturally quick, but there was no way he could move faster than the speed of electricity.

The entire room seemed to explode then, in a riot of energy discharges. Violet, blue, white, gold, and red lightning arced, crisscrossing the chamber. There was no pattern to the barrage; the first strike, which seemed to have been a lucky one, had come the closest. Shade, not being a trained and augmented net-head, had acquired the ship's power, but hadn't the skill to wield it. His shots were wild, random.

With any luck, Trouble could use that against him.

He holstered the gun and rolled into the dubious shelter of a workstation. Its chair was anchored to the deck. He disengaged the base from its track. Sensing the movement, Shade tried to zap it, but the bolts again went awry—which made them no less dangerous.

With a powerful thrust of his legs, Trouble sent the chair flying toward the lift shaft, letting out a roar of only half-feigned pain as he rolled part of the way after it, coming to rest directly beside Shade's cryo pod. Lightning followed the chair's progress to the threshold and across. The chair plummeted into the abyss, making an ungodly racket as it careened off the walls.

Shade filled the room with static discharges. Trouble could feel his skin tingling, and every hair on his head and body rising. The smell of ozone was strong enough to make his eyes water. From across the room near the door, came screams from Morgan and Lucas. Lucas's shriek cut off suddenly. Morgan's died to a whimper.

The lightning ceased.

Trouble lay still, barely breathing.

"Trouble?" said Cyber's voice. "Trouble, that you? Morgan? Where are you guys? Who fell down the shaft? Please answer me."

Trouble lay motionless. Which lunatic was doing the talking —Cyber or Shade? There was no way to be sure—it was entirely conceivable that the captain was mimicking Cyber's vocal patterns.

"Trouble, you've won. You've worn him out. All those pyrotechnics took their toll. He's unconscious. You can come out now."

Trouble shot to his feet beside Shade's couch, bringing the

staff around to fire. Every light in the chamber, blazed on, blinding him completely for a second.

"Uncle Erasmus!" The ragged cry came from near the door and was answered with a zap of electricity.

In that instant of distraction, Trouble reached blindly out and found the pod cover control. The couch snapped open. Trouble shoved the staff against Shade's shoulder and triggered it.

"Oh!" Shade's voice said, as if he'd just had an epiphany. Which, in a way, he had. The room was plunged back into darkness.

Trouble dropped to his knees, blinded, but the effect lasted no more than a second before his eyes adjusted. Someone rose from hiding near the door and moved toward him. Morgan. She held a steel rod that used to be part of a cabinet frame, wielding it like a club.

"I am sorry," said the Cyber/Shade voice then, and Morgan froze.

The lights came on at about two-thirds their normal brightness. Trouble came slowly to his feet, freeing the laser cutter from his belt clip.

"I fear I was disingenuous," Shade continued. "How did you know, Trouble? How did you know that was me and not Cyber?"

"You've been running this ship for hours now without even breaking a sweat. I didn't think a few fireworks were gonna 'take their toll.' Besides, Cyber wouldn't have put it quite that way."

"Where's Lucas?" Shade asked. "Please tell me I didn't hurt the boy. I didn't mean—"

"I'm okay," said Lucas, emerging from hiding. His hair was singed, and one cheek bore a red weal, but he seemed otherwise sound.

"Ah. Good." The voice sounded honestly relieved. "So tell me, Mr. Trouble—what do you intend to do now?"

"First, I'm going to give you some anti-rad meds Pike cooked up for us." He pulled an infuser from his pocket and activated it against the older man's neck. "Second, I plan to shoot everybody up with Druud joy juice. You had a pretty good plan, there. I figure we'll stick with it."

Shade chuckled mechanically. "As you so aptly pointed out, Mr. Trouble, my plan was conceptually sound but logistically ridiculous."

"You were missing a piece of the puzzle. This piece." Trouble patted the control panel that connected Erasmus Shade to his ship.

Morgan had lowered her weapon and come to stand beside him. "What are you thinking?"

"If the hull conducts electrical charges, why not a charge from this?" He held up the Druud staff.

Morgan shook her head. "Damn. Tell me what we need to do."

"First, give Cyber his Lerandia juice." He handed her the second infuser; she took it and moved to Cyber's couch. "Then we need to disconnect the captain from the network. That all right with you, Cap?"

"Yes, of course. Whatever you must do to save the ship."

"We'll leave him hooked up to life-support though, right?" Lucas asked.

"Yeah. Can either of you disconnect him?"

Lucas nodded. "I can. Dr. Pike showed me what he did ... in case something happened to him."

"Do it."

"Before you disconnect me," Shade said, "I should warn you that Cyber is somewhat ... incapacitated. And the ship's systems have been reduced to purely autonomic and algorithmic functions. In other words, once I'm out of the loop, there will be no one piloting *Moonraker*."

Lucas paused, his eyes meeting Trouble's over his uncle's body, his hand hovering over the neural net connection.

"Are you piloting the ship, Captain?" Trouble asked.

"Not exactly. I'm piloting Cyber. I can have Cyber do ... whatever I please."

There was something in the tone of his voice that made Trouble's skin creep—the sense that Shade was already fighting his way out from under the effects of the staff. He traded glances with Morgan, then gave Lucas a brisk nod. The boy pulled the plug.

A shudder ran through the ship.

"I'll go to the bridge," said Morgan. "Take control manually."

"And then what? You can't manually pilot a ship through a wormhole. We've got to get Cyber back online."

"How?"

There was an empty cryo pod on Cyber's left. It had a standard neural helm with a set of non-intrusive surface sensors and a single hair-thin cortical probe. As much as the thought of having that thing inside his brain disturbed him, Trouble slid into the couch, grabbed the helm, and slipped it over his head.

Morgan loomed over him. "What the hell are you doing?"

"I told you. We need to get our pilot back online and I'm the best man for the job."

"Why? Why are you the best man for the job? You don't even know what that thing is going to do to you. Hell, you may not even know how to pilot a ship."

"Yeah, I do. It's one of my hidden talents. Help Lucas with Shade."

"You can't go into cryo—"

"I'm not going to." He smiled grimly. "Get out of my face, Madelen."

29 / GHOSTS

THE CRYO POD CONTROLS WERE AT THE END OF EACH ARMREST. A trained and augmented cybertech would use them to connect with his software and hardware. Trouble was not trained and had no clue about his augmentation except that he had enough to exert far more control over his mental and physical processes than the average human. Now was the time to put his mods to a real test.

He activated the helm and felt the icy sting of the cortical probe pricking the back of his neck just above the first vertebra, imagined he could feel it sliding up into his brain. He quashed his imagination viciously and concentrated on his breathing—deep, focused. He was an island made of rock—impenetrable, eternal. He had complete control over his body, his mind, every thought, every sensation. He was inside himself. Everything else was outside.

Beyond.

Inside, there was only Ridley Matthews and his connection to the ship.

He became aware of the *Moonraker* then, the simulated breathing of her life support systems, her fiber optic synapses, her virtual musculature, her steel bones, her alloy flesh. And within it, her brain—a living entity connected to her by the same neural net he now shared.

Trevor Marsden. Cyber.

Trouble could feel him, an amoebic collection of muddled thoughts and feelings. Frustration, regret, anger, fear. Trapped. He was trapped. Exiled to the neural network that guided the ship, caught like a rat in a maze. And everywhere he turned, a barrier.

Get a grip, Cyb.

Who ...? Trouble?

In the flesh ... sort of.

Lost. I'm lost in here.

Get un-lost. This tub needs you. The crew needs you.

How? I don't know how to get out.

You tell me.

I'm too weak. He scrambled my brain. Disconnected. Me. Disconnected me.

What's that mean? He disconnected you from the net?

No. He ... the sleep drug—Noctrafin. The shunt. Left arm. Deep. I'm too deep.

Trouble let his mind surface, emerge from the connection just enough to give him some control over his inert body.

"Morgan," he mumbled.

"Here."

He felt her leaning over him—smelled her perfume. No, Morgan didn't wear that perfume. Jani wore it. He bit the inside of his lip, tasted blood.

Focus.

"Cyber's left arm. A shunt. Shade jacked up his dose of Noctrafin. He's too far under."

He sensed her moving away. He was submerging again when she said, "Got it," her voice sounding as if he had dived into the waters of a lake.

How much fight have you got in you, Cyb?

Fight? No fight. Too tired.

We don't have time for tired. This ship needs a pilot. You're it.

No.

"I'm feeding him a little adrenaline," said Morgan's voice. "To counter the Noctrafin."

C'mon, Cyber-man. Count to ten. No, make it five. We don't have time for ten.

Okay, okay. Yeah. Right. I'm it. I'm Moonraker. I'm ... whoa, that's got some kick.

Cyber's voice was more animated. suddenly—less dense; Trouble assumed that the adrenaline infusion was having its effect.

Oh ... oh, man... Not good, not good, not good...

The ship yawed. Trouble wasn't sure how he knew this to be the case; an artificial gravity field kept everyone feeling as they were on *terra firma* even if the vessel was doing barrel rolls. Yet somehow he sensed that yaw.

You back with us? he asked Cyber.

Not ... Yeah. Oh, yeah.

Need you to get control of this thing. We're in deep shit and you're the only one who can pull us out. Do what I say. Got it?

Got it. Oh ... oh, wow, there are ghosts here. Did you know that? All the ships. All the crews. Everyone this bitch has swallowed.

He meant Pilgrim's Passage, of course. Now wasn't that just dandy? The ship was hallucinating.

So many of them ... Trouble? Are we ghosts?

Not yet. I guess that's up to you ... up to us.

Trouble swam back to the surface, smelling the faint odor of char and sweat, the crisp scent of machinery, the lingering tang of ozone ... Janina's perfume.

"Morgan, you got the Druud staff?"

"Got it."

"How much charge is left?"

"One, maybe two shots."

"Cyber? Can you hear me through comms?"

There was a silence during which Trouble tried not to feel the cortical probe as a presence in his body.

Cyber's voice came to them through the ship's audio systems. "I'm here. Still a little disorganized thought-wise, but here."

"Praise Brahman," Trouble muttered and disengaged the neural helm. The probe withdrew. The contacts that lay, icy, against his scalp warmed. He took the helmet off and slid out of the chair with vast relief, raking hair out of his eyes.

Druud staff in hand, he stood next to Cyber's pod. "Here's the plan—or at least *a* plan. Morgan and Lucas, go grab onto a workstation or something. Something metal. Cyber, when I say 'roll,' you dial down the inertial dampers and roll this ship—you got that?"

"Roll the ship?"

"Forty degrees port, then back."

"But—"

"Just do it, okay? No time to argue."

Cyber didn't hesitate. "You got it."

Trouble shoved the business end of the Druud staff up against the connection between Cyber's optic cables and the control panel. He braced himself against the plastic cowling of Cyber's pod, careful to touch nothing metal.

"Roll!"

The *Moonraker* yawed suddenly to port. Trouble felt the deck shift beneath him as the stabilizing power of the inertial dampers was momentarily reduced. He discharged the staff into the connection, saw the panel glow with golden light. When the ship rolled back to starboard, he discharged it again.

Morgan, clinging to a nearby data console, yelped as an amber aurora danced up her arms to engulf her. Lucas lost his grip on his own anchor and fell beneath one of the station chairs. He was bathed for a moment in Druud radiance, then looked up at Trouble with a beatific smile.

"Hey," he said, "that feels great!"

"You still seeing ghosts, Cyber-man?" Trouble asked.

"Not a one." Cyber's voice was calm, uncertainty gone. "Trouble, we need to get out of here. Even with the effects of the Druud energy, the stresses on my hull and systems are extreme."

"No shit."

"Language, Trouble. 'No shit' is hardly a loving way to address a comrade in arms. Now, if we're going to get out of the Pilgrim's Passage, someone needs to restart the Keplinger."

Which was a task Trouble already knew had to be done manually. "Can you cut the radiation leak?"

"Ah. The leak. Yes and no. Mostly no, I'm afraid. I can keep the radiation from leaking out of the drive core—there, taken care of. But I can't cut it off at the source. Whatever the captain did, it was sort of catastrophic. Someone has to go into Engineering and fix it."

Of course. It couldn't be easy. Trouble dropped the spent Druud staff and glanced over his shoulder at the lift. "Great. Okay, two things: First, Sanchez's telltale is in his office behind Hydroponics. He said it was on the console or in it—disguised as a data chip."

"I'll send snoops. What else?"

"Can you get the lift back online?"

"No sooner said than done."

The lift control panel lit, the doors slid shut momentarily, then opened again as the car arrived at Epsilon.

Trouble turned to Morgan and Lucas. "Go find Doc Pike. He's short an infirmary and is about to have a lot of patients. Find him someplace to set up shop. Retreat, maybe." He handed the slap gun to Morgan. "You might need this."

"Where are you going?" she asked.

"Engineering." He turned on his heel and headed for the lift. "I'm going to give this ship a good kick in the ass," he added as the lift doors closed.

30 / DEAD MEN

WITH THE GRAVITY BACK ONLINE, TROUBLE MADE ALL SPEED TO Engineering, literally sprinting the length of the ship. He encountered a few of the crew, now engaged in helping their less fortunate fellows—those who had not been thrown into contact with metallic objects when Trouble had discharged the Druud staff and those who had run head on into the surreal effects of the Pilgrim's Passage.

Trouble ignored all pleas for assistance, just as he ignored Jani, just as he ignored Pocket Watch, just as he ignored the Dead Man, who had not left his side since he'd stepped out of the lift on Beta. He seemed to stand in every intersection of every cross-corridor, bleeding silently. Trouble still had no idea who he was —he just knew he was *supposed* to know.

He had purposefully kept himself from lapping up the Druud energy; he was afraid it would distort his judgment, make him more susceptible to the plight of the crew and to the hollow eyes of his personal psyquams, whom he suspected would be with him whether he could see them or not. They weren't in the atmosphere; they were in his head, and he suspected his future—if he had one—would involve letting them fully in so he could get them out again.

Rusk's mangled body was not where he had left it. Between

the changes in gravity and the rolling of the ship, the two sections of the corpse had been levitated and flung about, coming to rest separately in the transverse corridor. Trouble barely gave them a glance as he passed through into Engineering.

Jiang wasn't where he'd left her either, but the smeared hand prints and speckles of blood between the inner and outer hatches told him she had left under her own power.

Peering through the flexiglass into the drive chamber, Trouble saw immediately why the drive was offline. One of the drive rods had come loose from its collar at the top and was leaning at a crazy angle, held only by the bottom collar. If it slipped that restraint, it would fall, destroying itself and taking out its nearest neighbor to the bargain.

There was no time for a rad suit and no need. His dose of Lerandia serum should be effective for at least an hour of exposure. That gave him roughly half an hour before he was in any danger from the effects of the displaced rod. He expected to be long out of harm's way in ten minutes at most.

A sudden shiver ran through the hull of the ship, reminding him how close they were to utter destruction. If the *Raker* came into even the most fleeting contact with the exotic matter lining the Pilgrim's Passage, it could conceivably result in a chain reaction that might rip her very atoms apart.

Trouble slipped into the drive chamber, glancing at the control console. The levers were in the ON position—if he rotated the rod back into its collar with the drives engaged, the power build up could blow the whole rod array. He moved swiftly to the console and brought the levers back to idle, then turned to make the climb to the drive gallery, glancing up as he did. Behind the softly glowing rods, something moved in the shadowed recesses of the gallery.

Trouble froze. Jiang? But the trail she'd left led *out* of Engineering.

He slipped into the stairwell, his hand going to his belt.

Without the slap gun he'd given to Morgan, all he had was his shiv and the laser cutter, which was worse than useless in here. He unclipped it anyway, disengaged the power source, and grasped it by the barrel. Made of metal and all angles, it should make a decent cudgel.

He stepped out onto the gallery on the side across from where he'd seen the movement, and opposite the loose rod. He began a silent passage around the outer railing, his eyes on the shadows on the other side of the core. The lights were still at about fifty percent.

He paused by a comms panel, put his lips close to it and murmured, "Cyber, your channels still open?"

"Yeah. What's the situation?"

"I'm on the drive gallery. One of the rods is loose. And there's someone up here."

There was a moment of silence, then Cyber said, "No. No, there's not. I've got snoops all over the place. I don't see anyone."

"Then your lenses are fogged, mate. Because someone is up here."

"If you say so."

"Can you zero the lights in here?"

In answer, the lights went out completely, leaving the drive core in darkness relieved only by the ambient glow of instrument panels and the idling drive rods. To Trouble's augmented eyes it was almost as bright as day. He started toward the drive array, and almost immediately saw movement near the displaced rod. He paused.

"Hey, come on out where I can see you." He made his tone casual, even friendly.

No answer. He quickened his pace and had gone halfway around the gallery when a figure appeared at the railing, framed in the inverted triangle between two of the rods.

It was Rusk.

For the briefest moment, Trouble questioned his senses and

his sanity, but almost immediately realized it had to be Rusk's psyquam, since the real Rusk was in two pieces. Both pieces very, very dead.

Oddly, Trouble did not find that thought reassuring. His experience with Janina's psyquam had convinced him of their power to deke the senses. He'd seen the lacerations and bruises on Glass's body in Medbay; he'd seen a crewman eaten by decking. He knew that, in some cases, what you thought you were only imagining was real and could kill you.

Trouble was more than capable of controlling his thoughts, his feelings, even his physiological reactions; he had known the Jani that thrust herself into his path wasn't real. Yet, neither of those things stopped him from seeing her, feeling her, smelling her scent ... loving her.

He shook himself. *No more of that.*

He circled the gallery, shiv in one hand, makeshift laser club in the other, wondering if either weapon would do him a damn bit of good. Just because the psyquams could *feel* solid when they wanted to (or when he *expected* them to), it didn't mean they would behave as if solid if he whacked one.

He kept his eyes on the Rusk psyquam, which stood grinning at him as he approached, as if it could see as well in the dark as he could.

As if.

He cursed himself for the lapse in logic. It couldn't see a damn thing. It wasn't real. It was a mental construct. *His* mental construct. A phantom dredged out of his half-blind emotions. Which meant he should be able to predict it, control it, defeat it.

As if in response to these thoughts, the psyquam's grin deepened and it reached up to grasp the skewed drive rod and give it a twist. The rod moved ... or seemed to. Trouble wasn't sure which. He decided to believe it hadn't budged an inch.

He rounded the curve of the gallery and stopped dead in his tracks. The psyquam wasn't Rusk—it was *half* of Rusk. The mate's upper torso, arms, and head floated in mid-air as if gravity had not been restored. The lower half was missing.

What the hell.

Before he could recalibrate, something struck Trouble viciously behind the knees, sweeping his legs out from under him. He hit the deck hard, and found himself looking up at a pair of legs and a torso that ended at the waist. Rolling to his knees, he lashed out at the psyquam's legs with the laser cutter. It met resistance, then passed through.

Damn.

Trouble flipped himself into a backward somersault. He landed on his feet, facing the bizarre half-phantom. He could see the interior of the truncated torso. There were no exposed viscera, just a solid, gunmetal gray nothing. It reminded him of an ancient flat-vid cartoon he'd seen once, in which the villain had been cut in half lengthwise, leaving the two halves to hop around on one leg until they could rejoin. The villain's interior had been that same fuzzy shade of gray.

If I start laughing, I'll never stop.

Trouble sensed movement behind him, knew the upper half was attacking, and dove for the gallery rail. He grasped it and turned the dive into a one-armed handstand, his mind working. The psyquam's legs had felt solid for an instant, then had not. Why? Because he'd lost focus?

He whipped his body into the air again, attempting to put himself between Rusk and the displaced rod. He'd no more than landed when the psyquam came at him. He grasped the switch laser's barrel with both hands and swung it at the psyquam's head. He willed it to meet solid muscle and bone, willed the phantom to be stopped. It did stop, rearing back and bobbing in the air like a grisly balloon.

Trouble unsheathed his shiv and thrust it into the phantom's torso. Solid. The psyquam shuddered, the knife sticking grotesquely out of its chest. But there was no blood.

Because I didn't expect any. I sabotaged myself.

The half-Rusk grinned, pulled the shiv from its side, and plunged it into Trouble's ribs, right where the shrapnel from Medbay had caught him. Pain—hot and searing—shot up and down his side like flash fire. He grasped the psyquam's hand where it covered the knife's hilt, but after a moment of resistance, his fingers went right through the phantom flesh and bone to the knife. He yanked it out.

There was more pain, if not as much as he'd expected. There was definitely blood.

No time, he told himself. No damned time to play cat and mouse with this hellish cartoon character. He gathered himself with a will, then executed another backward vault, flipping himself up and over. He landed just short of the gallery rail. Glancing over one shoulder, he saw the disconnected end of the rod; it would be just reachable from the rail. In front of him, the two pieces of Rusk had rejoined and started toward him.

"You. Are. Not. *Real!*" Trouble snarled, putting the full force of his will behind the words.

The Rusk psyquam stopped.

Trouble spun toward the rail and found himself face to almost familiar face with the Dead Man. Were they tag-teaming him now?

"You screwed up, Trouble," the Dead Man informed him. "You got me killed."

"Y'know, I really don't have time for this."

Trouble stepped through the Dead Man, vaulted to the gallery rail, and moved along it to the loose rod. Taking it in both hands, he twisted it into its socket. The rod slid in, but refused to lock into place. He was off balance, trying to keep his eyes on the two psyquams. He needed to turn his back on them, when instinct told him that would be stupid.

Instinct was going to screw him.

He forced himself to turn his back just long enough to lock the rod into place. Then he did an about-face. Through the glow of the rods, he could see not just two, but three psyquams moving toward him: Rusk, the Dead Man … and Sanchez.

Where had he come from, Trouble wondered, then understood. He'd had a stray thought for the efficacy of the serum, he realized, and its creator had appeared. You couldn't afford stray thoughts in the Pilgrim's Passage. And you couldn't afford to feel you were even tangentially responsible for someone's death. It stood to reason that if Sanchez was here, he must've perished in the Medbay fire.

Trouble danced backwards on the railing beyond the reseated rod. The psyquams kept coming. He glanced back over his shoulder at the lower deck. He'd survive a controlled fall that distance. But would he be in any condition to get to the drive controls?

"Cyber, you with me?" he murmured.

"At your service."

"Two things: One—cut gravity to seventy percent."

"Now?"

"Now."

He felt suddenly lighter.

"And the other thing?"

"Ninety degree turn to port on my mark."

"No can turn. The *Devi* is coming right at us and I'm not under power."

"You will be."

"Great. Anything else?"

Trouble glanced at the phantoms. No time to deal with them.

"That'll have to do," he said.

He dove off the gallery rail, down between the splayed drive rods, rotating once in the lighter gravity. He landed feet first, grunting in pain, then tucked, rolled and leapt for the drive console. He found Rusk suddenly and unexpectedly in his way.

Trouble had the momentary impression of Sanchez standing inside the Rusk psyquam, and within him, the Dead Man. He knew that even this was some manifestation of his own thought.

He stared through the melded psyquam at the drive levers, and shut down all thought, all sense. He saw nothing but those levers, heard nothing but the breathing of life support. In all the universe there was nothing but Ridley "Trouble" Matthews and those levers.

Trouble reached through the psyquams, grasped the levers and thrust them forward.

"Mark!"

The drive engaged, the *Raker* went superluminal, the psyquams winked out like smothered flames, and the proximity alarms screamed to life. They cut off seconds later, leaving a throbbing silence behind. There was no sudden vertigo to indicate that Cyber had executed the crash turn, but Trouble heard the hull groan and vibrate under the strain.

"Eeeeeeeeeeee-haw!" Cyber shrieked through the comms. "Damn you, Trouble, you crazy son of a bitch! We are freakin' out of there! Out, out, *out!*"

Out.

They were out of the Pilgrim's Passage.

Trouble sat on the floor of the drive chamber, feeling curiously light-headed and reflecting that 'out' was a good word. Possibly his favorite word, at least for the moment. There was no time for rest, however; his time of grace afforded by the serum was almost up.

As he rose to make his way forward again, the drive rod he'd just reseated split lengthwise with a sound like breaking ice. A second later it exploded into powder, raining tiny crystal pellets onto the deck and spraying the chamber with radiation. A second after that, the Keplinger made an emergency shut-down.

Moonraker was dead in space.

31 / HELL

"WE'RE LOOKING AT ABOUT A FIVE HOUR JOB," SAID MORGAN, "JUST
to get Engineering cleaned up and replace that shattered rod.
Normally, it wouldn't take so long, but the explosion warped the
collar pretty badly. The subluminal drive is damaged too, so we
can't even limp off into the sunset."

Sitting in the command chair, Morgan was unusually
subdued. So was Lucas. It probably had a lot to do with their
finding Blackwood lying on the command deck when they
entered, barely alive. The Bridge still smelled of burnt flesh.
There had not been the faintest trace of residual heat anywhere
in the vicinity, and for the amphibian to have been fried the way
he had, the temperature would have had to have been impos-
sibly high—every metallic surface would have been glowing
cherry-red. Nevertheless, the infrared readings had been well
within normal limits.

Cyber had pronounced what had happened impossible.

Tell that to Jay Blackwood, Trouble thought.

Or to Rainor Glass, who'd been electrocuted and crushed by
a one-gee fall down the shaft on top of that. Or Kai Jiang.
Concussed and inexplicably burned almost as badly as Blackwood, she lay next to him in one of three bio-beds Pike had

salvaged from Medbay and installed in the Retreat. Or tell any crew who had collided head on with the Passage's bizarre manifestations. All in all, the Passage had killed four, injured five, and left even more people in fetal positions sucking their thumbs.

Life in a wormhole bore a striking resemblance to the Medieval human's idea of Hell.

That left running the ship to a skeleton crew: Cyber, Morgan, Lucas, Doc Pike, Trouble, and crewman Redfield, who'd saved himself from the worst of what the Passage had to offer by locking himself into a cubicle at the Retreat with a flask of honey brandy. This had Pike muttering about endorphins and making copious notes on his datapad.

Trouble was of the opinion that Lucas and Morgan were in such good shape because they'd been focused on saving the ship. And they'd damn well better *stay* focused or they could still tank. It would be only too easy for everyone to let down now—to give into the sense that, having escaped Pilgrim's Passage, the worst was over.

The worst was probably riding their wake right this minute.

"Somehow I doubt we've got five hours," Trouble replied to Morgan's assessment. "We've already been sitting here for nearly two. We could've painted a bull's-eye on the side of the ship in that amount of time."

"Yeah," Cyber said from comms. "We almost plowed into the *Devi* on our way out of the Passage. There's a slim chance Chowdury could calculate approximately where we exited."

"How slim?" Trouble asked.

"Astronomically slim, actually. Especially now that he no longer has Sanchez's telltale."

"But not impossible."

"Well ... not if he was tracking us in the first place. Which he probably was. Not if he had a sensor lock on us at the moment we exited the wormhole. Which he probably... Okay, maybe not so astronomically slim. I guess we have to hope the Passage did as much damage to his ship and crew as it did to ours."

Trouble looked around the bridge at the other two members of the ad hoc command group and asked, "What's the status of the weapons?"

Morgan answered. "Vishnu pretty much kicked the crap out of them. They're completely unresponsive from the bridge stations."

"They're completely unresponsive, period," said Cyber.

"Can they be fixed?"

"I was coming to that," Morgan said. "As far as I can tell, if we have to fight any more battles, we're screwed. The crew is so messed up I doubt if we could repel another boarding party."

Trouble didn't remind her that he had repelled the last one pretty much single-handedly. Even so, an extended hand-to-hand battle wouldn't be his first choice. Chowdury could be counted on to send more boarders this time and maybe not care if they punched holes in *Moonraker*'s hull and instrumentation. That is, if he had anyone of able body and sane mind left to send. Sure, they could hope and pray that everyone aboard the *Devi* was mad as a Hatter, but that wasn't a plan.

"What about the ion thrusters?"

"Starboard's working," Cyber reported. "Port, as you may recall, is clogged. Besides, those are for quick starts and maneuvers, not sustained travel. But I've got sensors and external cameras working again. If Chowdury does find us, we'll have a heads up."

"Peachy," said Morgan. "Then I'll have time to comb my hair and put on a fresh uni."

Trouble ignored the gloomy sarcasm. "Morgan, why don't you and I see what we can do about the weapons systems. Lucas, find somebody—anybody—who might know how to at least get sublight back on line."

"Aye, sir." The kid nodded and left the bridge.

Trouble had just popped the top off a weapons panel so Morgan could dig into its guts when Cyber said, "Uh-oh," in a tone that made both Trouble and Morgan look up at the view screen.

The *Agni Devi* had leapt into being off their bow and was coming at them dead on. The proximity alert blared, making everyone cringe.

"Distance!" Trouble shouted over the din. "And dammit, Cyber, turn that thing off!"

"Five thousand kilometers," Cyber said, loudly. "And can't right now."

Morgan let out a frustrated yowl. "This panel's fused! We're not going to get weapons restored in time!"

Trouble moved to stand by the empty command chair, where he could see the forward and aft screens. "Cy-man, can you fire the starboard thruster?"

"Yeah, but if I do, we'll just go around in a circle."

"Fire it!"

"Huh?"

"So he has to come up astern! Bring us around!"

Cyber's reaction was instantaneous; the ship started to come about.

Morgan scrambled to Trouble's side, watching the view screen adjust to keep the *Devi* in sight. "What are you thinking?" she yelled over the siren's blast.

"Who can think with that—!" Trouble pulled his slap gun out of his belt, turned and fired it at the bridge klaxon mounted over the lift. The speaker grille crumpled and the siren muted to a disconsolate wail. He fired again and it cut off.

"I'm thinking," Trouble said, into the resulting silence, "that the hunk of slag we got stuck in the port thruster is as good as a torpedo at close range."

"Damn," said Cyber, admiration in his voice. "How do you come up with this stuff?"

"I think I'm used to strategizing ... and improvising." Hell, his whole life was an improvisation at the moment. "But I'm no good at math or spatial dynamics, so you'll have to figure out when to fire."

"How stuck is it?" Cyber asked.

"Glass and I had it almost free when you went into hyperdrive. I figure maybe we had about five more minutes cutting."

"We didn't have five minutes then," Cyber recalled, "and I'm not sure we have them now. Okay, a sustained burn is at least as good as a couple of laser cutters. It'll take the *Devi* about six minutes to reach us at her current speed."

"She'll have to decelerate to come alongside and grapple us," Morgan reminded him.

"That's the variable," said Cyber. "We've got no way of knowing her braking rate. We may have mere seconds to play with; we may have minutes."

"Even I can do that math," Trouble said. "You better start firing now. See if you can loosen it up."

"Aye-aye, sir," Cyber said. There was no irony at all in his voice.

Trouble watched the readout bars on the *Raker*'s ion propulsion level. The glowing orange bar representing the port thruster should be growing. It wasn't.

"Cyber?"

"It's not firing."

"I can see that." Trouble's eyes were on the view screen in which the *Devi* grew steadily larger. "Can you fix the circuits?"

There was silence.

"Can't hear your head rattle, Cyb."

"It's not in the circuitry, Trouble. The circuitry is fine. It's just not obeying the firing sequence."

"Which means?" asked Morgan.

"Which means it might be some residual causality effect from the Pilgrim's Passage—in which case we're all screwed—or it's mechanical—in which case we may be only half-screwed. That's probably it. There's something wrong with the engine itself—

something severed, maybe. It'll have to be repaired manually, which means someone'll have to go down there."

"This day just gets better and better," Trouble muttered, and turned toward the lift.

Trouble had lost track of how many times he'd sprinted the length of this misbegotten scow in the past seven or eight hours. He'd lost track of time, period: the day, the hour, the minute. Time was measured in heartbeats now. So many heartbeats to go here, to do that; so many heartbeats to wait and see if the result was survival or destruction.

When this was over—if he was still alive—he was going to sleep. For days. Maybe he'd have them put him in one of those cryo pods and not wake him until they found someplace they could strand him safely. Some out-of-the-spacelanes mining or religious colony. If they survived this, he figured they'd owe him that much.

He reached the aft lift and slowed, opening his mouth to hail Cyber. The lift doors opened before he could utter a sound. He didn't even have to break stride to enter.

"Where's old Vishnu now?" he asked.

"About five hundred kilometers off our port stern."

"What if he tries to board from starboard?"

"I'll fire the starboard thruster again and move us out of reach, as many times as it takes for him to give up and go to port just to keep us from juking out of his way."

Cyber opened the lift doors onto the aft corridor of Epsilon Deck. Trouble stepped across the threshold into a transverse hallway that was a mirror image of the one on Gamma. There was a hatch directly in front of him.

"Go through the hatch," Cyber told him. "You'll find yourself on a catwalk above Hydroponics."

Trouble did, and was immediately bathed in the miserable stench of the Lerandia grove.

"Who designed this boat? Is this the usual way you get to the thruster engines?"

"No, but it's the most direct. Besides, the Lerandia expansion up onto Epsilon is a kludge."

Trouble moved out onto the catwalk, listening to Cyber's running instructions. Below, he could hear the drip and gurgle of the nutrient bath.

"About halfway along the walk there are a pair of ladders."

"I'm there."

The ladders canted at a forty-five degree angle away from the catwalk, forming a wide 'V' above the Hydroponics bay. Each ladder ended at a round hatch just below the chamber ceiling.

"Take the port ladder. It connects to the thruster access tunnel."

Trouble was already a quarter of the way up the ladder. "Are you about to tell me I gotta climb into the thruster?"

"Ah ... not exactly. Worst case, you'll have to get into the thruster interconnect. I'm hoping it won't come to that. First, you'll need to check the firing circuitry on the outside of the tube. The optics might have gotten disconnected from the firing mechanism. At least that's what I'm hoping."

"Then I just reconnect it?"

"Maybe. The *Devi* is braking. She's about two hundred klicks to port. You want me to dance around a little bit to buy some time?"

"Not unless you have to. There's actually a benefit to looking like we're dead in space—it will make Chowdury less inclined to cripple us further."

"I could let him come alongside and then ram him."

"Good idea. Blow us all up. Don't know about you, but I was hoping to avoid that."

Trouble reached the hatch; Cyber had already opened it. A short, perfectly round tunnel angled away toward the outer hull.

"*Devi* closing at one hundred kilometers," Cyber said, and the tube seemed to double in length.

Trouble moved up it swiftly. One hundred kilometers could be covered easily in less than two minutes, even if Vishnu wasn't in a hurry.

"What's the optimum firing distance?"

"Between one and three kilometers. That gives us the best shot at hitting the target with enough force to do significant damage ... if we get lucky."

Trouble had reached the top of the tube and climbed out into a cramped maintenance landing. The inner wall of the chamber curved outward, echoing the cylindrical shape of the thruster tube.

"I'm here."

"I see you. Look aft. The control panel is mounted on the port bulkhead."

The control panel was dome-shaped with a sprinkling of yellow lights ... and one blue one that appeared to be moving.

"Damn!" said Cyber. "They're all yellow."

"What about this blue one?"

"That's me." The tiny cam bot waggled its light at him.

"So, they're all yellow. What's that mean?"

"It means power is getting through to the firing mechanism, so the problem is mechanical. You'll have to go into the interconnect. The access is on the aft bulkhead."

Trouble turned to the last barrier between him and the thruster tube—a small, circular iris barely large enough to admit a man of his size. It opened without his intervention, letting him into a wedge-shaped chamber. The curving inner wall was a tangle of tubes and fiber optic cables. Falling from a port in the ceiling, they connected with the coolant jacket that protected the *Moonraker* from the intense heat of the thruster's firing.

The bulkhead had clearly sustained damage from the *Devi's* attack. It was rippled—almost pleated—and a cluster of red lights, like glowing droplets of blood, announced that a major system was in crisis.

Trouble leaned in to look at the data panel. "Coolant. The damn thing's not getting coolant."

"Then it won't fire."

"So override the fail-safes."

"It would superheat to critical in a matter of seconds and go 'ka-boom.' We were trying to avoid that, you may recall ... seventy-two kilometers. *Devi* ETA two minutes."

Trouble made a quick survey of the hanging tubes and saw nothing obviously out of place. Frustrated, he ran his hands down each of the coolant lines, looking for a break, a kink, anything that would keep the coolant from flowing into the buffer jacket between the inner and outer walls of the thruster. His questing hands found the disconnected ends of several major feeder lines that had been torn completely free and now hung tangled among their fellows.

"Twenty kilometers," said Cyber. "ETA one minute and—"

"Do me a favor, Cyb," Trouble said amiably. "Shut up."

He grabbed the first tube that came to hand. It had a metal collar that clamped into a receptacle on the curving bulkhead. He reconnected it. The second had a collar that was slightly warped, but he was still able to get it to seat. The third had ripped from its receptacle with such force that it had left its collar behind.

"What happens if one of these coolant tubes can't be reconnected?"

"You get coolant in the interconnect chamber."

Trouble reconnected the fourth tube. "Then we have coolant in the interconnect. No big deal, right? Can you override the controls here and get the coolant flowing?"

"I could—but I can't."

"We don't have time for riddles, mate."

"It's not a riddle. If the interconnect floods with coolant, it will eat through the fiber optics, not to mention all of the soft fittings. The system will shut down anyway. Catastrophically, I might add. What's the problem?"

"You got snoops in here?"

"I do now."

Trouble turned and saw a blue light winking at him from near the hatch. He held up the collarless line. "Looks like I'll just have to hold it in place."

"Well, there's a problem with that, Trouble. I need to fire that thruster in the next thirty seconds. But there won't be enough coolant in the jacket by then to keep the outer bulkhead from heating up. A lot. It's going to get damned hot down there."

"Figures." Trouble shoved the broken end of the coolant line into the thruster mechanism, tilting it so that the coolant would flow downward into the jacket. He wrapped both hands around it. "It's in."

"Hit the reset switch. Next to the coolant monitor."

"You can't do it?"

"Sorry. A little short on physical things like fingers right now."

Holding the coolant line with one hand, Trouble reset the system and watched as coolant began to flow. "Whoever designed this scow should be spaced."

"I think he was. And the *Raker* wasn't so much designed as patched together. This system was added about two years ago when the original one failed."

Trouble glanced around the crowded, dingy chamber. It kicked a memory out of hiding—a cell. A tiny, cold, gray cell in a prison. He remembered thinking it was a wretched place to die. This wasn't much better, but at least he felt useful.

"Fire at will, Cyber-man."

"Trouble, I'm not kidding. It's going to get hotter than hell in there."

"I think I've been to hell. Who knows, maybe I've even been augmented for hell."

"Trouble, there aren't any mods for exposure to that extreme temperature."

Trouble ignored him. "You've got about ten seconds, I figure."

"Mad Morgan is going to think I did this on purpose just to get rid of you."

"*Are* you doing it to get rid of me?"

"Pretty sure I'm not."

"Good, because I kind of thought we were becoming friends. Fire it up, Cyb."

"Trouble? Cyber?" Morgan's voice broke into their conversation, sharp with panic. "He's practically on top of us! When are you going to fire?"

"Now," said Cyber. And did.

Even on the bridge, Morgan could feel the unnatural vibration of the ship as the thruster's burst of raw, irresistible power met the immovable object jammed in its maw. She gripped the arms of the command chair and stared at the view screen where the *Agni Devi*, battered but whole, bore down on their port flank. Seated in front of her at the useless helm, Lucas threw her a look that was half determination, half raw terror.

The screen flickered momentarily, then the view split between the *Devi's* approach and a dimly lit cranny where Trouble knelt amid a mare's nest of cable and coolant lines. His skin was glossy with sweat, his hair was matted to his head, and his eyes were closed. Above his head, where the curving outer wall of the chamber met the ceiling, the metal glowed dull red.

Lucas gasped aloud and Morgan murmured, "Oh, my God!" She swallowed convulsively. "Cyber, what the hell's going on! What's he doing?"

"Saving our collective asses. It's over two hundred degrees in there and, it'll get worse before it gets better."

"You've got to do something!" Morgan tried not to let panic control her, but she was helpless on the bridge, an entire ship's length away from where a man was being slowly cooked—a man whom, she was coming to realize, she cared about a great deal. "There's got to be some—some sort of emergency fire system down there, right? Something that's supposed to kick in if the interconnect chamber gets too hot or—or there's a fire in the hold?"

"Jammed," said Cyber. "I checked."

Morgan swore a series of oaths that scorched the air. "He's not going to die!"

She stroked and tapped the controls on one arm of the command chair. A schematic of the aft section blossomed up in holo before her. She isolated the support systems network, rotated it, studied it—

"There!" She pointed. "The nutrient system grid. If you reroute the flow here, and blow this hatch—"

"The layout's wrong," argued Cyber. "Water won't flow uphill."

"Isolate and reverse the grav field!"

Cyber's voice was hesitant. "If I do this, the Lerandia will be short on nutrients. Some of it—maybe all of it—will die. The captain won't—"

Morgan slammed a fist onto the arm rest, making Lucas jump. "*You're* the captain, dammit! Do it—or I will come down to the computer core and flatline you with my bare hands."

Cyber didn't reply. Morgan watched the readouts tensely— then relaxed as she saw the warning flash that indicated the hatch had been blown. More warning lights fired on several consoles. She looked at the screen monitoring Trouble in the interconnect chamber, and saw the nutrient liquid beginning to rain down on him. It probably smelled worse than a dead hell-hound at high noon, but it might cool the chamber down enough for Trouble to survive ... or it might simply boil him to death.

Morgan felt limp with relief as she watched. In a matter of seconds steam billowed up, obscuring her view. The last she saw of Trouble, he was gazing balefully up at the cam bot, but the corners of his mouth were twitching.

Morgan turned her gaze to the *Devi*, a little over five kilometers away now, her grappling ports open, her weapons trained on the crippled *Moonraker*. She thought her heart would burst, it was beating so fast and hard. Her chest muscles felt like clamps, squeezing it. She made herself breathe. In, out. In, out. She wanted to take her eyes from the view screen, but couldn't. Lucas seemed to be similarly transfixed.

Two kilometers now. It seemed to Morgan that she could count the leaves on the golden tree that decorated the other ship's starboard bow.

"Five ... " murmured Cyber. "Four ... three ... two ... one."

They only heard a dull thud on the bridge when he hit zero, but the ejection of the slag core from the *Raker*'s port thruster sent a jolt through the ship that nearly threw Morgan from the command chair. The chunk of metal shot from the *Raker*'s torn thruster port, riding a boiling river of plasma that arced across the dwindling space between the two ships.

Vishnu Chowdury never had a chance of evading it. He may have never even seen it coming. What was, to all intents and purposes, a metal meteor slammed into the pirate's bridge, opening it to space with the ease of a master chef filleting a fish. Even though sound couldn't carry across vacuum, it seemed to Morgan that she could hear the horrendous screech of metal against metal and the screams of the dying crew as they were blown into infinity.

The *Raker*'s stern swung up and to starboard. Cyber compensated by firing the starboard thruster. The *Raker* shot away from her nemesis, leaving the pirate in her fiery wake.

Morgan watched the view aft, as explosions wracked the

other ship, rippling from stem to stern like a series of festival fireworks. When at last the pyrotechnics dwindled to a fitful spattering of quickly smothered sparks, Vishnu Chowdury's fire goddess was little more than a tangle of blackened, twisted metal, still spewing debris into the vacuum.

Morgan's fingers had locked painfully around the padded arms of Erasmus Shade's command chair. She loosened them and rose, her eyes on the view screen.

"Trouble," she said numbly and headed for the lift with Lucas on her heels.

32 / CAPTAIN SHADE

LUCAS SHADE STOOD IN THE STINKING HYDROPONICS BAY FOR WHAT he hoped was the very last time, inspecting one of the mutagenic devices which crewman Redfield was holding up out of the wretched swamp. They called them Sanchez Boxes now. After all, saboteur or no, the man deserved some credit for inventing them.

Hands dripping with smelly ooze, the crewman eyed Lucas cautiously, almost nervously. Lucas savored that faint glow of trepidation coming from Redfield, but only momentarily. He shook the feeling off.

That way be dragons.

He'd read that somewhere, and wasn't quite sure what it meant, but it had never sounded more true.

"They seem to be functioning," said Redfield. "At least, they're doing what they're programmed to do. Are you sure that's what we want?"

"Positive," Lucas said, and allowed himself to savor this new sense of confidence with no guilt whatsoever. "These plants are going to give all of us a super nice payday."

Redfield nodded and slipped the Sanchez Box back into the nutrient tank. "Um, Lucas ... about what happened. With Hackett and all. I ... ah ..."

Lucas turned back to stare at the man. Holy shit, was he trying to apologize? With the exception of Cyber expressing regret for not being able to salvage Erasmus Shade's over-whelmed mind after their escape from the Pilgrim's Passage, no one had ever apologized to Lucas. Hell, he didn't even know if he would accept an apology from Redfield or Duff—or anyone else who'd caused him so much misery over the past few months.

The comms pinged just then, interrupting the awkward moment.

"Lucas," Cyber said, his voice subdued, "you've got an incoming hyperwave from Guild HQ. It's your father."

His father! Lucas felt the familiar rush of blood from his head, the sudden iciness of his extremities, the overwhelming desire to run and hide.

He didn't run and hide; he took a deep breath, glancing at Redfield, whose eyes still watched him with that glitter of uncer-tainty—and, possibly, of fear. He straightened his spine and got his legs moving.

"I'll take it in the Hydroponics break room."

He sat at the computer terminal in the break room, gathering his thoughts, back ramrod straight, stomach quivering.

I survived a beating. I helped stop pirates. I helped Trouble take back the ship from Uncle Erasmus. I can sure as hell talk to my own father.

He touched the keypad, opening the terminal to the incoming signal. His father's handsome face appeared in trivee, seeming to project outward from the screen. His brows were knit, his jaw flexed.

"Father," said Lucas, pleased that his voice neither quivered nor broke. "You ... look well."

Julian Shade did not acknowledge the compliment. "I read the report. I'm not clear; is your uncle Erasmus dead?"

"No. But he's ... not all here, either. I think the Pilgrim's Passage messed him up pretty badly. He sleeps, mostly, and doesn't make much sense when he's awake."

If Julian felt any regret for his brother's state, he showed no trace of it. "So, then—by Guild law and right of primogeniture, the ship will be yours when you come of age."

His father's tone and expression were neutral—the same neutrality Lucas had experienced most of his life. Except for the cold rage and icy contempt that was worse than physical brutality.

"Right now, however—"

"First Mate Marsden—Cyber—is in command right now. The crew elected him before we ..."

"Before your uncle made the disastrous decision to take the *Moonraker* into the Pilgrim's Passage."

"It was the only thing he could have done. Vishnu had us outgunned six ways from Sabbath and we'd taken a lot of damage."

"Cyber ..." his father interrupted in a musing tone. "Isn't that the stim addict net-head your uncle snatched last year? Hardly a sterling choice for second-in-command. I'd expect you to—"

"He's not a stim addict," Lucas interrupted.

His father raised an eyebrow, and Lucas recalled that there had been a time when even that subtle expression would have sent him into panicked hyperventilation. Part of his mind—the part that sat up in the bleachers and watched his life—was frankly surprised that he wasn't hyperventilating now. Was it because he was separated from his father's physical presence by several lightyears?

No. There was more to it than that. In fact, though he wasn't sure how or why, he somehow knew that his father would never have that effect on him again.

"Cyber piloted this ship better than anyone I've ever seen. We'd have all died three times over if it wasn't for him."

Julian Shade regarded his son. "Your loyalty to your crew is ... commendable."

"My loyalty to this crew is necessary," Lucas told him. "If

you don't have loyalty, you have chaos. I learned that from Uncle Erasmus."

His father's eyebrow again rose quizzically. "And where did you learn to be a smart ass?"

Again, the faint amazement that he wasn't cowed. "That I learned from Trouble."

"Who? Oh, yes, in the report. Ridley Matthews—the crewman who led the takeover. Conscripted on Herron's Hope. I'm surprised a crewman who so recently came aboard by force would be trusted with command decisions."

"You'd have to meet Trouble to understand. He just ... has a way of taking command. I don't think you'd like him. Look, Father, we've got a lot of work to do. The *Raker's* pretty shot up. I've got to help Doc Pike get the infirmary back together."

Shade glanced down and to one side as if he were consulting a second monitor. "I'll send you some supplies and reinforcements. If you give me your coordinates, I can have the *Quantum Rose* there in—"

"No thanks. We're fine. We can do this ourselves."

For once he had his father's full attention. "What did you say?"

"I said, thanks, but no." He was feeling almost giddy now. "We don't need your help. Don't send anybody."

Julian Shade sat back in his chair, his expression unreadable. "Really?"

"Really. So, if you don't have anything further to tell me, I'll get back to work." Lucas rose.

"Certainly—Captain Shade."

Lucas froze. There was no trace of irony in his father's voice. "What did you call me?"

"You seem to already be in command in the hearts and minds of your crew. Therefore, as owner of the *Moonraker*, I'm making it official." His father moved as if to end the transmission, then stopped. "One last thing, though, that might be of benefit to you." He glanced aside again. "I just got some interesting information about your Mr. Matthews."

He was burning, but he couldn't remember why. He recalled having told someone that he'd been in hell before. Maybe that's where he was again.

I don't believe in hell.

He seemed very certain of that, but if there was a hell, it wasn't supposed to be humid. If not hell, might he be in a jungle? Had he been dumped back on Herron's Hope? But no jungle heat could be this searing. And not even a jungle smelled this strongly of citrus.

Why would they have dumped him in a jungle?

They who?

In answer, his life aboard *Moonraker* tumbled through his mind in a chaotic roil. Erasmus Shade and his young nephew, Rusk, Cyber, the stalking pirate ship, the dive into the Pilgrim's Passage, Sanchez and his stinking plants, and…

Morgan.

His mind stuck there, as if he'd hit a mental reef, on a vivid memory of Morgan and a shower cubicle. Shower cubicles were hot and humid. Maybe that's where he was now. But that didn't explain why he felt as if his skin had been boiled off. Not to mention why he didn't have any immediate memories of hot, steamy sex.

He took a deep breath, his throat feeling as if he'd swallowed a sandstorm. Oh, hell. That felt worse. He let out an involuntary groan and tried to open his eyes. They seemed to be stuck shut.

"Sip," said a woman's voice. A familiar voice.

He felt a pipette slip between his lips and sucked reflexively. Chill, viscous liquid coursed down his throat, coating it and quelling the fiery storm. He'd never tasted anything so good.

Sensation began to return to other parts of his body. He felt as if every inch of his flesh was covered in cold slime, yet the overall effect was not disgusting—it was, in fact, pleasant. There was a faint smell of char in the air, overlaying the citrus.

He felt twin dabs of moisturizing liquid touch his eyelids. Then the same voice said, "Open your eyes. It'll be worth it."

He did. It was.

Morgan hovered over him, freshly showered, her hair curling about her face, which glistened with glamour spray. She smelled of a spice he couldn't put a name to. She was wearing a dark, body-hugging outfit that made her blonde hair look like spun gold. He had to admit, she was definitely one of the better things he'd woken up to recently.

He had a stray thought of Jani. Pushed it aside. Jani was dead.

"Where...?"

"Medbay—what's left of it. You've been out for over a week. Most of it in cryo, growing new skin and hair follicles, which you've done with amazing speed. Doc says you can wash this salve off in another day or three." She smiled. "I get to help."

He moved his eyes experimentally. He seemed to be in a dimly lit cubicle in the corner of the larger chamber. From where he lay, he could see swathes of soot on the ceiling. That explained the charred smell.

He was lying in some sort of shallow gel bath, naked, his pale, new skin shiny with a translucent blue-green goop—some kind of regenerative salve, obviously—that smelled faintly of limes. His head was slightly elevated—so he wouldn't drown in the goop, he supposed. Intravenous and monitor lines ran to several stents and plugs attached to his arms and chest.

Over a week and the ship was still in one piece ... more or less.

"So, it worked," he croaked.

"It worked. The plug took out the *Devi's* bridge and the main drive reactor. It was pretty much chain reaction after that. Vishnu's dead. We rescued a few survivors from the after section of the ship, but that was it. Some of them were ... well, a little less than sane."

She stood. "We managed to get the Keplinger back on line enough to limp off. We're on our way to port with, I should note, a perfectly healthy cargo of super-Lerandia plants. Damage to the ship, notwithstanding, it should be a pretty lucrative trip. Congratulations."

"Sanchez?"

"He didn't make it, but his sporules and serum did. Enough for Doc Pike to be able to reverse engineer, we hope."

"Why reverse engineer? He'd've left notes."

She gave him a *look*. "I thought he told you not to kill him because he was the only one that knew—"

"Sal Sanchez was a lousy liar, but a good scientist. He'd've recorded the procedure. Check his lab."

"I'll do that." Morgan glanced back over her shoulder. "Oh. It looks like the captain wants a word with you, and I have work to do. Later."

She exited the infirmary, but the man who took her place was not Erasmus Shade. It was Lucas.

"Captain?" If Trouble had had eyebrows he would have raised them.

Lucas blushed, but raised his head and looked Trouble in the eye. "My father insisted on it, and the crew ... well, Morgan and Cyber are going to help me with them." He looked away then and lowered his voice. "You should be captain, Trouble. You put your life on the line a dozen times, and I know we wouldn't have made it if you hadn't."

"No, thank you. I don't want to be captain of anything. I wouldn't mind an all-expenses-paid trip to an isolated planet, though. Nothing fancy, just someplace that's off the main routes."

"Somewhere they don't post bounties for fugitives, you

mean?" Cyber had come up behind Lucas, looking even more translucent than when Trouble had last seen him.

Trouble licked his lips.

Okay. They know …

Hell, he had no idea what they knew about him. Probably more than he did.

Lucas faced Trouble again, but didn't meet his eyes. "We're … we're bound for Acre. It's a bit of a backwater, but it's got a full-service space dock and we need one pretty bad right now. We'll put in for temporary repairs there and harvest and sell some of the cargo. You'll get your share, I promise. You should have enough credits to go wherever you want after that."

"But not on the *Moonraker*," Trouble surmised.

Lucas raised his eyes to Trouble's face. "If it was my decision, I'd take you any place you wanted to go. I'd let you stay on the crew if you wanted. But …"

"But what? You're the captain."

The boy lowered his eyes again, his cheeks reddening.

Cyber glanced at him and said, "But not the owner. If he were an adult, the ship would belong to him. But because he's a minor, his father exercises ownership rights. And Lucas's father wouldn't want a…"

Trouble sat up, pulling out several IV stents. "A what?" he growled. "What did I do?"

Cyber and Lucas exchanged glances, then Lucas asked, "You really don't remember?"

"What I remember … what I *think* I remember … is that I was supposed to kill someone. That I … backed out of the deal. I failed to follow through as the psyquam put it. Then he … I think he killed my wife. Jani. Janina. I remember being in a cell. Then nothing. Nothing, until I found myself walking into Porphyry. That's when I remembered my name. Until we went through the Pilgrim's Passage, that's about all I knew about myself. Except that I've been heavily modded."

Cyber's expression was grim. "You know what? I believe

you, but that's not the way the authorities have it. According to the report Lucas's dad got, you assassinated Chaz Carldon then murdered your wife in a jealous rage. You escaped from a prison ship and disappeared. Until now."

He killed...

"Chaz Carldon. I don't even know who that is."

"Chaz Carldon," said Cyber quietly, "was Primary of the Consonance and a minister of the Heartworlds Parliament. He was also favored to become Heartworlds Prime Minister in the next election. You were ... you were his chief security officer."

"I don't remember any of that." Trouble looked past Cyber to Lucas. "Cyber said he believed me, Lucas. What about you?"

Lucas met Trouble's eyes again, his own gaze steady. The kid was no coward, Trouble had to give him that.

"I do believe you, Trouble, but my dad owns this ship. I told him what you did. You saved my life. You saved my uncle's life —or what's left of it. You all but sacrificed yourself to save us and salvage our ship and her cargo. You got rid of Vishnu Chowdury—my father should thank you personally for that, because Vishnu was roguing all over the space lanes and causing the Guild six kinds of agony. None of that changed his mind. He wants me to turn you over to HASA."

Trouble frowned. That almost meant something to him.

Apparently catching Trouble's confused expression, Cyber said, "The Heartworlds Alliance Security Agency—chief player in a big, fat manhunt. And you're the man."

Lucas's dark eyes looked haunted, trapped. Desperation rolled off of him in waves. "Trouble, people in my father's organization know where you are. If we shelter you, every bounty hunter between here and Herron's Hope will be after you. And us. We won't be able to make port anywhere. If it weren't for that, I'd ..." Tears glittered in the kid's lashes. "Trouble, I have to look after my crew."

Trouble lay back in the gel and closed his eyes, feeling unutterably weary. Lucas was right, damn him. Even in disguise,

Trouble couldn't go through any port that checked DNA profiles. That severely limited where he could go. He had hoped the *Moonraker* might be a place where he could recover the rest of his memory. Where he could pause to figure out what to do next— where to go. He'd thought about finding a hiding place—a pioneer planet circling a star far from the Trunk Line. But that was a child's fantasy—a coward's escape. He hated the thought of being a coward. Hated the idea that after all he'd been through, after all the things he had faced, and lost, he was most afraid of his own memories.

Damn it, that was not going to happen. Whatever he had or had not done, whoever had died as a result, he was going to find out. There were ways a man could hide in plain sight with enough money and the right cosmetic surgeon. He took a deep breath and blew away any lingering sense of disappointment. What had happened to him wasn't their fault.

He glanced up at Cyber. "Tell Mad Morgan I'll have to pass on the shower."

Cyber glanced at Lucas, then back at Trouble. "If she made you an offer, she did it knowing ... everything we know. I'd take her up on it if I were you. Might be the last shower you get for a while." He looked down at his feet. "I mean, at least until you're able to put some distance and time between you and the authorities..."

Trouble propped himself up on his elbows. "What are you saying, Cyb?"

"I'm just saying..."

"He's just saying," Lucas interrupted, "that if our paths should cross again, we'll owe you. *I'll* owe you. And I won't be a kid that much longer."

"Lucas, you're not a kid now," Trouble told him, and meant it.

33 / MEMORY

THERE WERE NO SNOOPS IN THE SHOWER THAT MORGAN COULD SEE. Cyber had finally kept a promise. She didn't doubt that they'd be back the next day, though. She'd brought along some scented oil she'd bought in a bazaar on Acre ages ago. It smelled of evergreens and rain.

Trouble laughed when he saw it. "What're you planning to do, make a salad? I had something else in mind."

"It'll be good for your new skin," she said, suddenly shy about admitting how hungry she was to relive the pure pleasure he'd given her before.

"Yeah, but it'll look better on yours."

It did look good on her too, she had to admit. It coated her pale flesh with a glossy sheen that accented every curve. And it felt incredible. The vendor had told her there was something in the oil that stimulated nerve endings. She hadn't believed it then. She did now.

She responded to Trouble with passion, her ardor increased by the knowledge of his imminent loss. And yet, to her surprise, she found herself distracted by the thought of Cyber's snoops. She was still suspicious of Cyber, and found it hard to believe he would have removed them all. She had better not, she told herself, find out he'd left some behind. The thought of him watching them ... watching her ...

The thought was followed by one even more unwelcome.

"What's wrong, Morgan?"

Morgan came back into her skin, her back pressed into the supple, padded tiles by the weight of Trouble's body, her eyes looking up into his. They gleamed pure silver in the dim light of the steamy cubicle.

She smiled at him, letting sensation flood her. "Sorry. I was looking for cameras. And could you please call me Mad? Or Maddie? Or Madelen? Considering what we've been through— and what we're doing—calling me by my surname feels ... impersonal."

"Impersonal? Does it strike you that this is impersonal to me?"

She shrugged. "I don't know what it is to you."

He levered himself higher, his eyes narrowing. "Whoa. Mad Morgan suddenly unsure of herself—after all we've been through? This isn't about cam bots, really, is it?"

She closed her eyes. "The whole thing about your wife. You seeing her as a psyquam. The way she died..." She was careful not to make it sound like "the way you *say* she died."

She glanced up into his eyes and could see him withdrawing.

"I'm sorry, I shouldn't have said anything, but I was thinking about Cyber watching us and had this sudden ... fear that maybe you felt watched too. But by ..."

"Jani," he said, his voice rough. "It was three years ago ... yeah, three years. And a lot of the memories are shredded. I loved her. I know that. And yeah, I feel ..." He lowered his head until his forehead rested on Morgan's shoulder.

She listened to the steam jets for a time, then reached up to stroke the back of his neck.

"I'm sorry," she said inadequately.

"No reason you should be." He raised his head. "No reason I

should be either. Not for this, anyway." He touched her cheek. "Jani is dead. I didn't kill her and I don't know for certain who did. Or maybe I do know but I can't or won't remember. Maybe that makes me haunted. And maybe that also makes me an emotional wreck. But it doesn't make me sorry I'm here with you."

He kissed her, deeply and savoringly. Heat reignited, licked up through her core. She dove back into the moment, remembering that he'd be gone as soon as they made port. She would not mention love, or hope aloud that they'd meet again somewhere down the line. She would just take these moments and stow them.

She opened her eyes briefly and thought she saw a tiny flash of blue on one of the shower's sonic emitters.

Damn Cyber, anyway.

Fine. They'd give him a show that would burn out his circuits.

The shower was good. The sex was better. The emotional intimacy ... a mixed bag. When Morgan—no, Maddie—said she'd never forget him, he could honestly repay the compliment. At least, he hoped he wouldn't forget her. He'd forgotten far more permanent parts of his life, so who knew?

He didn't answer her when she asked where he would go. He *couldn't* answer her with any certainty.

Now they stood in the airlock of the shuttle Morgan had flown down to Acre's capital city, New Haifa, setting down expertly in an area so crowded with like vessels that their landing skids nearly locked with the shuttle directly aft.

"Safety in numbers," she said. "If there's someone looking for you, they're probably not looking someplace quite so public."

Through the airlock window, Trouble could see that the shuttle terminal was abuzz with people of all shapes and sizes, mostly pilgrims bound for the religious shrines on the slopes of the mountains that cupped the city.

"I don't exactly blend in," he told her, suddenly overly conscious of the paleness of his skin. He looked so new, so freshly scrubbed.

"Yeah, but on the other hand, you don't look a damn thing like the man they're hunting."

That was true enough. He'd been several shades darker, for one thing, and his hair, which had been a nondescript light brown, was growing in almost black. If he could get his eyes colorized, he'd be unrecognizable as the Ridley Matthews whose image was engraved in law enforcement records.

"Here, these should help." Morgan held out a pair of mirrored eye-shades. "You can buy these at just about any kiosk on any corner in this city. 'Tenth-credit a dozen,' as the old saying goes. And there's a long-sleeved hooded coat in your pack. You should probably put it on before you hit the streets. Protect that brand-new skin." She grinned at him.

He opened the pack and drew out the tunic, pulling it on over his vest and leggings while Morgan watched.

"It's more fun watching you take your clothes off," she said.

He put on the eye-shades. "If you're not in a hurry ..."

She grimaced. "Actually, I am. Cyber wants me back aboard the *Raker* in ten minutes."

"Cyber wants you—period."

"You noticed? How flattering."

"You given any thought to it, Maddie?"

"Cyber? What—are you trying to pair me off with another man?"

"A *good* man, Mad. Cyber's a *good* man. A little odd, but good."

She smiled. Shook her head. "I'm going to have to get you out of my system first. Which isn't going to be easy. And ... I'm

not sure Cyber isn't happier watching than he'd be participating."

Trouble slung the pack over his shoulder, then reached out
with his free hand and touched Morgan's cheek. "Maddie,
Cyber's gone pretty deep into the ship. He more than identifies
with her. I think he's going to need some solid human contact to
keep him in the real world. You're real, Mad. You're solid."

"Doesn't mean I can or will or should fall into bed with him."

"No, but I think he's going to need—if not a lover—at least a
friend."

She put her hand over his. "That I can do." Her smile went
cockeyed. "Hell, after all, we've been through life and death and
life together."

She kissed him.

Looking at her, regretting that he had to leave her, Trouble
realized he'd gotten comfortable with Mad Morgan. Too
comfortable. And too comfortable on the *Raker*. He'd beat
himself up for that pretty thoroughly since coming to in Medbay.

It was best, he decided, to think of this whole happening as a
wake up call—a reminder of what 'solitary' meant. If you were
in solitary confinement, you didn't get friendly with the prison
guards. If you were at solitary liberty, you didn't get too friendly
with your fellow travelers. In his case, given what he knew—and
didn't know—about himself, friendliness could be dangerous for
all concerned. There were still ways in which this already lousy
situation could get a whole lot worse ... for everybody.

"What are the chances of me stepping off this launch without
being nabbed by cops or Guild enforcers?"

"Pretty good. Julian Shade wanted Lucas to promise to notify
the authorities and turn you over to them when we made port.
Lucas didn't make that promise. He just said he'd consider it.
And, of course, he didn't. Not for a moment. None of us did."

"Shade might have notified them himself."

Morgan shrugged. "He might've—but he'd be notifying the
authorities on Idris. That's where Lucas told him we were bound

and that's what the flight itinerary would say if his pa looked it up—which I'm sure he did. Lucas is a pretty savvy captain, wouldn't you say?"

"Cyber's not jealous? He deserved that promotion more than Lucas did. Hell, you deserved it more. Way it worked out, you didn't even make first mate."

"Thanks. But no, there's no jealousy. Cyber's just fine with being first mate; he legitimately wants to help Lucas be a good captain. He's an all right guy in most ways. In other ways … well, he needs work, but then, we all do. As for me, you're looking at the new Chief Engineer."

"Yeah? Congrats. You get a stateroom out of that?"

"Naw. Just a cabin. But it's *my* cabin."

"I don't know, Maddie. I'm pretty sure if you wanted a stateroom, all you'd have to do is give the first mate a shower."

Her eyes glinted wickedly. "You're a terrible matchmaker, Matthews. And are you really that bloodless about me moving on just like that?"

"No. Not bloodless. I just … I like to think of you *with* somebody. Someone who's got your back. Cyber … Cyber's that kind of man."

"I know."

She'd never forget him, she'd said. And here he was, trying to shove her into someone else's arms.

"I'm sorry. I must be an incorrigible romantic."

"Great," she said dryly. "You can add that to your catalogue of 'things we've learned about Trouble Matthews'."

Trouble cycled the outer door open and turned to watch the ramp slide out. Morgan laid a firm hand on his arm, turning him back around. Her expression was solemn, almost wistful.

"I'm sorry you couldn't stay with *Moonraker*. That we couldn't even take you to that frontier planet you were hoping to find."

That stopped him. "How the hell do you know about that?"

"You talk in your sleep." She wrapped a hand around the

back of his neck and drew his head down for a kiss that was long, slow, deep, and tasted of mint and coffee.

He held her for a second or two longer than he'd intended to. Then he turned, adjusted his shades and walked out into the hard, bright sunlight.

TROUBLE DIDN'T LOOK BACK AT THE END OF THE LANDING RAMP. He heard the ramp withdraw and the external hatch seal. He'd gone maybe twenty strides when the shuttle lifted off again. In another five, he was sucked into the stream of people leaving the spaceport's shuttle bays.

He pulled up the hood of his tunic and adjusted the pack on his shoulder. It was filled with clothing, a couple of hand weapons, supplies—and enough credits to buy passage anywhere he wanted. Enough to have his face changed so that no one would recognize him. Enough to do some clandestine digging around the murder of a certain Minister of Parliament.

He decided he would find a room first, a nice one, some-where pricey—a place where no one would think to look for Ridley Matthews, fugitive. Then he could arrange for transport to a less crowded planet … or not. There might be advantages to starting his search here, on a world with a large temporary population of religious pilgrims.

He was moving with the multitude, making his way toward the spaceport's broad plaza, when he saw a vaguely familiar figure lounging near the white arch that framed the pedestrian exit. It was the clothing that drew his eye first; the man was dressed in a black thigh-length cutaway coat over gray breeches, his face partially obscured by a dark broad-brimmed hat. His black boots were knee-high and looked new. But what captured Trouble's entire attention was the gleaming brass timepiece that hung from the breast pocket of the man's coat.

Breath left Trouble's lungs in a gust. It couldn't be. It could not be the man he'd seen with Jani's psyquam in the Pilgrim's Passage. The man he connected to her murder. That man was a ghost, an hallucination.

You're being damned paranoid, Matthews. Cut it out.

The man lifted his head for a moment to scan the crowd, and Trouble got a clear look at his face. It was a face he was certain he'd never forget again.

How was this possible? Psyquams were dead people. Weren't they?

He managed to keep moving, pretending to be engaged in conversation with the nearest knot of travelers. They chattered. He turned his head toward them, nodded as if listening to them, gestured with his hands. He had no choice. If he stopped suddenly in this press of bodies, he would draw attention to himself. Most of the people around him—men and women— wore hooded tunics, robes, or cloaks. In a climate that couldn't decide whether it wanted to bake you or freeze you, such garb was common. Trouble was just one more hooded form in a herd of hooded forms. There was no reason for anyone to notice him.

He continued on through the exit and into the plaza, putting the impossible man behind him. The skin between his shoulder blades crawled.

When was a ghost not a ghost?

Trouble shook himself. He had to separate reality from lore. Ghosts were lore. Populating the Passage with them was hallucination, if not superstition. All anyone knew about the Passage was that it caused subatomic displacement and delirium. He already knew that that delirium was guided, to some extent, by the hallucinator's mental state. By fears and desires that a man or woman might not even be aware of. By inner truths struggling to emerge.

What inner truths had produced *that man*? What part of Ridley Matthews had believed the man had somehow been complicit in Jani's murder?

Had any of it been real?

That thought almost stopped him in his tracks. What if his recovered memories weren't memories at all? What if he was lying even to himself? What if he had actually caught his wife with another man—a man named Chaz Carldon—and killed them both in a jealous rage? Worse, what if he was an assassin?

Stepping out into the plaza, Trouble dared a glance back at the man with the brass timepiece and realized he wasn't the only one interested in him. A woman stood roughly three meters from the guy in the shadow of a light standard, ostensibly checking her cloud of raven-black hair in a mirror she held just above eye level. Trouble had to assume that it was one of his mods that allowed him to be certain that her gaze was not trained on her own image, but on Pocket Watch.

Agent? Bounty hunter? Pickpocket?

It was tempting to keep his eyes on the two, but Trouble knew doing so would risk curiosity directed back at him. He stayed with his adopted traveling companions until he reached the center of the plaza. Then he wove his way across the glittering stone toward a row of cab stands, struggling with the ideas that danced and sparred in his head. Whatever the truth, he could not allow self-doubt to take root. He had to believe—or at least pretend to believe—that he was neither a murderer nor an assassin. He knew one thing: From here on out, he could rewrite himself—*would* rewrite himself, starting with his first steps into this city of pilgrimage.

Ironic. Here was another pilgrim's passage, possibly more dangerous than the first, in its own way.

He felt an urge to look back, to see if Pocket Watch was still standing at the port exit—to see if the woman was still studying him. He ignored the impulse, mind mulling this turn of events. It could not possibly be a coincidence that this man was on this planet, in this city, at this spaceport, at this time. He suspected that Julian Shade hadn't trusted his son and had reported the ship to someone who had felt it was worth tracking. If so, the man had good instincts.

A small, insidious voice inside Trouble's nearly bald head asked how far he could trust Lucas Shade. Or Madelen Morgan. Or Cyber Marsden. Or anyone else aboard *Moonraker*. He mentally shouted the voice to silence. If he started thinking like that, it was all over for him.

He resisted the urge to look back as long as he could. But finally, as he was approaching the cab stands, he shot a glance back at the port exit with its gleaming white arch.

Pocket Watch was gone.

There was no way to tell where he had gone. He could be halfway to an off world shuttle. He could be tucked into the crowd behind Trouble. Or he could be somewhere ahead, waiting. The woman, too, had disappeared.

Trouble chose a cab, slipped a credit chip into its pay slot, stepped into the vehicle, and looked straight ahead as it pulled silently away from the curbing.

"Where can I take you, sir?" the bot's voice was courteous and pleasant.

"I need a nice place to stay. The more luxurious, the better."

The more defiant of expectations…

"The Bengurian comes highly recommended, sir," the cab bot replied.

"Bengurian it is."

Once again, Trouble looked back, scouring the plaza for signs of Pocket Watch. By the time he reached Hotel Bengurian, he had almost convinced himself the whole thing had been a figment of his fevered imagination.

Almost, but not quite.

Tonight, he would eat well and sleep in a real bed. Tomorrow, he would begin working out why he, or anyone else, would have wanted to kill Chaz Carldon, and looking for the man with the brass timepiece.

PART 2
THE HAUNTED MAN

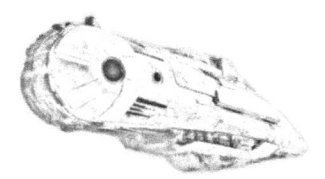

35 / NEW MAN

TROUBLE SLEPT FOR AN ENTIRE DAY, THEN WOKE TO ORDER breakfast (or whatever meal it was) from the hotel's kitchen. He ate that on a balcony that ran the width of the posh suite on the opposite side of floor-to-ceiling windows that offered a stunning view of the lake port and the immense lake—Teykh Akhdus— itself. The suite was tastefully decorated in mauves and plums; the furniture was real wood. There was even a little fireplace carved of pale stone that activated with a motion sensor whenever he entered the living area.

He did not look at himself in the vanity of the stylishly spartan bathroom until after he'd eaten and showered (in real water) and resigned himself to considering his next move. He stalled somewhat in that endeavor. How could you plan anything if you couldn't even work up sufficient courage to look at yourself in a damned mirror?

In the end, he made himself look, knowing a stranger would be staring back. He hadn't looked at his face in a reflective surface—real or holographic—since he came to in the *Moonraker's* infirmary. Then, he'd thought he looked a lot like one of those archaic Asian ceremonial masks he'd seen once in a museum. What were they called? Noh. He was pleased to have remembered that, and to know that he'd visited a museum at least once in his life.

Now, though his flesh was still as pale as an eggshell, his brows, lashes and hair had begun to grow in earnest. The hair covering his scalp—about an inch in length after roughly two weeks—had a black cherry sheen. His face was gaunt—all cheekbones and brow ridges.

Hey, it's a good thing, he told himself. If you don't recognize yourself, chances are no one else will recognize you either.

His eyes were the only thing he did recognize, and that *wasn't* a good thing. They were still silver, and had an unnatural sheen, even in the light of the bathroom. They were an identifiable feature. Especially so, he suspected, to anyone dedicated to finding him.

He'd have to do something about that. Problem was, doing something about it meant going to an Enhancer or a cosmetic mod salon. That was clearly out. Those places kept records of their clientele/patients. Trying to solicit illegal mods would be ... well, illegal, and likely to draw unwanted attention. Of course, so would skulking around indoors wearing dark lenses, and he needed clothing that befitted a swell. That meant shopping for clothing that befitted a swell in places where swells shopped. While it was likely that his pursuer wouldn't be looking for him in places like that, it wasn't impossible that their paths would cross.

Frustrated, Trouble turned his attention to that mysterious figure: Pocket Watch. Who was he and who did he work for? If—big if—the visions that had assaulted Trouble in the Pilgrim's Passage were to be taken as warped memories, then it stood to reason that the guy worked for whatever military or law enforcement body had been tasked with running him to ground.

For murder. For a murder he had no memory of committing, though he knew somehow he'd been hired to commit it. A murder that the psyquam Pocket Watch had told him he'd failed to follow through on.

Well, that was a show-stopper.

Was the guy after him because he'd assassinated Chaz Carl-don, or because he *hadn't*? It seemed a pretty important distinc-tion. If the guy was an agent of Heartworlds Alliance Security, then there were rules he had to abide by, presumably, that would make just shooting the escapee a no-op. If he was an agent of whatever party Trouble had stiffed by *not* assassinating Chaz Carldon, then there might not be any rules at all.

Trouble pushed finding out who Pocket Watch worked for to the top of his Important Things to Know list. That meant finding Pocket Watch in the first place, and *that* meant he'd need to go out in public and somehow not look, in any way, like a certain escaped convict. Which meant he needed to mod his eyes further, which meant going to the very sort of place that Pocket Watch would be surveilling, hoping his quarry would do exactly that.

It's a freaking snake eating its own freaking tail.

The only solution Trouble could think of was to purchase some cosmetic contact lenses, but even that was risky. Pocket Watch would very likely have feelers out in shops that sold those as well, and the number of feelers would be proportional to the resources of whatever party he worked for.

Trouble looked at the stranger in his mirror, wryly thinking how much simpler life would be if his built-in augmentations ran to changing such things as eye color at will. If he could just think *Eyes! Be brown!* and his eyes would just…

What the hell.

He stared in utter fascination as the irises of both eyes began to darken. He repeated the tongue-in-cheek command with a lot less cheek and a strong image in his mind of the color of a cup of black coffee. His eyes responded to the suggestion and settled into a pleasingly generic brown. It seemed to him the room got a shade darker.

Okay, but did that cancel out his night vision? And would the color hold? What if they went back to "normal" in the middle of a conversation with someone?

He paused to think about the rationale behind such an augmentation; logic dictated that it was unlikely to just shut off when you weren't thinking about it or had a stray thought. It was a mod that would be highly useful in spy craft; if it could be undone by mere inattention, it would be useless for that. It would have to be a mod you could switch on, then leave until you directed another thought at it to switch it off again.

That was easy enough to test. Trouble stopped focusing on his eyes and took a step back to survey the entire picture. Except for his height, he quite literally looked nothing like the man who'd gone into that thruster interconnect chamber. Lanky, pale, with dark eyes, dark hair and brows.

He liked it. He was unrecognizable, anonymous, almost ordinary.

He moved back into the main room of the half-suite to sit at the desk in the small parlor area and picked up the datapad Cyber had given him. His intention was to finish cataloguing what he knew about himself and his circumstances against the possibility—however slim—that he'd lose pieces of his memory again.

Thanks to Cyber's diligence, he knew he was Ridley Matthews, Chief of Security for one Chaz Carldon, Prime Minister of the Earth-centered Consonance and an MP in the Heartworlds Alliance. Carldon had potentially been Heartworlds' next Prime. Most significantly, he'd been a man it had been Trouble's job to protect.

According to what Cyber had pieced together, Trouble had not always been employed as a security officer. In his twenties, before he'd aspired to work for HASA, he'd been in a Mars-based Solar System Guard unit, serving as an engineer aboard a patrol vessel mandated to foil the efforts of smugglers, priva-teers, and outright pirates.

There was some weapons-grade irony in that. Not much

more than a decade ago, he might have helped board and impound the ship he'd just left. He wondered if his tour of duty in the Solar Guard explained his vague memories of having been in a space battle.

After he'd exchanged the Guard for a similar guard unit within Heartworlds Alliance Security Administration, he'd left engineering behind and focused entirely on security, working his way up in HASA. Carldon had chosen him to head his personal security detail after he'd been assigned to organize and command a joint Consonance/Alliance security team for the MP's administrative junkets.

Some people were of the opinion that Ridley Matthews had killed his boss and his wife in a jealous rage. Others thought the timing was suspicious, given the upcoming election, and theorized that he'd been bought by one of his client's enemies and had used his position to carry out the assassination. His wife had been collateral damage.

Carldon had made quite a few enemies in his young career. He was a high profile law and justice activist and had alienated any number of corporate entities who habitually indulged in practices that skirted the law. Lucas had commented that his father, Julian, was no fan of the man he called "Crusader Carldon".

Curious about the timing of the assassination, Trouble used the datapad to do a lookup of causes Carldon had been involved in at the time of his death and legislation he had proposed or favored. There were a number of policy positions that might have made him *persona non grata* with the power players from a variety of commercial sectors. He was behind probes running on the Freeman's Guild, a major Earth-based financial institution and three major bio-tech firms. Trouble wondered if Julian Shade's machinations ran to removing pesky pols and statesmen from the scene.

If Trouble had not murdered Chaz Carldon out of jealousy and a thirst for revenge or money, then someone else had for other reasons. He saved off the list of companies Carldon had been investigating, and seriously considered the possibility that he had been the one who'd ended the man's life. More damning than his possible motives was the fact that he'd had opportunity and access. The murder had been done at close quarters with a service weapon that had Trouble's DNA and fingerprints on it— a beam pistol found stored with a small collection of other weapons in his gun safe. Beamers were issued only for special missions—manhunts involving criminals who were considered armed and dangerous. Keeping one for personal use was illegal.

He had been convicted and incarcerated for the double murder and had somehow managed to escape the prison transport when it was blown apart in a suspicious accident. That validated his memories of being in the slam, but other than the remembered chaos of that event, how he'd escaped was still a total blank.

Not important.

He tried to move on from that, but a pair of stark, vivid memories hit him like a one-two gut punch: His wife's body stretched out on a highly polished floor, her upward-staring eyes reflecting the dappled sunlight from a wall of floor-to-ceiling windows. A little girl no older than four, making dolls and figurines ice skate in almost exactly the same spot.

His stomach clenched, and breath left his lungs in a rush.

My child? Our child?

She had to have been, and she must have had a name, but he couldn't remember it. The absent fragment of memory opened a deep pain in his breast. Tears stung his eyes as he pushed against a seemingly impenetrable wall. How could he have forgotten his own daughter's name? Was she even alive, or ...?

Stop this. Now is not the time.

He clawed his way back out of the well of memory, focused his attention on the datapad, and went about cataloguing his mental and physical landscape.

He'd been genetically modified in a variety of ways that he was still discovering. His reflexes, strength, and senses were heightened to unsettling extremes; his body seemed infinitely adaptable, and in ways he was fairly certain were experimental at best, and possibly illegal. The question was: *Why?* Why had he been modified in this way, and how was that connected to the other things he knew? Had he been complicit in the modifications? Surely, he must have been.

Had he also been mind-wiped? That seemed most likely. He couldn't imagine a memory fog this impenetrable being the result of an accident. Possibly it was part of his punishment, but it might have been done for another reason altogether. His current situation inclined him toward the idea that his amnesia was both intentional and malign.

He knew at least one agent of an unknown entity was after him and had tracked him this far. And he knew that this mismatched hodgepodge of information was about to compel him to do some dangerous and possibly stupid things. He needed to know more about … hell, he couldn't name one thing he *didn't* need to know more about.

He switched focus to the now. Thanks to Cyber's lack of creativity in the real world, Ridley Matthews was now Adam Newman, a weapons design engineer and a native of Herron's Hope—hometown, Peatville, a bog town about half an hour's journey from Porphyry. He had to admit that was a good call; every weapon that had come into his hands since he'd begun to resurface from his personal sea of Nepenthe had felt natural and familiar, and now he knew why. A weapons engineer could write his own ticket on just about any world, so the absurd amount of credits in his shiny new financial account would seem perfectly natural.

He considered that. Considered that the sane and safe thing to do would be to take the new identity and wealth bestowed on him by *Moonraker's* new captain and disappear from everyone's sensors. But, if there was one thing this new man understood about himself, it was that he was highly resistant to doing the sane and safe thing.

He had the better part of a day to play with, and decided that he was going to use it to prepare for just the sort of activities that he suspected had earned him the nick "Trouble." In a nod to a semblance of sanity, he'd take it easy today—acquire a new wardrobe and arm himself with something more potent than the hotrod and slap gun Lucas had afforded him from the *Moonraker's* armory. To that end, he suited-up in the best clothing the *Moonraker's* grateful crew had been able to assemble, checked his still brown eyes in the bathroom holographic mirror, and headed out to collect more of the trappings of a life.

Tomorrow, he would begin a search for Pocket Watch.

It was really too bad, Trouble thought, that his talents didn't run to fabricating clothes. It would have saved him the torturous experience of having to shop for them. Standing in a high-end store, faced with display after virtual display of garments for every occasion, he wondered how Jani had managed it—even enjoyed it.

A recollection came to him in her voice, as present as if she'd been standing at his shoulder: "It's instinct, T, like hunting and gathering. I like to hunt and gather. Don't you?"

The memory froze him for a moment, causing his reflection in the kiosk display—currently wearing a sleek suit with a sleek jacket and aggressively tight breeks—to look more like a mannequin than a man. Was that what life was going to be like from now on? Having his past drip on him like a freezing and inconstant rain? A drop here, a drop there?

He shook the droplet off, but not without contemplating the message.

Hunting.

Well, he *was* hunting, or at least he was going to be. Hunting the hunter, which he could best do by hunting himself. To find Pocket Watch, he reasoned, he'd look for Ridley Matthews, fugitive, and be just unsubtle enough so as to attract the other hunter's attention. Pursuant to that, he bought the suit his virtual self was modeling, along with a number of other items from the dressy to the businesslike to the casual. He suffered no more icy droplets of memory, but he was aware that he was comfortable in all of the clothing he bought, as if he might have possessed garments like these before. He concluded that security chiefs made good money ... or maybe whatever Jani had done was lucrative. He couldn't remember, didn't try.

Wearing one of the more knockabout outfits, he paid to have his new wardrobe delivered to his hotel, then found his way to a quarter of New Haifa as unlike the area around the Bengurian as his new "look" was unlike the old. Here, in a sector called simply Al Suq (the Marketplace) clothing stores did not have virtual fitting kiosks (VFKs), or AI shopping assistants that literally sized you up and automagically delivered the appropriate garments in whatever size and color and fabric you desired. Nor did they all take their payment from a credit stream. They had racks of physical garments from which you had to choose what you wished to try on and required you to pay in coin, barter, or with a credit chip.

In these depots, Trouble purchased the trappings commonly worn by those who lived and/or worked in the desert to the north of New Haifa—the miners, merchants, and wind-farmers. He had researched Acre, and New Haifa in particular, before he'd left *Moonraker*. The fact that the city was a place of pilgrimage for millions of souls who subscribed to a faith called Mabirati (which meant "illumined" in some forgotten tongue), had factored in its favor when Trouble's friends were seeking a place to deposit him in relative safety. The sheer amount of diverse traffic in and around the spaceport was its own smoke screen.

On his way back to the hotel, Trouble's taxi crossed the broad avenue that led to the Mabirati shrines. They sat halfway up the slope of a mountain in the range that served as the city's backdrop and windbreak. A temple, an immense library, a school, a hospital, an elder-care hospice, and a pilgrim house poked through the trees like jewels in a bed of green velvet. The taxi's AI sensed him looking up the boulevard at the shrines and informed him that, while the place of pilgrimage was lovely by day, it was breathtaking at night when the lights on the buildings and grounds looked like a sea of stars. He felt an impulse to visit the spot, but discarded it. He might pretend to be a pilgrim, but he wasn't one. He had a job to do and he was going to start doing it this very day.

Back at the hotel, Trouble appraised his new wardrobe and considered his next steps. First order of business was to think like a bounty hunter. If he were himself, doing what it might be supposed he would do—hide—where would he go? Mod salons, most certainly. Clandestine arms dealers, likely. Skeevy dives and cheap hostels, that too. Were he a desperate criminal on the run, he might consider leaving the urban area behind and venturing into the desert. Or he might cross the Teykh Akhdus—the huge lake along whose shore New Haifa sprawled—to her sister city, Mirrorton. He might try to leave the planet again. Pocket Watch would also be considering these options and would no doubt exhaust those before searching farther afield.

How thoroughly Trouble's hunter covered these various options depended, again, on the depth and breadth of his physical resources. Chances were good he wasn't the only agent in the field, which led Trouble to wonder anew about the woman he'd seen at the spaceport.

A few minutes of thought provided him with a healthy list of places he might expect to find someone who was tracking him and a likely sector of the city in which to begin his search. He settled on a change of clothing that suggested he was from off-world—breeches, boots, a thermal shirt, and an all-weather jacket—and headed to a colorful part of town officially known as Bayside Cross. Locals, according to conversations Trouble eavesdropped on, referred to the place as Double Cross as if to remind themselves of its untrustworthy nature.

He tailored his search to look aimless and meandering. He wandered into a number of taverns for a drink, poked his nose into an employment center, and browsed two small arms and hunting supply dealers, buying himself a backpack in one and, in the other, a hunting knife to add to his tiny arsenal. In each place, he asked the locals if they'd seen a man answering to his prior description, or a rather striking gentleman who was asking about him.

"Natty dresser," he described his hunter, "and wearing a shiny, gold antique pocket watch. Possibly a broad-brim hat."

As he expected, the response to his first question was a universal *no*. Unless the respondent was lying, they could not have seen him in this New Haifa *suq* since he'd never been here. The second question received *noes*, occasionally punctuated with "What's a pocket watch?" until he got a qualified *yes* from the bartender at the fifth tavern he visited—the Sassy Duck, by name.

"Last night," the guy said. "Around the eleventh hour. Weird gent. Downed a whole bottle of our best low country rum— Megiddo Red—then strutted out of here like it was water. It ain't water," he added, looking almost affronted at his guest's lack of drunkenness. "He should've been passed out on the floor."

"Did you talk to him at all?"

"Yeah. He said he was looking for a friend of his who, now that I think about it, sounds an awful lot like the guy you're looking for. I told him the same thing I told you—never saw the guy. He asked me to keep an eye out and said he'd be back."

"He leave you a way to contact him?"

"Yeah, gave me an ME number."

Trouble's memory caught that cultural detail. An ME was a Message Exchange, which allowed individuals to create essentially anonymous accounts by which people could reach them without them revealing their identity or their whereabouts.

"Care to share?"

The barkeep grinned. "How important is it to yeh?"

"Twenty-five cred important enough?"

The barkeep pursed his lips as if to whistle. "Cut to the chase, huh?" He pulled a small datapad out of his shirt collar on a chain, said, "MEs, prior week" to it, then tapped one of the addresses on the resulting list. While he was doing that, Trouble produced his own datapad and used it to extract the highlighted exchange address from the list and send 25 credits to the bartender's account.

"Thanks," he said. "If he comes back—"

"Yeah, yeah, I won't mention you."

"No, I *want* you to mention me. Tell him I thought we might be able to do business. Name's Newman."

The barkeep shrugged. "Newman. Got it."

Trouble turned and headed for the door. Intriguing. That bit about Pocket Watch's resistance to alcohol suggested strongly that he was also modded. An interesting choice of enhancement. Had it been the goal of the mod or a side-effect? Trouble supposed that having a digestive system designed to allow you to ingest food and drink that would debilitate most humans could be of great benefit. It made him wonder about his own internal modifications, though he wasn't of a mind to experiment to find out. He'd bought a single ale during his trekking about today, but had steered clear of other alcoholic beverages for the simple reason that he was a control freak, as Jani had so frequently reminded him.

That thought—that memory—quite literally took his breath away and stopped him in his tracks as he stepped from the Sassy Duck into the small plaza that served the tavern, the inn next-door, and a variety of other businesses. Shaking himself free of the aftershocks from the random recall, he made his way to the inn.

It was called the Starry Night, which was ironic considering that the light pollution in this quarter completely obscured all but the most brilliant stars. There he engaged an upstairs room with windows that looked out onto the plaza, which served as the hub of two of the neighborhood's main thoroughfares. This, he figured, would make a good base of operations away from his comfortable haven at the Bengurian. Pocket Watch had been here, and given the nature of his quest, it made sense that he'd return periodically. When he did, there was a good chance that one or two of the people Trouble had spoken to would mention him to his hunter. He was counting on it.

The room was spartan, but clean right down to the bedclothes. It had a working mag-lock on the door, so he left some token belongings and a change of uptown clothes in his backpack, then returned to the prowl, walking down several blocks to a bazaar he'd seen while traversing an adjacent neighborhood. He fielded a few more hits on his stalker, but the man himself was nowhere to be seen. Trouble continued his loitering late into the evening, then went back uptown to the relative safety of his room at the Bengurian where he sat down to craft a note to his predatory friend.

He created a Message Exchange account and sent a message, wondering whether Cyber's sense of irony in assigning his identity was a blessing or a curse. The message read: "It seems you and I are seeking the same goal. I'd like to set up a meeting to discuss possible collaboration in finding the elusive Ridley Matthews. - A. Newman."

By the next morning, he had received no response to his attempt to contact Pocket Watch. Counseling himself to patience, he conducted another experiment in camouflage, this time to see if he could also alter the pigmentation of his skin. He found he could, but it turned out to be trickier than changing the color of his eyes. After a half-hour of trial and error, he was able to achieve a tea-stained effect that did not quite make him look like a burn victim. Still, even dressed like a desert-dweller, his head and shoulders draped in a gauze burnoose, he knew he would draw too many closer looks. Until he could create the effect without mottling his skin, he'd have to settle for looking distinctly off-world until his skin darkened naturally. He returned to his nondescript travel clothes, and went out on another sortie, this time to the spaceport and the adjacent airport.

He spent his morning there, using the same methodology he had the day before—he asked if anyone named Ridley Matthews or matching his prior description had booked or attempted to book passage off-world or to another part of Acre by air. Possibly, he might be looking for work.

No one had seen Matthews (naturally), but several noted that another gent had also been asking questions about him. This included members of the port security detail who'd been on shift the day Trouble had landed on Acre. Pocket Watch had given all of his contacts the same ME number that Trouble already had. He'd also shown them a pic of his target, they said, and agreed that Ridley Matthews was one strange and scary looking fellow.

Trouble wasn't sure how he felt about that. He decided to be pleased that none of them had so much as given him a side-eye glance, let alone recognized him. He headed for the lakeport next, figuring that Pocket Watch might also consider the possibility that Ridley Matthews would try to disappear somewhere else on Acre. Logistically, that made a lot of sense. More sense than him trying to find his way back off-world with someone dogging his tracks.

Teykh Akhdus all but split Acre's second-largest continent. It was large enough that its opposite shore was invisible even from atop the port observation tower. Trouble checked with several commercial passenger carriers that offered highspeed travel across the lake, asking the same set cf questions. The results were the same as the other places he'd asked—a mixture of *nope* and *no,* on the scary guy and *yes* on the odd gent with the shiny antique timepiece.

He checked his ME account frequently, despite the fact that he'd set it to ping him if there was an incoming message. He returned to the Starry Night around sunset and asked if anyone had left a message or asked for him by the name he'd given out freely—Adam Newman. No one had. Apparently he'd not called enough attention to himself yet. He'd need to expand his field of search, possibly to mod shops and clinics.

He headed over to the Sassy Duck next, where he sat at a small table in an unobtrusive corner from which he could watch comings and goings while eating supper. He was engaged in that, wryly noting that he actually preferred the hearty, but plain fare at the neighborhood tavern to the over-produced meals at the upscale hotel, when the barkeep dropped by his table to refill his ale. The guy was obviously awash in curiosity, which pinged Trouble's radar.

"You," he told the barkeep, "look like a man with something to say."

"Yeah, actually. You asked about a guy with a prehistoric timepiece who was looking for this fugitive, Matthews?"

Interest piqued. "Has he come in again?"

"No, a woman came in asking about him too. A very pretty woman. Well, lotta sharp edges, but pretty. Definitely gives off 'Admire me from afar' vibes."

Trouble digested this with unease. "Was she asking about Matthews, or the man with the pocket watch?"

"Oh, uh … the fugitive, Matthews. I told her about you and the other guy, anyway. She didn't seem surprised."

Of course not. She'd already been surveilling Pocket Watch and probably expected others to join the hunt. Trouble let out a long breath. Well, that changed things. It sounded very much like the Mystery Woman was seeking *him*, not his pursuer. The situation struck him as ironic and darkly humorous. Pocket Watch was trying to find him; Mystery Woman was trying to find him by following Pocket Watch; he was trying to find Pocket Watch by pretending to look for himself. He'd seen both of them; neither of them had seen him—or at least they hadn't recognized him.

If there was only a way he could put in an appearance as Ridley Matthews… He wondered if his many talents ran to illusion. Probably not. He could buy a wig and return his eyes to their normal state. His face was different now—pale and gaunt—but still...

The barkeep dropped into an empty chair at the table. "So, what'd he do—this guy you're looking for? I mean, you're a bounty hunter, yeah?" Clearly, he was hoping for a good tale.

Trouble reasoned that could be of benefit if the tale spread and he was identified as the one who spread it. "You hear about the Consonance Primary's assassination?"

"Yeah, sure. We're not so much of an outworld that we don't get the news. It was all over the media. All the pundits were saying the guy was going to be the Alliance's next Prime Minister."

"Chaz Carldon," said Trouble, still not used to how his gut clenched up when he said the name, or thought it. "This guy I'm looking for was the trigger man."

"I heard the guy who shot Carldon was sent to Restitution."

Restitution, Trouble now knew, was a high-security, non-terra-formed moon from which it was claimed no one had ever managed to escape ... and where he'd likely been expected to die.

"He never made it to Restitution," he said. "He escaped the prison transport."

"No way. How?"

I wish I knew.

"No idea, but he was the only one who escaped."

"I gather he's really dangerous."

Trouble nodded, looking grim. Not hard.

The barkeep shook his head. "You're a braver man than I am. I only do that sort of dangerous shit in VR games."

"I recommend you keep doing that. They say this guy's death on legs."

The barkeep stood, picked up his pitcher and headed back to the bar, leaving Trouble to ponder his next move. Instead of chasing ghosts and mysteries, he needed to draw his pursuers to him. How, he wondered, could he use his old self as bait without getting caught?

He polished off his supper, and had risen to leave when his datapad pinged. He pulled it out and looked at the message. It was from Pocket Watch's account and comprised of a single word: *No.*

37 / DADDY ISSUES

MAD MORGAN SHIFTED UNEASILY AS SHE WATCHED THE SECURITY
Dude go over a schematic of the *Moonraker's* lower decks under
the Shade patriarch's gimlet eye. Security Dude had a name—it
was Curtis Arkitsis. *Inspector* Curtis Arkitsis, if you please. He
was a member of the Heartworlds Alliance's much-vaunted
security apparatus, HASA, and he had boarded the freighter
with a team of six forensics specialists the moment she made
port on Idris. Julian Shade had accompanied him and was horrified (*horrified*, I tell you) that one of his fleet had unwittingly
harbored a dangerous and possibly sociopathic criminal.

Standing beside Arkitsis in his ready room adjacent to the
bridge, the young captain of the *Moonraker* pointed out all the
places on the ship he knew Matthews to have been.

"Crew's quarters, obviously," he said, tapping a red dot of
light into place in the holo-schematic currently displayed above
the map table, "the Retreat, canteen, hydroponics and engineering—he did shifts in both. And during the crisis he was in
the computer core, Medbay, and the aft thruster ignition tube, of
course." Lucas glanced up at Morgan. "Did I miss anything,
Mad?"

She shrugged. "He went up to the observation deck a lot,"

she said. She slid her gaze to Shade senior and let a smile play across her lips. "And he *really* liked the showers."

He gazed back at her with bland arrogance. The man was cool, she had to give him that. His expression hadn't changed since he'd come aboard with Security Dude. She wondered if it was possible to get Julian Shade to show some emotion beyond stern, if that was even an emotion.

Challenge accepted.

"He died in the ignition tube, you said." Arkitsis fixed Lucas with a dark gaze. "You're certain."

"Inspector, there was nothing left of … well, there wasn't much left of the thruster assembly, so you can imagine what would happen to a human body…"

Morgan had to admire the way the kid lied without actually saying anything untrue. He looked young and guileless as hell, and yet, there was something different about Lucas Shade since what they now referred to as "The Crisis." He stood taller, held his head higher, looked people directly in the eye … like he was doing to Security Dude Arkitsis just now.

"Let's focus on the ignition tube and Medbay first," Arkitsis said. "We're likely to find the most DNA samples there."

He split his team; two to the Medbay, two to crew's quarters, two to the ignition tube. He accompanied the third team. Lucas and Morgan followed.

"Are you the First Officer?" Arkitsis asked her as they made their way down through engineering to the thruster assembly.

"No. Chief Engineer. This is my bailiwick and I'll be overseeing repairs … as soon as you and your tech-heads are out of the way."

"Is that how you speak to an officer of HASA?" asked Julian Shade.

Morgan glanced over her shoulder at him. His brow was just the tiniest bit furrowed. She decided to call that a score. "Well, I just spoke that way to an officer of HASA, so … yes?"

Arkitsis ignored the by-play. He turned to Lucas as they

made their way through Engineering, past the now dormant Keplinger drive. Its rods were colorless and dull—a giant's set of Pick-up Sticks.

"Where is your second-in-command?" he asked Lucas.

"He's in the comms, lining up repair contractors. Did you need him?"

"We'll want to interview him, of course—along with the rest of your crew. Your father tells me he's a net-head."

"Yes. Trevor Marsden. Goes by Cyber. We would never have made it out of Pilgrim's Passage without him."

"I'll definitely want to meet with him, then. He likely saw things none of the rest of you did."

You can bet your shiny blue uniform he did, Morgan thought and felt heat ripple up her spine.

"And we'll want to see his video records of the incidents leading up to Matthews's death."

Morgan yanked a glance over to Lucas. His face was still completely composed—a sixteen year-old version of his dad's. She'd never tell him that; it would insult the hell out of him. The only way she could tell he was at all perturbed was the tiniest twitch at the corner of his mouth.

<Got it covered.>, said Cyber's voice, from the middle of her head. It tickled, not unpleasantly.

She glanced up along the spot where the bulkhead joined the ceiling and caught the almost invisible scuttle of tiny cam bots tracking their progress through the engineering bay. One of them paused to blink a blue light at her. She smiled at it.

The thruster ignition tube was a gutted, burnt out wreck that reeked of chemical cinder, the bitter tang of once-superheated metal, and charred flesh.

"If I may ask," said Inspector Arkitsis, as his team scraped char and anything else from the chamber's surfaces, "what was Matthews doing in the ignition tube to begin with?"

"I thought I answered that, already," said Lucas, his voice

level and laced with what sounded like annoyance, but might have been fear.

He was standing just in front of Morgan on the catwalk leading to the thruster assembly, with his hands clasped behind him. Her gaze was drawn to his hands and she realized, for the first time, how nervous he really was. His face was eerily composed, but his fingers were twisted together so tightly behind his back his knuckles were white. That he was holding it together this well was impressive. That he was doing it in front of Julian Shade was almost unimaginable.

"You said he went down because your thruster wasn't firing, but weren't there other crew who could have gone? Matthews was new to the vessel, wasn't he?"

"Yes, but he was the only one we thought had a chance of surviving long enough to get the thing to fire."

Morgan thought Arkitsis almost rolled his eyes. "I suppose what I'm really asking is how did you induce him to do that?"

Lucas looked at the man as if he was slow-witted. "We didn't induce him. He volunteered."

"Why would he volunteer? It was a suicide mission."

"To keep the ship from falling into the hands of Vishnu Chowdury and all of us possibly being killed. Isn't that obvious, inspector?"

Way to lay on the heavy sarcasm.

"It seems an odd bit of altruism for an assassin who knows he can survive things that would kill most men."

"I doubt even Trouble could survive a zat bolt directly to the head," said Morgan. "Which is what he would've gotten if the *Agni Devi* had caught up with us. It was already a little personal with Chowdury *before* his synapses got scrambled by the Passage."

Arkitsis glanced at her, and opened his mouth to say something else, but Lucas cut him off.

"What is your point, Mr. Arkitsis? Do you think we're lying about him being in the ignition tube? Why?"

The inspector flicked a glance at Julian. "Your … your owner suggested that among his other enhancements, Mr. Matthews was considerably personable. Even charismatic. That he had effectively worked his way up from rank newbie to Captain's right hand man in the course of one voyage."

Lucas gave his father a side-eye. He flexed his fingers before sliding his hands into the pockets of his coveralls. "He did that by being honest and honorable. By being someone the captain and crew could rely on."

"Plus," added Morgan, "he didn't take shit from anybody, and hated bullies. Gotta love that in a man."

"Yes, perhaps you do," said Arkitsis. "Love him enough to fabricate a death scene?"

"Well," said Morgan, shrugging, "I guess your little team of experts will tell us."

Moments later, the experts climbed out of the thruster assembly and handed Arkitsis a tricked out medpad, apparently one for specialized uses like analyzing tiny bits of charred human on bulkheads. Morgan could feel Cyber's excitement through her shiny, new comms implant.

"Mm," she murmured to no one physically present. "I bet Doc Pike would love one of those."

Shade threw her an annoyed look, then watched the inspector inspect the data.

"Yes, I can see that the subject was indeed in the chamber when it superheated," Arkitsis said. "The tissue samples show no residual activity as might be expected of…" He paused and looked up at his avid audience. "It appears that Mr. Matthews is indeed, deceased."

Morgan was only half-convinced she was imagining his disappointment.

<I would really like to know>, Cyber said in her inner ear as she trailed the inspector and his team out of Engineering, <how he was going to end that sentence.>

"Which one?" she murmured.

<The one about residual activity. 'As might be expected of' … what?>

"So." Back in the ready room, Lucas looked across the map table at Inspector Arkitsis. "Anything else you want your forensics guys to check, or are you done here? I'd like to get the repair crews started."

His father turned a cool eye on the man, as well. "Yes. It would seem you have sufficient evidence that Matthews was in the ignition tube when it fired, and died there."

The inspector looked up from his datapad, flicking a glance from Julian to Lucas. "It would seem," he repeated. "I am concerned about the amount of DNA in your infirmary that Tech Wong found. Can you explain that?"

"I'm pretty sure I already did, at least once," Lucas responded. *And that you're trying to catch me in a lie.*

It was a wry thought; he'd become less and less anxious about the presence of these snoops as their visit wore on. Besides, he'd had plenty of practice lying to his father, though admittedly, that had been long distance.

Arkitsis's expression could only loosely be called a smile. "Humor me."

"Okay, fine. During the Crisis, we used Medbay as a sort of home base. The executive crew was all present, plus Dr. Pike and Trouble … Matthews. My uncle Erasmus … Captain Shade, that is, was under the influence of the Passage. He blew up Medbay with us in it and turned off the gravity. Our botanist was killed; Matthews was wounded. There was blood literally floating in the air. So, I'm not surprised he left a … a presence. You can ask Dr. Pike."

"I intend to. In fact, I believe I'll conduct that interview immediately, then speak to your first mate."

Lucas groaned inwardly. Why is this guy being such a hard ass?

They'd effected only the most crucial structural repairs to the thrusters and the drive while orbiting Acre. Right now, he wanted nothing more than to complete the repair and retrofit of the rest of their systems, and be about their business.

"I'm telling you, inspector, you're wasting your time and ours. Trouble Matthews died in the ignition tube."

"Under normal circumstances, Captain Shade, I'd accept that," said Arkitsis. "But these aren't normal circumstances. This man escaped a prison ship on which every other person—inmate and crew—died."

Julian shifted. "Survived how?"

"We don't know how."

"We know he was modded," said Julian. "Heavily so, if my son's experience of him is any indication."

"Obviously, but have you ever seen mods that could keep someone alive in space? That prison transport was turned inside out, exposed to the vacuum. Nobody had any chance of surviving it, but somehow Ridley Matthews did."

"Which suggests what?" Julian asked.

The inspector shook his head. "Not something I can speculate about, Mr. Shade. It's above my pay grade. Now, if you don't mind, Captain," he added, turning to Lucas, "I believe I'd like to interview Dr. Pike next."

Lucas nodded and looked into the red light of a cam bot that was perched atop an antique armillary on the map table. "Cyber, tell Doc Pike he's wanted in the Map Room. Oh, and you might want to unlink. I think you're next."

Morgan was studying a star chart on the map table when Lucas and Cyber entered the ready room. She looked up, scanned their faces, and found them both uncommunicative as hell.

"Well?"

"They're gone," said Lucas. "My father is seeing them off the ship."

"D'you think they bought our tale of adventure and woe?"

Cyber shrugged his bony shoulders. "Happens it's all true … right down to that last little white lie. I still want to know what sort of 'residual activity' he expected to find. And why. In fact…" He trailed off, his angular face taking on a thoughtfully vague look.

"Cyb," said Morgan, "you have to keep your mouth moving if you want us to actually hear what you're thinking."

He blinked and looked at her. "Oh, yeah. I was just thinking there was a lot of Trouble's DNA in Medbay. I wonder what Doc Pike would find if he, y'know, scraped some off the walls and analyzed it."

"You could always ask," said Morgan.

Lucas seemed disturbed by the thought. "Do we really want to do that? I mean, what would we do if we found something … I don't know … bad. We owe Trouble a hell of a lot."

"Yeah," said Cyber, "which is exactly why I think we owe it to him to fill in as many of the blanks in his life as we can. If we can get some idea of what HASA is looking for, we might actually be able to help him. In any event, we should let him know about the visitation."

Lucas nodded, but he still looked troubled. "Yeah. You're right. Good call. Do that."

Cyber had been gone for mere seconds when Morgan caught the sound of shoe soles in the short passage that led from the bridge to the ready room. She made a sharp hissing sound. "Incoming."

Two seconds later, Julian Shade stepped through the open hatch. He scanned the two of them with his colorless gaze, his face giving up nothing of what he was thinking.

"I've come to take my leave of you, Captain Shade," he said, and Morgan was certain there was an undertone of pride in the man's voice. "But I first need to know if there is anything you want to tell me that you neglected to share with the inspector."

"No, sir." To his credit Lucas did not even glance at Morgan for support.

She smiled and moved to lean against the bulkhead next to the hatch, from which vantage point she could see the faces of both father and son.

"Are you sure? Did you notice nothing ... unusual about Matthews? Something beyond what you told Arkitsis?"

"Like what, exactly?"

"A behavior or ability you'd never seen before in a modded human."

Lucas seemed to go inside himself for a moment, then said, "I know you were responsible for the inquisition—I mean, welcoming committee. Why are you so curious about Trouble? He's dead."

"To be honest, I'm skeptical of their story about him surviving in space and wondering why HASA is so interested in this particular dead man. That is, beyond the fact that he assassinated a major statesman."

"Maybe they thought he might've left behind evidence of coconspirators," suggested Morgan.

Julian looked at her as if she had performed an unexpectedly clever trick. "You may be right. Still, *can* you think of anything particularly unusual about Mr. Matthews's enhancements?"

Lucas shrugged. "He was really strong. Lightning fast. Nimble. Flexible."

Morgan snorted.

Lucas gave her a swift glance, then added, "I suppose the most unusual thing about him was that he had a whole inventory of physical enhancements, but without having his body permanently and specifically altered to accommodate the modifications. You know what I mean? He just looked like a regular human. Tall, buff, but normal."

Julian nodded slowly. "Not like a Hardbody or a Slinky, you mean?"

"Yeah. We … had several crew that were modded that way. Rainor Glass was a Slinky, modded for zero or light gravity, but he had bird-bones and wore an exo in standard grav. Trouble seemed just as capable in zero-g as full gravity."

Julian studied him for a moment, then said, "That's all?"

Lucas shrugged again. "He seemed able to handle radiation better than most folks without having to take meds. He recovered from the Passage quicker than the rest of us. And he was really, really smart. Good at reading people."

"Well," said Julian. "I see I'm to be no wiser when I leave than when I arrived. Except to note that I am pleasantly surprised by your performance, Lucas. You have acquitted yourself well in getting this ship to port. And you did it with enough cargo intact to bring in far more profit than I could have expected. I'm impressed, too, with the way you handled the inspection. You did not let the authorities intimidate you."

Morgan thought he sounded puzzled, as if Lucas had morphed into something alien and inexplicable right before his eyes.

"No, sir. Thank you, sir." Lucas looked up and met his father's gaze. "Trouble taught me that. He thought being intimidated was a waste of time and energy and that I should trust my instincts."

Oooh, you brazen little brat, thought Morgan fondly.

Julian's eyebrows rose so far they disappeared under his forelock. "You liked him, didn't you?"

"I did."

"Lucas, the man was an assassin."

"That's not the way I choose to remember him. He was my friend. *That's* the way I'll remember him."

Julian shook his handsome head and put out his hand. "Good-bye for now. I'll see you again when the retrofit is done. I want to make sure the ship is in good shape." He paused and smiled. "I plan on offering you some … particularly rich, but potentially dangerous commissions. Will you need help replacing your crew?"

Lucas shook the proffered hand. "No, sir. We're good."

Julian seemed strangely reluctant to go, but at last he started toward the hatch. He paused just short of leaving and turned. "Oh, yes. I meant to ask you to keep an eye open for one of those medpads the inspectors brought aboard. It seems one of them went missing."

"I'll put Cyber right on it, sir."

Morgan, still standing by the hatch, caught the elder Shade's eye as he turned to step out into the corridor. "There's one thing Lucas didn't tell you about Matthews, probably because he didn't know." When he raised a quizzical brow, she leaned in and whispered, "His eyes glowed in the dark."

She enjoyed the dawning distaste on Julian Shade's face even more than she'd expected to.

The moment his father stepped off the ship, the moment he saw him in the ready room monitors striding down the *Raker's* debarkation ramp, Lucas felt as if every bone in his body had turned to goo. He realized, only then, how tightly he'd been holding himself. He shuddered, took a deep, cleansing breath and then blew it out.

He felt a hand on his shoulder and turned to see Morgan grinning at him.

"That was impressive. I think your old man was legitimately proud *and* perplexed. You handled that really well. I'm proud of you—proud to be serving with you … Captain."

Lucas could feel his cheeks going hot with pleasure. "Aw, c'mon, Morgan. Call me Lucas."

"That," Morgan said, "would be inappropriate. What if I call you Cap. 'Kay?"

He nodded, not trusting himself not to blurt out how much her approval meant to him. He didn't remember his mother well, wasn't completely sure why she had suddenly disappeared when he was still small, but this felt the way he'd imagined it would feel if he'd done something to make her proud.

He moved to return to the bridge when Cyber pinged him.

<Hey, Lucas—I mean, Captain.>

"Cap," said Lucas, glancing at Morgan. He could tell by the way she was looking at him that she was receiving the communication as well. "What is it?"

<Are you available to talk to an investigator?>

Lucas rolled his eyes. "Shit. *Another* one? What does he want?"

<She, actually. And she wants to talk to you about the subject of the day: Ridley Matthews.>

"Did you tell her he's dead?"

<I'm not sure she believes me.>

"Put her through. Morgan and I will try to convince her."

BUYING THE SKIN-DARKENING SPRAY WAS NO BIG DEAL. MANY WORE foundation, face and body paint, and other cosmetic devices in the world Trouble pretended he belonged in. Returning his eyes to their natural (or unnatural) color was as simple as flipping a mental switch. He still didn't look quite like himself—his face was too angular and gaunt, his body thin—but it was enough, he thought, to catch the attention of the people on his trail. He'd padded the lines of his body with a desert-dweller's gear, the folds of the burnous concealing the lower half of his face.

After his success with his eye color, he worked on growing his hair and managed a messy, every-which-way coiffure that he gave up on after he'd achieved a length approaching four inches. He could make the hair grow, but didn't seem to be able to affect the color. He ended up using a cosmetic spray to lighten it to its original chestnut brown. Since he had no idea of the actual mechanism that allowed him to do these things, he was uncertain if he was doing something wrong, or if the mod simply wasn't supposed to work that way.

He spent several hours in the morning and early evening letting Ridley Matthews be seen around a particularly promising area in which there were a surfeit of mod shops, tattoo parlors, and armorers. He was particularly interested in the tattoo artists, he watched one woman work on a fellow's forearm, imbuing it with figures and lines of gleaming "ink." He wondered if his own talents ran to mock tattoos that he could learn to change at will. Would he have to get a real tattoo to manipulate, or could he fake that too? He caught himself just short of becoming fascinated with his unknown alterations and left the shop before he could talk himself into an experiment.

Leaving the quarter—a run-down district ironically referred to as Kiryat Amiram (town of lofty people) or Lofty Town—he shed the Ridley Matthews "costume" in the darkest stretch of a poorly lit alley and tucked it into his shoulder pack. It was Adam Newman who haunted the "lofty" neighborhood by night.

After several days of this, he saw Pocket Watch again. He had been loitering at an open-air chop house in his bounty hunter drag for perhaps an hour when his hunter/prey appeared around a corner and proceeded to enter the tattoo parlor Trouble had visited the day before as himself (more or less). He fought the urge to dash down the street and nonchalantly pop into the place. Instead, he rose, took a last sip of his drink (something called prickly tea) and wandered aimlessly in the direction of the tattoo parlor.

Aimlessness wasn't enough; Pocket Watch was long in reappearing, Trouble supposed this was because he was getting an earful from the artist with whom Trouble had had a brief conversation about the luminous ink she used. To kill a bit more time, he crossed to the side of the street the shop was on and paused to make a pretense of reading his datapad. Pocket Watch emerged from the shop in due time, bristling with purpose. He radiated agitation, notwithstanding the deadpan expression on his face. He made a beeline for a tavern halfway down the block on the same side of the street.

This time Trouble followed him.

When Trouble entered the place, the guy was already at the bar, demanding the attention of one of the two barkeeps—a diminutive middle-aged woman. Trouble hesitated to draw closer, then caught a glance at himself in the mirror behind the bar. He barely recognized himself. Hesitation evaporated and he made his way to the bar a bare three feet from where Pocket Watch stood.

The second barkeep, a younger, taller woman, was with him immediately. "What can I get you?"

"I'm new around here. How about your favorite soft ale?"

"Coming right up." She flashed a smile and spun away with a whisk of her long braid.

"I'm looking for someone," Pocket Watch was saying, pulling a datapad out of his jacket pocket.

The barkeep laughed. "Isn't everybody? Name's Delilah. Any chance you're looking for me?"

He shot her an annoyed glance. "A particular someone. Guy named Ridley Matthews. May go by Trouble or just T."

"Don't know anybody by any of those names, fella. Sorry. You gonna buy a drink?"

Pocket Watch held the datapad out to her. "This man. If you can't tell from the pic, he's a bit over two meters tall, muscular, looks like he could handle himself in a fight. His hair may be longer than this. He's got pale eyes. Strange eyes."

The younger barkeep had returned with Trouble's ale. He smiled his thanks, and transferred the credits to the house account.

Delilah, meanwhile, had stopped to give the image in the datapad a long, narrow-eyed look. "Strange, how?"

"Sometimes they seem to … shine or gleam. Especially in dimly lit places." He gave the dimly lit room a meaningful glance.

She was already nodding. "Yeah. Saw him … two days ago and again earlier today. Can't forget those eyes. He was desert-dressed, so I didn't get a good look at his face, but those eyes were a stand-out. He looked like he was getting ready to hike into the dunes. Hadn't gone yet, though. Clothes were too clean."

She seemed proud of her observation and Trouble had to allow he was impressed that she'd noticed that.

Note to Self: get dirty.

Now Pocket Watch was fairly vibrating with predatory angst … or glee—it was hard to tell. "Was he alone? The whole time?"

"Yeah. Came in, got a bowl of the house chowder and a drink, asked for a good mod shop that wasn't too expensive. I told him about Soheyl's over in the next block. On Saffron Street." She indicated "that way" with a gesture.

Well, that ratcheted up Pocket Watch's heart rate a bit.

"Did it seem to you he intended to go there directly?"

She shrugged. "He thanked me and left right away. Gave me a nice tip."

"Thank you, Delilah," said Pocket Watch, keying something into his datapad. "You've been most helpful. I've left a tip, myself, on the house account under your name … along with my ME number, in case Mr. Matthews should return." He gave her a dismissive nod, pocketed his pad, glanced at his timepiece and turned to leave.

"Hey," said Delilah to his retreating back, "you got a name?"

He didn't stop, but turned his head slightly. "Raimi," he said, and was gone.

Trouble watched him through the door, took a long pull on his ale and left the tavern himself. Clearly, his stalker had left Delilah the same ME contact he already had, but now, at least, he had a name: Raimi. It might be his real name or an alias, but it was something. It was an unfamiliar name, though … unless Raimi was a part of Trouble's memory that hadn't surfaced— except under the influence of the Pilgrim's Passage. He smiled grimly; with his luck he'd remember who Raimi was just before the guy zatted him out of existence.

He followed Raimi to the mod shop on Saffron and stood just to one side of the front door, listening to his exchange with the clerk, effectively concealed by a holographic ad for DeNA-Gen's "new and improved" line of facial enhancements. It went pretty much as his conversation with Delilah had gone, except this guy hadn't seen Trouble and had to ask his technicians if they'd seen him. Two of them had, and reported that Raimi's quarry had inquired about a certain set of mods but had left without booking any services. Finding out which mods the fugitive had asked about had required Raimi to cough up significant credits —which gave Trouble some enjoyment.

The look on the man's face when he left the shop was a contrarian combination of excitement and frustration. Trouble got it. He was feeling something like that, himself. Having raised the stakes, he wanted to act now, to confront Raimi and find out who he was working for. But this next part had to be executed with great care.

Trouble settled for following Raimi at a distance from concealment, until the man finally disappeared into an inn about four blocks from Trouble's low-rent digs. He did not come out. Trouble figured he could go in and ask what room belonged to the odd-looking gent who'd just checked in. But if he did, the chances that the concierge would tell Raimi about him were high. That wasn't a big problem; he wanted to be seen as competition or a possible ally in Raimi's quest. But how would his stalker react if he literally showed up on his doorstep, clearly spelling out how closely he'd been following him?

Trouble chose to return to his own lodgings.

The next morning found Trouble sitting in the simple little eatery just off the foyer of Raimi's inn, enjoying an early breakfast. Raimi appeared in the lobby as Acre's sun was pouring warm golden light into the narrow streets and alleys and polishing the walls of the buildings with a grime-concealing glow. He entered the cafe and ordered a hand pie and a coffee.

Raimi looked up when Trouble came to his table and said, "Mr. Raimi, I was wondering if I might have a word with you about a mutual interest."

Raimi tilted his head slightly to one side and regarded Trouble through narrowed, wintry eyes. "I can't begin to imagine what mutual interests we might have. I don't know you. And I'm pretty sure you don't know me."

This close up, Trouble was chilled by the fact that this was, without doubt, the face of his nemesis in Pilgrim's Passage. Long and angular with pale eyes, high cheekbones, a nose as sharp as a sailing ship's prow, the wide, thin-lipped mouth bracketed by long lines. He'd call them smile lines, but he was pretty sure this guy didn't smile so much as he bared his teeth to ward off strangers.

"I do know why you're in New Haifa," Trouble told him. "Same reason I am. You're looking for a man named Ridley Matthews."

An eyebrow flicked upward. "And why would I be doing that?"

"Because he's a murderer. An assassin. And I've heard some scuttlebutt that he's pretty heavily modded, so I figure you might just need help if you ever locate him."

"What makes you think I haven't located him?"

Trouble shrugged. "You're not dead and you're not on a ship back to wherever you came from with a prisoner or a corpse in a cryo pod."

The twitch of the thin lips might have been Raimi's version of a smile. "And what do you hope to get out of 'helping' me?"

"Seriously? C'mon. There has to be a bounty right?" He hesitated then said, "If there weren't, you and Mystery Woman wouldn't both be looking for the guy."

The pale eyes were suddenly riveted on Trouble's face. He was aware of the uptick in the other man's heart rate, sensed a minute rise in his body temperature. felt the quiver of his interest like prickles up the back of his neck.

"What woman?" Raimi asked.

"Young, pretty, lethal-looking, black hair, dark eyes. She's been asking about Matthews too. I've caught her watching you a few times. You didn't notice her?"

Raimi didn't answer. "Why don't you try to partner up with *her* then?"

Trouble didn't answer, but simply observed, "I like your taste in antiques." He nodded at the pocket watch gleaming from its fob.

Raimi fingered the crown of the watch, "You are in error, Mr..."

"Newman. Adam Newman."

"Mr. Newman, I am not a bounty hunter. I have no idea who your mystery woman is or why she's looking for Matthews or why she's stalking me. Nor do I care. I am a private detective hired to find Matthews and return him to Earth."

"Earth?" Trouble was unable to hide his own surprise at the mention of humanity's original homeworld. He realized that his model of the universe had shriveled to Herron's Hope and Acre, and that he tangentially knew of Restitution, which wasn't even a planet, and whose population consisted of criminals and those hired to keep an eye on them.

"Matthews committed an offense against the Heartworlds Alliance. Where else would I be taking him but the Heartworlds' capital?" Raimi paused, regarding Trouble through half-closed eyes, then said, "Still, you are correct—Matthews is supremely dangerous. I'm not in a position to join forces with you, Mr. Newman, but perhaps we can share intel. Were you to glean any information about this woman you say is following me, I will reward you for it. And, if you should happen across Ridley Matthews, I'd pay well for his location."

Raimi rose from his seat, straightened his coat, checked his watch, then leveled an icy look at Trouble. "If you should happen to encounter Mr. Matthews, I highly recommend you do not engage with him. He's got at least forty pounds on you and even I am not certain about the extent of his modifications. Good day, Mr. Newman."

Raimi lifted a small backpack to his shoulder, gave Trouble a nod, and strode out of the inn. Trouble waited a moment, savoring the irony of being offered money to find himself, then followed.

Raimi rented an electric bike and headed out of the city toward the mountains. Trouble followed in a robotic rickshaw. He was puzzled by this seeming digression at first, then realized that the man was headed to the Mabirati shrines on Mount Carmi. The air cooled as they climbed; lowland foliage gave way to conifers that overshadowed the road and covered the flanks of the mountain in a deep green blanket. The scent of the trees was intoxicating, and Trouble allowed himself to simply enjoy it until the gleaming buildings of the Mabirati complex came in sight.

The rickshaw swept into the circular approach and let Trouble out in front of the main temple which was apparently where most people—whether tourists or pilgrims—began their visit. It, and the other buildings around it, were set among red-gold spires of native rock that rose, sentinel, above the dark trees. Pathways and plazas of pale stone connected the various buildings—the schools, the hospice, the library and its adjuncts. Everywhere, there were people walking the paths, sitting in the many arbors and pavilions. Their activities identified them as tourists (gazing and taking pictures), or students (reading or tapping on datapads), or devotees (praying or meditating).

As he disembarked from the rickshaw, Trouble saw Raimi's rented bike parked in a line of similar conveyances. He had donned a burnous in the rickshaw, and now pulled the hood up over his head before he went in search of the alleged detective. Entering the temple approach with its reflecting pools and flower beds, his puzzlement returned, but with a different emphasis. There were two reasons Raimi would come here;

either he was a Mabirati, which was unlikely, or he thought his quarry might come here.

Would he? Why? Was Ridley Matthews a Mabirati? Was this place and the faith it symbolized another piece of his missing self? He searched his mind for knowledge, but found none, only the quivering sense of being suspended, frozen, in the desire to know.

He stepped into the temple through tall double doors and found himself on the pale, gleaming stone of a circular gallery that ran around the perimeter of the sanctuary. The cavernous room was without abrupt angles or corners and was crowned by a sun-filled central dome. At the very apex of the dome, a symbol had been affixed—a golden cup spilling silver stars into a night sky. The cup was encircled by a border made up of a double-helix, also decked with stars. The vault, itself, rested on a series of pillars carved to represent DNA strands.

A wave of familiarity struck Trouble so hard it stopped his breath, and all but pushed him a step backward. He'd seen this. This was familiar, comfortable, *known*. At least, the symbols and architecture were. But the scenery he could see through the tall perimeter windows that formed the outer wall of the gallery was off. He did not expect the view to include the rocky spires between which he could see an expanse of desert stretching out from the foot of the mountain.

What had he expected to see?

He shook himself free of the *deja vu* moment and stepped behind one of the DNA pillars from which he swept the large chamber for Raimi, his eyes flitting along those seated in the circular tiers that rose from a central dais. He found Raimi just as the man was moving from one pillar to another on the far side of the hall. Trouble smiled. Both of them were, once again, engaged in the same activity in similar fashion. Only the object of their search was different. The only thing missing was...

The thought stalled as his eyes found her in the top row of seats just below the perimeter colonnade—the Woman. She had her head tilted to one side, seemingly focused on a set of prayer beads in her hands, but even from here he could see that she was watching Raimi's progress along the walk to her left. When the "detective" had reached the next pillar and stopped to scan the room again, she rose and ascended to the gallery. She turned as if to follow Raimi, then disappeared behind one of the pillars. When she reappeared on the opposite side, she had affected a burnous not unlike the one Trouble wore, with the hood pulled up to conceal her hair and the lower half of her face.

Trouble moved a few steps toward the doors that opened into the exterior plaza, glancing back and forth between the Woman and Raimi. The third time he looked in her direction, she was looking back at him. He froze for a split second, then made a gesture he had no conscious knowledge of learning. He cupped his hands at heart level, extended them toward her as if offering a gift (or asking one), and bowed his head. When he looked up again, she was gone.

39 / VOICES

NEEDLESS TO SAY, NEITHER POCKET WATCH NOR THE MYSTERY Woman found what they were looking for at the Mabirati Shrines. Trouble couldn't help but find humor in that, considering that he was standing only yards away during the entire day—sometimes closer. He used the opportunity to watch both of them, make lists of observations, and ponder imponderables. Who were they? Who were they working for? Clearly not the same entity. Unless it was a very paranoid entity that had enlisted one operative to spy on the other.

No. He had the sense they were in competition, not collaborators.

Assuming that the Woman was aware of the re-emergence of Ridley Matthews, that she was still shadowing Pocket Watch could be significant in a variety of ways. Maybe she hoped to snatch their quarry from his grasp, or—more disturbingly—kill him before he could be returned to custody. It had not escaped Trouble's notice that someone wanted him dead. Either of these stalkers could be working for that someone.

Trouble's next task, he figured, was to try to find out who Raimi was working for. The pretext was simple enough: Bounty hunting (or detecting) gigs were hard to come by for a freelancer. It made sense that Adam Newman would like to work for someone willing to offer a decent contract just to find disappeared persons.

The morning after the trek to the holy places, Trouble was prepared to waylay Raimi at his inn with a simple question: "Who's your boss? I'd sure like to work for him too." He came ready with a series of "leads" to misdirect his would-be captor, intending to focus his own efforts on maneuvering an encounter with the Mystery Woman.

"You again," Raimi said when Trouble sat himself down at the same breakfast table.

"Me again," Trouble agreed. "So, did you see her? Yesterday at the shrines. Did you see the Woman?"

"You followed me."

"Well, yeah."

"There were many women at the shrines yesterday."

"Yeah, and she looked like four or five of them. She kept rearranging her clothing so you'd never see the same woman standing three feet away from you."

Raimi's face went very still. "She was never that close."

Trouble smiled amiably. "Whatever you say, Mr. Raimi."

"How did you come to notice her so easily?"

How did he? Probably mods. Possibly training. He couldn't say that to this guy. "I know what to look for now. I've seen her face, her body language." He shrugged.

"And you came here to tell me that?"

"No. I came to tell you that I saw your Mr. Matthews last night."

Now he had the other man's full attention. "Where?"

Trouble stopped just shy of scratching his suddenly itchy nose. "How badly do you want to know?"

Raimi regarded him silently for a moment, then said, "What are you asking?"

"A connection. To whomever you work for. Your agency, your boss. I'm tired of scrabbling for work on Acre."

"I work for a rather large agency that doesn't tend to hire

freelancers off the streets. Especially not the streets of a tourist-infested backwater like Acre."

Trouble tipped his head to one side, shrugged, and stood. "Fine. I'll just go follow up on this myself then … or maybe share it with our Mystery Woman." He'd do it too, he'd decided, as much as he was hoping to send Pocket Watch off on a wild Trouble chase.

The corners of Raimi's mouth twitched, possibly in recognition that the threat was not an idle one. "I work for a man named Thorn. He's … an officer in the Heartworlds' security apparatus."

Thorn. Trouble couldn't pair the name with a face or an identity, but he had the vague, unsettling feeling that those things existed somewhere in his blasted memory. He supposed he should be relieved. He wasn't. He'd been concerned that Julian Shade might have hired a bounty hunter once he learned that a convicted assassin had traveled aboard one of his freighters. Of course, Raimi could be lying. Thorn might not be a real person.

"Thorn, huh? That's it? Is that a name or a description of his personality?"

"Funny. Like I said, he's got some rank in HASA. I suppose you want me to recommend you to him. Hard to do when I have no idea how valuable your intel might be."

"Fair. I found your guy and followed him down to the lakeport last night. Watched him board a ferry to Mirrorton."

Raimi's eyes narrowed. "What time was this?"

"It was the last ferry—so twenty-two hundred hours. He was carrying a well-filled pack and a short staff. May have been a weapon of some sort masquerading as a walking stick. Not sure about that. Gave the impression of a man intending to be gone for a while."

"Were you planning to follow him?"

"Not on my own. I've done some research on this guy. I doubt I could take him by myself."

Raimi's eyes took on a shrewd gleam. "You might tell this

Mystery Woman what you insist you've seen. Partner with her to go after Matthews. Isn't that why you wanted to know who I work for? You capture Matthews, swing a deal with Thorn, and split a bounty with your lady friend?"

Trouble shook his head. "I can see why you'd think that, but no. I was gonna ask to ride along with you, but I suspect you wouldn't go for that."

"Your suspicions are correct. I don't do partnerships or ride-alongs. But I will keep my agreement to let my boss know I met someone with a shrewd eye who's looking for work. In fact, give me your ME code and I'll pass it along." He rose, pulling out his datapad and extending it toward Trouble, who reciprocated, tapping his pad gently against Raimi's.

"Thanks." Trouble rose, as well. "Good luck with the manhunt."

Raimi nodded curtly, turned and strode from the cafe back into the foyer of the inn. Trouble watched him go, then sat back down and ordered some breakfast. He was just finishing his coffee when someone said right into his ear, "Hey, Trouble. Need to talk."

It was like being hit with a jerkstick. He spun out of his chair and glanced around, his hand on the knife in his belt. There was no one even remotely nearby, but the other diners were now staring at him.

<Trouble, hey,> said the voice, sounding as if the person behind it was murmuring inside his head. <Did I catch you at a bad time?>

He realized that he recognized the voice. "Cyber?"

<Who else?>

"Shit."

<Well, that's a fine way to greet a friend.>

Trouble muttered a few more choice expletives under his breath, said, "Give me a minute," and left the cafe.

Once out in the street where the ambient noise was enough to cover conversation, and he was headed toward a main thoroughfare, he murmured, "Where are you? How are you talking to me?"

<I'm on Idris. We put in to offload some of the cargo and finish repairs. You should see *Moonraker*. Less than a week in and it's already a world of difference. When you see the old girl again, you won't recognize her.>

"Cyb, there was a second part to that question."

<Oh, right. I'm using your comms port.>

"My—" Damn. This constant parade of Things Trouble Matthews Doesn't Know About Himself was going to drive him mad. "You mean to tell me that I came with a built-in comms system on top of everything else?"

<Not exactly,> Cyber said. <I knew you wouldn't ask for help, so I sort of took things into my own hands. You had a socket for a communications array, so while you were in Medbay regenerating, I filled it.>

"Okay." Not okay, but what could he do about it now? "What did you need to tell me?"

<Bunch of stuff. First, I guess, Papa Shade showed up on the *Raker* wanting to commend Lucas and help us crew up. Lucas accepted the accolades but nixed the help part every-which-way. The proceeds from our trip were more than adequate to get the old bucket an upgrade and crew.>

"And?"

"And Julian also brought with him a HASA inspector who had his minions crawl all over the ship looking for you, or signs of you. Lucas listed you among the casualties and it seems they didn't believe you'd bagged it, Pike's death certificate notwithstanding. Your reputation apparently preceded you. Took letting them loose in the thruster assembly before they seemed convinced. Hopefully, news will get back to the folks who're hunting for you."

"No sign of that yet."

There was a pause, then Cyber said, <There's someone looking for you on Acre?>

Trouble had reached a roundabout that had a cab stand and queued up behind a family who, judging from the toy drones the two kids were leading on fiber-optic leashes, were sightseeing.

"Two someones. A man named Raimi and a woman I fondly refer to as my Mystery Woman. She's following him, hoping to find me, it seems. He had no idea she existed until I mentioned it to him just now."

<A woman? You wouldn't happen to know her name.>

"Uh, no. Hence, Mystery Woman."

"<Right. Well, Cap—Lucas—got a chat from a woman intelligence agent several days back. An Agent Sharaf. She's not HASA, she's from COI.>

"Try to remember that I can't, Cyb. COI is…"

<Oh, Consonance Office of Intelligence. What are the odds she's the same as your Mystery Lady?>

"Probably just a coincidence. I'm sure COI has battalions of female agents."

<You think either of these people recognized you?>

"Nope. I just sent Raimi off on a wild Trouble chase across the lake and the Woman—" He was suddenly struck with the possibility that instead of pursuing the leads he'd created by posing as himself, the Woman would follow Raimi across the lake. "Oh, shit."

<What?>

"Look, we'll need to catch up later, Cyb. I need to make sure my Mystery Woman doesn't track Raimi across Teykh Akhdus. He says he's working for someone named Thorn who's an officer in HASA. Not sure any of that is true."

<Kind of rings a bell. I can check it for you—easy. How about Mystery Woman?>

"No idea who she's working for … unless she's your Agent Sharaf."

<Wren,> said Cyber.

"What?"

<Agent Sharaf's first name is Wren. Not very agent-y. Sounds

more like a vid star. Looks a little like one, too. Here, I've got her file. I'm sending you a mental pic so you can see if she's your mystery lady.>

He did exactly that. The file image of Agent Wren Sharaf appeared in Trouble's mind's eye as if he was reviewing her file himself. It was the same woman—dark eyes, elfin face and thick black hair. In the file pic she was wearing a deep green uniform with a COI logo patch on the left shoulder and an ID badge on the right.

"Yeah," said Trouble. "That's her."

<Huh,> Cyber said. <And she's still hanging around? Makes me wonder if maybe Inspector Arkitsis didn't believe us as much as we thought.>

"Yeah, or I complicated things by putting in an appearance as myself."

<Oh, you did not…>

Trouble watched as the family pulled away in their cab and another arrived to take its place. "I wanted to draw my stalkers out. Look, my cab's here. I need to focus."

<Wait! There's something else you need to know.>

Trouble wondered how many more surprises he could take today. He climbed into the cab and directed the bot to take him to the Bengurian. "Go ahead, Cyb."

<The stuff Arkitsis was saying about you got Doc Pike to wondering what they were looking for in your … uh, your residue. He had some tissue samples and blood so he analyzed them. Doc says, you've got elements in your blood and tissue that he didn't recognize right away. He thought it must be nanites at first, but just about everyone has some nanites in their blood these days, so that shouldn't have caused Arkitsis's mind to wrinkle so hard. So, Doc used this new medical tablet we, um, acquired, and he found something else. Something organic. But Pike doesn't know what it is. Or he knows, but he's not telling.>

Well, that was unsettling. "D'you think he'd tell me?"

<I can ask.>

"Do that," Trouble told him. "In the meantime, I'm going to try to figure out why my two new friends are hunting a dead man."

<Trouble, really, it'd be best if you'd lie low. Just a for a week or two, max. Then … then we'll come by Acre and pick you up.>

"I'll consider your proposal," said Trouble. "But for now, I need to sign off and figure out how to keep Mystery Woman on this side of the big water."

<Why don't you just let her follow the other guy around? Wouldn't that be safer?>

"Most assuredly. But I've discovered that it's hard for me to lie low. I think I may be constitutionally incapable of it. Now, how do I turn this comm port off?"

<Trouble…>

"How, Cyb?"

A cybernetic sigh. <You just think, 'Comm One off.'>

Trouble frowned. "Is there a Comm Two?"

<Maybe…>

God Almighty. "Comm One and Two *off*," he said aloud.

There was silence in Trouble Matthews's head, but he was pretty certain Cyber had not set up his comms without some sort of emergency override. He was loath to admit that the certainty brought with it a sense of comfort.

BLAKE RAIMI WAS AN INTENSELY CURIOUS MAN.

As he waited for the ferry at the New Haifa terminal on the shores of Teykh Akhdus, his curiosity centered on the odd behavior of Ridley Matthews. Specifically, why would Matthews have left the safe haven of a Freeman's Guild vessel to wander around the seamier boroughs of the city before crossing the lake for ... what? Did he hope to lose himself in some rural tide pool, hoping that the people looking for him would just give up and go away? That was bloody unlikely. He must have been forced from the ship when they'd realized he was a wanted man. That would have happened the moment they emerged from the Passage.

He knew Matthews was a Mabirat, that he'd accepted the faith after marrying a woman who'd been brought up in it. Maybe that was what had drawn him here. Maybe the mind wipe hadn't been as effective as Thorn supposed. Maybe the same thing that gave Matthews his ability to survive what would kill most men had caused his memories to rebuild themselves. Raimi had to admit some curiosity about what that something was.

The ferry arrived and Raimi boarded. He sought a place at the bow of the boat that would offer a view of the vast expanse of sparkling, surreally blue water and the streamers of white mist that perpetually floated across it, listing this way and that in eddies of air. The locals called them "water whimsies" and "lake angels" and granted them some form of sentience, based on the seeming willfulness of their movement. He was pretty sure no one really believed they were sentient, but it probably made the tourists and pilgrims happy.

He smiled wryly at the thought of that Newman character. *God, what a naif.* A naif who apparently had good powers of observation. Or something else entirely. That woman the guy talked about was a complete mystery. So much so that Raimi wasn't certain she existed. In fact, he was inclined to believe she didn't. He surely would've noticed some femme following him around. But then, he'd been so focused on his quarry that he hadn't noticed Newman until the guy wanted to be noticed.

Still, chances were good that Newman had made the woman up out of whole cloth as a form of leverage.

Raimi had no more than settled into a bow-facing deck chair when the comm link in his ear went off. It was Thorn.

"I'm on my way to—" he started to say, but Thorn cut him off.

"It's over. Come in. I've transferred the credits to your account to pay you what you've earned so far—you're done. But if you come back to Earth, you've got a permanent place in my organization waiting for you."

"What the hell are you talking about?" Raimi started to ask, but Thorn cut him off again.

"He's dead."

Just like that. Delivered in a voice that sounded like it was wearing lead boots.

"Matthews? Matthews is dead?"

"Apparently, he did something idiotic and heroic and got himself barbecued in the thruster housing of that rust bucket he was on. There's nothing left of him but soot and bloody smudges on the bulkheads."

Raimi opened his mouth, started to say that couldn't be true because people around here had seen Ridley Matthews in the days after the *Moonraker* had allegedly come and gone. He stopped himself from saying that and instead said, "I have reason to doubt that."

Thorn snorted. "You have reason to want to squeeze more money out of me, you mean. I know you were hoping to score the bounty on this job, but that's no longer an option. As it is, I was paying you for a fool's errand. Just be thankful I'm not cutting you loose. I have hard scientific evidence that Matthews died of his own sacrificial stupidity. Now are you going to come in? I have other work for you."

Raimi didn't answer the question. "You haven't asked why I think the reports of Matthews's demise might be exaggerated. That surprises me, considering you seemed to really want to get this guy alive."

"I did."

"I don't get that. I mean, he's been mind-wiped, so he can't tell tales on you. So, this isn't about shutting him up. He failed to execute, but you don't seem like the type to indulge in revenge."

"I don't give a gnat's eyeball about revenge, in this case. He was ... a valuable asset."

A failed assassin and (ironically) convicted murderer was a valuable asset? A variety of suspicions queued in Raimi's mind. He pushed one out of his mouth. "Because of his mods? Guy was impressive. To get blown out into space like that and survive—that's nothing I've seen anywhere but science fiction. Something special about him, is there?"

Thorn's laugh was as deep and smooth as his speaking voice. "I'm certainly not going to tell you what makes—or what *made*—Matthews special. Let's just say his death was a very costly end to a very costly experiment."

"Experiment," Raimi repeated.

"Your earned credits have been transferred to your account. Now I need you to come in."

Raimi considered that option ... for about a nano-second. He had no interest in being part of someone else's organization. Sure, he might be able to wangle another freelance contract out of the man, but that meant starting fresh with a new "project" and he was pretty sure he wasn't really finished with this one. "I'll pass. I have some loose ends to tie up here on Acre. Besides, I kind of like New Haifa. The sector I've been snooping in is a regular den of thieves. My kind of people."

"Loose ends?"

"Yeah. I'm a real thorough kind of guy. When I find a bunch of odd rocks, I like to turn them *all* over before I move on."

There was a twitchy silence on the other end of the connection, then Thorn said, "Okay, I'll bite. Why do you doubt that Ridley Matthews is dead?"

Raimi chuckled. "No good reason, I'm sure you'd say. Just ... things."

There was a long silence before Thorn said, "What things? His DNA was all over that thruster assembly. Not just smears or particles. He was cooked. Burnt to a cinder. We had to scrape the ash off the bulkheads."

"Yeah. But you already thought he was dead once."

"Yes, but that was different. We pronounced him dead—hastily, I admit—because of a complete *lack* of DNA ... from any of the people aboard that prison transport. What do you have to show me or tell me about besides a gut feeling?"

"I'm not the only one still looking for him."

Again, the silence. Raimi swore he could hear gears turning.

"I get it, Raimi," Thorn told him. "You're trying to sell me the moon. I'd say 'nice try,' but you're a very blunt instrument. Stay on Acre, then. It's your loss."

Thorn closed the connection, leaving Raimi to sit and ponder the situation. He was certain Ridley Matthews was very much alive, and Thorn's insistence that he wasn't and that Raimi's services were no longer needed rang false. Thorn was lying; Raimi was sure of it. He'd been only too willing to believe

Matthews had fled to Acre until ... what? He hadn't said how he came by "scientific evidence" that Matthews was really, truly dead—this time.

Raimi knew enough about how Thorn operated to suspect that he was intending to use his "regulars" to swoop in and capitalize on Raimi's work. The money for time spent was substantial, but it wasn't anywhere near what he would've been paid if he'd brought in a live Ridley Matthews. Or even his corpse.

Which left Raimi to wonder if Thorn had always planned on finishing this with someone on his regular payroll, after Raimi had done ... well, everything. He'd pulled Thorn's chestnuts out of the fire when it was clear Matthews meant to betray him to the authorities, finishing the security chief's assignment, then framing him for two murders. He'd been paid handsomely to do so, but he knew he wasn't the only hunter in the field, and it occurred to him that Adam Newman might be one of those other hunters. Maybe the woman (if there really *was* a woman) was one, as well. It made all kinds of sense that they'd be working together.

The more he thought about the possible permutations of this, the closer he looked at the fact that it meant a much leaner payoff for him, the tighter Raimi's jaw clenched. The tighter his jaw clenched, the more determined he became to finish his assignment in a way that would maximize his profits ... and protect him from his knowledge of Thorn's secrets.

He watched the far shoreline through the morning meanders of water whimsies, and sorted through what he knew. He knew that Ridley "Trouble" Matthews was very much alive and living up to his nickname on Acre. Did he also know that the fugitive had booked passage on the ferry to Mirrorton the night before?

No. Because Adam Newman had told him that and he had no idea who Adam Newman really was and whom he might work for. At the moment, the theory that he and his mysterious woman worked for Grant Thorn seemed most likely. As did the

unsettling idea that Raimi might well have a target on his own
back.

Yeah, and maybe you're just paranoid.

A man got that way when he worked in the torn, sooty edges
between law and anarchy and occasionally stepped all the way
into the bloody red of criminality. He still felt like his belly was
full of lead when he thought about Matthews's wife. He had
assassinated people before. Men mostly, but occasionally a
woman. They'd been like Carldon—lawmakers, corporate actors,
other mercenaries, criminals embedded in corrupt systems,
someone's political enemies. He had never before taken a life out
of someone else's desire to control a narrative. A life that had
nothing to do with anyone's self-protective schemes. He had
disliked the job. Even hated it. But it went far beyond hatred of
the job when he'd heard the child's voice wondering why
Mommy was sleeping on the floor and imploring her to
wake up.

He'd made the mistake of looking back, of registering the
image of the little girl curled up next to her mother's lifeless
body, singing it a lullaby: "Hush now, Mommy, don't say a
word. Baby's gonna buy you a mockingbird."

As soon as he'd returned to the safety of his hotel room, he'd
left an anonymous tip with the authorities that he'd heard a
child crying inconsolably at the Matthews's address. He hadn't
realized until later that night that the figures reflected in the
gleaming tile of the Matthews's dining room floor would also be
reflected in his dreams.

Maybe Grant Thorn didn't give a gnat's eyeball for revenge
or justice. Neither did Blake Raimi. But it was suddenly important to him to understand why Grant Thorn found Ridley
Matthews so very valuable … and dangerous. Instinct and experience told him that it had to be more than a potential reawak-
ening of Matthews's memory.

41 / BIRD OF PREY

Wren Sharaf had arrived in New Haifa on Blake Raimi's coattails, trusting that he had some reason to be there. The COI agent had her own reasons to be seeking Ridley Matthews.

When Chaz Carldon had been assassinated, the Consonance Parliament he had headed found itself taking a back seat to Alliance operatives in the investigation. More than that, it seemed to Consonance officials that HASA was keeping them at more than arms' length in the investigation of their own Prime Minister's death. Consonance law enforcement agencies—including COI—had not even had the opportunity to interrogate Matthews when he was arrested and tried. They had been forced to watch everything from a distance, and any appeals to the Heartworlds' guiding council had been met with apologetic shrugs and sympathetic assurances that HASA had very good reasons for keeping everything under wraps. Those reasons were never addressed, and Wren and her superiors had the distinct impression that the Alliance's upper echelons didn't really know what they were.

Now, she had explicit instructions to locate Ridley Matthews if possible, and to find out why Grant Thorn, the head of HASA, was sitting on top of an investigation and man hunt that should have included participants from Consonance investigative agencies.

She had a theory. Chaz Carldon had drawn Ridley Matthews out of Thorn's operation at HASA to head his own security team. That his security chief had then turned around and assassinated him couldn't help but reflect negatively on Thorn's organization and the process by which they vetted their agents. He'd taken some public heat for it, but had brushed it aside by noting that Matthews had been working for Carldon for the better part of three years before the assassination. How could Thorn be held responsible for it?

Wren had decided early in her own investigation that monitoring the movements of HASA operatives would be a good place to start, and she had done just that, following them to the wreckage of the prison ship and thence to Porphyry on Herron's Hope, where she'd gotten her first look at Ridley "Trouble" Matthews in the tavern wherein he'd connected with Erasmus Shade—the man responsible for her trail going cold just as she was preparing to make a move on her target.

Matthews was a puzzle. He'd been convicted of murdering two people, yet had been concerned about getting a stolen credit tab back to its rightful owner. She could only imagine he had expected to receive a greater reward than a meal and an ale. She'd seen the old spacer blunder into him, but had been unable to sort their brief exchange from the background noise. Matthews disappeared not long after that interaction while Wren and most of the other patrons had been distracted by a loud altercation near the tavern's front entrance. She was convinced that neither Shade's clumsiness nor the altercation had been coincidental or accidental, but a cover for a transaction that got Trouble Matthews off-world.

She'd searched the bar after Matthews's disappearance, frustrated and angry with herself for allowing him to slip through her fingers. That was when she'd seen Raimi … and not for the first time during her tracking of Chaz Carldon's assassin. She had trailed the mercenary (and his reputation as a Bloodhound) to Acre.

If Raimi ran the fugitive Matthews to ground, she wanted to be as close by as possible, because the very presence of a merc sniffing at Matthews's back trail suggested that something was not right. Sure, there were legit HASA agents in the hunt, but they seemed too content to document their near-misses at Porphyry, on the *Moonraker* and Acre, and move on or withdraw from the field. The HASA contingent was down from a dozen agents to one or two since Wren had begun shadowing them.

Meanwhile, Raimi forged on.

The newest wrinkle in the situation had Wren deeply puzzled. Word had come to her from her superiors that Ridley Matthews had died aboard the *Moonraker*. She put in a call to the captain of the ship and had spoken, ultimately, to him, his first officer, and his chief engineer. All three had told her without hesitation that, yes, Trouble Matthews had died in the old freighter's thruster assembly attempting to thwart a pirate attack. His few belongings had been snapped up on Idris by an inspector named Arkitsis.

End of story.

Except it wasn't. Inexplicably, someone matching Matthews's description had been spotted in and around Bayside Cross and the Suq. Wren was willing to grant that this could be a red herring or mistaken identity or even an intentional misdirection on someone's part (which theory opened up a Pandora's Box of questions). But Blake Raimi had stayed put, as if he knew something that others in the hunt did not.

Hence, Wren Sharaf also stayed put, and now wondered if the someone—a pale scarecrow of a man she'd seen stalking Raimi on at least two occasions and talking to him on one—had seen Matthews himself and might be able to lead her to him.

She knew what she'd do if she found Matthews—zat him to unconsciousness and call for backup. That was what Agent Sharaf of COI would do, at any rate. Wren Sharaf, human being, wanted to throw the man against a wall and demand to know what sort of monster murders his wife in front of their child, then leaves her alone with the body.

Of all the things she did not know about Ridley Matthews, that was the most disturbing. It brought back to mind the conversation she'd had with the officers of the Guild freighter *Moonraker*. What they'd told her was perplexing, and exploded her pet theory about Matthews using *Moonraker* to escape. They admitted he'd been drugged and shanghaied, yet described the new "recruit" as a steady, reliable crewman who detested bullies and defended the vulnerable. Reading between the lines, Wren assembled the image of a patient big brother, a mentor, a friend, possibly a lover, and a hero willing to sacrifice himself for people who had, by their own admission, wronged him.

Granted, it was harder for her to read people through an uplink, even with video enabled—her particular mods worked best when she was in the same room with her subjects and could read subtle biological signals—but though the net-head first officer was twitchy in the way that net-heads tended to be, the *Moonraker's* officers seemed sincere in their praise. Nor could Wren come up with a rational reason they would lie about Matthews's character. He was either dead or he was alive on Acre. In any event, he was nowhere within striking distance of the *Moonraker* and her crew, so she doubted fear was a motivator.

One thing they had all agreed upon was that Trouble Matthews had had no idea who he was until they had told him. That might have been an act calculated to put them at ease, or a truth that left Wren with three possibilities:

1) Ridley Matthews was a monster pretending to be human.

2) Ridley Matthews was a monster who had forgotten he was a monster.

3) Ridley Matthews was innocent.

That last one was profoundly disturbing because it meant the real assassin was still out there and that the Alliance justice system had failed profoundly. The second possibility also discomfited her, but for different reasons. What if Matthews had no memory of having murdered his wife and assassinated a man beloved and admired by billions of souls? What if whatever had brought him to commit that horrific crime had been stripped away?

Would it matter? Should it?

That avenue of thought only raised more questions: Innocent or guilty, if Ridley Matthews had been mind-wiped in some fashion, who had done it, and for what reason? She did not like the possibilities that bubbled to the surface. She shoved them back down and headed for Bayside Cross.

42 / ENHANCEMENTS

BLAKE RAIMI HAD NOT ATTEMPTED TO PURSUE HIS QUARRY IN Mirrorton. Instead, driven by insatiable curiosity, he'd returned to New Haifa on the next available ferry, using his time on the boat to compose a list of the major enhancements he knew Ridley Mathews had been endowed with.

- Night vision, accompanied by apparent bioluminescence in the iris.
- Abnormal speed and quickness.
- Abnormal strength and stamina.
- Resistance to sigma radiation, and possibly other varieties as well.
- Able to function in extremes of heat and cold.
- Temporary existence in the vacuum of space.
- Rapid healing.

These were at the top of Raimi's list of Matthews's enhancements. Some of them he had thought—if they were at all possible—required structural modification of the body. Hardskins could survive some climate extremes, but they bought a chitinous epidermis along with that enhancement. Slinkies could navigate Zero G far better than other humans, but it meant giving up life in normal gravity without an exo-suit.

He checked his assumptions first thing the next morning by inquiring at a series of mod shops from the government-sanctioned clinics found in most med-centers, to the seedier ones deep in the less respectable districts of New Haifa. The first clinician he spoke to—the chief modeler at a clinic in the Port sector —nodded as Raimi read the first several items on his list.

"Yes, of course. We can do most of that. Although, I'd note that giving some of those enhancements to a single individual would be impossible because the modifications made for one circumstance would rule out those made for another. For example, extraordinary speed and strength and the ability to work in Zero G are impossible to impart to a single individual. The modifications to the body are specialized, you see. The mods that would allow someone to survive a fire or freezing temperatures, are going to make them less effective in Zero G."

"So," said Raimi, "you're telling me that there's no way to give all of the mods I just read to one person?"

The doctor shook his head. "Except the enhanced sight. That pairs well with just about any other mods. Though I have to admit, I've never seen it coupled with bioluminescence of the iris. That's … different."

Raimi pondered this information, staring at the crystal caduceus on the wall behind the doctor's head. It was backlit with an array of moving colors that raced up the etched traceries and suffused the staff's interwoven serpents with light. A bit hypnotic.

"And I suppose," Raimi said, "that there's no way to give most of these mods to someone without altering their body visibly."

The clinician chuckled. "You suppose correctly. Some mods, yes, we can make without the differences being noticeable. Eyesight, hearing, bone density and strength, resistance to certain conditions or diseases, say, but some modifications alter the body's structure. Even something as simple as fitting someone for a different atmosphere will potentially change the shape of the torso due to alteration of the lungs, for example."

Raimi glanced down at his list. "What about survival in a vacuum? Specifically in space."

The doctor's brow furrowed. "I know of no legal mods that would allow that."

"Ah, I see. I find that a bit strange. Those modifications would seem to be essential to a space-faring species."

The frown deepened. "Yes, they would be, but the means of obtaining them is not available to state-sanctioned clinics."

"Because?"

"Because the only way we've found of integrating those particular modifications into the human body is to introduce tardigrade DNA which, as I suspect you know, is highly illegal."

Raimi nodded. "Yes, I do know that. What I wasn't sure of was if another means of achieving those mods might have been developed. I guess not."

Tardigrades—also called water bears and moss piglets—were minute creatures that possessed a dizzying array of capacities that rendered them virtually immortal. They were the most extreme of extremophiles—even able to exist in the vacuum of space, which, naturally, made them of much interest to space-faring humans. Alas, the use of tardigrade DNA in human modification was illegal for a number of reasons, including the discovery that the tardigrades possessed an unmapped and peculiar form of sentience. Researchers had been placing entire colonies of the creatures into a subject's bloodstream, bone marrow, and brain tissue, where they effectively became a subsystem of the subject's body. Augmentation with nanites was programmable, with tardigrades it was not, because tardigrades literally had minds of their own. This called into question whether the augments were any longer strictly human.

The doctor was regarding Raimi suspiciously now. "Why are you asking about this?"

"I'm working with the Heartworlds Alliance Security Agency on a case. We suspect a person of interest has been modded in ways that—"

"Are on that list?" The doctor's eyebrows had risen and his eyes gone wide.

"Yes. Do you know of any mod shops of the non-sanctioned variety that might provide this tech?"

"I suspect there are many who *would*. I pray there are none that could." He made a circular motion over his heart, marking himself as a Mabirati. "I have to believe that access to tarditech is limited."

But was it? That was the question Blake Raimi took into his scouring of the Suq, and the even more obscure commercial areas of the Altananir—also called simply "The Skirts." There he was told that those mods were possible, but hard to come by and costly. He got more head shakes than he could count before one vendor told him where rumor had it, one could purchase such illegal mods. Raimi paid for the name and address and hoped the expense would turn out to be worthwhile.

He was on his way to the mod shop when he got another ping from Thorn, nagging him to come in. The man apparently still believed the news of Ridley Matthews's demise.

Raimi's response was straight and to the point: "You're no longer paying me, so I can do as I please."

There was a moment of silence, then Thorn said, "What's your angle, Blake? What are you after? The assignment is over—"

"Not from where I stand, it isn't. It's over when I've satisfied my curiosity about the allegedly dead man who's skulking around New Haifa and why you really want him."

"You know why. His memories are literally lethal to me and my interests. If he's able to retrieve them…."

"Ah, no. That would be highly unlikely under normal circumstances. I've never heard of a mind wipe coming undone. I think there's more to it than that."

"No. There is not." After a beat, Thorn added, "I never took you for a paranoid sort, Blake. What can you be imagining?"

"You called him an experiment. An expensive experiment."

Thorn laughed. "You really are suggestible, aren't you? I was referring to the experiment of grooming HASA agents, assigning them to private clients and expecting them to be controllable. Trouble Matthews lived up to his name. I'll never make that mistake again."

He cut the connection.

Raimi pondered his situation, which seemed to be a good one. The only question, now, was whether he captured Matthews and sold him to the highest bidder, or used what he now suspected to squeeze a lot more credits out of Grant Thorn ... or deal with him in some other way.

Which path he chose, he thought, depended on whether Thorn's last words about uncontrollable agents had been a veiled threat.

43 / Q & A

ULTIMATELY, WREN FOUND HER NEW MARK THE SAME WAY HE'D NO doubt found Raimi—by asking about people who were looking for Ridley Matthews. Which was how she ended up at the Sassy Duck tavern around twilight on the third day of her search, asking the barkeep if he'd seen Matthews since the sighting some days earlier. He had not, so she showed him an image of the tall, pale man she'd seen at the shrines. His head had been covered by a burnous, but she'd managed to capture him as he'd turned and looked up into the light falling from the crown of the temple, illuminating his angular features.

"Oh, yeah," said the barkeep. "That's Newman. Adam Newman. He's here now." He tilted his head toward the dining area to the left of the tavern's long bar. "He favors the back corner of the room. Likes to watch the entrances." He leaned toward her across the bar, lowering his voice. "He's a bounty hunter, too. Seems you're looking for the same guy."

"Seems," Wren agreed. "I believe I'll go introduce myself."

She did just that, using the walk across the dining area to assess the man sitting at a small table in the rear corner of the room. Without the concealing burnous he'd worn at the shrines, his appearance was even more striking. He was pale and thin. His face was gaunt—the high cheekbones standing out in stark relief below large, dark, watchful eyes. His hair was relatively short, riotous and wavy. His full lips curved upward in an expression that was less a smile than a grimace of resignation. He wasn't looking at her, but she knew he'd seen her and recognized her.

She reached the table and stopped, looking down at him, reading him. She canted her head toward the second chair at the table, raising an eyebrow askance. He nodded assent, the corners of this mouth turning up even further. This time it was a genuine smile. He was looking directly at her now, as well; she felt him assessing her as thoroughly as she had read him.

"Let me guess," he said. "You're going to tell me that you're a bounty hunter or maybe a HASA agent looking for a guy named Ridley Matthews who allegedly assassinated a high profile head of state, murdered his own wife, and orphaned his child. Am I close?"

She nodded. "Pretty close."

He seemed to consider that. "Well, we have something in common, then, 'cause I'm looking for him too. So, are you here to make me some sort of offer … Agent Sharaf?"

He had surprised her. He knew that only by her elevated heart rate and slight dilation of her pupils. Her outward posture —relaxed and watchful—remained the same.

After a moment, she gave him a rueful half-smile, and said, "You're pretty good."

"Thanks. Now, what do you want? Intel? A piece of the bounty on this guy? Full partnership?"

"Just some answers if you have them … for now."

He shrugged. "Sure. Why not?"

She crossed her legs and eased back in her chair. Trouble noticed how slender she was and suspected she was often underestimated by the unobservant. He sent a thought to enable his comm ports, though he was pretty certain Cyber would have programmed a way around them being disabled. If the net-head wanted to listen in on this conversation, that was fine with him.

"I have to warn you," she said. "I have a few mods that are specialized to interrogation. My boss tells me I'm the best little lie detector on her staff."

"Ah. Is that supposed to precondition me to tell the truth?"

"No. It's supposed to scare you down to the depths of your soul."

It didn't do that, but it did concern him. That he had similar modifications hadn't escaped his attention, and they made sense for a man whose job it had been to guard a statesman's life. It struck Trouble, suddenly, that his association with Chaz Carldon had not been merely master and guard dog. A vague notion that they had been friends did not rise to the level of memory, but it conjured the *sense* of friendship and a mental image of shared laughter in a casual setting.

"Consider me warned. If I answer some of your questions, will you answer mine?"

"Depends."

"Same here. You work for COI, don't you?"

"You're well-informed."

"In my line of work, I have to be. There were a few HASA agents underfoot when I first got here, though they seem to be pretty thin on the ground now. Also, some guy who seems to be an entrepreneur … or an antique collector. Jury's out on that one. You're the first Consonance agent I've run into."

He caught the slight downward drift of her eyes; she had to think about her answer. "That's because we don't get noticed until we're ready to be noticed."

Trouble gave Wren Sharaf a toothy grin he was certain would give her nightmares. "Really? Then you were aiming to be noticed at the Mabirati Shrines yesterday … and at the spaceport a while back? As I recall, both times you were chasing that natty dresser with the antique pocket watch."

This time her reaction caused her breathing to ripple and one side of her mouth to twitch.

"So, who is he—the pocket watch guy? I know his name," Trouble said as she considered her answer. "Blake Raimi."

They spoke the name in unison.

"He tells me he's an indie operator," Trouble said. "D'you know if that's true?"

"It is. I've been trying to connect him to some known individual or group…"

"Thorn," said Trouble, and her response to that bit of news surprised both of them.

The agent sat up straight, both feet hitting the floor. "Say again?"

Okay, that was a reaction. "Thorn… You know that name."

"He's…" She hesitated.

Trouble gave her a nudge. "Raimi swears the guy works for HASA."

The woman almost growled. "Yeah, you could say that. He runs the entire organization. To all intents and purposes, Grant Thorn *is* HASA."

Trouble was certain his face had gone blank for an instant. If everything he knew about himself was true, then the man who was doing his damnedest to find Trouble Matthews and kill him had once been his superior officer.

He managed to keep his voice steady and casual as he asked, "Wasn't Matthews HASA once upon a time?"

She nodded. "I have a theory about that. I think that's the reason Thorn is putting private operatives in the field and keeping a lid on his investigation. He knows how bad it looks for his organization that an assassin came up through his ranks. He's at least in part responsible for Matthews ending up as Carldon's security chief."

What's that old saying: Someone just stepped on my grave?

Trouble shook the creeping sensation off. If he'd reneged on a plot to murder his employer, someone had approached him and those conversations might still be locked up somewhere inside his head ... unless the mind wipe had obliterated them.

"You ever meet the guy Matthews is supposed to have assassinated?" he asked.

The COI agent sent Trouble a disconcertingly piercing look. "Yes. I did meet him. Several times. At Consonance state functions mostly, when I was on event security detail."

Trouble tried not to let his own gaze become too focused. If she did security for events Chaz Carldon attended, then there was every possibility that he had seen her or even met her. He didn't remember meeting her ... but then, she was a master of disguise, and he still barely remembered what he'd looked like in a mirror before he'd died and been resurrected as Adam Newman.

"What sort of man was he?" he asked.

"A good one," she said without hesitation. "He was the sort of calm, deliberative soul you want at the head of government. Non-partisan, strongly principled. Careful. By which I do not mean indecisive," she added wryly. "Too many people—especially when whispered to by politicians—mistake the application of reason for indecision."

Trouble nodded, keeping his face noncommittal. Inside, he was feeling a sort of sick dread and realizing he'd been half hoping that Carldon had been a trash bag or an insincere smirk of a human being. Deeper inside, he knew that was a forlorn hope; he'd been friends with the man, he was certain of it.

"Why?" she asked next. "Why do you care?"

He tilted his head and took another swig of his beer. "A little extra incentive, I guess. I kind of have it in for bad people who kill good people. I take it this guy—Carldon, right?—was in line for the Heartworlds throne, as it were."

"He was."

"Which meant he had enemies."

"Apparently."

"You have any idea who Matthews was working for?"

She shook her head. "If anyone knows, it's Grant Thorn. But if he does, he's not sharing. The fact that he hired someone like Raimi to find Matthews suggests that he doesn't trust people in his own organization."

"Is that what it suggests?" Trouble asked.

She cocked her head, not unlike her namesake avian. "What does it suggest to you?"

Given that Trouble was fairly certain Raimi had been Plan B for Chaz Carldon's murder—which had implications he didn't even want to consider—it suggested something a good deal darker. He watched Agent Sharaf watching him watching her and wondered how honest he could be.

"It suggests to me that he wants to keep his search for our fugitive out of sight of … well, of everybody. One of those right hand not knowing what the left hand is up to situations. Maybe he's doing it because he's not sure who to trust. *Or* maybe he's doing it because *he* can't be trusted."

That observation earned him a prodigious scowl. Sharaf leaned forward, her elbows on the table. "Look, Mr. Newman, do you have any idea where Ridley Matthews might be? Assuming he's not dead."

He considered that for a moment. Maybe telling her he'd heard he was dead would make her go away. "I've heard that rumor, actually," he said. "What do you think?"

"He was seen here on Acre after his alleged demise. I think he's still among us."

Oh, the irony. If he hadn't used himself as a lure, Raimi and Agent Sharaf might both have taken the first ship back to wherever they'd come from.

"He might've moved on," Trouble observed. "Blake Raimi thinks so, anyway. He's gone over to Mirrorton." He didn't mention that he had been instrumental in that development.

"And you didn't go with him? That surprises me."

Well, hell.

"I had a hunch Matthews might be laying a false trail and I kind of wanted Mr. Raimi out of my business. Besides, there's no going *with* Raimi. He works alone. Hell, if he'd caught me tailing him, I have every reason to believe he'd shoot me out of sheer annoyance." Trouble had lifted the beer mug to polish it off when his comms port fired and Cyber's voice poured into his head.

<Hey, T, Doc Pike wants to jabber with you. He's got something he needs to tell you about your blood. And before you ask, he hasn't told me squiddle.>

Trouble realized he'd frozen in the act of drinking, swallowed the last mouthful and set the mug down carefully. "Gotta go," he told the COI agent.

"Yeah, I get it. You just got a ping. I recognize the glazed look in the eye. Girlfriend?"

"Informant." He rose, looking down at her from his considerable height ... until she stood up, too. She had to be at least five-foot-ten.

"Meaning," she said, "it could be about Matthews?"

"Look, Wren—may I call you 'Wren'?—even if it is about Matthews, doesn't mean I'm gonna share. I have a stake in this too, right?"

"Point taken." She didn't so much as blink at his use of her first name.

"See you around, I'm sure," he said, and left the Sassy Duck, knowing with utter certitude that Agent Sharaf would follow. Did he let her? Or did he disappear? Did he go to his room at the Starry Night or anywhere but?

He made the decision quickly, turning into the foyer of the inn, bounding up the stairs two at a time to his room.

"TALK TO ME, CYB," TROUBLE MURMURED.

He was in his room at the Starry Night with the door closed and locked, but still kept his voice low. He thought odds were good the COI agent had followed him. Odds were better she was telling the truth about being modded, if not to the extent that he was, and he had no idea what those mods might be beyond sensitivity to physical responses. He could guess.

<Hey, like I said, it's Doc Pike who needs to talk to you. I'm putting him on now, okay?>

The line went completely silent, then Doc Pike came on over audio, his voice sounding deep in Trouble's ear instead of (seemingly) the middle of his head. In typical Doc fashion, he did not screw around but got right to the point.

"Trouble, I'm sitting on one doozy of a report on what makes you tick."

"Sitting on it? Why sitting on it? What's so dire you haven't told Lucas and—"

"I wanted to check with you first. Make sure you really want them to know."

Trouble went cold down to the soles of his soul. Felt like an icicle was lodged in his belly. "Damn, Doc. Just spit it out. Are we talking about a ticking time bomb or something?"

"Legally speaking, yes. Trouble, your upgrades are highly unorthodox and illegal to boot. Along with the usual nanites, son, you have a house full of tardigrades."

The icicle in Trouble's belly became an iceberg. "Tardigrade DNA? I have tardigrade DNA in my system?"

Doc's laugh sounded like a creaky hatch. "Tardigrade DNA is the least of it, boy. You have entire colonies of the little buggers in your system—brain, spine, muscles, blood … bone marrow."

"Hair follicles?"

"Probably. Who knows?"

I do. Now.

"Tardigrades are sentient. I know that much. Experimenting with them…"

"Yeah," said Doc.

"How?" Trouble asked. "How is that possible?"

"I think it would have to have been done over a period of time—maybe years. You really don't remember?"

"I really don't. And I can't … well, at the moment, I can't imagine that I would've done that to *myself*. I was Chaz Carl-don's security chief. Would *he* have…?"

"Doesn't matter how they got there at the moment." Doc hesitated, then said: "Trouble, you have significant numbers of another lifeform living pretty much everywhere in your body. Lifeforms that you did not come by naturally … or legally."

"Is there any way I can get them removed?"

"If you did, I doubt you'd like the result. They're part of you, son. They've taken over a number of processes that I *can* see and probably ones I *can't*. The technology for inserting them in the first place is rare, if relatively simple. Removing them once they've spread out in your system … I don't even know where you could go to have that done. But I doubt you could survive it. Huh. May be the one thing you *couldn't* survive."

"Great. So, if I can't disappear convincingly…"

"Yeah. That's a problem."

"Doc, you have a talent for understatement. But … but

thanks. Thanks for letting me know. And … feel free to let Lucas and the others know."

Doc was silent for a moment, then said, "Thank you. For your trust." He signed off.

As much as he wanted to sit and ponder the ramifications of what he now knew about himself, Trouble decided to keep moving. He snatched up his backpack, then slipped out a rear exit and down an evacuation shaft.

Wren Sharaf spared a tendril of thought to shut down the telephoto mod in her left eye and pondered what she had just witnessed. Her position on the roof of the building quarter-corner to the Starry Night Inn had given her an on-again-off-again view of Adam Newman's face during his remote contact with his "informant"; his growing tension was not lost on her.

He'd come across as a laid-back opportunist, looking to coat-tail on someone else's work in hope of reward. But the man she was now watching apparently prepping to bug out, was anything put laid-back. And he'd gone from surprised to stunned to grim in mere seconds. Why? What might his infor-mant have told him to send him into frenzied flight?

Something about Ridley Matthews? About Raimi?

About her?

Though her aural mods were state-of-the-art, she'd caught no words, only the timbre and modulation of his voice. She had, however, through the mundane discipline of training, been able to read his lips when his face was raised toward the window. She'd caught only snatches of the conversation, a phrase here and there: *Talk to me (a name)? Why? What's so dire (something)? … Why haven't you told (another name—was it Lucas?) … ticking time bomb … degrade DNA. I have … experi-menting with them … how is that possible? … I can't imagine I would … If I was Carldon's (something), would he… get them removed … I can't disappear…*

And that was that. He'd thanked the person for letting him know whatever it was he'd been told. But what had been the message? What was the ticking time bomb? "Degrade DNA"—what did that mean, and what did it have to do with Chaz Carldon and a strange bounty hunter from God-knew-where?

The mention of Carldon's name raised the hair on the back of Wren's neck. In this context it was surprising and puzzling. Adam Newman, of course, knew that Matthews had assassinated Chaz Carldon, but why invoke the late Prime Minister's name now?

If he was Carldon's … what?

There was no time to puzzle it out now. Newman had bundled his backpack up under his jacket and was exiting the room. When he left the inn, Wren followed his circuitous path, keeping to rooftops and balconies where she could, and making full use of her own mods to track him by heat signature as well as sight and sense. She had everything under control until she lost him in the Suq when he blended into a group of pedestrians that vanished into a narrow lane between rows of buildings. One moment she had eyes on him wending his way past kiosks, stalls, and food carts, and the next he had turned and passed out of sight beneath the myriad canopies and banners that spanned the lane.

Here at the fringes of the sector—at the boundary between the chaotic and the circumspect—the narrow passage was teeming with heat signatures. Wren hastened across the rooftops to take up surveillance above the far end of the lane where it emptied into a main thoroughfare.

She'd not long to wait. Within minutes, a group of five men strode out into the main street, clearly in a party mood. Two men in the pack were above two meters tall. Either *could* be Newman, but height was where their resemblance to her mark ended. One was broad-shouldered and wore his silver hair in a brush cut. He appeared to be above fifty. The younger man's hair was longer, had artful streaks of color among the dark strands, and he was dressed like a swell in a trendy, knee-length coat, cream breeks and tall, gleaming burgundy boots. He held his body as if his surroundings were alien enough to cause discomfort. When he and his companions paused at the curb, he peered up and down the street as if seeking a cab. She realized his eyes were a different color than Newman's.

How the hell could he have managed such a complete change in the brief time she'd lost sight of him? She couldn't see the backpack, but it could be hidden beneath the loose coat. A more reasonable conclusion is that she'd lost him completely in that alley.

Wren Sharaf experienced an unfamiliar moment of uncertainty. Could this be Newman, or had he turned about in the lane and gone back the way he'd come? The only thing this man had in common with the alleged bounty hunter was height.

Clenching her jaw in frustration, Wren watched as the man at the head of the group flagged down a robotic carriage, tapped his datapad to the pay point sensor and climbed in. Three of his companions followed; the tall man stayed put on the curb. He watched the vehicle out of sight, then hailed a rickshaw and got in. His voice was pitched low, but Wren recognized it and clearly heard him direct the drive-bot to Hotel Bengurian.

Alright. That explained the creme-de-la-clothing. If the guy had tried to enter the Bengurian looking like a bounty hunter, he'd've been bounced right back out again. Chances were good he was meeting someone there—his handler maybe.

Wren was determined to find out who that was, so she hailed her own cab and asked to be taken to the Bengurian as swiftly as possible. On the way, she did a quick-change of her own, winding her shoulder length hair into an up-do, turning her black jacket inside out to expose the silky interior of verdant green, and folding over the tops of her knee high boots to show the quilted inner lining of the same color. She tucked the collar of her jacket under to reveal a necklace with small iridescent stones that lay casually over her collar bone, then fished a pair of dangling fan-shaped earrings out of her belt pouch and hooked them over her ears. Lastly, she tapped a stone on her necklace that turned on a dazzle screen. It wasn't intended to give her a new face, just adjust the one she had enough to make her unrecognizable to the casual observer.

She grimaced. Adam Newman was not a man whose observations were casual. She would need to keep her distance from him.

She somehow managed to make it to the Bengurian mere seconds after her mark alighted on the stone plaza in front of the hotel. There were two cabs between his and hers and she waited until he'd done a visual sweep of the forecourt before slipping out of her ride. He seemed to be in a hurry, so she lengthened her stride and followed him into the lobby, where he headed back toward the lift tubes at the rear. Mentally, she was already working on what she'd do if she lost him in a lift. She knew she didn't dare get into the same one. She had no doubt he'd recognize her in a heartbeat.

She was going over options when Newman glanced to his left, across the broad, opulent space toward a seating area just outside the premiere floor lounge and restaurant. His steps slowed, then he simply stopped, staring in that direction. Wren couldn't see his face from her angle, but slowed her own pace and followed his gaze.

Three well-dressed men stood and chatted just outside the entrance to the restaurant, possibly waiting for a table in the crowded lounge. She had no idea which one of them had drawn his attention or why, but when a handful of seconds passed without Newman twitching a muscle, Wren turned and pretended to be looking for someone, while keeping her attention fixed on her quarry.

One of the men in the subject trio seemed to spot Newman over the shoulders of his companions, to whom he turned and spoke. She lip-read, "There's a guy staring at you, Vic. Is he someone you know?"

The other two men turned to look in Newman's direction, something that caused him to quickly do an about-face and angle back toward the lifts again. Wren followed, hoping he would have a car to himself; it would make tailing him much easier. She might have to figure out which floor he was on by watching the display over the doors. But if his room was close to the lifts or he was in too much of a hurry, she'd have to come up with a Plan B. If he was a frequent visitor, she could resort to charming the Concierge. They might know him by name and be able to give her the name of his contact. If he used a different alias when he visited his handler, she was going to have to find another way of locating him.

Wren was in luck; Newman stepped straight into a lift tube that had just disgorged a family of four. He was the only passenger for the skyward journey. She stepped out of his line of sight as he turned back toward the lobby, so she clearly heard him say "Nineteen," to the lift.

"Nineteen," the lift repeated in a melodious female voice.

Wren waited until the doors to the tube had closed, then tapped the Up button on the next car to the left, praying it was on the Lobby level. It was. She darted into the lift the moment the door slid back.

"Nineteen," she told the car before it could ask.

"Nineteen," it repeated in the same musical tones as the first car. The door slipped shut and the car shot silently up the transparent tube.

Wren ignored the splendid view of New Haifa that lay before her; gleaming buildings, pools of darkness, trails of lights that wended up into the hills like discarded necklaces of glittering gems. It blurred before her eyes as she worked out her potential next moves.

The door slid back with a whisper of sound and the voice intoned: "Nineteen."

She stepped out into the long, broad hallway and glanced both ways. There was no one in sight.

Damn. He must've *sprinted* down the hall.

To her left, she heard a soft click as a door mechanism engaged. She turned to see light fan out across the carpeted floor of the cozily lit corridor; a long shadow flickered within it. A moment later, the light and the shadow were gone. Noting the distance between the recessed doorways, she realized these were suites, which limited the possibilities. The shadow had been thrown from the left side of the corridor, which eliminated the suites to the right.

Wren hurried down the hall to where she thought Newman had entered one of the suites. She'd taken only a few steps before she realized that the doorways were paired, two to a recess. The suites were mirror images of each other. She understood the economics of this for the hotel—it meant less redundancy in the environmental, power, and plumbing systems—but it made her current task a bit more challenging. Newman could have gone into either of two suites whose entrances were side-by-side in their shared alcove.

When she reached the suspect doorways, there was no indication which one of them had recently opened and closed or which rooms might be currently occupied.

Not a problem. Standing at the center of the corridor so as not to engage the suites' privacy systems, a flick of Wren's tongue fired her mods, and the walls of the two sets of rooms seemed to fall away into darkness. She swept the suites with her altered gaze and found three heat signatures—two in the suite on the left, one in the suite on the right. She turned her attention to the left hand suite. She was expecting Newman to connect with someone, so this seemed more promising. But, while one figure was taller than the other, it was nowhere near as tall as Newman. Both signatures were moving away from her viewpoint and, quite suddenly, tilted to the horizontal, where they merged energetically.

She turned her attention to the suite on the right; the heat signature here was in motion too, pacing back and forth as she had just seen Newman do in his Starry Night digs. And it was obviously generated by someone of good height. Had he arrived early and been forced to wait?

If so, the person he was waiting for might be along at any moment.

Wren flicked her sight back to normal, then took a swift step toward the right-hand doorway, stopping just shy of entering the recess it occupied. Pulling out her datapad, she turned and leaned her back against the wall, striking a casual pose and a petulant expression. Anyone approaching would see a young woman wiling away the minutes on her device while she waited for someone.

Behind that façade, Wren pushed her audio enhancements to the maximum and focused on the room behind the door of suite 1911.

45 / FLIGHT

WHEN HE CONSIDERED ALL THE THINGS THAT SHOULD HAVE KILLED him but hadn't, Trouble thought it ironic that the one thing he was afraid actually *would* kill him was the stuttering return of his memory. Halfway across the lavish lobby of the Bengurian, he heard a man's laughter. It was painfully familiar and his gaze followed it, unbidden, to the ghost of Chaz Carldon, standing with two other men in a tight cluster just outside the entrance to the off-lobby lounge.

A cold, heart-clenching stab of memory followed, stopping Trouble dead in the middle of the gleaming quartz floor to stare at the Dead Man. Half-formed thoughts tumbled through his head. Was he hallucinating? Had the Pilgrim's Passage done him permanent damage? Was this a psyquam that had somehow followed him from the wormhole?

The laughter came again, and the ghost said, "Why do you need so many—" The last words were blurred by the laughter of his two companions, but Trouble's mind supplied them: "Damn physicals."

He vividly recalled Chaz asking him that several times, the emotions behind the question wavering between curiosity, concern, and something darker. "Why do you need so many damn physicals? Hell, Trouble, I only get one a year."

One of the two companions noticed Trouble staring, and called the ghost's attention to it. It was only when he turned face on that Trouble realized the man really didn't look like Chaz at all. He shook himself out of the fugue and all but ran for the elevators.

Once in a car and on his way up to the nineteenth floor, he realized he was sweating. It was a cold, teeth-chattering sweat, accompanied by a sharp sense of how vulnerable he was in those unmoored moments. The stranger's laughter had triggered recall and he had seen what he expected to see—a face that matched the laughter. A face that he knew he would not forget again, because it now resided in his head in three-dimensions, not just the watery translucency of Passage psychosis. The Chaz Carldon now etched by memory was sharp and painful as a shard of crystal.

Why do you need so many damn physicals?

Why that memory?

He knew, damnit. Tardigrade DNA. Had he done that to *himself*? Had Chaz suspected him of it?

He wanted answers to those questions more than he didn't want them, and he knew he wouldn't find them here on Acre … at least, not before he got himself killed. He was being stalked by a COI operative who had found him once and likely could again. He had little doubt she would eventually track him to the Bengurian, if she hadn't already. And if Raimi returned to New Haifa suspecting he'd been given disinformation, he would most certainly want to know why. There was nothing for Trouble to do here, nothing more to know. Nothing but a soul-deep urge to return to the mountain shrines, which he dared not do.

Once alone in his suite, he pinged the *Moonraker*, pacing away the few eternal seconds until the connection was made in front of the floor-to-ceiling windows. The fireplace had sensed his presence and sent flames dancing for his entertainment.

"Cyb," he said tersely when the net-head came online, "I

need to get off Acre. I don't know if you can get here fast enough, so I may have to arrange transport—"

Cyber cut him off. <We're already incoming. Cap cut the refit to essential systems and the drives, and we shipped out early. Can you hold out until tomorrow night?>

"I guess I'll have to," Trouble started to say, then realized how defeatist that sounded. "Yeah. I can. I'm pretty sure Sharaf knows where I am, but Raimi should still be out on his fool's errand."

<Good. I'll send down a skiff and let you know—>

"No, no skiff. I should take a commercial hopper. Sending down a Guild skiff could draw too much attention from the wrong people."

<Like that Thorn character? Turns out he's—>

"The head of HASA. I know that now. Our little COI bird confirmed it. He's the one that hired the bounty hunter. ...He's also someone I used to work for before I worked for Chaz Carldon."

<Wait. Thorn's the one who placed you with Carldon and then turned around and framed you for his assassination? I can see why he'd want you mind-wiped.>

"I think he knows the mind wipe is coming apart. Now I'm pretty sure he'd settle for a swift death."

Cyber's alarm came through the connection like a virtual bleat. <I can arrange the hopper,> he assured Trouble. <I'll just appropriate another ship's ID. I'll let you know which ship so you make it to the right hopper.>

Though he knew better than to count his escape plots before they hatched, Trouble could feel the tension in his chest uncoil. He took a breath that went all the way down to his diaphragm. "Thanks. Thanks, Cyber."

<Our pleasure. Oh, uh, Cap would like a word. I'll put him on.>

Lucas, unlike Cyber, was not jacked directly into the comms, so Trouble heard the kid's voice in his ear. Even so, his senses told him there was something different about Lucas Shade. There was a depth and steadiness to his voice that had not been there the last time they had spoken.

"Hey, Trouble. Doc Pike told us about your … your situation. I decided we needed to be on our way back to you. If the wrong people find out about what's in your blood, the entire Alliance will be hunting you."

Trouble sank onto the sofa in front of the cheerful fireplace. "Yeah. That had not escaped me."

"Listen, something came up that I think might be related to your situation. My dad had been trying to get Uncle Erasmus to carry cargo for a bio-tech company since I can remember, and he's started in on me about the same commissions. We're talking highly illegal contraband. Prohibited stuff. Dangerous, maybe. Stuff Uncle Erasmus refused to take on."

The significance of that was not lost on Trouble. "Really? I didn't get the sense that contraband was a problem for Erasmus."

"It wasn't, but he refused this. He never told me why, except to say that it wasn't 'safe' contraband. I didn't really know what he meant by that, but I've been dodging the issue with Julian until I could find out more about it. Here's the deal: the company that wanted the transport was DeNA-Gen. Ring a bell?"

"Yeah. I gather they've about cornered the market in bio-modification."

"Right. A lot of people use DeNA-Gen nanites and prostheses. But they were also the corporation that sank the most of their R and D budget into—"

"Tarditech," said Trouble, in perfect unison with Lucas. He came to his feet again and paced around the seating area. "You think DeNA-Gen might have something to do with my illegal mods?"

"I think chances are good they're the source of those mods even if they didn't have anything to do with you getting them."

"You refused the commission, you said."

"Yeah, I did. So I know only what my father was willing to tell me before he got my buy-in. But based on the equipment he wanted to install aboard the *Raker*, the contraband material was going to be in stasis. I've had Cyber doing some weasel work on DeNA-Gen. Turns out they sank just about everything they had into tarditech and hold most of the patents on it. *And* they've been trying for several years to move legislation through the Heartworlds Parliament to legalize it."

Why do you need so many damn physicals?

A door seemed to open in Trouble's head. "Chaz Carldon was a hard no vote," he murmured.

"Was he?"

"More than that. He was investigating DeNA-Gen. He suspected them of continuing prohibited lines of research."

Like me.

"Wow. Really? How do you—?"

"I did some research of my own and ... I remember, Lucas. I *remember*."

The speeches before Parliament. The vid interviews. The campaigning, for which Ridley Matthews organized every stitch of Chaz Carldon's security coverage. Coverage that had apparently failed spectacularly. It was a mere fragment of what he suspected he knew; the rest stayed achingly out of reach.

He heard Lucas swallow hard. "Okay. Okay, we're gonna get you out of there. Tomorrow night. Cyb will set up the shuttle and we'll let you know what bay it's in and give you the passcode."

Trouble rubbed at his temples, his head suddenly feeling as if it had no more room in it for memories or thoughts or plans. "Lucas..."

"Yeah?"

"I ... I think I have a daughter."

Jani lying on the polished stone floor looking sightlessly at the ceil-

ing. The child curled beside her, stroking her face. The security guards suddenly all around him, taking him into custody.

"I don't remember her name."

"Oh." The sound came out sounding like the mew of a lost kitten. "I'm so sorry, Trouble. I'll get Cyb on that, too."

Trouble paced across the living area to the floor-to-ceiling window that looked out on the shimmering waters of the Teykh Akhdus. The lights of the city and marina were mirrored and multiplied in the dark water, stars dancing around his reflected image. That revealed him as a shadow being, hollow inside, light behind and around, darkness within.

"Lucas … Am I that man? Am I a man who killed his wife and left our daughter alone with her body? What if I—?"

"You're not that man, Trouble." Lucas said the words without hesitation and with an absolute certainty that Trouble could hear and feel through the distance between them. "Say it," he added, his tone one of uncompromising command.

Trouble laughed at that coming from Lucas Shade, his laughter catching on a gasp of mixed grief and gratitude. "Aye, Captain."

"Say it."

"I'm not that man."

"Tomorrow night," Lucas said. "Be ready to move right after dark."

"Tomorrow night," Trouble confirmed. "After dark. See you, Lucas. Thanks."

They ended the communication, and Trouble sat down again, trying to school his thoughts. It would be best, he figured, if he could just stay in the hotel until tomorrow evening, take a cab directly to the spaceport and get off world as Adam Newman. He was glad of his instinctive decision to remove the backpack from the Starry Night. The few things in it were not important, but the DNA he'd left on them was. For all he knew, he sweated tardigrade DNA—left a trail of it wherever he went.

The only thing he knew even mostly for certain was that a

fire like the one in the *Moonraker's* thruster assembly could expunge it. Even if he was evil enough or mad enough to burn the Starry Night and the Bengurian and half-dozen other businesses to the ground, he couldn't create a fire hot enough to erase Trouble Matthews from Acre.

WREN SHARAF STRUGGLED TO MAKE SENSE OF THE HALF-DIALOGUE she'd just overheard. The first she'd caught were the words "No skiff," and gathered from what followed that Newman was arranging to be retrieved from Acre and didn't want a guild skiff involved.

Which guild? There were literally hundreds, if not thousands, of them in a wide variety of disciplines and industries. Logic suggested a bounty hunters' guild of some stripe.

When Newman referred to the head of HASA, Wren was intrigued. Was Newman one of Grant Thorn's HASA operatives, then? Even as she was being wryly amused at his reference to her as "our little COI bird," Newman said a string of words that flipped her perception of the situation on its head: "He's the one that hired the bounty hunter. ...He's also someone I used to work for before I worked for Chaz Carldon."

The bounty hunter in question could only be Blake Raimi— no surprise there—but if Adam Newman really had worked for Chaz Carldon, that was too much of a coincidence to actually be a coincidence. She began to wonder if his connection to the hunt for Ridley Matthews wasn't more personal than professional. Was he a colleague? A friend?

He said something about a mind-wipe coming apart, about

Thorn settling for a swift death. She assumed both referred to Matthews. Confusing. A mind-wipe was not part of standard criminal punishment, any more than was an outright death sentence. What Newman's words suggested was grotesque: that Thorn meant for Matthews to be run to ground and killed rather than serve his time on Restitution, cognizant of his crime. That was revenge, not justice, but it certainly could explain why Thorn had been keeping his investigations so close to the vest.

The destruction of the prison transport suddenly acquired dark significance.

Wren gave these stunning new ideas a moment's thought, which produced two new questions: What was the mind-wipe intended to conceal? And if Blake Raimi had been hired to give Matthews that swift death, where did Adam Newman fit in?

She brought her mind back to the dialogue within the room, which seemed to be wrapping up. When Newman thanked whomever he was talking to, he said what was clearly a name: Cyber. Wren knew one person of recent acquaintance who went by Cyber—the First Officer of Lucas Shade's *Moonraker*. Given what Shade and his command staff had told her about their friendship with Matthews, it surprised her that they'd aid someone hunting him to collect a bounty.

But if that wasn't Newman's real intent, if he was a friendly…

Things clicked together like a puzzle: Adam Newman didn't want to capture Matthews; he wanted to rescue him. That was why he'd sent Raimi off across the lake. He was running interference, which suggested a whole different array of approaches Wren might take to further her own search.

She'd begun to consider those approaches when Adam Newman uttered the words "tarditech" and "my illegal mods." When he followed that with an observation about Chaz Carldon's investigation of DeNA-Gen, it shifted the foundation of her perceptions yet again.

As she was trying to sort the new information into some

semblance of logical order, Newman said, "I remember, Lucas. I *remember*." His voice was broken, frayed, as if he barely possessed the power of speech.

Wren's thoughts staggered.

Mind-wipe.

Unease was clamoring in her back-brain, trying to push an impossible idea to the fore, when Newman spoke again and derailed her thoughts completely.

"I think … I think I have a daughter," he said. "I don't remember her name."

Wren levered herself away from the wall, pivoting to stare at the closed door. She knew the name. It was Amalia. And the man on the other side of that door could only be Ridley Matthews.

As the new pieces fell into place, other pieces—pieces she thought she knew as fact—shifted and warped because they no longer fit in the puzzle. If Ridley Matthews was a monster, he had been forced to forget it. She almost laughed at the simple truth of his alias: Adam Newman. A New Man.

Wren fought her breathing and heart rate back under control, her enhanced senses picking up the minute sounds of movement in the room. Was he getting ready to bolt? Was he pacing again?

She checked her weapons, considered how best to get to him, to take him down without killing him. She now knew the sort of mods Ridley Matthews had; hers could not match them. She would have only the element of surprise as an equalizer.

She unholstered her zat gun and took a step toward the door. It was a standard weapon for a COI operative; unless fired directly into the head or heart at close range, it was non-lethal. She'd been offered the option to carry a more lethal beam pistol for this mission, but had rejected the idea. She almost wished she had not. Almost.

She was taking aim at the door's electromagnetic locking mechanism when Matthews asked the question she had wanted the answer to from the beginning: "Am I that man? Am I a man who killed his wife and left our daughter alone with her body?"

The inconsolable grief poured out of Ridley Matthews's soul into Wren Sharaf's enhanced hearing and took her back a step. This was not what she'd expected when she'd asked for this assignment, or hoped when she'd been granted it. She'd wanted this to be cut and dried. Simple. For Amalia's sake.

The next sound Wren was conscious of hearing was Matthews's laughter. It ended in a sob. "Aye, Captain," he said, then, after a beat: "I'm not that man." A moment later he said, "Tomorrow night. After dark. Thank you, Lucas."

He'd be taking a commercial hopper to the ship; she knew that. Now she knew the day and time. It was a relief, really. Confronting him here, with her thoughts so disorganized, would be a mistake. To do it anywhere with so many people around, with the local authorities involved, was dangerous. She needed time to consider the best tactic. She needed time to think.

Wren holstered her weapon and withdrew. In the lobby, she went to the registration desk and took a room at the Bengurian. Then she returned to her previous lodgings, which were at a hotel less luxurious than the Bengurian, but closer to the space-port. She took a hotel rickshaw there and back, trying to keep her mind focused on sorting and cataloguing her new set of givens. She considered contacting COI headquarters and filling them in on the newest developments, but she was reluctant to do so before she was more certain of the situation. She could debrief when this was all over—whenever that was.

The rickshaw was less than a block from the Bengurian on her return trip when she saw Blake Raimi sitting in a bistro on the same side of the street as the hotel. He was watching the traffic, his gaze casual.

Pretense.

Wren leaned back in the vehicle, turning her face toward the opposite side of the avenue. At this distance—roughly thirty feet

—she couldn't tell if he had seen her or, if having seen her, recognized her as anyone of note.

It was as she pondered the connections between Matthews, Raimi, and Thorn that Wren stumbled over a couple of puzzle pieces that had fallen off the board: Ridley Matthews had worked under Thorn in HASA before he'd been assigned to Chaz Carldon. Grant Thorn had sent the mercenary after him. Why? To bring him in or to make sure he stayed missing?

If the destruction of the prison transport was connected, it suggested the latter. It also suggested that Thorn was responsible for Matthews's mind-wipe, which led Wren to wonder what else he was responsible for.

The possibilities that clamored for recognition were all horrific, and they brought Agent Wren Sharaf to another realization: More than she wanted to capture Trouble Matthews, she wanted simply to talk to him.

47 / CONTRABAND MAN

WREN WAS AT THE NEW HAIFA PORT AUTHORITY OFFICES WHEN they opened. She wore her dress greens, her insignia of rank clearly displayed on the collar, her service patch over her left breast. In case that wasn't sufficient—for she'd certainly seen enough children adopt this as a costume for All Halloweek—she showed her credentials, as well, and allowed them to be scanned. The COI dress uniform was especially popular on Earth because of a holo-stream series about COI agents. People loved cloak and dagger fiction; the original series had lasted for generations and spawned a raft of spin-offs.

"What do you require of us, Agent Sharaf?"

The question came from the Officer in Charge of the New Haifa Port Authority. A silver-haired whipcord of a man Wren guessed must be in his late nineties, Carter Hansen had been summoned to the main office the moment she had shown her badge to the shift supervisor. He now seemed to waver between concern and curiosity. He had taken her aside into his office once he understood the nature of her mission and his part in it. He offered her a seat across from his desk; she remained standing.

"I am tracking an inbound Freeman's Guild freighter named *Moonraker*. She's under the ownership of Julian Shade and captained by his son, Lucas Shade. I require access to your flight control center and I need to know the disposition of your commercial shuttles. Specifically, I need to be informed of any commercial shuttle that is reserved by *Moonraker*. In fact, I need to know the moment she requests an orbital position."

Hansen nodded, his gaze going inward, where she knew he was processing the logistics of her request.

"I'll tell you what, Agent Sharaf, I'll escort you to Ops, myself. Do you have a window in which you expect this vessel to arrive?"

"I'm not completely certain of the arrival time, but I do know they plan to make contact this evening after sunset with someone here in New Haifa—a known criminal whom I intend to arrest."

"Is it your intention to wait here until this evening, then?"

"No, but I would like to inspect your hopper docks, get a sense of how they're laid out and how quickly I can get from your Operations center to the pads."

"Of course."

The OC rose and led the way from his office to the Ops center several floors above the public terminal. The heart of New Haifa's port was a large circular chamber whose curving walls were dominated by a series of video screens and tactical displays. The wall opposite the entrance showed the placement of vessels in geo-synchronous orbit somewhere above New Haifa and its environs. To the left of this display, were arrayed a map of the shuttle docks—both commercial hoppers and private skiffs—and video feeds from the berths. To its right, was a similar display of the port's "suburbs"—a series of large pads and hangars where ships of various sizes could dock for repairs or load and offload cargo and passengers.

The center of the room was occupied by an impressive cohort of air and ground traffic controllers. Their workstations fanned out from a central point roughly four meters from the entry, each grouping of specialists monitoring a different sector of the port.

The lights were low so the staff could clearly see both the wall displays and the screens at each of their stations.

The patterns of shadow and light suggested the room ought to be hushed, but it wasn't. There was a subtle symphony of sound: murmured voices, the delicate tapping of keyboards, the soft tonal input of alerts as the status of different vessels updated.

Officer Hansen ushered Wren into the operations theater, introduced her to the shift lead, Officer Ferrar, and concisely explained what the COI agent needed from her.

"Do you have a *Moonraker* in orbit now?" Wren asked once she'd filled in any blanks Hansen had left. "I don't have her ident codes, but she's registered with the Freeman's Guild."

Officer Ferrar glanced up at the orbital tactical display, then turned to a young man sitting at a workstation facing the display.

"Jess, could you check for a *Moonraker*? Registry is with the Freeman's Guild. Could be a recent arrival."

The man tapped the name into a search bar, studied his desktop display for a moment, then shook his head. "Afraid not. We have a *Moonbeam*, but she's on her way out. Our most recent arrivals are the *Champion* and the *Moriah*."

Wren shrugged. "It was a long shot. I'm really not expecting her until later in the day, but I figured it wouldn't hurt to check. I don't know if she'll request a hopper right away when she gets in, or will wait until sunset to make the request. Timing is … unknown."

"So, to confirm—when the request comes in, you want us to approve the shuttle. You're not going to make the arrest on the ground?" Ferrar seemed puzzled.

"I may, but I want my target to believe he's getting away. If his crew can't give him a docking pad address with a prepped hopper on it, it will spook him." Wren saw the skepticism in the other woman's eyes and added, "This guy is modded to ridiculous extremes, Officer. Trapping him in an itty bitty boat might be the ticket to an arrest that doesn't put anybody else in danger. When *Moonraker* makes contact I need you to assign them a hopper and tell me which one it is. I'll take it from there."

Ferrar nodded. "Yes, ma'am."

Wren swung back to face Officer Hansen. "What's the fastest way to the hopper pads?"

Hansen inclined his head toward the far right rim of the circular room. "There's an elevator over there that will take you right down to the shuttle level. Let me show you."

He suited action to word, taking her to the shuttle pads and explaining how the reservation system worked.

"We assign hoppers beginning with the ranks closest to the terminal." He gestured to the gleaming building of steel, glass, and native stone positioned directly beneath the Ops tower. "I'm thinking it may make your job easier if we pre-assign *Moonraker's* hopper. I'll have Officer Ferrar assign one close to the terminal."

Wren appreciated the gesture. The sheer number of hoppers and shuttles, in sizes ranging from tiny two-seaters to larger vehicles that could hold two dozen passengers, was daunting. They were arrayed in semi-circular ranks around the operations facility, smaller ones to the fore, larger ones further out. They were terraced, too, so that they looked like a giant's amphitheater. At this time of day it was a hive of activity. Passengers were arriving on the broad concrete sidewalks, or coming up from the parking areas below the bays via lift tubes.

"Thank you, Mr. Hansen. With a 'go' time of 'after dark,' the timing of this whole exercise is far less precise than I would like."

He offered Wren a thin smile. "I empathize. In an operation like the Port Authority, improvisation can be … dangerous."

Indeed it could, but at this point in the catching of Ridley Matthews, improvisation was really all she had.

48 / CONFLUENCE

BLAKE RAIMI HAD BEEN ON HIS WAY UP FROM THE SUQ TO THE SASSY Duck, determined to find Adam Newman, when he'd seen the guy all but sprint from the rear entrance of the inn next door. He did not miss the opportunity to follow, and because he did not, he saw something both puzzling and intriguing. Newman entered the cluttered alley populated by the Suq's less prosperous vendors and almost immediately showed interest in a kiosk selling a variety of likely stolen goods. He circled the kiosk ... and disappeared.

It had taken Raimi a handful of seconds he couldn't afford before he realized that the tall swell emerging from the opposite side of the booth was his quarry. The body language and carriage was completely different, but it was Newman nonetheless. Raimi questioned his own intelligence in obscene terms and took off in pursuit. He caught up with Newman when he'd inserted himself into the rearguard of a group of partiers, and watched him flag down a jitney.

He'd been waving down his own transport when he saw the Woman appear as if she'd just materialized at the curb. He would have noticed her for her striking good looks under normal circumstances, but now, it was her body language that caught his attention. She radiated tense, expectant energy, her gaze on the vehicle that had just borne Newman away. Raimi watched as she'd expertly procured a jitney and took off after a target he was certain they shared.

The next time he saw the woman, when she stepped from her taxi in front of the Bengurian, he would not have recognized her if he had not watched her enter the vehicle. Two quick-change artists in the same place at the same time? What were the odds?

Raimi's ideas about who these characters were and who they worked for took yet another hard turn. If the woman was a COI agent, following the professing bounty hunter, then Newman was not working for the same boss. What was it Thorn had said: "I don't have any female agents in the field?" A cagey way to answer a yes or no question.

With the two unknowns in the same place at the same time, Raimi took up a series of positions in the street outside the Bengurian, observed the woman's going and coming, and settled in to wait. The stakeout tested his patience and his decision-making processes. The woman left the next morning; Newman was nowhere in sight. Raimi almost followed her, but thought better of it. He'd wait out Newman.

That took until the early evening. As Acre's sun was bathing the horizon in a blaze of color, Adam Newman finally appeared, carrying a pack and dressed in clothing somewhere in the continuum between the swell and the bounty hunter. He was wearing a wig, apparently, a collar-length mop of black-cherry curls that looked real and that drastically altered his appearance. The guy was a grab-bag of surprises, but Blake Raimi was determined not to let him out of his sight again.

49 / LOOKING FOR TROUBLE

THE SUN WAS SITTING LOW ON THE HORIZON, CASTING A RUDDY glow over Port New Haifa, when the Freeman's Guild freighter *Moonraker* appeared on the mid-range tactical display and requested an orbital position. Wren felt her adrenaline begin to surge and reined it in. She was going to need that edge later, she suspected, and didn't want to waste it on waiting games.

Still, her expectation that *Moonraker* would immediately request a hopper went unmet. While a number of requests came in for the small shuttles around the time the freighter and several other ships settled into geosynchronous orbit, none of them came from *Moonraker*. The control team fielded requests for shuttles from a *Morro Castle* (wanting a skiff to transfer first-class passengers planet-side), *Volturno* (needing a hopper for colonists from New Haifa bound for a recently founded outpost) and *Moriah* (requesting a hopper for crew returning from pilgrimage at the Mabirati shrines). All the while, *Moonraker* sat serenely in her orbital nest, doing exactly nothing.

Wren went from fearing she'd waste her edge on small stuff to fearing that she'd throttle it waiting for *anything* to happen.

This could take all night, she thought.

<Hey, T.>

Cyber's thoughts echoed in Trouble's head, making him wish he could reach in and scratch his brain. He was on the long, gently sloping ramp that led from the port's ground level down to the shuttle bays. Lights had come on all around the terminal as the light of Acre's star had drained from the sky. It was now fully dark—not even a ribbon of twilight graced the star-strewn sky. Trouble tried not to think of all the things that could go wrong between here and his shuttle.

"Hey, Cyb. If you're not jacked in can you go to vox? It's creepy when you're in my head like this."

<Oh, sure, uh...> "There, is that better?"

"Great. What's the news from on high?"

"The hopper you want is registered to an ore carrier named *Moriah*. We didn't want to announce that we were retrieving someone from Acre, in case Daddy Julian, or someone equally nasty was watching. The hopper's on Level 3, Bay A-7. Pretty close to the terminal. Should take you twenty or thirty minutes to get there if nothing holds you up in security."

"How're you going to keep the *Moriah's* shuttle from going to the *Moriah*? I ask because I really don't want to end up working in a mine on some frozen ball of rock."

"Don't you worry your pretty head about that, my friend," said Cyber, sounding seven kinds of cocky. "*Moonraker* and I are really, really good at being sneaky."

Don't I know it.

"How's Morgan?"

There was a moment of hesitation then: "Tasty. But you already knew that."

"Ah. I take it you've made some progress in the Morgan department."

"I think so. I hope so. She's ... uh ... Well, you know."

Another hesitation. "Are you gonna want ... I mean, if you want to pick up where you left off..."

"I hadn't planned on it. I'm still ... figuring things out."

"Take all the time you need."

"Gee, thanks. ...Level 3, Bay A-7, you said."

"I did."

"I'm almost to the terminal. I'll ping you when I'm aboard the hopper so you can do your navigational magic."

"See you soon," said Cyber, with more confidence in his voice than Trouble had in his whole body.

Asking the net-head to switch to voice hadn't stopped the itching in his brain as it usually did. Maybe his enhanced senses were trying to tell him something else was cocked up.

Wren Sharaf stood on the upper gallery in the flight control center, monitoring the shuttle requests being received by the ground-to-air transport team with every alarm in her head going off. It made no sense. *Mocnraker* had been in orbit since before sunset, it was now coming up on half an hour after, and no call had been made for a hopper. It didn't feel right.

She swung around to look at Officer Hansen, who had returned to Ops just before sunset. "Can I see the security feed from the entrance to the shuttle bays?"

She knew her quarry to be a master of disguise, but she also knew at least some of his tells, the tricks he used to mask his height and body shape. There was a good chance she could spot him. Hansen set her up with two feeds—the one that began right at sunset and the current one. Her mods allowed her to split her attention between the two, not simultaneously, but through rapid switching back and forth. Her vision AI spotted and flagged several individuals who shared some characteristics with Matthews/Newman, but a swift, direct look eliminated them.

A full ten minutes after she started her surveillance, the real-time feed came up with a hit. The stride was wrong, the hair was too long, his carriage constrained and tentative in a way that she'd never seen her target wear. He looked like a provincial boy from Goshen province who'd accidentally pitched up in New Haifa and had never seen so many people in one place in his life. This, notwithstanding the busiest part of the port's day was long behind it.

Yet, there was no mistake; it was Matthews. She stepped off the gallery to stand at the shoulder of the shuttle ops team lead. Her name tag identified her as "Keyes."

"Anything from *Moonraker*?"

"No, ma'am," the woman told her. "Not a peep."

Wren looked up at Hansen, standing above her on the gallery. "How long does it usually take to get through security and into the embarkation concourses?"

"Twenty minutes minimum. Longer if you're carrying something suspicious."

Wren ran a swift calculation in her head. Matthews was here and he was passing through the security checkpoints. *Moonraker* had not requested a shuttle, but three of her orbiting neighbors had. One was a skiff and taking on paid passengers, so she could let that one go. Two were taking on passengers or crew on a one-way ticket. What if *Moonraker's* request was wearing some other ship's transponder ID? What if *Volturno* or *Moriah* was being used to cover Matthews's escape?

And how long do I wait until I play a hunch?

She had a finite set of minutes, which were flying by as Matthews made his way through security. Wren thought of having port security stop the man, but there were risks to that. Too many innocent people were in the way; she wanted to confront him in the enclosed space of the hopper, where no one else would get hurt.

Wren glanced up at the big screen where the assigned transports were monitored. The *Morro Castle's* skiff was already loading. She considered the two viable options: *Volturno* or *Moriah*?

She turned her attention back to Keyes. "How long has *Moriah* been in orbit?"

The other woman checked her stats. "Since about 1500 hours."

Far longer than the other two. Odd that it would've been in orbit that long before ordering up a hopper. She went with it.

"Thanks for your help, Mr. Hansen," she told the duty officer. "You and your crew. I'm going to check out the *Moriah's* hopper. You may wish to route people around that landing."

"You're sure that's the one your target will take?"

She gave him a slanted smile. "Not sure, but it seems the most likely candidate because *Moriah's* the least likely to have suddenly decided to request a shuttle after being in orbit for hours."

Hansen nodded and ordered Keyes to unlock the transport.

Wren headed for the lift tube.

THE THING ABOUT A CROWD OF PEOPLE ALL MOVING IN THE SAME direction, is that they're easy to fade into, even if you're taller than most of them. Trouble folded himself into the herd, made his way through the security check point with minimal nerves, and headed for the shuttle gates. He really didn't expect to be stopped in the terminal; after all, anyone who might suspect his real identity would expect him to be a dangerous sonofabitch and wouldn't want to confront him where the people around him would be put at risk.

He did not feel watched, beyond the moment he passed through the entrance to the terminal. There were at least half a dozen cameras there, and he imagined as many people watching from the Ops center. He made his way to the shuttle concourse, went up to the third level and strode purposefully toward pad A-7.

Through it all, he carefully held up a firewall between his neocortex and reptilian core. His body wanted to break into a dead run; he kept his adrenal gland in check with a will. The flesh between his shoulder blades would not creep, he would not turn and look behind him, no matter hcw insistently his instinct told him to, and he would not change pace. He would not look like a man on the run.

The shuttle was a square and squat quad-boat with two seats fore and two seats aft. The simple airlock on the port side could soft-dock with just about any craft. The airlock was so small it could fit only two people side-by-side and so shallow, you could reach the lock mechanism for the inner hatch standing with your back against the outer one. Trouble eyed it skeptically as he stepped through it onto the tiny craft, glad that he wasn't claustrophobic, happier still that he wasn't going to have to execute an EVA from it.

The airlock was bracketed by a pair of stowage compartments. He tossed his duffel into the forward compartment as the double airlock hatches closed behind him.

"I'm aboard, Cyb. Bring me up."

<Aye-aye,> Cyber returned. No use asking him to go to vox now—he was clearly jacked directly into *Moonraker's* systems. <We are cleared. I'm going to try to steer from here, but if Ops tries to override when they realize you're off course, I'll have to kick it into manual and have you follow our transponder beam. You ever pilot a shuttle?>

Trouble turned to look at the nav board in the bow of the hopper; it was flushed with green light as the craft lifted from its pad into the air. The only sounds in the craft were the swish of the air filtration system coming online and a contralto hum from the Dresden magnetic repulsion system that Trouble imagined only someone with his mods could hear.

"I don't remember, I …" But he did remember. Vaguely. "Wait. You know what? Yeah. I have piloted … something like this… Weird."

<What's weird?>

"Memory. It's creepy."

<Why don't you strap in? I'm gonna punch it when you clear the port. Might be too much for the inertial dampers in that little dinghy.>

"This little dinghy," Trouble said wryly, sliding into the pilot's chair, "is state-of-the-art."

<Sure it is. *I'm* state-of-the-art. Your little dinghy is a—>

"Who the hell are you talking to, Newman? Is it be Grant Thorn by any chance?"

Trouble spun the chair around and stood, bringing himself nearly nose to nose with Blake Raimi. He did not miss the fact that the guy had a slap gun aimed at his belly. Mods or no, getting hit with the sonic blast from one of those would cause major damage.

He raised his eyes to Raimi's face. "Why would I be talking to Grant Thorn?"

<Is that a rhetorical question?> Cyber asked.

"That's who you work for, isn't it?" Raimi demanded.

"Listen," Trouble said tersely, speaking more to Cyber than his adversary. "I don't work for anybody, Raimi."

<Oh shit,> said Cyber. <He's on the boat with you? Are you strapped in? I can drop the dampers and flip the thing—>

Trouble let Cyber "see" his situation—standing in the bow of the hopper, less than an arm's length from Raimi.

<Oh, shit,> Cyber repeated.

"Really?" said Raimi. "And I suppose you're going to tell me you don't know who the woman works for either."

"No, I do. The woman is a COI agent who's investigating Chaz Carldon's murder. She wants his assassin. ...That's you, isn't it?" He added, and saw a sudden flare of wariness in the other man's eyes.

<Trouble! F'Godsake, strap in!> Cyber insisted.

No time, Trouble thought back. Flip it to port, NOW.

"I don't know what you think you know," Raimi was saying, "or where you got—"

"Inertial damper failure," said the shuttle's AI in a pleasant female voice. A half-second later, the hopper rolled suddenly to port, flinging both men against the door of the forward stowage compartment. Trouble, who'd expected the wild ride, had sprung forward a split second before the roll and caught Raimi's wrist. As their bodies collided with the stowage compartment, the slap gun flew from Raimi's hand, ricocheted off the upper bulkhead, and spun off aft.

Trouble didn't bother to track its flight. He suspected Raimi was modded, but had no idea to what extent. The fact that he'd been able to cloak his entry to the hopper in ambient sound, and damp down his biological telltales hinted at his enhancements' sophistication.

Now, pressed against the wall that had become a deck, the two men struggled for advantage. Trouble won that battle, ending up on top of Raimi and in possession of his wrists. He noted that the guy was wearing a pair of black gloves woven with silver webbing that hinted at hidden tech. Another unknown.

Trouble did the math: Raimi still believed he was Adam Newman, bounty hunter—at the moment more good to him alive than dead. That should give him some room to negotiate.

"Simmer down, Raimi," he said. "Why the hell are you trying to bust me?"

"You work for Thorn," Raimi snarled. "He's using you put me off the trail and cut me out."

"You've got it backwards, Raimi. *You* worked for Thorn and he cut you out because you're a liability. You're an assassin. I'm just a guy with his own agenda."

"Yeah? You wanna tell me about that agenda? How you want to capture Ridley Matthews and reap the benefits of all my hard work?"

Trouble felt Raimi relaxing his grasp—setting up a move of some sort.

"If I was going to do that, why would I be leaving Acre?"

"Maybe because you know that Matthews is off-world. Maybe he's on the ship you're headed to."

"S'pose it could look that way," Trouble said, agreeably. "Maybe I'm leaving because he's dead."

Deep down in Raimi's eyes, something shifted, as if he had just remembered that the main reason he believed his quarry hadn't been killed aboard *Moonraker* had him pinned to the airlock hatch.

"You sonofabitch," Raimi growled, going even more slack in Trouble's grasp. "What're you playing at? If you knew he was dead—?"

"That's the thing. I didn't know. I needed you out of the way so I could figure it out." Some truth there.

"So he *is* dead, then?"

Trouble took a split second to wonder why he found outright lying so unpleasant, then said, "In all the ways that count."

Raimi's pale eyes narrowed. "What the hell is that supposed to mean?"

"What if we stop trying to kill each other and discuss that?" *Cyb*, he thought, *can you put us on an even keel again? Gently?*

The hopper righted itself and Trouble found his feet once more on the decking of the little boat. He let go of Raimi's wrists and held him against the airlock door with a forearm across his throat. A second later, the DMR drive gave way to the ion propulsion system, announcing that they were free of Acre's gravity.

"Ready to have a civilized chat, Mr. Raimi?"

Raimi smiled, nodded, then made a move Trouble had not seen coming. He grasped Trouble's restricting arm in one hand, then reached up with the other and activated the airlock's inner door. Then he pulled.

Cyb! Kill gravity! Trouble thought.

Too late. Raimi had had enough time while his feet were planted on the deck to yank Trouble into the airlock. Trouble's reaction was instinctive; as he shot past Raimi he got an arm around his torso and dragged him into a collision with the outer hatch. The inner door slid shut, trapping both men in the narrow space, with Raimi closest to the control panel.

"What now, Raimi?" Trouble asked. "You're going to have to open the inner hatch to get back into—"

"Am I?" Raimi freed one hand long enough to trigger something on what Trouble had mistaken as a lapel pin. A soft EVA hood deployed from the collar of the emergency escape suit the man apparently wore beneath his street clothes. Before Trouble could do much more than register admiration for his enemy's preparedness, Raimi cycled the outer door.

It was a strange sensation, suddenly being enveloped in the vacuum of space. It was, Trouble realized, a familiar one, and not because he'd experienced it in a small way during an EVA from *Moonraker*. He remembered, with crystal clarity, that he had once before been thrown into the void and had felt his body taking reflexive measures to protect itself. A warm flush of pleasant heat poured from the crown of his head and out from his spine to every extremity. His eyes did not cloud with frozen moisture, his lungs did not ache for air; in fact, he felt no need to breathe.

The momentary fear that washed through him ebbed as quickly as it had come.

He turned his attention to Raimi, still locked in his hostile embrace. He knew the form-fitting emergency EVS the other man wore would support him for roughly ten minutes—fifteen at most—and that its capacity to do so would begin to deteriorate almost immediately. The hopper was hovering roughly two meters away, thanks to Cyber. But the two men were almost four meters aft of the airlock. Raimi's only chance of survival was to get back aboard.

Trouble saw the realization in the bounty hunter's eyes; a moment later, he saw them register the fact that Trouble was not a human popsicle, very much alive, and in no immediate distress. What Raimi made of that, he literally couldn't say since space didn't transmit sound. Did he realize that he was stranded in space with his worst enemy, just meters from safety?

If there was a more perfect circumstance for an interrogation, Trouble couldn't imagine it. The irony of not being able to ask a single question was bitter comedy.

Raimi mouthed something that could have been "Matthews" or could have been "Flak you." Regardless of who he thought

Trouble was, they both knew that Raimi's moments of life were limited if they couldn't get back aboard the shuttle. Presumably, they both knew that Trouble could hold out indefinitely. What Trouble didn't know was if there was a limit to how long he'd remain conscious and able to move. He suspected that, at some point after he'd escaped the prison transport that would have taken him to Restitution, he had lost consciousness; what had happened between the time he'd been blown into space and been reborn on Porphyry was still a closed book.

Didn't matter now. What mattered was that he needed to get back aboard the hopper and get to *Moonraker*.

<T?> Cyber's query came to him in quivering uncertainty.

Here. Gotta get back aboard. Anything you can do besides keep the boat nearby?

<I can operate the airlock, I think. ... Maybe ... I'm not sure. I'm not connected to every system directly. Just navigation and propulsion.>

Propulsion. They'd need a little of that if they were going get back inside the hopper. Trouble knew the craft's reverse thrusters weren't made for such tiny shifts.

<Raimi's EVS!> Cyber chirped. <The puffers!>

Raimi had been very still, thoughts that Trouble could only imagine flickering behind his eyes. Trouble had no way to communicate with him except...

He let go of Raimi's jacket and gestured at the hopper. He mouthed the words, *Your EV suit,* and tapped the soft helmet.

With a grimace that told Trouble he'd forgotten about the suit, Raimi shot a glance back at the hopper and used the left glove to activate the suit's propulsion unit—pressing together the thumb and middle finger of his left hand. The cuffs of the suit's legs exuded a puff of air and Raimi drifted toward the hopper, leering back at Trouble as if he expected to make a clean getaway. But Trouble had anticipated the move and wrapped both hands around the other man's left leg just above the knee.

Raimi kicked out with his free leg, attempting to dislodge his adversary. Instead, the two men began to tumble and twist in space, and not in the direction of the airlock. When Raimi continued to fight; Trouble could only conclude that he was having an unpleasant confrontation with his own mortality. It had apparently stripped him of rational thought; fighting was suicidal. He was taxing his EVS and pulling them further toward the stern of the hopper.

Trouble grasped Raimi's arm and hauled himself further up his torso. He knew the controls for the propellant were in the left glove, so he reached for it, managing to capture the other man's wrist. Trouble was in no mood to be gentle at this point; he hauled the hand toward him while Raimi squirmed. When he failed to dislodge his captor, the assassin tried to throttle Trouble with his free hand.

Trouble ignored him, keeping his focus on that glove. He managed to mash the two fingertips together, using his legs to reorient Raimi's body in the right direction. But the bounty hunter refused to give up, even though he was clearly out of his element. Their journey toward the hopper was erratic, and carried them into a sharp collision with its flank roughly a meter and a half behind the airlock. Trouble lost his grip on Raimi's hand, which caused the man to explode with sudden energy, twisting, jack-knifing, trying desperately to unseat his rider.

Stop fighting, you dumb bastard. You're killing yourself, Trouble thought, wishing he had some way to communicate that to Raimi. He tried to get at the gloved hand again, but Raimi was waving it so wildly, it was a losing proposition.

Ready to open the airlock outer door, Cyb.

<Uh, yeah. I'll try.>

Hardly comforting. Trouble focused on the goal. Only a meter now. With one arm around Raimi's chest, he used the other to grab handholds and pull them forward. Two feet. One.

Cyb, the airlock!

As if he'd heard the urgent thought, Raimi twisted in Trouble's one-armed embrace, trying to get to the airlock first. Maybe he thought he could activate it somehow and leave Trouble outside. Who knew. But in his mad attempt to reach it, he dislodged his emergency helm, causing it to slip upward on his head. Instead of trying to secure it, he reached beneath the hem of his jacket and produced a laz blade.

Cyber! Anytime now!

Trouble had no idea whether the blade would work in space and he had no desire to find out. But if Raimi tried to slash him with the damn thing, it would give him ample opportunity to grab the man's hand again. Splitting his attention for a second, Trouble realized that the soft helm that was feeding Raimi oxygen was continuing to loosen.

The laz blade lit up with frenetic green arcs of light.

Trouble reached up and got one hand around Raimi's throat, thrusting him against the side of the hopper. With the other he blocked the other man's attempt to slash him with the laz blade.

In a matter of seconds, Raimi went limp. The laz blade tumbled into space, inert.

The outer hatch slid open. Trouble grabbed the sill of the airlock and shoved the man in, using their combined momentum to get them both completely within the narrow space and into the arms of gravity. The outer door closed, the airlock cycled, and the inner door opened. Trouble dragged Raimi in and collapsed beside him on his hands and knees, feeling the changes in his own body as it registered that it now had oxygen, warmth, and gravity.

"Thanks Cyb, but your timing needs some work."

<Yeah. Um ... that wasn't me.>

"What d'you mean it wasn't you?"

Suddenly aware of another presence, Trouble raised his head to find himself looking at the muzzle of a zat gun that was, almost inevitably, in the hands of a certain COI agent.

51 / STAND OFF

TROUBLE IGNORED THE WOMAN WITH THE GUN. HE PULLED OFF Raimi's soft helm, caught him under the armpits, and hauled him to one of the aft passenger seats.

"He needs oxygen," he told the COI agent. "Behind you, in the forward stowage."

She hesitated for a only a second, then reached into the already open compartment—which was where she must have been hiding—and brought out one of the oxymasks that were stored in a bracket just inside the stowage hatch. She tossed it to Trouble, without once taking her eyes—or her gun—off of him.

"Thanks." He sensed the hopper's renewed forward movement and thanked Cyber silently for being Cyber. He also let *Moonraker*'s first mate in on the full flavor of his current predicament. He fixed the mask over Raimi's nose and mouth, then turned back to Agent Sharaf, gesturing at the bounty hunter. "I don't think I can trust him not to try to kill both of us. You have restraints of some sort?"

"Yeah. For you."

"I am no danger to you, Agent Sharaf. He is."

"I know who you are," she told him, the zat gun never wavering. "You're not Adam Newman. There is no Adam Newman; you're Ridley Matthews."

Trouble let none of his surprise—and admiration—show. "I'm sure there are multiple Adam Newmans somewhere in the universe, but you're right. I'm not one of them. You have my buddy Cyber to thank for that unimaginative alias."

<Hey!>

"This guy," he indicated Raimi, "is a bounty hunter, a murderer—"

The words foundered in a moment of lucid recall so horrific it almost sent him to his knees. His home. His safe haven invaded. Broken. Jani's body lying as if she only slept, but empty, her spirit already gone. His may as well have been. His life had shattered into a million pieces, most of which had been stolen from him. And his daughter. They had taken his daughter to a safe place, they said. He had not seen her again. He still couldn't remember her name.

"Hey! Matthews!" The COI agent's voice cut sharply into his waking nightmare. "Talk to me."

He took a deep breath. Tried to find some sort of center. He felt like a clay sculpture with mismatched pieces only barely held together by … by what?

Talk to her.

He pointed at Raimi. "I can't prove it, but I am certain this is the man who killed Chaz Carldon. And my wife."

She frowned at him over her gunsight. "That's not the common wisdom."

His laughter was without even a molecule of humor. "Yeah. I get that. But it's *my* wisdom. Hard-earned, because whatever they did to me—whatever Grant Thorn did to me—it took my memories. But they started coming back, believe it or not, in Pilgrim's Passage. Just bits and pieces, at first, and they didn't make sense. Then."

"And now?"

Raimi moaned and his eyelids fluttered.

Trouble shot him a glance. "You really need to make a decision about this, Agent."

Sharaf muttered something beneath her breath, then reached up under her jacket and produced a set of restraints. She handed them to Trouble. "Secure him to the chair—both wrists. You might want to relieve him of any further weaponry he's got. I saw the laz blade."

Trouble did as she directed, connecting Raimi's wrists to each other and one arm of the chair and removing the impressive collection of weapons he had concealed on his person.

"If Blake Raimi is the assassin," said the COI agent, "and your wife's murderer, why bother to drag him back in here after you'd tried to strangle him?"

Trouble shook his head. "I never tried to strangle him. His hood was coming off. I tried to keep him from losing all his oxygen. He still lost enough to knock him out."

"Okay. Reverse that question: If this is the man you say murdered your wife, why would you save his life?"

"Well, first because I'm not, generally speaking, inclined to kill people if I don't have to. Second, because I want him to face justice. And I want him to give up the people he works for, starting with Grant Thorn."

"Why Thorn, in particular?"

"Because I used to work for him too, apparently. And he … had me turned into … whatever this is." He swept a hand up and down his body. "Because I think he tried to have me kill Chaz Carldon and when I refused, he sent Raimi to convince me by destroying my life. My wife is dead and my daughter—"

He couldn't speak for a moment; it felt like the emerging memories had gotten stuck in his throat and were choking him. He met Sharaf's eyes. "I don't know if my daughter is alive or dead. And *I can't even remember her name* "

The COI agent pursed her lips, then lowered her weapon and holstered it. "Your daughter's name is Amalia," she told him. "She's alive and well—physically, anyway. If you give yourself up, I could arrange for you to see her."

Trouble could only stare at the woman for a moment before

his legs failed him and he sat down hard on the deck. He vaguely registered, through the surface beneath him, that they had changed course. He didn't much care.

Amalia. Her name was Amalia. He had a flash memory of naming her when Janina was five months pregnant, their hands pressed together over her belly. Amalia meant "God's work" in several of Earth's languages. She was alive and he might see her if…

"If I turn myself in," he said finally, his lips feeling as if the iciness of space had finally caught up with them, "the man she sees will be in shackles. She'll see her father as a criminal. Which he's not." He looked up at Sharaf sharply. "What have they told her about me? About her mother's death? Did she see—?"

The agent shook her head. "She didn't see anything or anyone. She heard a strange noise, came into the dining room and found…" She hesitated. "We didn't tell her any of … what we thought had happened. She knows her mother is gone, and that we didn't know where you were, but we knew you were alive."

"Where is she?" He didn't mean to sound demanding, but knew he did.

"She's in a safe house on Earth."

Trouble "heard" a burst of chaotic emotions from Cyber's end of their connection, and tuned it out.

"Who's caring for her?"

"Your wife's parents, at the moment. Before that, I was her guardian."

That surprised him. "You? COI assigned—"

"I volunteered. I'm a trained psychologist, as well as a finder of lost persons." The corner of her mouth twitched. "She calls me 'Aunt Birdie.' Wren—Birdie? Get it?"

Trouble nodded, still finding it difficult to breathe. "I don't want her to see me in shackles, Aunt Birdie. I think I'd rather she believe I'm dead."

Wren Sharaf's ideas about the man she'd been hunting for the better part of a year had exploded one after the other since she'd overheard his conversation with *Moonraker's* first mate at the Bengurian. Now they seemed to be caught in a repeating cycle of explosions and implosions that left her without logical recourse.

Then I rely on my gut, she thought, and moved to sit in the chair next to Raimi, who had now begun to turn his head from side to side and murmur unintelligibly. She glanced up at the viewport with its tactical overlay. They were drawing close to *Moonraker;* docking maneuvers would begin in a matter of minutes.

"Maybe," she told Matthews, "there's a way she can see you without the shackles. I want you to tell me everything—everything you recall or have pieced together "

He did, including both the abstract information he'd gotten in Pilgrim's Passage, his fragments of memory, what Doc Pike had found in his system and what Cyber had dug up about Thorn's investments in DeNA-Gen.

"Chaz Carldon was investigating DeNA-Gen," Wren said when he'd finished. She took another glance at their distance from the *Moonraker,* and knew that docking maneuvers were imminent.

"Yeah," Matthews said. "And as near as I can tell, Thorn wanted Chaz out of his way and I was a handy mole to have modded. Chaz twitted me a couple of times for the number of physical exams I'd had. I don't remember, but I'm thinking that was when they had the illegal work done."

"No lost time?"

"Apparently not. After all, they didn't actually have to do a full physical. Just put me in the exam tank and let the machine and nanites do their work."

Wren nodded, turning things over in her head. "So Thorn

wanted Chaz Carldon out of the way because he was getting too close to DeNA-Gen and their involvement with the illegal tech it was doing on the sly."

"That's as clear as I can make it. They apparently approached me about the hit, but because I first learned about that in the thrall of Passage psychosis, I didn't trust it. I can only imagine I said I'd do the hit hoping I'd be able to bring them down. My … perception of Chaz from the Passage was that *he* blamed me, too. He said I should've warned him and apparently, I didn't." He took a deep breath. "I didn't warn him, and I should have. Chaz wasn't just my employer, he was a friend. But even knowing that, I was afraid I was gaslighting myself—that the idea that I'd backed out of the hit might've been wishful thinking."

Wren gave him a searching look. "How could you not know?"

He shrugged. "I had no memory of who I'd been. It seemed like something the-the new me wouldn't do, but I didn't know that with any certainty, until I started to remember my relationship with Chaz. I wasn't certain, I think, until Lucas was certain."

She shivered a little at the idea of not knowing such a thing about yourself, of fearing that you might actually be a killer. "Lucas Shade," she said. "*Moonraker's* captain?"

He nodded.

"You trust Captain Shade?"

He smiled wanly. "With my soul. We've gotten in the habit of saving each other's asses."

"You're him." Raimi's voice creaked like rusted metal on rusted metal. "You're Ridley Matthews."

"Allahluya," said Matthews wryly. "Finally had your 'come to Buddha' moment, have you?"

"I see why Thorn wants you dead," Raimi snarked. "Glib sonofabitch."

"Oh, I'm pretty sure that, at this point, he wants both of us dead." He quirked an eyebrow in Wren's direction. "Possibly all three of us."

"Docking maneuvers initiated," said the hopper's computer.

"Any chance your trusted captain is going to shoot me as soon as he sees me?" Wren asked.

Matthews tilted his head to one side for a moment, then frowned. "I can't raise *Moonraker* right now, but I assure you, shooting first is not something Lucas Shade does."

Docking took several minutes, during which Wren took possession of Matthews's duffel, positioned both men in front of her, and considered drawing her sidearm again. Just as they were making their final turn to soft dock with the freighter, she caught the view toward *Moonraker's* bow. There was a HASA skiff docked to the freighter.

"Well, shit," said Raimi. "Looks like our ex-boss might be here."

"Were you expecting him?" Wren asked.

Raimi shook his head. "No, Agent. I wasn't. Far as I knew, he was still on Europa ... and that I was done with him."

Wren took a deep breath. "Matthews, your friends aboard *Moonraker* have anything to say about this?"

Matthews shook his head. "Gone silent." He looked uneasy.

Not good.

"Okay," said Wren, drawing her zat gun. "Here's what we're going to do."

GRANT THORN STOOD IN THE SHUTTLE ACCESS WAITING FOR HIS long-sought quarry to appear and musing that no human being had ever lived up to an epithet with more flair than Trouble Matthews. At least his damned sidekicks had the sense to be cowed in the face of HASA authority. "Captain" Shade was as passive and pliant as might be expected of a teenager with his history.

Lucas Shade and Chief Engineer Morgan—an attractive woman with a badly concealed chip on her shoulder—accompanied Thorn and his quartet of armed guards to the airlock. Captain Kid called his engineer Maddie; Thorn was willing to bet the boy saw her as a mother figure. That was not at all the way *he* saw her. She was attractive in the same way a mountain lion was attractive; even dressed in her company jumpsuit she exuded an aura of feline danger. The green eyes and tawny hair enhanced the picture.

Thorn recognized the way those eyes followed him. He had crossed paths with a mountain lion once, while trekking up in the Sierra Nevada on Earth. He remembered the watchfulness of the beast, recognized the same type of sharp regard in Maddie Morgan. He returned her interest, letting her know the attraction he was certain she felt was mutual. She flashed him a toothy smile.

The ship's doctor hovered in the background, armed to the teeth with tranq pellets in case Matthews came out fighting. Shade's First Mate was a net-head. True to his stereotype, he hadn't even bothered to put in an appearance. Probably hiding in his sensory-free tank like a nervous fish.

Everyone who knew Grant Thorn thought he was paranoid. He didn't deny it; paranoia was why he'd set off for Acre right after his first conversation with Blake Raimi. Once he'd realized Raimi wasn't the only participant in the hunt for Ridley Matthews who'd refused to accept his demise, his paranoia informed him that something was off kilter and that he'd better get to Acre to figure out what it was.

Thorn rolled his shoulders and waited for the airlock to cycle. He'd been prepared to just shoot Matthews dead the moment he stepped aboard *Moonraker*, but he'd thought better of it. He'd make one more attempt to salvage his investment by offering the ex-agent a chance to redeem himself and come in from the cold. While it was true that Matthews would never have anything approximating a normal life on any Consonance world, he could at least have a new identity and lucrative work. His enhancements and skills had been calculated for exactly the type of job he'd blown when he'd revealed his real agenda to the wrong person—an agenda that would have brought down Thorn, his lieutenants, and at least half of DeNA-Gen's board of directors.

Theoretically, it was a deal Matthews could not refuse, given that the alternative was death.

It still burned Grant Thorn that he, with his own subtle modifications and training, had not intuited that a man like Ridley Matthews would not be easily turned. He didn't know much about the Mabirati, but he'd always thought all religions were pretty much the same and all believers were inherently weak-minded. He'd viewed Matthews's religious zeal as a malleable substance that could be molded to equate Carldon's politics and policies with evil—to view the Consonance Prime Minister's universalism as a lack of patriotism for the home sector.

Big mistake; Matthews's particular form of religiosity apparently only stiffened his sense of duty and loyalty.

What Thorn had learned from the whole affair was that Trouble Matthews was a damned chameleon who could deadpan and charm his way into making you believe he was exactly what you wanted him to be. Thorn had wondered frequently over the last months if some of the mods he'd insisted Matthews be given during his physicals hadn't also given him some heightened powers of persuasion, along with the ability to reverse a mind-wipe. He didn't see how that was scientifically possible, but tarditech continued to provide surprises. Which was, he wryly acknowledged, one of the reasons it had been banned.

The light above the airlock went green and Thorn tensed. He had positioned himself off to one side so he wouldn't be the first person Mathews saw when he stepped onto the ship. Instead, he'd see the friendly faces of Lucas Shade and Mad Morgan ... just before Thorn's guards took him into custody.

The hatch rolled back on a tableau that Thorn could not have imagined if he'd been under the influence of spaz, or some other entertaining hallucinogen. Two men stood in the airlock, manacled together. One was his freelancer, Blake Raimi. The other, by process of elimination, had to be Ridley Matthews, though with his wild mop of dark curls, brown eyes, and pale, gaunt features that seemed a stretch of imagination.

Before he could quite make sense of the anomaly, Thorn's gaze was drawn to the woman standing behind the pair, a zat gun trained on them and a ferocious light in her dark eyes. His security detail turned to him, silently requesting new orders in the face of this unexpected turn of events. Thorn raised his hand to gesture them to stand down for the moment.

"Well," he said, "this is a surprise, Agent..."

"Agent Wren Sharaf," she said, prodding her captives out of the airlock.

"Sharaf, yes. May I ask how you happened to—"

"Not important at the moment. What's important is that I have captured these two men and intend to transport them to Consonance HQ for processing."

Thorn made a quick assessment. Sharaf was young, earnest, by-the-book, right down to her regulation non-lethal weapon. The kind of young zealot whose experience had yet to temper her naivety. He could work with that.

"I can provide transport, of course, Agent Sharaf, but not to Earth. I will deliver your prisoners to Heartworlds headquarters on Europa."

The woman moved her charges forward, then stepped around them to meet Thorn eye to eye. "No," she said.

He smiled. "No? I don't think you understand who your prisoners are. Or who I am."

"Really? You're going to play the 'do you know who I am' card? I'm disappointed, Chief Thorn. My prisoners are Ridley Matthews—currently wanted for the assassination of Consonance PM, Chaz Carldon—and Blake Raimi, a mercenary I believe you may be acquainted with. Mr. Raimi has been hunting Mr. Matthews for some time. I expect he has an interesting story as to why."

Thorn felt as if a colony of ants wearing crampons were rappelling down his spine. "Mr. Matthews isn't just an assassin, he's a traitor."

"No, I'm not," said Matthews. "And you know damn well I'm not."

The ants' fervor increased. Thorn swept a glance at his guards. He could put an end to this violently right now, killing both Raimi and Matthews, but if he did that, and the COI agent or the captain of the *Moonraker* got caught in the crossfire, there would be hell to pay. He knew who the kid's father was. Knew how powerful his Guild was.

Beneath his uniform, Thorn began to sweat.

He glanced at Lucas Shade and saw that the boy had surreptitiously drawn a small handgun. He met the kid's eyes and nodded slightly. Shade nodded back.

"Agent Sharaf, I commend you for having the audacity and skill to take two such dangerous men into custody, but I must insist on exercising my right as head of Heartworlds Alliance Security to take charge of this situation." He started to gesture his guards forward, but Sharaf stepped in closer, putting herself even more thoroughly between him and her two prisoners.

"As you said, these are *my* prisoners, Chief Thorn. But, if you have a sound reason to claim jurisdiction, I'm willing to hear it. Perhaps, Captain Shade would lend us his ready room for our discussion?"

The bitch had ovaries of steel, he had to admit, but he was past being willing to admire her moxie. "Stand down, Agent," he said, making his voice as biting as he could.

She did not stand down. Instead, she turned and gestured at Matthews. "The crimes allegedly committed by this man were committed against the Consonance. Chaz Carldon was the head of my government. I will hand his assassin over to my government. They will decide his fate. As to Mr. Raimi, he tried to kill my target and interfere with an official investigation. I had to arrest him. It's my intention to interrogate him."

Thorn made the mistake of glancing at Raimi. Their eyes met in a malevolent collision that convinced Thorn that he now had no choice. Raimi and Matthews would both die.

Sharaf caught the glance and smiled. "I don't think Mr. Raimi is particularly fond of you right now, Chief Thorn. I think he knows if he ends up on that HASA vessel, he's a dead man. Don't you, Mr. Raimi?"

The merc nodded, his eyes still on Thorn.

There was no mistaking what he saw in the COI agent's gaze; she knew. Raimi must have already given him up. Fine, then she would die, too. And if necessary, the Boy Captain and his engineer. The whole thing could be explained; The prisoners had tried to escape, there was weapons fire. People died.

Thorn took a step back from the COI agent, drew his sidearm —a non-regulation and potentially lethal beamer—and nodded to his security team. "Take them," he ordered.

The two guards closest to him stepped forward. There was a whisper of sound like a couple of indrawn breaths and the two guards collapsed to the deck. Their comrades froze, stunned, then folded up and hit the deck, as well. Each had a neat hole drilled into the back of his uniform jacket.

Thorn spun, seeking the shooter. The ship's doctor leaned nonchalantly against a bulkhead, a tranq pellet gun in each hand. The old fossil had the audacity to smile at him.

"Are you ready to stand down, Chief Thorn?" Sharaf asked him. "To discuss this like professionals?"

He swung back around to face her and found her zat aimed at his heart. He believed his mods would keep the weapon's electrical charge from killing him or rendering him unconscious, and he was coiling to test that theory when he realized she wasn't the only one aiming something at him. Her two prisoners had discarded their apparently unlocked manacles and had drawn weapons.

"Discuss?" Thorn snarled. "There's no discussion. You're committing an act of treason—"

"Well, that's my dilemma, Chief. These two gentlemen have suggested to me that *you're* the one who's committed an act of— well, treason doesn't begin to cover it. If Mr. Matthews's returning memories are accurate, you had him illegally augmented without his consent and set him up to assassinate the head of my government."

"Matthews's memories are fantasy. ...Aren't they, Blake?" He turned his gaze to Raimi.

"What do you think you can offer me," Raimi said, eyes smoldering with banked fury. "More money? My freedom? I'm a liability, Thorn. You're only safe if I'm dead."

True enough. Thorn made a move to turn his gun on the mercenary, then grunted as the muzzle of another weapon dug into his ribs.

"Your gun, Mr. Thorn," said *Moonraker's* captain from beside him. With the muzzle of his weapon pressed against Thorn's ribcage, the kid no longer seemed the least bit pliant. He held his free hand out for the gun.

Thorn let his shoulders slump and held the weapon out before him. When Shade moved to retrieve it, Thorn took a half step back, grabbed the kid's arm and pulled him across his own body, using him as a human shield. One arm around the boy's neck, he fired off a shot at Raimi, aiming for his heart, but catching him in the shoulder. The bounty hunter went down with a roar of pain, his jacket smoking from the energy round. Thorn started to take aim at Matthews, but the younger man had raised his weapon in a two-handed grip that reminded Thorn of the many awards the guy had won for marksmanship.

Thorn dragged Lucas Shade backward down the corridor in the opposite direction from the medic and his tranq pistols. His only hope was to get to a safe place to call his ship for backup or to make his way to it, using Shade as leverage. He had a half dozen more modded agents on the HASA vessel. That would be enough. It would have to be.

53 / MISTAKES WERE MADE

TROUBLE NEVER TOOK HIS EYES OFF THORN AND HIS YOUNG hostage. Seeing the older man again had flooded Trouble's brain with memories and sensations that made him feel as if he was emerging from a warm, soporific bath into chilling clarity. He had looked up pics of the HASA chief that had tugged at the door to recall without opening it, but now he was assaulted with memory: how he'd seen the personable, seemingly rock-solid senior agent as a mentor, how that image had been shattered when Thorn's conversations with him about "Carldon the Crusader" had begun to drift from political differences into open contempt … and worse.

He remembered the sick sense of horror as he watched Grant Thorn morph before his eyes from benign to malignancy— remembered the moment he decided to play along so that he would be Chaz's shield even as he worked behind the scenes to bring Thorn down. What he did not know was which one of the three people he had informed of the threat to Chaz's life had informed Thorn that he was being played.

Weapon aimed, ready to fire if he got a clean shot, Trouble followed his ex-mentor down the corridor toward engineering and the cargo bays. Above Thorn's restricting arm, Lucas's face contorted in a rictus of fear and pain. But his eyes, locked onto

Trouble's face, betrayed a level of faith that Trouble found hard to accept.

I may be superhuman, but I'm not God, he wanted to tell the boy. I can make mistakes. Have made mistakes.

"Matthews!" Sharaf called to him from behind. "What're you doing?"

"Making sure Lucas survives this. Get Thorn's goons secured!"

"Matthews, you don't give the orders—"

"Please," he added, and focused his attention on Thorn and Lucas.

He heard Morgan say, "Don't argue with the man. You can't win," then, "You got any manacles that actually work?"

He knew the HASA chief did not dare try to take a shot while in motion. It would expose his arm and his head and his chances of actually scoring a hit were low while trying to grapple Lucas. Thorn might be good with a gun, but he did not have Trouble's mods. Trouble was sure of that with the strength of returning memory.

"Let Lucas go, Grant," he called to the HASA Chief. "This is about you and me."

"Let go of my leverage, Ridley? I don't think that would be wise, do you? You'd just shoot me."

"No I won't. Not if you don't do something stupid. Don't you know me better than that yet?"

Thorn's restraining arm jerked and Lucas choked a bit, his feet scuffling on the deck.

"Don't mess with me, kid," Thorn told the youth. "I'll shoot you, then put down your damn guard dog."

"He's not messing with you, Grant. His eyes are rolling back in his head. Loosen up."

Apparently he did. A little color returned to Lucas's face and his expression went from fearful to determined. Trouble knew that look. Knew that it meant Lucas Shade was thinking of doing something bone-head risky.

"Where do you think you can go, Grant?" Trouble asked. "You don't know this ship like I do. You don't know her crew."

"I know enough to avoid the crew. Did you think I didn't study the layout of this boat so I'd know the places you might hide if, by some outrageous fluke, you got to *Moonraker* before I did?"

"Then you know you have to go up a couple of decks to get back to your ship. We're on Zeta deck. It doesn't connect to the skiff dock."

"I do know that. And I know that if I take the lift from Zeta— a lift that should be coming up on my left in a few yards—you'll be stranded down here with only guesses about where I've gone."

He had a point, and indeed there was a lift tube coming up on the starboard side of the corridor.

<Yeah,> said Cyber in the middle of Trouble's head. <Except you won't be guessing.> There was a pause, then Cyber added, <Don't tell *him* that, though.>

Trouble managed not to let his facial expression change, not to show his relief that Cyb was able to talk to him again.

I'll try to remember that sage advice.

Every step brought them closer to that lift tube and when Thorn drew abreast of it, he shot Trouble a smug grimace, and hauled Lucas level with the control panel.

"Activate it, kid."

"Activate it, *Captain Shade*," growled Lucas.

Thorn chuckled. "Gotta give it to you, kid—I mean, Captain Shade. You're unexpected."

Lucas punched the lift panel ... and nothing happened. Well, something happened, it just wasn't what Thorn was likely expecting. All the lights in the control panel went out.

"Hit it again," said Thorn.

Lucas did, but the lights remained stubbornly dark and the doors remained stubbornly shut.

Swearing, Thorn continued down the corridor past Engineering and Cargo Bay A. Trouble reasoned he didn't want to have to deal with the crew, who'd likely take offense at him holding their captain hostage. That left him one place to go—the hydroponics bay.

Trouble tensed, remembering that *Moonraker's* accommodation of an entire Lerandia grove meant its top level catwalk let out onto Epsilon Deck. He was pretty sure that detail hadn't escaped Thorn's notice.

On the heels of that thought, every light in the corridor went out, leaving it in complete darkness. Or rather, nearly complete. A tiny flash of light on the ceiling above where Thorn had been standing caught Trouble's attention. He looked up to see a cluster of Cyber's little bots there. Several of them flashed red and did a brief synchronized dance.

Trouble had no more than registered this, than there was a sudden explosion of movement from the spot Thorn had been standing. His modded eyes already adjusted to the lack of light, Trouble saw Lucas plummet toward the deck, punching upward into Thorn's groin as he dropped. The head of HASA emitted sounded like the roar of a wounded bear. Lucas, freed, took off aft.

Trouble leapt forward, hugging the bulkhead. He doubted Thorn could see him, which meant this might be his only opportunity to bring him down without killing him.

Thorn dropped to one knee and fired off an energy round at the ceiling of the corridor, bringing down a rain of sparks that fell on Trouble's head and shoulders and illuminated the spot where he stood. Exposed, he hit the deck and fired back, but Thorn was already fleeing toward the hydroponics bay. The doors had opened for Lucas, and before they could close again, Thorn disappeared through them.

Cyber quickly opened them again.

"Crew?" asked Trouble as he launched himself after Thorn.

<No one on duty now. Thorn put all non-operational personnel in the Retreat.>

Trouble sensed the outer office and lab of the hydroponics bay were empty before he stepped over the threshold. The door into the steamy Lerandia jungle was still open from Thorn's passage. Trouble slipped through it, wrinkling his nose at the sweet stench. It smelled just as bad as he remembered.

He hunkered down by door and scanned the path that ran back into the grove. It had been upgraded in his absence. The entire bottom of the immense chamber was filled with the trees' nutrient bath, and the solid, raised planking had been replaced with plates of steel mesh, each set into a frame of silicon padding that could be rearranged into different configurations as the size of the grove waxed and waned. There was a constant mist here. It wafted languidly among the trees ... except the two places where it eddied and coiled as if annoyed at being disturbed.

One such spot was down the main corridor Thorn had just passed, the other was halfway up a catwalk on the starboard side. Would Thorn spot that telltale? If he did, would he choose to track down Lucas, or would he make a beeline for the exit up on Epsilon?

The unknown factor was whether Lucas was heading for that exit as well, or had the sense to find a hiding spot and stay put. Lucas was smart as a whip, but Trouble had seen that determined look on his face. He might be considering escape, but his deepest desire would be to take Thorn out, or at least to cause him as much grief as possible before Trouble took him out.

Heartily wishing he could communicate with the boy, Trouble considered his own priorities: protecting Lucas and capturing Thorn—killing him if it became necessary.

<I have complete control over that exit, you know,> Cyber observed. <It doesn't have to open ... at least not for our prickly friend. And I'm also on comms with Lucas>

If Lucas reaches it first —

<Well, duh.>

Trouble felt the static of Cyber's indignation. He rose slowly to his feet, wishing he could make himself invisible. If he could blend in with the plants… He took a couple of steps forward and grasped one of the great, crimson, plate-sized leaves of the nearest tree. He willed the hand to mimic the leaf, putting all effort into being red. He watched in fascination as his flesh steadily changed color, becoming the same shade of deep crimson as the leaf he held. Here, the strange mottling that he'd been unable to completely banish was an asset—Lerandia camo.

He checked his other hand; it was mottled in shades from carmine to maroon. He slipped carefully out of his jacket. His arms were the same. He took off his shirt, too, and considered stripping further but didn't want to waste time. His pants were brown. Not quite the same shade as the Lerandia branches and trunks, which were more rust-colored, but close enough in the mist.

He set off after Thorn.

Lucas hunkered beneath a canopy of Lerandia leaves and thought through what he had seen and heard and what those things told him about the situation he was in. He knew Thorn had studied the *Raker's* schematics. Which meant he would know that there were two ways out of the bay—back the way he'd come, or up a series of ramps and catwalks leading through the dense, aromatic jungle to the exit on Epsilon. He also knew that his net-head First Mate had been paying close attention to what Thorn had been doing since he boarded *Moonraker*, and had intentionally herded the guy down here. Cyb was in control of entrances and exits, but Lucas doubted Thorn had realized that yet or had seen the army of cam bots Cyber had stationed all over the ship.

Of course, Trouble had to have figured all this out, too, and would know that the surest way to catch this sonofabitch would be to make sure he arrived at the hatch on Epsilon. Lucas decided he might as well give Thorn some added incentive.

He rose and grasped the spreading Lerandia branch he'd been sheltering beneath. Then he waved it up and down, stirring the mist around it to a frenzy. Then he let go of it and moved to the top of the last ramp he had climbed, hand on the railing, ready to bolt. Some yards below, he heard a stealthy tread stop, retrace its path, then stop again. A second later, the steel rail vibrated beneath his hand.

Lucas smiled fiercely and faded further into the misty grove.

THORN'S PERIPHERAL VISION CAUGHT THE EDDYING OF THE MIST near the top of the ramp he'd just passed. He'd avoided that ramp because it was the first one he'd encountered and Matthews might expect him to take it with the hope of getting to the highest catwalk more quickly. He wanted to do nothing that Matthews expected, but he saw the indication that someone was up there as a game changer. If it was the boy captain, he could catch up with the kid and continue to use him as a passkey. If it was Matthews, taking the next ramp he encountered might put him in the dangerous position of emerging right into his nemesis' path.

Grant Thorn knew, better than anyone, the sort of abilities DeNA-Gen's tinkering had given his one-time protege. He knew the mind-wipe had hidden many of them, but it was clear that they were coming to light as Trouble Matthews met with obstacles to be overcome.

Thorn had alerted his remaining troops aboard the skiff to the situation the moment he'd been able to conceal himself in the hydroponics bay's stinking mist. He expected they were even now sweeping aft to rescue their chief. All he had to do was reach them. He activated his comms again and murmured that he was going to be moving toward the bow on Epsilon deck.

Then, he did an about-face and returned to the bottom of the first ramp, pausing to listen before he began to climb.

At the top, he paused again. To his right, something made a light metallic sound as it tapped the metal framework. He figured that was the kid. Trouble Matthews wasn't heard unless he intended to be. This, of course, was problematic. If that tiny sound had been Trouble trying to draw Thorn toward the exit, then he was being baited into an ambush. He put his finger on the trigger of his beamer; he might just shoot whoever stood between him and the exit when he reached it.

He went up the ramp with great care. Three feet or so from the top, he reoriented and surveyed his options. The ramp continued up into the foliage; the catwalk that divided it from its upper segment ran left toward the stern and right toward the bow. He hadn't studied the layout of the hydroponics bay in exhaustive detail, but he did know that the series of catwalks and ramps were laid out in a grid that the two people in here with him both knew from experience. It was possible that one or both of them were waiting for him up there—waiting for him to turn toward the bow so they could attack his unprotected back.

He gave a moment's thought to going back the way he'd come in, but that would only work if Trouble Matthews was in front of him somewhere and not stalking him through this stinking, clammy mist. He desperately wanted to scratch between his shoulder blades, but could not. The urge did give him an idea though. He shrugged out of his uniform jacket and continued up to the axial catwalk. He took a swift series of steps toward the bow, then hung the jacket over a Lerandia branch, giving it a little tug to get it bobbing up and down, then he slipped back to the intersection and moved swiftly up the ramp to the next level. He chose to head toward the stern along the next catwalk, then took the final ramp up to the top level of scaffolding. He crouched in the mist for a moment, unmoving, his cheek pressed to the metal railing to catch any vibrations, and wondering why he had not heard the hatch on

Epsilon open and close. Had neither of his adversaries reached it yet?

Didn't matter. He needed to get out, and that was the way out. He padded the length of the top catwalk, the ceiling of the hydroponics bay not much more than an arm's length above his head. The mist moved around him as if possessed of sentience, opening up a bit before him, curling around him, brushing his face with moist fingertips, then closing up at his back. He felt suffocated, intruded upon, and surveilled. He wanted out.

He saw the green guidelight centered over the hatch before he could make out any of its other features. On the control panel to the right of the hatch, status lights of various colors pulsed. As he drew nearer, he saw that the catwalk widened right in front of the hatch, basically forming a balcony that bracketed its two-foot-deep frame. He was maybe six feet away when a slight figure came out of the mist to stand at the center of the door. It was Lucas Shade. He was unarmed, so Trouble must not have caught up with him yet.

Thorn leveled his gun on the kid. "What're you waiting for, Captain? Why haven't you opened the hatch?"

"I can't. It's locked and it's not recognizing my handprint or bio-signature."

"You don't seem scared."

The kid shrugged. "What would be the point?" he asked, deadpan.

"So, it looks like all your running and hiding was a waste of time for both of us. I don't take kindly to having my time wasted, kid."

"*Captain* Kid," said the kid.

"That's what you want for your epitaph, is it? 'Here lies Captain Kid, smart ass?'"

"On the other side of that door," the teenager said, "you're going to need me. That is, if you make it to the other side of that door."

"Move. Up against the rail." Thorn waggled the narrow

muzzle of his gun to indicate the far left-hand side of the balcony.

Shade moved, allowing him to access the hatch frame. Working with one hand, Thorn tried a standard HASA override.

The hatch did not open.

He pulled his ID badge off its magnetic mooring and tapped it on the sensor.

The hatch did not open.

He tried the badge a second time. The hatch still did not open.

He tried a verbal recognition protocol. "This is Chief Grant Thorn, Heartworlds Alliance Security Agency. Read and identify my fingerprint."

The ID reader on the door panel flashed blue, then displayed a bright white circle to which Thorn pressed his right index finger. The ID reader flashed red, then shut down entirely.

The hatch did not open.

"Sonofabitch!" swore Thorn. "Come here, Captain. We'll do a *manual override*." He spoke the last two words as a command to the hatch AI.

"Sure," said Shade.

"Manual override," repeated the ship's computer, and the lights on the control panel began to flash.

The manual mechanism consisted of two round gears—one set on each door, and each with a handle meant to be grasped, pulled out, and turned to release the central locking mechanism. At that point, the handles were to be used to pull the two sides of the hatch apart.

Thorn stood back and waved Shade into the frame. "Do it," he said.

The kid complied, grasping the handles, pulling them out about three inches, then turning them until the handles were upright. When they'd clunked into their new position, he tried to pry them apart.

"I'm not sure I can do this. I'm not strong enough. You'll have to help me."

Thorn chuckled. "That's not going to happen. Stop screwing around and open the damn hatch."

The kid shrugged and turned back to the task, but Thorn had seen that swift glance back down the catwalk, the look of momentary confusion in the boy's eyes. He spun to find himself looking at something as inexplicable as it was creepy. It was a man—it had to be a man—but the color and texture of the flesh was wrong. Bark-like, it was mottled in shades of red, rust, dark green and brown and seemed one with the trees and the mist that eddied around it, almost lovingly, leaving behind a glistening sheen on the alien muscle and sinew.

Thorn's mind tried to tell him that somehow, improbably, it was Matthews, whose adaptations and modifications had now gone beyond Thorn's intent or imagination. But his reptilian brain chittered that it could not be a man, that one of the Lerandia had developed autonomy and mobility, or that the Lerandia grove had a hitherto unknown power to construct a golem or avatar to protect it. Thorn's mind reminded him that he had read something once about a forest that had come to life and killed an entire army of its enemies.

The golem's eyes—chill, glowing moons—were trained on him as it moved toward him, its gait fluid and menacing. Thorn took swift aim and fired.

The energy beam clipped the thing's shoulder, bits of the bark-skin exploding into the air like biological shrapnel. The creature (no, *not* a creature, Matthews) stopped short, glanced at the shoulder ... then grinned at him, its eyes bright, chaotic points of silver fire. It was an expression he'd never seen on a face in his entire life and it drove a thrill of reflexive terror deep into his gut. Into his soul.

Then it took another step closer.

Thorn uttered an inarticulate sound of terror-induced rage and raised his gun again. Lucas Shade shot out of his corner and chopped at Thorn's hand, knocking the gun muzzle aside. The shot went wild, slicing through the forest canopy, setting branches, leaves, and mist in motion. The entire grove seemed to tremble, its canopy rippling as if a breeze played across it.

Beneath Thorn's feet, the catwalk vibrated as his carefully constructed killing machine moved inexorably toward him. He was no match for the monster he had created. He knew it and did the only thing that made sense: He dove for the starboard side of the balcony, vaulted the railing, and plunged through the Lerandia trees toward the manmade swamp below.

55 / NO EXIT

TROUBLE SPRINTED TO WHERE LUCAS STOOD ON THE CATWALK, peering down through the Lerandia to the aromatic pool below. He reached the boy's side just as Thorn's noisy downward plunge ended in a huge splash, followed by the sound of falling branches.

"Whoa," Lucas breathed, giving Trouble the once-over. "You are freakishly scary."

Trouble grasped the kid's shoulder and turned him toward the hatch. "Get out of here, okay, Cap?"

"I wanna help."

"Best done on the outside where you have resources. I'll go after Thorn." He turned and sprinted back down the catwalk toward the stern.

"But, aren't you gonna—" Lucas gestured at the railing Raimi had just leapt.

"Out!"

Trouble continued down the catwalk until he reached the aft-most ramp, then bounded down three levels, his ears picking up the sounds of Thorn's thrashing below and to his left. He thought about letting his body revert back to its normal form (whatever that meant), but he'd found the alterations he'd won by imagining himself as a Lerandia tree had definite benefits.

Especially if Thorn had managed to hold onto his beamer. His shoulder felt bruised, but the pain was negligible.

As he stepped onto the catwalk one up from the deck, he realized Thorn, holding his sidearm well above the noisome water, had nearly reached the far end of the waterlevel walkway. Okay, he was still armed. That changed the math a bit. The door to the lab—

<Way ahead of you,> Cyber told him. <The door is locked down.>

Upon reaching the walkway, Thorn lay his sidearm on the steel grating, keeping it well away from the water. Trouble, meanwhile, slipped over the rear railing of the catwalk and lowered himself onto a tangle of thick Lerandia roots. From there he slid down to immerse himself in the pungent nutrient bath. Shielded from Thorn's view by the drooping branches with their broad leaves, he submerged and half-swam half-crawled toward the walkway very near the entrance to the lab and outer office.

Thorn had pulled himself onto the steel grating, dripping, his clothing heavy with swamp goo. His pistol still lay on the steel plating.

Before he could do more than drift in that direction, Trouble saw an arm snake up out of the swamp and toward the gun.

Damn it, Lucas!

He admired the hell out of the kid's intelligence and courage, but this adolescent false sense of invincibility was new. Had he leaned a little too hard into teaching the kid he had a spine? If he'd created an ego monster that got Lucas killed…

Pushing up the sleeves of his sodden shirt, Thorn leaned down to retrieve his sidearm. He saw Lucas at the same moment the teen's fingers touched the weapon. Cobra quick, Thorn reached down and caught Lucas's arm, wrenched the gun out of his grasp, then hauled him up onto the walkway. In the blink of an eye, he had him in a blood chokehold and began to march him toward the hydro-lab.

Trouble shot toward the struggling pair, no longer caring

about stealth. Thorn turned just as Trouble heaved himself out of the water and up onto the steel grating. Trouble could only imagine what he looked like, and if the flash of rank fear in Thorn's eyes was any indication, it wasn't pretty. But Thorn didn't waste time or energy trying to shoot Trouble. Instead, he turned the gun on Lucas, his hand shaking.

"Don't even think about it, Trouble. I know how to wound this boy in a way that won't kill him outright, but will saddle you with the choice of whether he dies or *maybe* lives if you can get him to your medic fast enough. So, here's how this is going to work—you're going to let us get past you. You even so much as inhale too loudly and I will maim this kid." He dug the muzzle of the gun into Lucas's ribs. "You hear me?"

"I hear you." Trouble was already calculating how he could blindside the HASA chief.

<Don't do it, T,> Cyber warned him. <Let him go on by.>

You can't be —

<Serious? I am sometimes. This is one of those times. Let him by.>

Trouble did, pulling back against the outer wall of the huge chamber. His eyes never left Thorn's face as the guy maneuvered Lucas past him on the walkway.

<Stay on top of him,> Cyber said. <Keep his attention on you … and wait for it.>

Wait for what?

Trouble straightened and followed Thorn as he edged backward toward the doorway. The man's returning smugness, visible as a crooked smile, was damned annoying.

They were perhaps two meters from the door when the 'ponics bay disappeared in darkness so thick, it felt like someone had pulled a blanket made of black holes over it. Trouble dropped into a crouch as a brace of wall-mounted emergency lights flashed on, the concentrated beams hitting Thorn full in the face. He threw one arm over his eyes—the one he'd been using to restrain Lucas—and flinched backward.

This was the "it" Trouble had been waiting for. He shot forward, grabbed Lucas by his soggy jacket and yanked him away from Thorn. Then he pushed the boy behind him and rose to his full height with every intention of giving Thorn the beating he so richly deserved.

Cyber let out a high-pitched <*STOP!*> and Lucas wrapped himself around Trouble's legs. One of those things alone might not have halted him in his tracks, but together they did an admirable job. Trouble's frustrated annoyance evaporated when the metal grate beneath Thorn's feet lit up with a kinetic dance of electricity. Tiny blue-white bolts of lightning arced between the metal plating and the HASA chief's body. Hair and clothing smoking, the man who had so carefully and cruelly decon-structed Ridley Matthews's life uttered a horrific shriek and toppled to the deck.

<Well,> said Cyber. <That went well.>

"It went well?" Trouble repeated. "I was trying *not* to kill him, Cyb."

<He's not dead, just ... a little toasty.>

BLAKE RAIMI WAS ONLY TOO HAPPY TC CUT A DEAL WITH THE Consonance Court of Justice. His testimony, along with Wren's, Lucas's, and Trouble's erstwhile crewmates had led to the full and horrified attention of the Court being focused on Grant Thorn and one or two of his direct reports. Of course, his behavior aboard *Moonraker* had added to the aura of guilt; Trouble was convinced that, even without Raimi's confession, this would have led to the HASA chief to being arrested by his own forces. Not every place aboard the old freighter had squads of cam bots stationed permanently, but the hydroponics bay did.

The Court took mere days to determine that it was Thorn, his lieutenants, and a pair of well-paid doctors who belonged in jail, not Trouble. Thorn did his best to convince the panel of judges that Trouble had been complicit in his illegal mods. The fact that he'd been mind-wiped, Thorn claimed, had been the result of a malfunction in one of the processes. Possibly, Thorn testified, that had also resulted in Ridley Matthews becoming mentally unmoored which, in turn, had led to him killing his own wife and the man he had been assigned to protect.

Hearing Thorn say those things had filled Trouble with a toxic mixture of anger and fear that the panel of three justices might believe him. It had taken every ounce of his training to balance the heavy weight of those emotions—that, and what he had just now begun to see as a sort of partnership or collaboration with his onboard team of tardigrades. They seemed helpful in regulating the sort of adrenaline surges that came with a human's inherited fight or flight response. He hadn't mentioned that view of his "cargo" or "crew" to anyone but Cyber, who had jokingly suggested that he name them all.

Trouble knew he had presented his case well to the Consonance COJ. He no longer looked like a vagabond or a bounty hunter; he had put on weight, adopted his "normal" appearance (at least what more or less matched the images of his original self Wren had shown him). He had spoken in well-modulated tones. He had been calm, composed, rational.

Both fear and anger were dispelled when the judicial panel made it clear that Thorn's testimony was suspect, at best. His investment in DeNA-Gen was known, including the resources he had funneled into the tardigrade experiments before they were declared illegal and unethical. The amount of his investments had not slacked off, but now they were allegedly for legal R&D. Thorn's goose was well and truly cooked when one of the physicians involved cut his own deal with the Court and made it clear that Trouble had no hand in his illegal upgrades. As far as Ridley Matthews knew, the doctor testified, he was receiving subtle upgrades to his legal mods and having his general health monitored. Thorn had been the one driving the use of tarditech, which he'd gotten directly from DeNA-Gen. Clearly, that was going to open an additional line of investigation in the corporate world.

Listening to the doctor testify, Trouble was reminded again of the times Chaz had questioned the need for the frequency of his security chief's examinations. Trouble now recalled having asked Grant Thorn and his doctors that very question: "Why am I here, again?"

They had cited the use of cutting edge technology and the

contractual agreement to report on that tech to its creator, DeNA-Gen.

At the end of the hearings, Grant Thorn was remanded to COI's law enforcement wing to be held for trial. The Heart-worlds COJ recognized Consonance's purview, and stepped into the role of oversight board and collaborator. A fact-finding commission was mandated for a deep look at DeNA-Gen's part in the production of illegal tarditech.

Ridley Matthews was pronounced "completely exonerated."

And yet, he knew that this exoneration did not cover the millions or billions of tiny creatures living in his body and brain. While one axe had been returned to its sheath, another remained to fall.

As he left the courtroom after the final session, Wren Sharaf—who had been at his table through the entire process—escorted him to a chamber adjacent to the courtroom and asked him to wait for her there. It did not escape his attention that there were two armed guards standing just outside the chamber. He took a seat on a settee and tried to make his mind blank.

As usually happened when he did that now, he had vague ghost images of Janina and Amalia appear behind his eyelids. Jani stood out in sharp relief, looking just as lovely as she had in life and in his Passage psychosis. Amalia was more a ghost; a tiny, bouncy ghost with a shock of short, curling golden brown hair and a foggy blank where her face should be. Trouble suspected he could not see her face because he didn't want to see it. He feared what it might reveal—bottomless sorrow, distrust … terror.

He did not know—because Wren had not told him and he couldn't bring himself to ask—what Amalia thought had happened to her mother. What had she made of her father's arrival on the scene of her mother's death, and his almost immediate arrest?

He had no idea how long he'd been sitting on the settee, his head tilted back, his eyes closed, when Wren reentered the room.

He sat up straight and looked at her, trying to read her expression and psyche. He was surprised to find he could not. At least, not until she'd crossed the room and sat next to him on the couch. This close, he saw the concern in her eyes, the tension in her face, the stiffness in her posture. He felt it, too—she was tentative in a way she had not displayed since he'd met her.

"They're not going to just let me go, are they?"

"They have … concerns."

He laughed. "They have more than concerns, Wren. They're terrified of me."

"They're more terrified of what you represent. The unknown. A-a chimera. You're a human being who's been egregiously wronged. *And* you're a science experiment gone wrong … at best. One that—were you not human—they'd consign to a lab. At worst, you're a lethal weapon with unknown capacities that cannot be deactivated."

He met her gaze. "Except that I *can* be deactivated."

She nodded, dodging his direct regard. "Which would maim you or even destroy you. Removing your mods…"

"Is that what the Court wants? For someone to de-mod me?"

She hesitated, then said, "They told me that they are considering that as one course of action. One they don't want to take. So, they've consulted with the ethics council at COI and have determined to make a final decision based on input from various sources, including your friends aboard *Moonraker*."

"That surprises me. They could just tranq me and stick me in a cell somewhere."

A smile touched the corner of her mouth. "Oh, yes. Because that's worked out so well in the past." She met his eyes again, directly. "They don't want to do you further injustice, Trouble. But they can't just pretend you're not … an anomaly. COI Ethics wanted me to ask you if you have an alternative to de-modding. A best-case scenario."

"Yes, actually, I do. I'd like to be allowed to return to the

Moonraker as crew. I would not return to Earth or any other worlds they put off limits."

Wren looked up at him sharply. "That would mean ... that you couldn't go home."

You mean I couldn't get my daughter back, he thought, and wondered if that wasn't for the best. He shrugged. "They say you can never go home again."

Wren stood. "I'll go relay your wishes to them. Then I'll take you to the safe house they've set up for you while they're deliberating."

"A safe house? Why?"

She hesitated before answering. "Well, obviously they want to treat you ..."

"Like an unexploded landmine?"

She smiled and shook her head. "I was going to say 'with care,' but yeah. And also because, right now, we have no idea how many 'associates' Thorn has or how they might take his being arrested. We don't know whether he's the kingpin of a criminal organization that existed to serve his interests, or whether he's part of a larger criminal blackmarket in illegal tech."

"And illegally modded mercenaries?"

She took a deep breath. "*And* that. Point is, if he was a central cog in a larger machine that's under the control of person or persons unknown, that machine might still want you. Or what you represent."

"Which is another reason they can't keep me around home base with all my mods intact. I'm a-an expensive experiment. A prototype. An asset." He closed his eyes—put his head in his hands. "Maybe de-modification is the best solution for everybody involved."

She reached out—impulsively, he thought—and pressed his shoulder. "Not everybody," she said, then turned and left the room.

The safe house was in a gated residential neighborhood several miles from the spaceport in South San Jose, California. San Jose boasted the largest and busiest spaceport in the coastal nation, largely because of its annoyingly perfect weather. Just now that weather was springlike—it being spring in Earth's northern hemisphere—and the rolling hills were an indescribable and glowing shade of green. Trouble remembered that he preferred them in autumn when they gleamed golden, wearing copses of oak and elm and varicolored maple like boutonnieres.

The two-story house was at the end of a cul-de-sac and behind a tall hedge. There were maples in the front yard, deodar cedars in the back. A carport was set at right angles to the house, supported by thick stuccoed columns. There was a car in the carport already—a silvery utility vehicle. Trouble assumed it belonged to whatever agents COI had assigned to monitor him. Wren pulled her car into the turnaround and parked next to the carport.

A short flight of stone steps led up to the front door. He followed Wren up them and into a foyer with flagstone flooring. Inside, she turned to look at him, opened her mouth to say something, then continued on into the house, stepping from the foyer into the living room.

Trouble followed. The first thing he noticed about the room was that it was full of light—light that filtered down from clerestory windows along one wall, light from a skylight set between the exposed beams of the steeply sloped roof. The second thing he noticed was the fireplace and fan-shaped hearth of sand-washed limestone ... or more accurately, the small child playing on the fan-shaped hearth, building something out of those interlocking block toys that seemed as impervious to time as the game of chess. She was wearing a pair of denim overalls and a bright yellow t-shirt.

She had her father's chestnut hair and her mother's stormy gray eyes and pale, heart-shaped face—a face he saw clearly now. He murmured her name as he thought it: "Amalia."

She heard him and looked up, her face still wearing the focused concentration she'd been giving the little tower she'd been constructing. That changed as she looked at him. Her eyes widened, her lips parted, and she leapt to her feet. From one heartbeat to the next, her face lit from within—a sun emerging from behind a cloud.

"Daddy!" she cried and threw herself at him, dashing across the room, her arms reaching upward.

He cast his burden of doubt and responded reflexively, sweeping her up and into his arms, closing his eyes, burrowing his face into her hair. She smelled of lemons and vanilla. He wished with the entire strength of his soul that he could just live inside this moment, always, and never have to move on from it. But time and turmoil buffeted him like a riptide, trying to suck his legs out from under him even as he struggled to hold his child above the wild and uncontrollable

"Daddy!" his daughter cried again, tightening her arms around his neck, as if making absolutely sure she had not imagined him.

"I'm here, Ama," he murmured into her ear. "Daddy's here."

He opened his eyes and met Wren's gaze. *But for how long?*

The woman's expression was thoughtful and filled with concern and compassion. "I'll leave you two alone for a bit. Let me know if you're up for seeing ... her gramma and grandpa."

Trouble exhaled sharply. Of course, she'd told him his mother and father-in-law were Ama's guardians. "I can't imagine they're up for seeing me."

Wren looked suddenly uncertain of herself. "They never believed you had anything to do with ... what happened. They've always believed in you."

Amalia let go of Trouble's neck and looked up into his face, using one small hand to pull his chin around so he was facing her. "Me too, Daddy," she said, then burrowed back under his chin. "Don't go away again, Daddy, please," she added, and broke her father's heart anew.

THE SENTENCING HEARING, AS TROUBLE HAD COME TO THINK OF IT, was held in COI headquarters in San Francisco. The emissary from the Consonance Court of Justice was in attendance to ascertain that the judgement of the security apparatus fell within the court's guidelines for both security and humanity. The contingent from COI included Wren Sharaf, who had been in Trouble's company daily since the hearing that had exonerated him, and two special high-level agents—one from Ethics and one from Risk Assessment. They were agents Camilla Saito and King' Wahome. The agents had ageless faces, hers so smooth, it seemed made of porcelain, his so dark, it seemed to absorb light.

HASA had sent a pair of representatives, as well: Fouad Chafik and Miles Doyle. They were in uniform, the COI agents were not, something that Trouble thought might account for his sense that the HASA agents were a bit stiff and uncomfortable. Then, too, they'd just had the Chief of their entire operation condemned for a laundry list of egregious sins, so it was possible they were just embarrassed.

Trouble and Wren found these worthies gathered in a comfortable, but entirely generic conference room as if they were having a corporate brainstorming session to decide a new product line and not a man's fate ... and his child's with it. It was an imposing group to walk into; the justice, Her Honor Rowan MacGillian, was seated at the head of the oval table, facing the doors through which Trouble and Wren entered. The HASA and COI delegations were seated around the opposite end.

Justice MacGillian waved Trouble and Wren to seats on either side of her, so that they faced the security delegation obliquely with a two seat buffer between them. There were polite greetings all around; Wren seemed to know the other COI agents.

MacGillian opened the proceedings, referring to a datapad in front of her on the table. As if reading Trouble's mind, she said: "I would like to remind all of us that this is *not* the sentencing hearing of a criminal. Rather, you were mandated to consult within and between your institutions and arrive at a just and compassionate solution to this very complex problem. The question before us is: What sort of life will Ridley Matthews live? He has been found innocent, by the Court I represent, of the murder of two people, yet, he has inarguably been transformed into a human weapon that cannot simply be deactivated in a way that leaves his person and his life intact. He is also innocent of that transformation. He has expressed a desire to rejoin the crew of the freighter *Moonraker*, and has offered not to set foot on Consonance or Heartworlds planets without the express permission of the Court and the security agencies of both administrations."

She looked down the table at the two security teams. "What has your consultation yielded?"

After an exchange of glances, King' Wahome spoke, his voice as warm and dark as his features and laced with the cadence of Kenya. "The risk in the situation lies completely and only in Mr. Matthews's modifications. His psychological profile—despite all that he has been through—does not reveal any tendency to use his modifications for ill, though he has used them in self-defense and in the defense of others. Our chief concern is that the ... abilities bestowed by these modifications are only slowly revealing themselves. We do not know, at this juncture, whether their emergence is driven by Mr. Matthews's personality or by the situations he encounters in which new abilities may be needed. In other words," he added, looking down the table directly at Trouble, "you are a work in progress, Mr. Matthews, and the risk lies in what direction that progress takes."

"May I speak?" Trouble asked.

Justice MacGillian nodded.

"In my experience, the new capacities I have discovered are a product of both need and my own sense of … of self, of who I am. If Necessity is the mother of Invention, then Character is its father. My abilities are just tools—tools I've used to survive, to help others survive, and in the course of my duties aboard *Moonraker*. I realize they could also be useful in other ways. Hell, if I'd known I had some of them at the time, I might even have used them to save Chaz's life."

"Would you suggest that you return in some capacity to your previous career?" asked Justice MacGillian.

"No! Never. I was commissioned to guard Chaz Carldon with my life. I failed to do that, even after Thorn attempted to enlist me in his assassination plot and I recognized the source of the risk to Chaz. I should have taken him into my confidence. I should have—" He broke off and shook his head. "To be honest, I have no memory of why I chose to behave like a spy instead of a security agent … or a friend. But whatever the reason, it was an error in judgement. Chaz and Jani paid for that error with their lives. So, no, I couldn't just go back to that life. Especially in view of what Agent Wahome said about the risk my evolution poses."

Again the agents at the end of the table exchanged glances. This time the HASA agent Doyle spoke.

"There is a flip side to that reality," he said. "Grant Thorn invested a great deal of resources in the creation of an asset. Yes, Mr. Matthews is an asset that was created for ill, but he, like the modifications he has been given, is merely a tool."

Across from Trouble, Wren, her face radiating outrage, opened her mouth to speak, but Doyle raised a hand.

"Please, let me finish. I am not ignoring the fact of Mr. Matthews's humanity. I'm simply saying that the abilities he houses can also be used in the pursuit of the public good. Especially if, as he says, they are marshalled, not by blind necessity, but by his sense of himself and his desire *not* to be a weapon."

Justice MacGillian gave the HASA agent a thoughtful look. "What are you suggesting?"

Doyle's partner, Agent Chafik, answered. "We understand Mr. Matthews's desire to avoid situations in which he might discover new capacities in a way that posed potential harm to others. But we would like to suggest that those capacities not go to waste. We've been reminded by scientists involved in genetic manipulation, that understanding what has happened to Mr. Matthews would be of great benefit to science. We are in agreement"—he gestured back and forth between the COI and HASA delegations—"that having Mr. Matthews de-modded would leave him irreparably maimed physically and mentally. Any benefit to science, to our knowledge of human potential, or to Mr. Matthews himself—to his family and friends—would be lost."

Trouble felt something deep inside begin to uncoil. They didn't want to simply turn him into a blank slate and erase whatever he had become or was becoming.

"What Agent Doyle is trying to say, Mr. Matthews," said Camilla Saito, meeting Trouble's gaze, "is that our scientists want very much to understand how the tardigrade presence and your human systems interact. They see you not as a weapon or a monster, but as an opportunity to understand. And, while neither of our organizations would have had you modded illegally, we might yet have need of you. So, your serving aboard the *Moonraker* makes sense. It would allow you to explore the extent of your modifications in an environment in which you feel welcome, if not safe. So, the deal we have arrived at and are authorized to make is this: You may return to your ship, but you must refrain from making planetfall on Heartworlds and Consonance worlds, as you proposed, without express permission to do so. You may freely make planetfall on planets and stations of the Filial Pact. We were made aware that you are of the Mabirati faith, and will also accord you dispensation to visit your religious shrines as you wish."

Trouble sat back in his chair and sucked in a deep breath. That was exactly what he'd asked for. There had to be a catch.

"And?" he asked. "What's the catch?"

"The catch," said the ethics agent, "is that, while we hope to give you the time you need to ... relearn yourself, when we need you, when we call you, you must come."

Exhale. "So, I live, but I live on a leash."

Agent Saito gave an almost imperceptible nod.

"I can live with that, but..." He looked across the table at Wren. "My daughter..."

"That," said Justice MacGillian, "is not in our purview. That is up to her legal guardians." The Justice met Trouble's gaze. "You signed a non-disclosure before this meeting, but I want to emphasize that you are not to contact anyone or speak to them about what took place in these chambers. You are to go directly to your ship—currently in the orbital repair facility—and begin a new life. I hope it will be a happy one."

"Repairs are complete and we're about ready to bust out of here. Cap'll want you in engineering. ... Trouble, did you hear me?"

Trouble turned from the observation decks seamless, curving window to find Mad Morgan standing next to him, looking at him with concern. He hadn't even realized she was there.

"Uh, yeah. Sure. I heard you."

She snorted. "No you didn't. Your mind is a million miles away."

He tried to smile, but his lips only seemed to twitch. "Not quite that far." He turned his gaze back to the mostly blue planet below.

She stepped closer and put a hand on his shoulder. "Your agent friend told me you didn't ask your in-laws if you could have your daughter back. Not even part time."

"I couldn't. Ama's been with her gramma and grandpa too long to disrupt her life. And she's been through so much. Losing her mother…"

"Losing you. Trouble, she may have been with her grandparents for the last year and a half, but she was with you since she was born."

He had no answer to that, so Morgan, being Morgan, just stared at the side of his head. At length, she said, "Wren says Amalia keeps asking when you're coming back."

He closed his eyes. "Mad, please. This is hard enough—"

"Uh, *yeah*. And you're making it harder. On everybody. Wren says—"

"Sounds like you and Wren have become bosom buddies."

"She's good people," said Morgan, then moved to stand between him and his view of Earth, "Look, Trouble, for all you know, your wife's parents were prepared to give her back. They may be wondering why you didn't even ask."

"Give her back to a man in exile? Aboard a-a tattered old freighter?"

"Hey! Watch your mouth, Matthews! That's *my* tattered old freighter you're disparaging. And I'll have you know she's been refitted with some pret-ty nif-ty upgrades. Now, c'mon. We need to get down to Engineering."

As if to belie that, the ship's intercom bleated and Cyber's voice said, "Trouble, Cap wants to see you in his ready room, STAT. Maybe he wants to make you first mate … I wish."

Trouble tried to shake off his melancholy, urging the tardi-crew in his brain synapses to pull him together. He wasn't sure it really worked like that, but it helped him focus. He turned away from the panoramic view of Earth and headed for the lift with Morgan keeping step.

"He's joking, right?" he asked her. "He's been a good first mate, hasn't he?"

"Yes, he has. But he doesn't like being in a position of author-ity. That's not his spice. He's a navigator. A problem solver. A communications guy."

"Does Lucas know this?"

"Let's just say this isn't the first time my sweet man has made such remarks over ship's comms."

Her sweet man? He shot her a sideways glance. "Your what, now?"

She refrained from answering, but her mouth turned up slyly at the corners.

Bemusedly wondering if Morgan might actually be right and he was about to be promoted, Trouble was completely unprepared for what met him in Lucas Shade's ready room. Wren Sharaf stood next to the captain's map table, while Lucas, a goofy grin on his face, was lifting a fascinated Amalia up so she could see the play of colorful data streams and tactical images on the half-sphere display.

"See that itty-bitty bright, white wedge?" he was saying. "That's us. That's *Moonraker.*"

Trouble felt as if his soul had plummeted through the deck and was in freefall toward Earth. It made sense that Amalia would have begged to be allowed to say goodbye to him and that Wren would do whatever she could to make it happen, but it was the last thing in the world he wanted to go through again.

"Wren, what—?"

He'd barely gotten the words out of his mouth when Amalia cried "Daddy!" in a voice so sweet, so joyful, that it gutted him.

Goofy grin still intact, Lucas set her down, and she ran straight into her father's arms and burrowed against him just as she had at the safe house. He could not stop the tears that came; he could only gaze at Wren through them, feeling his daughter's vital warmth.

"Wren why? I told you I didn't want to have to do this again. To say goodbye again."

Wren came around the map table to face him, meeting his silver gaze with her deep mahogany one. "You don't have to say goodbye. We're coming with you. We have Captain Shade's approval and the approval of Amalia's grandparents. They've appointed me Ama's guardian. Justice MacGillian has appointed me yours. To make sure you keep to the spirit—if not the letter—of the deal, and to make sure that Amalia gets to visit her grandparents from time to time."

Trouble opened his mouth, but nothing came out; he had lost

the ability to make words. A mad mixture of thoughts and emotions tumbled through his head, leaving him dizzy: lingering uncertainty, quivering joy, disbelief.

"Your family didn't deserve what happened to it," Wren said. "No one can compensate you for that in a truly just way, and the Court couldn't do more than it did toward giving you some semblance of freedom. It couldn't give you back what remains of your family. As it happened, I knew who could."

Trouble shook his head, feeling Amalia's hair soft beneath his cheek. "I didn't want to ask. I didn't think it would be fair to them, to—"

"Yeah, I know that about you, Matthews," said Wren. "You have a heightened sense of justice."

Trouble smiled. At least, he thought he did; his face still felt strangely disconnected from his emotions. "Blame it on the tardigrades."

"Oh, don't you dare blame it on the tardigrades," said Morgan from behind him. "Your eyes glowing in the dark, *that* you can blame on the tardigrades."

The sound of a throat being cleared seem to come from every comms transceiver in the room. "Y'know I hate to break up this lovely tableau," said the ship, in Cyber's voice, "but we are scheduled to vacate this refit slip at sixteen hundred hours. If we don't do this, we will be liable for additional charges. Which would make our dreaded captain—Lucas Shade, Scourge of the Space Lanes—really, *really* cranky."

The thought of Lucas Shade being cranky (or dreaded) struck Trouble as so absurd, he laughed out loud. It felt good, and it caused Amalia to raise her head, look at him and grin from ear to ear.

"Daddy's happy!" she said. "Look, Aunt Birdie—my daddy is happy again!"

In a moment of utter clarity, Trouble Matthews realized that, despite his still translucent memory, all past pain, and all future uncertainty, in this Moment, with these people, he was undeniably happy.

Whatever might come, he knew of one fixed point: He had the resources—human and otherwise—to meet it.

TROUBLE - THE SONG

The song "Trouble" was recorded for the author's original music album,
I Remember the Rain.

When you strolled into Porphyry

You knew exactly one thing about you:

Your name is Trouble

And you didn't have a credit or a clue.

The city's locking up

As the sun is going down.

The streets are empty canyons.

You're a stranger to this town.

Hell, you're a stranger to your life—

And that's trouble.

A run-in with some shady types

Puts you on a slow freighter to nowhere.

And there among your crew,

Some ghostly faces from your past—beware.

Do you really want to know

Why your memories slip like sand?

Why your reflexes are lightning?

Why there's thunder in your hand?

You're a very scary man—

And you're Trouble.

More — —>

You could build a life

If you could just tear down the walls of secret shame.

You could save your soul

If you could only make the ghosts give up their names

And tell you everything

You don't want to know—

Like who the hell you are.

Who's the man that dogs your tracks?

Who's the child whose laughter haunts your dreams?

It's cold consolation

That out in space nobody hears your screams.

Now you know you're running,

And you might not get away.

But you want to know the secrets;

You pursue them anyway.

You'll find a place to make a stand

And that's trouble.

You'll find a place to take your stand—

And make trouble.

You'll find a place to make your stand,

'Cos you're Trouble.

⬜

(lyric and music © 2015 Maya Bohnhoff)

From *I Remember the Rain* (Remixed), track released March 3, 2022

Produced at Mystic Fig Studios by Jeff Bohnhoff

Listen on Jeff & Maya's Bandcamp page:

https://jeffandmayabohnhoff.bandcamp.com

READ A SAMPLE FROM LALDASA: BELOVED SLAVE

CHAPTER ONE

She experienced her emergence through the layers of darkness and pain as an uphill struggle through an oppressive storm. Every breath came at a price; every movement was agony.

Had she lost her breather? She didn't remember. She gasped for air, expecting the sting of wind-driven sand on her skin, the taste of it in her mouth. But the air was too thick, too warm, too humid.

How could that be? It was autumn. Snow and ice were the only forms of moisture natives of the Kedar knew at this time of year.

Up through the muddle of sensations she climbed, groping toward light. She smelled vegetation, lush and sweet, heard the soft trill of water over rocks.

Wrong—that was wrong. Surely she was hallucinating.

Adrenaline seeped into her veins. She knew, too well, one familiar scenario that would account for hallucinations—that she had fallen through an old sink shaft into a pocket of manda gas. She willed the adrenaline to rouse her; manda fumes were slow poison. They fogged the mind, befuddled the senses, and eventually destroyed both.

She saw light and leapt after it. Made out indistinct shapes—a play of sunlight and shadow. But the sunlight was too bright, the shadows too dark.

She came to on a surge of near panic, disoriented by surroundings that made no sense. She was lying on a bed of grassy turf, overshadowed by softly waving greenery. Ferns—alien, and dripping with dew.

Wrong. Oh, wrong. There were no plants like these …

She tried to lift her head and all but swooned again at the pain. Memory rode the storm of agony. Fragmentary, but complete enough that she knew she was not on a mountain slope in the Kedar. She was not even on Avasa. She had come to the inner planet of Mehtar to …

There the memory failed. She rolled onto her back, slowly, carefully. Her right hand and forearm plunged into cold water.

Gasping in surprise, she rolled again onto her right side, bringing all her senses to bear on the stream. It was no more than a rill, wending its way through the foliage, sparkling where the sun kissed it. But it was clear, cold, and liquid.

She brought her face close to the surface of the water, used a cupped hand to fling it into her face, carry it to her mouth. Her senses steadied and cleared. The pain in her head steadied too, seeming to subside with every breath she took of the warm, moisture-laden air.

The nape of her heck stung when she trickled water over it. She touched it gently with trembling fingertips. They came back spotted with blood. How had that happened?

She breathed, drank water, bathed her face, and waited for the answer to come. It did not. Finally, she dared to sit up. She was at the bottom of a little slope in a tree-shaded glen choked with ferns. The air was heavy with the sweet perfume of alien flowers. Sitting, she was challenged to see over the nodding fronds.

Above her, clouds roved the sky, fat with the threat of rain, now masking the sun, now revealing it. Below her a jumble of colorful carts, tents, and stalls were scattered across an open meadow. People scurried around and between the little nomadic shops, rolling out awnings, setting out wares. On any world that was recognizable as a bazaar.

Memory fluttered. She had come to Mehtar, to the capitol city of Kasi, to buy mining supplies.

The flutter became a flood. She had had money, but no more. It was gone along with her pack, her cloak and—she put a hand to her throat—the necklace that had held her leaf, her personal identification.

Despite the warm air, a hard chill settled in the pit of her stomach. She knew who she was—she was Anala Nadim of Onan, Kedar province, but on this alien world she was no one. She had no identity, no money, no family, no friends. And she had no idea what to do or where to go.

But go, she must.

Shakily, Anala got to her feet and stumbled down slope toward the bazaar. Before she had taken two uncertain steps, it began to rain.

Get *Laldasa: Beloved Slave* at the BVC bookstore!

Bookviewcafe.com

ABOUT THE AUTHOR

Maya is the New York Times Bestselling author of *The Antiquities Hunter (a Gina Miyoko Mystery)* and *Star Wars Legends: The Last Jedi* (with Michael Reaves). She became addicted to science fiction when her dad let her stay up late to watch *The Day the Earth Stood Still*. Since then her short fiction has been published in *Analog, Amazing Stories, Century, Realms of Fantasy, Interzone, Paradox* and *Jim Baen's Universe*. Her debut novel, *The Meri* (Baen), was a *Locus Magazine* 1992 Best First Novel nominee. Since, she has published over a dozen speculative fiction novels.

Maya lives in San Jose where she writes, performs, and records original and parody (filk) music with her husband and awesome musician and producer, Chef Jeff Vader, All-Powerful God of Biscuits. The couple has produced three children (all of whom have performed with them) and seven music albums: *RetroRocket Science, Aliens Ate My Homework, Grated Hits* and *Shrödinger's Hairball* (parody), and the original music CDs *Manhattan Sleeps, Möbius Street, I Remember the Rain* and *Labyrinth*.

Visit Maya's writing website Making Reality Behave: htpp://www.mayabohnhoff.com

Visit Jeff and Maya's music site: https://jeffandmayabohnhoff.bandcamp.com

You can find their parody videos at: https://www.youtube.com/@mysticfig

ABOUT BOOK VIEW CAFÉ

BVC

Book View Café is a professional authors' publishing cooperative offering DRM-free ebooks to readers around the world. With authors in a variety of genres including mystery, romance, fantasy, and science fiction, Book View Café has something for everyone.

Book View Café is good for readers because you can enjoy high-quality DRM-free ebooks from your favorite authors at a reasonable price and find links to their hard copy works.

Book View Café is good for writers because 90% of the proceeds goes directly to the book's author.

Book View Café authors include New York Times and USA Today bestsellers, Nebula, Hugo, Lambda, National Readers' Choice and Philip K. Dick Award winners, World Fantasy, Kirkus, and Rita Award nominees, and winners and nominees of many other publishing awards.

BOOK VIEW CAFE

www.bookviewcafe com